26/12/09

for my birthday, from
James + Vickie

THIRTY and
FABULOUS!

GW00372082

Women's Aid

Women's Aid Is an Irish Registered
Charity No: 6491, with its address at
Everton House, 47 Old Cabra Road,
Dublin 7, Ireland.

National Freephone Helpline 1800 341 900
Website: www.womensaid.ie

THIRTY and FABULOUS!

30 Great Stories Celebrating
30 Bestselling Years From Poolbeg

Celebrating 30 years

POOLBEG
1976 - 2006

Published 2006
by Poolbeg Press Ltd
123 Grange Hill, Baldoyle
Dublin 13, Ireland
E-mail: poolbeg@poolbeg.com

© Poolbeg Press Ltd 2006

Typesetting, layout, design © Poolbeg Press Ltd

1 3 5 7 9 10 8 6 4 2

A catalogue record for this book is available from the British Library.

ISBN 1-84223-266-5
ISBN 978-1-84223-266-8 (From Jan 2007)

Typeset by Type Design in Bembo 11.8/14.2pt
Printed by CPD Wales, Ebbw Vale

www.poolbeg.com

Contents

Foreword
MARIAN KEYES

It's an honour to write the introduction to this wonderful collection of short stories by Ireland's best and most entertaining women writers. All the authors involved are giving their royalties to Women's Aid, a stalwart charity which has been working for over 30 years on domestic violence.

I'm delighted that Women's Aid is the recipient of these royalties, because domestic violence is an appallingly ugly problem which pervades Irish society and which isn't treated with anything like the revulsion it deserves. It's an issue which goes to the heart of what we value and what we disregard in Ireland and it's an issue which is surrounded – indeed, to a certain extent obscured – by myths: for example, the myth that it happens only to a certain class or ethnic group of women, that almost all perpetrators are themselves victims of violent homes and that alcohol is always a factor.

To my shame, over the years, I bought into the myths. I suppose I found the reality too unbearable: I didn't want to believe that, in 21st century Ireland, a woman can still be beaten to the point of hospitalisation or even killed by the man who 'loves' her.

The myths are just that – myths. Women's Aid

supports women from all socio-economic groups in Irish society – for that reason, domestic violence is called the most democratic of crimes. The abusers come from a variety of backgrounds and alcohol is not a causal factor (although it's easier for some men and women to believe that the violence wouldn't have taken place if alcohol hadn't been present).

The root cause of violence against women has nothing to do with alcohol, class, ethnic group, or the behaviour of the woman. It is a widespread and serious social problem which has to do with social and cultural attitudes to women and women's place in society.

It affects a huge number of us: during their lifetime nearly one in five of Irishwomen will experience mental, sexual or physical abuse at the hands of their partner or ex-partner and one in seven will experience severely abusive behaviour.

- On average a woman will be assaulted by her partner or ex-partner 35 times before reporting it to the police.

- The single biggest reason (88%) why women do not leave violent partners is because they have nowhere else to go.

- Two in every five women who sought refuge accommodation in 2003 were not accommodated. The principal reason for non-admission was that the refuge was full.

- Domestic violence has a higher rate of repeat victimisation than any other type of crime.

- One in eight pregnant women (in a sample of those attending one Dublin maternity hospital) reported experiencing abuse while pregnant.

- 64% of women who had experienced violence reported that their children had witnessed the violence.

Women's Aid is there to help abused women in all kinds of ways: from their helpline, to supporting women through the court system, to facilitating access to crisis and long-term accommodation.

But they're seriously underfunded. In 2004, almost 2 out of every 5 calls to the helpline had to go unanswered due to understaffing; this is a terrible worry because many women have only very small pockets of time in which it's safe for them to make that call. Women's Aid needs an extra €100,000 per annum to expand their phone capacity and to cover current shortfalls.

The work of Women's Aid is vital. Because, let's remember, any one of us could be a victim. It could be the woman beside you on the bus, the woman next to you at work. It could be your best friend, it could be your sister. It could be you.

Marian Keyes

1

Someone Should Tell Her

Maeve Binchy

Oh, we could tell each other *anything* when we were fifteen, Angela!

Couldn't we?

You and Maggie and I.

You two could tell me that white lipstick was tarty.

We two could tell you that the short skirt gave you thunder thighs.

We could both tell Maggie that the frizzy perm didn't work.

We were always together: Maggie, Angela and Deirdre. M–A–D.

They used to call us MAD back then. We thought it was a scream.

And when we got a bit older we could tell each other *almost* anything.

Like we told Maggie that the fellow Liam she was

seeing was also seeing a lot of other people. We only told her because she was actually starting to talk about weddings and we couldn't let her go down that road.

And we told you that your boss Eric, who you fancied, was a con man. And we had to tell you because you were about to invest all your savings in some scam.

And you both told me to go back home and live with my mam because my lovely bedsit that I was so proud of was actually a room in a brothel.

And back then we never really *minded* being told that we were wrong or foolish or silly or whatever. We didn't *like* it now, but we didn't get upset or sulk or anything.

It was what friends did for each other.

So why has it become so difficult now that we are 29? It's not that 29 is old.

Or that the dreaded 30 is creeping up on us.

We've lost something along the way.

I don't know what happened but we seem to be walking on eggshells with each other.

And there's no reason for it.

We've all done fine.

Well, as regards work anyway.

Not quite so well in the Men Department.

But then women marry much later nowadays.

And some don't marry at all.

It's not like it was back in our mothers' time when they still had the notion of being old maids or spinsters or whatever.

And of course we'd all like to have children.

But when we're ready, not like half the kids we were at

school with who had kids of their own just to get out and have a flat, and now they're tied down and can't go anywhere.

And I mean you have to admit we're not doing badly. You run a hair salon on your own. And you go out to movie sets and meet the stars and do their hair. You have your picture taken with them. That's pretty good, Angela, by anyone's standards.

And I'm doing okay as well.

Nobody in my family had even heard of a career in Marketing and yet here I am in a consultancy, doing very nicely, thank you.

Long way from the classroom when poor Miss O'Sullivan said that we would all end in the gutter because we had no 'get up and go'.

And, of course, Maggie's doing fine too.

In a way.

You know.

Considering everything

And really *her* family was much more difficult than ours were, so she more or less had to help out all the time.

And she couldn't get any real money together for a training course like we did when we all worked stacking shelves and serving tables back then. And honestly, Ange, we did try to tell her.

Remember when we said we'd all stand up to her father when he came down to take her wages from her? We said we'd speak to him straight out and tell the authorities that he was taking every penny his daughter slaved hard for, but Maggie begged us not to, said it would be worse for her mother if we did.

So we did nothing.

And then, when her mother got sick, Maggie said she *had* to stay at home and mind the younger ones. Who else was there? And we did say to each other then that someone should tell her we didn't get all that many chances in life and she should have gone to college. She was brighter than all of us – she could easily have got a place.

But would she listen? Would she what? It was all this about the young ones wetting the bed, what with her mother being so long in hospital and her father being so drunk. And somebody had to be there and do it and she was there and did it.

I mean she's marvellous, is Maggie, and what she did for those sisters and brothers was fantastic – some of *them* are actually in college now . And she was tough too. She got her father onto some alcoholics' programme and he did stop eventually, I think.

Didn't he? Anyway, it was all too late for Maggie and somebody should have told her that it's not so easy to go back to studying when you're older, and they want babes nowadays not mature women.

But it was getting harder to talk to her. All the old easy feeling had gone.

And that's what has her where she is now.

Not that there's anything wrong with it, working in a tacky kind of shop like that, selling all kinds of rubbish. But you know the way Maggie goes on – it's lovely, she meets great people, they get marvellous bargains, it's near home, one of the younger sisters has asthma or something and she likes to put a good meal on the table for her father . . .

And honestly she doesn't seem to remember that we're

all out for each other's good.

And that ever since we were the group they called MAD back at school, there was literally *nothing* we couldn't say to each other.

You get the feeling she's become touchy.

We never did touchy before. Did we?

But I didn't like the way she reacted when I offered to give her my old jacket. It was a million times better than anything she had.

A million.

But Maggie said she wouldn't have a call to wear it anywhere.

What a strange phrase, instead of saying thank you and being delighted with it.

Like we all would.

If we were in a position to, I mean.

And remember that time we went to have lunch with her in the posh hotel? It was almost embarrassing. Well, it wasn't really embarrassing what with her being Maggie and everything.

But she seemed so out of place, and asking could she take home the little sugar packs and paper napkins with the name of the place on them to her sisters.

They were giving us such pitying looks. Did you notice? No? But then, Ange, to be honest you're as blind as a bat these days.

Anyway, it was impossible to get a thing out of Maggie about her own life and her plans or anything. She just kept saying she'd see what happened, as if that were any way to get anywhere.

I don't know whether you noticed but she never answered a direct question. I know I asked her if her father was still off the sauce and she said something totally waffly about him being marvellous all things considered, which was neither a yes nor a no. So I asked again and she said that to some people drink was as natural as breathing.

Where does that leave us? Then she was asking all about *my* mother and father and whether I should tell my father that my mum had been for tests. He might want to know.

I said he had wanted to know very little else about her over the years since he left.

She remembered everything, Maggie did, about when he left. More than I do.

We were all twelve then. You'd swear it was her own family – honestly, it was spooky.

And she's been to see my mother more often than I have.

And it wasn't only me. She knows all about your family too, Angela.

She said she heard from your brother who went to jail in Australia. I mean I know you told us all about it at the time but Maggie actually sends him postcards and things because he'd be lonely so far from home. She knows the name of the jail and all. And apparently he's got very interested in birds, like that film with Burt Lancaster. He writes to her about rosellas and galahs and things you'd never have heard of . . . oh, he does to you too? You keep in touch with him? That's great, great – well, he *is* family, of course.

No, I was just surprised that Maggie would.

Yes, of course, it's kind of her.

Maggie *is* kind. That's what she does.

And, of course, if you wanted *me* to write to him I would – I just didn't think you had anything in common with him any more.

No, indeed, you're right, he probably wouldn't remember me. And too much water under the bridge really.

But that wasn't what I was talking about. I was saying that someone should tell Maggie for her own good that this kind of thing can't go on any longer. It's not fair, not on herself nor on anyone.

No, Angela, I *know* what you're going to say. That we should never try to come between lovers no matter how star-crossed they are.

Look, I know there's a point in that – I know that you often end up with egg on your face when it turns out to be a long-lasting affair.

But be honest – weren't you glad when we turned you against Eric, that con man who was going to take your money? What do you mean it was only money? You had worked for it, saved it.

No, that's ludicrous, Ange, you know it is. He couldn't have loved you. You couldn't have been the only one he didn't con. You were so well out of it.

It's not like you to look back and regret. Not like you at all.

And going back to that time, at least you'll admit that Maggie was lucky we pointed out that her fellow Liam had so many other girls. Look at the fool she would have made of herself and she had many more things to worry about – her sister with asthma, her mother not well, her father drinking. Oh, come *on*, Angela, how could that Liam have helped her with any of those problems? If he had been around he would have made things much much worse.

But now it's really important that someone say something.

This guy Hanif. I mean, Angela, he's an African. An Algerian. From Africa.

Oh, I know Maggie says he's a French citizen but the fact of it is that he's as black as the Ace of Spades and it won't work.

Well, it *can't* work. I mean marriage is hard enough anyway – look at all the disasters we see around us and that's even when they're from the same culture and background and race and religion.

I mean, what does Maggie know about Hanif's life before he came here? He could have lived in a hut in the desert!

No, stop it, Angela, stop telling me he's from Marseilles! That's not what it's about.

He can't go in and live with Maggie in her house, with her father poised to go back on the drink, with her sister whooping with asthma, with poor daft Maggie going to see *my* mother, writing letters to your brother. It's just ludicrous.

I know it's hard to do because we all like Maggie so much and we go back such a long way. But, *honestly,* someone should tell her before she starts organising a wedding.

She *has* organised a wedding?

I don't believe you.

You're serious? When? But that's only six weeks away! It can't be!

Angela? How do you know about it?

Have you been invited? And are you going? I see.

I see.

Okay. I haven't been invited. But I suppose you

8

know that.

What do you mean when did I see her last? She's our friend for God's sake! I'm always seeing her.

I saw her that time we went to the smart hotel where she took the sugar packets and paper napkins.

And then I saw her when we went to that weepy film and had a pizza afterwards

No, of course I haven't been to Maggie's house. Angela, listen to me. Who could go to that house with the chance that her father might come reeling in and the sister wheezing away in the corner?

You do.

I see.

Okay, I know she asked me, but honestly!

And that's true – I haven't sat down and talked properly to Hanif.

But what's the point? What would there be to say?

Oh. You do? You have? Good, good.

No, I mean it. I'm *glad* you like him and that you've found plenty to talk to him about. No, that's nice, really it is.

It's just that ... oh, come on, Angela, you and me, we don't have to talk Politically Correct to each other.

It's just that no matter how nice he is, he's an African immigrant and he'll bring Maggie down. Whatever hope she had before, she'll have none now.

And suppose she has children? Well, I mean.

But she's not seriously going to marry him, is she? She is.

And did she think I would never find out? I mean, was she ever going to tell me or anything? Was she going to wait until I walked in on her one day when she had a brood of African children by the hand?

What do you mean that's what she said? She said she wouldn't be likely to run into me because I never suggested any meetings.

That is *so* unfair!

That's so Maggie for you!

No, Angela, don't take her side.

Didn't I go along to that excruciating thing at the hotel and the movie and the pizza in that place with plastic tables?

You say nothing because there's nothing you *can* say.

I wouldn't want to go to her wedding anyway even if she did ask me.

It's all so petty, isn't it?

When you think what friends we all used to be.

If I were getting married I would have asked Maggie.

Probably.

And where are they having it anyway?

In a Registry Office. I see.

And you're going to be a witness. Oh, I see.

And are they having a reception?

Oh, really? Really? That's rather a nice restaurant – what made them choose that one? Won't they feel a bit out of place?

Oh, they both work there. Maggie left the other job. I see.

And will he have anyone there? Coming over from France. I see. 30 of them. Good heavens.

Well, well, well.

And does she know you're telling me about this or is it to be forever a secret? She *asked* you to.

Maggie asked you to tell me?

She said what? She said – "Someone should tell her!"
Those were her actual words. I see.

ALSO BY MAEVE BINCHY, PUBLISHED BY POOLBEG

Dublin 4, The Lilac Bus

2

Deliver Us From Evil
COLETTE CADDLE

The senior nurse stood frowning down at the girl, her arms folded across her chest.

"Mrs O'Connor, his temperature has been taken three times this morning – there's nothing wrong with him."

"He seems hot to me," Gráinne O'Connor insisted, "and he keeps crying."

"That's what babies do." There was a distinct note of irritation in Caroline Short's tone now. "If he doesn't settle, call Ann." Then, taking her student nurse to one side, she murmured, "I'm going downstairs for a minute. If there are any problems, talk to the staff nurse."

"Yes, Sister."

When she had gone, Ann smiled kindly down at the new mother. "Sister's a bit of a monster, but look on the bright side – you'll be out of here tomorrow but I'm here for at least another year!"

Instead of the smile Ann had been hoping to elicit, the

girl looked more terrified than ever.

"I can't go home. He's not well enough to go home."

Ann sat down on the edge of the bed and patted her hand. "Babies are a lot tougher than they look, honestly. Have you decided on a name yet?"

Gráinne shook her head. "Kieran wants to call him Patrick after his father."

"And what do you want to call him?"

Gráinne smiled for the first time. "Conor."

"Oh, that's lovely!"

"He looks like a Conor, doesn't he?" Gráinne pulled the blanket away from the baby's face and stroked the side of one silken cheek.

"He's gorgeous," Ann pronounced, "and he's going to have his choice of the girls when he grows up." She stood up and went to the door. "Just ring the bell if you need me."

"Could you take the flowers away?"

Ann looked at the beautiful bouquet of lilies that Gráinne's husband had brought in the night before. "But they're so beautiful . . . are you sure?"

"I hate them." Gráinne shivered. "Lilies stand for death, did you not know that?"

"I didn't and I'm sure he didn't either."

"Anyway, they're very overpowering and they're probably not good for the baby's breathing. He sounds quite chesty to me as it is."

Ann picked up the vase. "I'll take them down to the chapel, how's that?"

"Whatever." Gráinne gazed down into her baby's face, the flowers forgotten.

★ ★ ★

"Where are you going with those?" Caroline Short

looked surprised as Ann approached her in the corridor with the flowers.

"She doesn't want them in her room so I was going to take them down to the chapel."

"She's a right weirdo," Caroline said, shaking her head. "If I had a gorgeous husband like that bringing me in flowers I'd be over the moon. The woman doesn't know she's born."

"I think she's just a bit nervous about being a new mum."

Caroline snorted. "As if it will make any difference to her – with all her money she'll probably have a daytime nanny and a night nurse lined up from day one."

Ann said nothing but she had to agree. Gráinne was a bit odd. This should be the happiest time of her life but she seemed completely miserable.

Running downstairs, she delivered the flowers to the chapel and then headed back up to the ward, wishing it was time for her lunch. She'd been on duty since seven and, though it was only twelve now, she was already struggling to keep her eyes open. All this late-night studying was beginning to take its toll.

As she arrived back at the nurses' station a buzzer went.

"I don't believe it – it's the O'Connor woman again," Caroline groaned.

"I'll go," Ann volunteered and quickly went back down to the private room at the end of the corridor. She went in. "Everything okay, Gráinne?"

"No, he won't eat."

Ann went over to the bed and took the bottle from Gráinne. Gently, she rubbed it along the baby's bottom lip. "Come on, little man. Drink up! You're worrying your mammy."

The baby turned his face away and nuzzled into his

mother's breast.

"He's not stupid, is he?" Ann chuckled. "He prefers draught to bottle!"

Self-consciously, Gráinne moved her son away from her breast. "Maybe we should try a different formula."

"Let's give it a few hours," Ann suggested. "Babies don't eat much over the first couple of days – they're more interested in sleeping after the ordeal they've been through."

"He hardly slept a wink last night," Gráinne pointed out. "I really think there's something wrong with him."

"I tell you what, why don't I ask the paediatrician to take a look at him?"

Gráinne smiled gratefully. "I'd like that. I don't mean to be so much trouble but –"

"You're not," Ann said firmly. "That's what we're here for."

★ ★ ★

"Well, Mrs O'Connor, no cause for alarm. He has some fluid on the chest but that should clear up over the next few days." Doctor Tom Feeney handed the baby back to his mother. "When are you due to go home?" He looked from Gráinne to Ann.

"Probably tomorrow," Ann told him, "once the obstetrician has given Mrs O'Connor the all-clear."

"Well, maybe you should leave Baby with us for another couple of days," said Tom.

Gráinne stared at him. "I can't do that."

He smiled. "I assure you, we'll take good care of him."

Gráinne shook her head. "No, I'm not going."

"I'm afraid you'll have to," Ann said gently, "if the obstetrician says –"

"But this is a private room! I'm paying for it."

For the first time, Ann wondered if her boss was right and if Gráinne was just a spoiled wife used to getting her own way. Still, there was an undoubted look of panic in her eyes. "If you were breast-feeding, then maybe —"

"I can't breast-feed!" Gráinne snapped, folding her arms tightly around her.

"And that's fine, Gráinne," Ann soothed. "I'm just saying there's no reason for you to stay."

"I'm his mother!" Gráinne protested. "Isn't that a good enough reason?"

Tom smiled. "Look, why don't we wait and see what tomorrow brings? With a bit of luck, you'll be able to go home and take your son with you."

Inexplicably, tears filled Gráinne's eyes and started to spill over.

Tom looked at Ann. "Can I have a quick word, nurse?" He backed out of the room and started to walk towards the nurses' station.

Ann kept pace with him.

"I think you might want to have a chat with her doctor," he said. "It looks like a case of the baby blues to me."

"Who's this?" Caroline asked, overhearing him as they reached the nurses' station.

"Mrs O'Connor."

The Sister rolled her eyes. "All she wants is attention."

The doctor shrugged. "It was just a suggestion. I deal with the babies, not their mothers."

They began to discuss other matters and after a few minutes Ann slipped away and went back down to the private room.

"Gráinne?"

The baby was back in his cot but the bed was empty

and Ann could hear sobbing coming from the bathroom. "Gráinne?" She knocked gently and when the woman didn't answer she pushed the door open. "Gráinne, I just — oh, sorry!"

Gráinne's nightdress lay in a heap at her feet and she stood, naked, the tears rolling down her cheeks. "He puked on me."

"Oh, Gráinne, you poor, poor thing!" Ann gently wrapped a towel around the girl and led her back into the bedroom.

"It's not what you think."

"I think it is."

"Please don't say anything!"

Ann looked at the raw fear in the girl's eyes. "It's okay. Don't worry. We'll look after you." The baby started to wail and Ann smiled. "Why don't we get you into a clean nightie and you can have another go at feeding this little man. It sounds as if he's found his appetite."

★ ★ ★

"Where have you been?" Caroline Short barked at the student. "You were supposed to go round with the medication ten minutes ago!"

"Sorry, Sister, I was with Mrs O'Connor."

"What is wrong with the girl now?"

Ann hesitated. "Afterpains," she said finally.

"I'll be glad when she's gone home — she's been nothing but trouble. Now get a move on, Ann, and if Mrs O'Connor rings again, I'll see to her."

"Yes, Sister," Ann murmured and taking the keys went down to the drugs cabinet. She hurried around the ward distributing medication and was about to go back and check on Gráinne when Caroline called her.

"You take your lunch break now, Ann, but I want you back here in exactly one hour."

"Oh, I'm not that hungry – let Sue go first."

Caroline's eyes narrowed. "I'm running this ward and if I tell you to take your break then that's exactly what you do."

"Yes, Sister, sorry. I'll just drop this down to Mrs O'Connor – she's feeling sick."

Caroline took the kidney bowl out of her hands, her mouth set in a determined line. "I'll do it."

"But –"

Caroline raised an eyebrow and looked at the student. "Yes?"

"Nothing," Ann muttered and hurried off to the canteen. Gráinne was going to think that Caroline was mad when she arrived down with a kidney bowl. Ann just hoped she didn't drop her in it. She also hoped that Caroline didn't have a go at Gráinne because it would take very little to send the poor girl over the edge.

Ann took her tray to a small table at the back of the canteen but, though she was hungry and needed a rest, she couldn't concentrate on her soup and roll, too anxious about what was happening up on the ward. After thirty minutes she could stand it no longer and went back upstairs. She'd get a textbook from her locker and tell Caroline she was studying and that way, at least, she could sit at the nurses' station and keep an eye on things.

Caroline was nowhere in sight on her return and she risked slipping down to Gráinne's room, pulling up short when she saw Kieran O'Connor standing by the window with his son in his arms.

Ann turned to Gráinne and smiled.

"Hi, Gráinne, did the baby take his bottle?"

"About three ounces."

"That's great, well done. Do you need anything else?"

Kieran laughed. "She needs to get out of here! She's dying to get home, aren't you, darling?"

Gráinne nodded, smiling, but her smile didn't reach her eyes.

"I'm afraid that's up to the obstetrician and paediatrician," Ann told him.

"What time do they do their rounds?" Kieran asked.

"Usually first thing but it could be any time."

"And is Gráinne expected to just hang around here until they can be bothered to turn up?"

Ann bit her lip. "Emergencies get priority and if there are any deliveries, well," she smiled, "babies don't exactly keep a timetable when it comes to popping out."

"I suppose not," he conceded, smiling down at his son. "You weren't exactly punctual, were you, mate?"

"I'll leave you to it." Ann met Gráinne's eyes. "Just call if you need me."

Ann went back to the nurses' station and was relieved to see that her boss was nowhere in sight. Sitting down at the desk, she opened her book and bent her head over it, but it was a pointless exercise. She just couldn't concentrate. She couldn't get Gráinne's frightened little face out of her mind and her eyes kept darting towards her door.

Sue walked out of a room across the corridor, grumbling to herself, but she brightened when she saw Ann sitting there. "Oh, good, you're back. Do you mind if I go to lunch? I feel awful."

"What's up?"

"Just a bad headache. It's been getting worse all morning."

"Poor you!"

"Caroline's gone to a meeting with admin," Sue told

her, "and then she's going straight into the senior staff meeting – so if you've any problems, page me."

Ann couldn't believe her luck. This was definitely a sign. She smiled kindly at Sue. "You go on. I'll be fine."

"Thanks, Ann, you're a star."

As Sue was gathering her bag and cardigan together and muttering about getting some Solpadeine, Ann watched Kieran O'Connor walk out of Gráinne's room and up the corridor towards her. When his eyes met hers, she smiled. He really was a very handsome man.

"Keep an eye on them for me," he said with a wink as he passed her.

"You can depend on it," she promised.

As soon as she had a moment, Ann went back down to Gráinne. "Are you okay?"

Gráinne nodded.

Ann pulled a chair over to the bed and sat down. "Okay, then, let's talk."

★   ★   ★

The next day, Ann was sitting alone at the nurses' station when Kieran O'Connor walked through the door and headed straight for his wife's room without looking right or left.

"Shit!" Ann muttered under her breath as Caroline Short rounded the corner and joined her behind the desk. She cleared her throat and turned to face her boss. "Sister, there's a bit of a problem."

Caroline sighed. "What is it now, Nurse?"

Ann swallowed hard as Kieran walked back out of the private room and strode purposefully towards them. "Can you just follow my lead, Sister, and I'll explain everything later?"

"What on earth?" Caroline looked outraged.

"Please, Sister, I can't begin to tell you how important this is."

Caroline looked at the sheer desperation in the student nurse's eyes and gave a curt nod.

Ann turned around and smiled broadly. "Mr O'Connor, hello! Has Gráinne forgotten something?"

He frowned. "What are you talking about? Where is my wife?"

Ann's brow furrowed in confusion. "At home? She left about an hour ago – isn't that right, Sister?"

Caroline blinked and then nodded slowly. "Yes, that's right, about an hour."

Kieran's mouth tightened. "Who collected her?"

"No one, she asked me to call a taxi for her." Ann held his gaze, her eyes wide and innocent.

"Is there a problem, Mr O'Connor?" Caroline asked.

"You should have called me," he muttered.

"I'm sorry." Ann looked upset. "She said she wanted to surprise you. I didn't think –"

"It's not up to my staff to stop a patient from leaving the hospital once they've been discharged by a doctor," Caroline said briskly. "I'm sure your wife will explain her actions when you get home."

Kieran nodded slowly. "Yes, of course, I apologise. I was just looking forward to taking them home myself. I'm sure you understand."

"Of course," Caroline said graciously.

"Well, goodbye then and thank you for everything."

Ann smiled. "You're very welcome. Goodbye, Mr O'Connor."

As she watched him walk away, her boss turned to her,

arms crossed. "This had better be good, Ann. What the hell is going on? Why on earth did you lie to the man? You know perfectly well that Mrs O'Connor discharged herself last night."

"And hopefully by now she's far away and he won't be able to hurt her ever again."

"What?"

"Kieran O'Connor was abusing his wife."

Caroline's eyes widened. "Are you sure? You know that woman is very self-obsessed – you wouldn't want to believe everything she says."

Ann shook her head. "I'm afraid there's no doubt. I've seen the evidence with my own eyes."

"What? Bruises? But she's been having check-ups with doctors and midwives throughout her pregnancy – how come no one noticed any injuries before now?"

"When she found out she was pregnant he laid off for a while and then when he started again . . ."

"Yes?" Caroline prompted.

Ann swallowed hard. "When he started again, he used her breasts as an ashtray, knowing no one would see the marks."

Caroline closed her eyes and shook her head. "The bastard!" She opened her eyes and looked at Ann. "And that's why she wouldn't breast-feed."

Ann nodded.

"He had me totally fooled," said Caroline. "He's so gorgeous, so charming, I'd never have thought he was capable of that."

"Abusers don't go around with a sign over their heads," Ann muttered. "It's the fact that they're so confident and charismatic that allows them to get away with it."

"So where did she go when she left last night – to a shelter?"

"No, she went to a hotel near the airport and got on a plane to Frankfurt first thing this morning – she has a brother over there."

"I suppose she should be safe enough with him. But why did she so suddenly decide to go?" Caroline's eyes narrowed. "Had it something to do with you?"

Ann nodded silently. She had been expecting this question and knew her answer would probably get her into trouble but, the way she saw it, she simply didn't have a choice.

"Ann? What did you say to her?"

"She said she was afraid to leave because of the baby and I told her she should be more afraid to stay, that it was only a matter of time before he started hitting him too."

Caroline frowned. "Oh, Ann, it really wasn't your place to say that. Why didn't you talk to me? Why didn't you call in a counsellor?"

"What difference would it have made? She had to get out of the situation – she had to get away from him, if not for her own sake then for the baby's."

"You know," Caroline said gently, "some men beat the living daylights out of their wives but never ever lay a finger on their children."

Ann looked at her, her eyes bright with tears, and pulled back her hair to reveal the long jagged scar going from her neckline up to her scalp. "But some men do."

ALSO BY COLETTE CADDLE, PUBLISHED BY POOLBEG

Red Letter Day, Changing Places, A Cut Above, Shaken & Stirred, Too Little Too Late

3

The Designer
BER CARROLL

"That's it, there!" shrieked Camilla, the bride and navigator.

Kirsty, her sister, driver and maid of honour, slammed on the brakes. The hatchback jerked to a sudden stop on the spindly inner-city avenue and three pairs of eyes assessed the house in question. Nobody said a word but for once there was an uneasy consensus among them: No. 52 was not at all as they'd expected.

Camilla was quite horrified at the sight of the two-storey terrace.

This does not look like the home of a designer, she thought with uncharacteristic panic.

The walls, a mustard yellow, were dulled with decades of grime and overrun with nasty-looking ivy. A crooked tree dominated the garden and cast a dark canopy over the lifeless soil.

Kirsty's thoughts were similar to her sister's. The house

oozed an eeriness that made her want to press down on the accelerator and tear off down the street.

Perhaps Camilla has made a mistake. Maybe, what with the pressure of the wedding and everything, she's written down the wrong house number.

"Angie, why don't you hop out to check that we have the right place?" she suggested calmly.

Angie, by nature a gofer, obediently got out of the back. Her legs, skinny and brown, crossed the street and her short denim skirt rose to an indecent level as she bent over to unlatch the rickety old gate.

Yuk! she thought.

The damp smell from the rotting garden made her want to gag and she hurried towards the weather-beaten door. It possessed neither a bell nor knocker and Angie rapped on the rough wood. Seconds ticked by. She raised her hand to knock again.

"Oh!" She almost lost her balance when the door was whipped back from the tips of her knuckles.

She righted herself and studied the pint-sized woman who had flung the door back with such unwarranted aggression. A wizened face with glassy green eyes returned her stare. The woman's scraggly grey hair was tied in a messy knot at the base of her neck and a tacking pin hung from her mouth, much like a cigarette. It seemed that they had the right place after all.

"Um . . . I'm Angie . . . Camilla's bridesmaid."

"Sheila," the woman mumbled while her cracked lips held onto the tacking pin. She didn't offer her hand.

Angie turned around and nodded to Kirsty. She saw her face set in a resigned grimace as she parked the car neatly next to the kerb. After a few moments' delay, just enough time for a quick conference, the two sisters got out of the car.

"Little and large," they used to be called at school. Kirsty, older by two years, used to hate her doll-like sister tagging along. With good reason, for, as witty as she was pretty, Camilla's charm could bridge any age gap and Angie hadn't been the first of Kirsty's friends to jump camp.

After a jostle to be first through the gate, which Camilla won, the sisters joined Angie at the doorway.

"I'm Camilla – the bride – we talked on the phone." Camilla's tone was more subdued than normal but Sheila wasn't to know that. "This is Kirsty, my sister," she added as an afterthought.

Sheila gave an imperceptible nod and stepped back to let them through. As she passed, Camilla noticed that the old woman was barefoot and, even more alarmingly, her gnarled toenails were painted a garish pink.

Sheila had come highly recommended by a work colleague. Yet Camilla could not reconcile the photographs she had seen of her friend's dress with this witchlike woman and her spooky house. Something had gone terribly wrong but she couldn't figure out what.

In an effort to calm herself, she recalled what Kirsty had said in the car. *"Go in there and be polite but non-committal. Then, call the woman tomorrow to say we've decided to buy off the rack."*

★ ★ ★

"Up the stairs," Sheila instructed. "Turn right at the top."

The stairs, unvarnished and deadly steep, creaked in protest as they ascended to the upper level of the house.

This is the last wedding party, Sheila promised herself as she gripped the banister. *I'm too old for the kneeling, the pinning and the theatrics.*

She could already tell from the look of them that it wasn't going to be easy.

Her workshop was at the back of the house and the pure light that shone through its bay window was like a salve to her tired old eyes. The contents of the room were simple: a cluster of regal-like mannequins in various states of undress, a floral lounger and an ancient rocking chair.

Sheila spat out the tacking pin and it immediately became lost in the sea of silver flecks on the floor. She caught a look of distaste on Camilla's face but she had dealt with too many haughty brides to be in any way perturbed. They all came down off their pedestal, be it sooner or later.

Sheila made no apologies to anyone. She didn't advertise for business, it all came by the hand of fate. She wouldn't be hurt if a client denied fate and decided that she didn't want her dress designed by an eccentric old woman. However, they never walked away. Not once.

The girls sat on the fat floppy cushions of the sofa and Sheila handed them a photo album that displayed her best work. Maximilian, her cat, sidled up to her swollen ankles and she bent over to pick up his heavy silkiness. He purred, his body vibrating deliciously. Sheila sat down on the rocking chair and stroked his sleek black fur as she observed her newest clients.

The sisters were vastly different to each other. Not only was there a dramatic difference in height, but Kirsty's fair hair was in marked contrast to Camilla's jet-black tresses. It seemed that the only thing they had in common was their milky-white skin. It complemented Camilla's dark hair beautifully but its effect was more unfortunate for Kirsty: her skin and hair combined to give her a very unhealthy, washed-out look.

Sheila turned her gaze to Angie. A slip of a girl with sun-streaked hair and berry-brown skin, she had a vague aura about her, as if the real world passed over her head. However, Sheila was an experienced observer of people and she recognised the glint of intelligence in Angie's eyes.

That one gets away with a lot by playing the dumb blonde — but she's neither dumb nor naturally blonde.

Sheila allowed the girls another few minutes before she asked, "Anything catch your eye?"

Camilla's inner struggle was evident from the quizzical expression on her face. The dresses in the album were testament to Sheila's extraordinary skill. And, after all, wasn't it only the end product that mattered?

"What do you think would suit me best?" she asked and her two bridesmaids exchanged an astonished look at the meekness of her tone.

Sheila smiled to herself. The change was coming about already.

★　★　★

Kirsty jammed the car into gear, gave an angry look over her shoulder and screeched the tyres in her haste to take off.

"What was that all about, Camilla?" she asked through gritted teeth.

Camilla, deliberately obtuse, replied with, "What do you mean?"

Kirsty took her eyes off the road to shoot her a furious

glance. "You agreed designs, had our measurements taken and talked money — why did you do all that when you've no intention of staying with her?"

"I *am* staying with her," Camilla sniffed. "The dresses were divine — you could never buy anything like them off the rack."

"Well, thanks for remembering to let *me* know that you'd changed your mind!"

Kirsty should have known that Camilla would scuttle away from the tacit agreement they'd made before going into the house. She was always the same.

Well, she only has herself to blame if it backfires, Kirsty thought vengefully.

A quiet descended in the car. It wasn't lengthy. Angie was also harbouring a gripe.

"I thought Kirsty and I would get a say in the colour of our dresses," she piped up from the back.

Camilla emitted an irritated sigh. The first fitting was in two weeks and she had to buy material, shoes and jewellery in that short space of time. Something told her that her bridesmaids were going to be more of a hindrance than a help.

"Well, Paul wants to wear a red cravat —" she started to explain.

Kirsty cut her off. "Red makes me look like a tart."

Angie giggled and Kirsty's lips twitched in response.

Camilla, however, didn't find it funny.

"Don't be ridiculous," she snapped. "It's my wedding and *I* say you're wearing red."

★ ★ ★

"Do you have that taffeta in a deeper shade?" Camilla

asked the sales assistant a few days later.

She hadn't admitted it at the time, but bright reds did make her fair-haired sister look tartish.

"No," the woman shook her head, "but, here, let me show you this satin. Perhaps it's closer to what you're looking for?"

She held out a square of burgundy, its edges frayed.

Camilla shook her head despondently. If only Paul wasn't so adamant about the colour of his cravat! Camilla wondered, not for the first time, if he was just winding her up. A bloke's bloke, Paul was an avid watcher of Sky Sports, loved gadgets, never hung his towels on the rack and treated his special beer-tankard like it was an old friend. Cravats were not part of his *modus operandi*. But then again, it wasn't every day that he got married, was it?

"Let me check the catalogue," said the assistant, looking fearful that a sale was about to slip through her fingers.

She flicked through the pages of a thick binder.

"Mmm . . ." Her smooth face frowned with concentration as her finger stopped somewhere around the middle of the page. "What do you think of this?" she asked and turned the catalogue around for Camilla to see.

Camilla knew it was right the minute she saw it. "I like it. What's it called?"

"Red Duchess Satin."

"Can you order it for me?"

"No problem." The assistant gave a relieved smile as she extracted the order book from underneath the counter. "It takes six weeks."

"The wedding is in four," Camilla told her.

The assistant's smile fell from her face and the order book remained unopened on the counter. "It has to come from Thailand – there's no way it would get here on time. You've left it rather late to organise things, haven't you?"

It's because Paul left it rather late to propose, thought Camilla as she left the shop.

Right from the start, it was distressingly obvious that Paul had no interest in getting married. It wasn't that he didn't love her; he just didn't see the need.

"You don't need a ring on your finger, babes," he'd say whenever she dropped a heavy hint. "We're happy, that's all that matters."

Paul was right, they were happy, but Camilla was sure they could be happier if they made that ultimate commitment to each other.

Then, around Christmas, Paul had become distant. It was a busy time at work for him and there was a lot of overtime, much more than last year. He unwound from the stress by watching TV.

"I'm going to bed now," she would tell him night after night.

"I'll follow you," he'd reply. But he wouldn't. At least not until she was safely asleep.

One time, Camilla had noticed that even though he was staring at the TV screen, he didn't show the faintest reaction when his side won a free kick.

It was the most horrible Christmas ever. She went through the festive motions, all the while worried sick that Paul was going to leave her.

She was at the point of confiding in Kirsty when it came to a head.

"Camilla, can we talk?" he'd said when he came home from work one night, late once again.

Her heart had plummeted. Never had Paul asked to 'talk' in that tone of voice before.

He wants to split up, she thought in panic as she muted the TV. He's got the three-year itch.

His expression was pained as he asked, "Will you marry me?"

Camilla got such a shock that she didn't reply at first.

"Yes or no?" he urged.

"I thought you wanted to split up," she replied dazedly.

"What kind of answer is that?"

"Yes," she'd declared with belated delight. "Yes, I'll marry you."

They'd set a date for the middle of February (the earliest date possible, really) and she'd been instantly caught up in a whirl of organisation. With only six weeks to arrange everything, there was no time to sit on her laurels.

Now, as she trudged into another fabric shop, she wished that she had given herself more time. And that she'd called Paul's bluff about the cravat.

★ ★ ★

"So you've no material yet for the bridesmaids," said Sheila as she took another pin from her mouth and slid it into the hem of Camilla's dress.

"No," Camilla grimaced into the oval mirror. "I did see the perfect fabric — but it would take too long for the order to get here."

Sheila leaned back on her haunches to study the fall of the dress. She was pleased with the way the silk folded softly down the length of Camilla's slender legs before it kicked out at her ankles.

"Did you get a sample of it?" she asked.

"No — I thought there was no point."

"Bring one along to the next fitting," Sheila told her. "You never know what I might be able to do."

Camilla's reflection showed her reluctance to go back to the fabric store. Sheila didn't try to convince her. She knew that Camilla, like all brides, would leave no stone unturned when it came to finding that perfect colour to complement her own dress.

She only hoped that a small part of Camilla would make the effort simply because she owed Kirsty the right to look her best.

"Um, Sheila . . ." There was a note of uncertainty in Camilla's tone.

"Yes?"

"When we get the right material, I'll need you to run up a few extra things for me."

"Like what?"

"A wrap for my mother . . . and a cravat for Paul."

It was then that Sheila knew for certain Camilla would be her last client. Fate had a funny way of providing closure.

★ ★ ★

If I look like a tart on Camilla's wedding day, then it's nothing more than I deserve, thought Kirsty as the wedding date came closer. *For when it comes down to it, what else would you call someone who kissed her sister's boyfriend and did not want to stop?*

The kiss had been so innocent but the feelings it had aroused were not.

It had happened on Boxing Day, Kirsty's 30th birthday.

Camilla was cranky from the moment she arrived at the party.

"She's hung-over from yesterday," Paul explained when his girlfriend lay across the couch and refused to socialise with the other guests out on the terrace.

Kirsty was used to the excesses of Christmas Day overshadowing her birthday celebrations.

"Just leave her there," she said resignedly. "Come and meet everyone, Paul."

"Happy birthday, Kirsty," he said once they were out on the terrace. He handed her the gift-wrapped box. "I hope you like it – I picked it out."

Then he kissed her. It was intended as a brotherly birthday peck but their lips fused and refused to part. Neither of them saw it coming and they were swept off their feet by the intensity of it.

Slowly Kirsty came to her senses and stepped back.

"Thanks for the present," she said breathlessly while noting that Paul looked as dazed as she.

The gift was a compass with an expensive chrome casing, a stark white face and scripted markings. Kirsty loved it. Hiking was her passion and the team would be green when they saw it at the weekend.

He picked this out, she thought in wonder. *He knows me better than my own sister does.*

Over the next few weeks she could see that Paul was torn.

"I love Camilla," he said on many an occasion, as if trying to convince himself, "but I can't get you out of my head . . ."

Kirsty admired him for his loyalty and wanted him all the more. The kiss had changed how she looked at him. Now his rugged good looks made her weak at the knees and she realised, for the first time, that they actually had a lot in common: sport, beer and TV for starters. Camilla's idea of sport was trailing around the shops, she drank only champagne and she usually spent her spare time beautifying herself rather than watching TV.

"How can you love Camilla when you and I are so compatible?" Kirsty had asked him.

"It's our differences that make us good together," was his unsatisfactory reply.

So while he and Kirsty talked about the kiss and the impact it had on them, they didn't repeat the experience. In fact, Paul went out of his way to avoid touching her.

But at night, when Kirsty closed her eyes, his lips were waiting for her. Soft, yet demanding. Connecting with her in a way that no other man ever had. And the best part about her dreams was that she had no conscience in them. There was no reason to stop.

★ ★ ★

Camilla's jaw dropped open when she saw the roll of Red Duchess Satin propped up in Sheila's workroom.

"How did you get it?"

"I have my ways."

"Thank you!"

Camilla slipped her feet from her leather mules and pulled her T-shirt over her head. As she undressed, Sheila pondered her lack of curiosity about the source of the material. Anyone else would have asked endless questions.

You shouldn't take your good fortune for granted, Camilla.

Camilla started. "What did you say?"

"Nothing." Sheila held out the bride's gown. "Here."

Camilla stepped carefully into the folds of ivory silk and held her dark hair up with her hand while Sheila did up the zip. She turned fully towards the mirror.

"I love it!" she exclaimed. "I think that maybe it needs some extra beading around the bodice, but other than that it's perfect!"

With little over two weeks to go, the bridesmaids' dresses were now Sheila's priority.

"When can the girls come to see me?" she asked.

"Kirsty is working nights this week," said Camilla as she examined her profile from both sides. "She's a nurse," she added by way of explanation.

"How about Angie?"

"She's got more regular hours." Camilla's voice dropped, with a note of condescension in its tone. "She's a check-out chick."

Who are you to feel so superior?

Camilla paled when the designer's thoughts were soundlessly conveyed to her for the second time in a matter of minutes. Shaken, she apologised.

"Sorry, that came out the wrong way."

"Well, there's no rule that says Kirsty and Angie have to come for their fitting at the same time," remarked Sheila, as if nothing out of the ordinary had happened.

★　★　★

Angie's life had been turned upside down these last few weeks. She was not the kind of girl who kept a diary or paid much interest to the passing of time. Her period caused a mild surprise whenever it made its appearance, but only because she didn't count down the days. As a consequence, it had taken a few months before she clicked that something was amiss. By then it was too late to do anything.

She didn't know who to turn to. Mario, her boyfriend,

would be appalled. After four months of casual dates, Angie knew that he was most certainly not the 'Daddy' type.

Camilla would be equally appalled. Angie could hear what she would say.

"How could you be so stupid? You're four months pregnant – what were you smoking to say you didn't notice? And now it's too late to do anything – you're stuck with it!"

Now, as Angie undressed for Sheila, she felt extraordinarily weary. She wanted nothing more than to curl up on the floppy sofa and sleep until her pot belly and aching breasts went away. Sheila slid the half-made dress over her head. The material bunched at her midriff, unable to fall past the roundness of her tummy. Angie teetered between frenzied laughter and tears. There was a lot of noise. She was making it. But yet she was unable to decipher what it was: laughter or tears.

In the midst of her hysteria, she felt a steadying hand on her shoulder.

"How long are you gone?" asked Sheila.

Angie went from full-blown hysteria to calmness. Just like that. It was something in the old woman's voice. She didn't know what.

"Four months," she replied.

The woman nodded. Angie realised that she wasn't the first unexpectedly pregnant bridesmaid she'd seen in her day.

"Camilla doesn't know, does she?"

"No."

All of her friend's efforts to create a classy wedding were going to be ruined by a pregnant bridesmaid.

"Better she doesn't know until after the wedding," Sheila commented. "But you should tell Kirsty."

"But Kirsty and I aren't close," Angie told her but the old woman didn't seem to hear.

"Kirsty will be a rock for you. She's the kind of girl who's good to have around when the chips are down. Don't you think?"

Angie nodded in a bewildered kind of way.

"Now," Sheila eased the dress back over Angie's head, "I'd better start over on this gown of yours."

"The cost . . ." Angie felt the threat of fresh tears. "Camilla will kill me."

"What Camilla doesn't know won't worry her," said the old woman.

Angie briefly considered the wasted material and labour. She should have asked how there could be no extra cost, but she didn't. She decided that she didn't want to know the answer.

★ ★ ★

Kirsty stifled a yawn as Sheila pinned the underarms of the dress. She had finished her shift just as the grey fingers of dawn started to squeeze the blackness out of the night. After a small meal, that constituted neither a breakfast nor dinner, she had fallen into bed. However, exhausted as she was, sleep had eluded her.

If I told Camilla about the kiss, she would call off the wedding.

Camilla used to be the taker: Kirsty's toys, friends and achievements. Now, Kirsty could turn the tables and take away Camilla's dream wedding. All she had to do was tell the truth.

"Paul and I kissed. It knocked us both off our feet."

It wouldn't have made a difference if she'd added, *"But*

he still loves you."

Another bride-to-be might have overlooked the kiss, but not Camilla. Details mattered to her.

A pin pricked the soft skin of Kirsty's underarm. She winced. Sheila didn't apologise.

"Don't do it," was all she said, her voice stern.

"What?"

"Don't tell Camilla."

Kirsty felt a chill down her spine. "What do you know about it?"

"I know that you're better than that. And I know you'll find a man of your own to love."

The old woman's cat leapt down from the rocking chair and Kirsty jumped from the fright of the sudden movement.

"Sisterhood is very special," Sheila reached down to lift the black ball of fur, "but it needs to be nurtured to reach its full potential. You and Camilla may not be the closest now but she will turn to you for help in the future and a wonderful relationship will be born from that."

"What about Paul?" Kirsty spluttered.

"Paul loves Camilla. Their destiny is to be together. Your destiny is to meet an intellectual man, a chess-player."

Kirsty gave a nervous laugh. "He sounds incredibly dull."

Sheila smiled mischievously. "Not in bed, I assure you."

★　★　★

Three weeks later, photographs of the wedding came in the post. Sheila sat on her rocking chair while she looked through the glossy snaps that Camilla had sent on.

The bride looked exquisite in her mermaid-like dress.

Her dazzling smile held no clue of the trials that lay ahead, the black days that would eat up years of her life. It would start after the birth of her only child, a boy. Sheila could do nothing to prevent it from happening, only ensure that Camilla had support in her husband and sister. Hopefully, it would be enough.

Angie's face had filled out but there was no sign of her rounded belly. She also had hard times ahead and Sheila could see no man around to share the load. She wished her well.

Then there was Kirsty. Taller than even the groom, she made the wedding party look a little skewed. Her smile had an edge to it. She was still hurting but Sheila knew that she would get over it. Kirsty was strong. Strong enough to carry Camilla and Angie through.

Sheila saved the groom till last. Young and handsome, but an old soul with a penchant for red cravats and vying sisters. Sheila, like Kirsty, had lost out and her grief had been as great as her sister's when he'd died young. However, this lifetime would not be cut short and Paul would stick by Camilla through thick and thin. And that was what marriage was about. Wasn't it?

Maximilian purred at Sheila's ankles, wanting to come up.

"Wait a minute, kitty cat," she said affectionately.

She carefully slid the photographs into the last page of her album. Just like for all the others, she had done her best for Camilla and her bridesmaids. But now she was done.

ALSO BY BER CARROLL, PUBLISHED BY POOLBEG

Just Business, Executive Affair

4

Still Crazy After All These Years
TRACY CULLETON

I met my old lover on the street last night. He seemed so glad to see me, I just smiled.

Well, that's actually not true. I mean, part of it *is* true, but part of it isn't. Sorry ... I'm getting flustered now. He always had that effect on me, and he clearly still does.

So, with apologies to Paul Simon for using his lyrics, let me explain properly. I *did* see my old lover on the street. Grafton Street to be exact. But it was yesterday afternoon, not last night. And he didn't get the chance to be pleased, or otherwise, to see me. Because, as soon as I spotted him I ducked into a shop doorway, pulling a surprised Ella with me, and surreptitiously peered out at him.

He was with a young woman, and as they walked he had his hand on the back of her neck and she was smiling up at him.

I thought of how it used to be with us . . .

★　★　★

I met him in an upmarket city bar. He was one of the Celtic Tiger's cubs – well off and sophisticated. You might even have heard of him. It's not that he's famous – he's not a household name or anything. But he's well known in business and finance circles. So I won't use his real name, just in case. I'll call him . . . Mark. Mark Whelan, let's say.

I was instantly attracted to him. He was tall – just about six foot – and Mediterranean-looking. I originally thought he must be foreign, but no, he was one hundred per cent Irish . . . but from the west of Ireland, and it's a family tradition that they're descended from survivors of the Spanish Armada. He was quite skinny, and that was his only flaw. His only flaw that I could see then, at least.

That evening I met him, there were many women there more beautiful than I . . . in fact, I'd say that every single other woman there was more beautiful than I. I'm not being falsely modest, and it's not that I'm ugly. But I'm just so . . . so ordinary I suppose. I'm like a little brown sparrow whereas the other women were confident, arrogant, iridescent peacocks.

So I was extremely grateful when he chose me. I didn't realise then that my lack of confidence was the very thing that attracted him. That air of fragile vulnerability . . .

He effortlessly drew me into his circle of well-off self-assured men and their clone-like long-legged, longhaired women.

As the evening wore on I marvelled at how much they all drank, and how well they were able to carry it. I couldn't keep up – skipping most of the rounds and clutching the same glass of warm white wine as I smiled timidly.

He whisked me off later that evening, and I, reared on fairytales of handsome princes rescuing waiflike princesses, relished the romance of the whisking. I flew into his arms and clung to him and became his woman.

Without even discussing it, we were a couple, and soon we were living together. It was tacitly understood that I was way out of my league, and I was continually grateful for the fact that he had picked me. I was like a royal consort, walking a few paces behind, content to be the moon to his sun, shining only courtesy of his reflection and glad to have it.

But still, the imbalance in the relationship worked against me. I owed him and he was like an unscrupulous moneylender – the debt grew bigger rather than smaller. And he collected ruthlessly.

He drank a lot, and I was his chauffeur, coming out with him while he met his friends, hanging around on the periphery of the group, unnoticed and overlooked, smile fixed to aching cheeks, until it was time for us to go home. He would wave a cheery unsteady goodbye and I would link his arm, trying to make it look as if he was supporting me rather than me supporting him, and steer him towards the car, pour him into it and drive him home.

It wasn't fun. But I put up with it because I was still so honoured to be the lover, the woman, of the great Mark Whelan – to be chosen and picked. I still felt I was getting my share of the bargain. And I never questioned the bargain, I didn't dare. Fear is powerful, and the fear of the unknown, of being alone, of going to a lonely rented bedsit rather than this plush well-appointed house, kept me there.

And maybe I even believed I loved him and that he

loved me. Maybe I believed it, or chose to believe I believed it. Layers of self-delusion like layers of *papier mâché* making a playschool version of a relationship.

It cost me my friends and my family too. I realise that now. At the time I thought it was about them being unreasonable and unfair when they tried to speak against him, and one by one I fell out with them all. The more isolated I became, the more I clung to him.

It was okay. It could have gone on like that. But over time he became jealous when he drank. As we drove home he would sneer at me, accusing me of eyeing up other men.

"I saw you looking at that guy at the bar."

"I wasn't looking at any man," I would tell him, keeping my voice calm.

"Don't deny it!" he would say, his voice rising. "I saw you with my own eyes! How can you deny it? Jesus, but you must think I'm awful stupid to deny something I saw myself!"

I would say nothing.

"Do you?" he would insist. "Do you think I'm awful stupid?"

"No, of course I don't, Mark. I don't think you're stupid at all," I would reassure him, trying to calm him, not to escalate the situation.

"Well then!" he'd say triumphantly, as though he had just proven something.

I'd say nothing.

"So you might as well admit it!" he would continue, menace in his voice, and determination. "Admit that you were looking at that man."

I tried different tactics. I tried to continue insisting that I had looked at no man, not in any special way. "I probably glanced at somebody, Mark," I'd say, trying to meet him halfway. "The place was crowded. No matter where I looked there would be some man in my line of vision, wouldn't there? But I wouldn't have been looking at anybody as such. Sure, why would I?" I'd say playfully, going for flattery. "Aren't you the most handsome man in Ireland anyway?"

For a while this tactic worked. Until the evening he harangued me for the whole journey, so much so that I was weeping tears of denial, and still he browbeat me to confess to the imagined crime.

And then, once we were inside the hallway, he abruptly pinned me against the wall in a travesty of passion. But this passion wasn't for me – it was for his obsessive jealousy.

"Now," he breathed down at me, and the smell of stale beer was hot in my face, "now we'll have the truth. I'm sick and tired of you lying bitches, you're all the same! Tell me the truth – you were looking at that blond man in the bar. Weren't you?" he hissed.

I shook my head in denial and fear, unable to speak through my terror. Who was this man staring down at me, hatred and fury in his eyes? Was this really Mark who had told me he loved me?

"Don't *lie* to me!" he yelled. "If you tell me the truth we'll say no more about it. But by God if you continue lying to me I won't be answerable ..."

Terror won over my own pride. "Okay, okay," I said, "I was looking at him, I admit it."

"I *knew* it," he said, satisfied now. "I knew you were looking at him. I knew I was right!"

I took a deep breath, thinking it was over now, that the lie was more worthwhile than the truth.

Until he continued, a new source of fury consuming him. "But you lied to me! You told me you had been looking at nobody. You *bitch!*" He lifted his hand and with all his strength he hit me across the face. My head was pinned against the wall, I couldn't move to dissipate the force, and the pain bolted through me.

Immediately he was contrite.

"Dear God, what have I done? Oh, I'm so sorry," he told me, weeping now. "I'm so sorry. I never meant to hit you. I was just so angry about you looking at that man – I love you so much; it just hurt me so much. I'm so sorry, please forgive me. I'll never do it again, I swear. Please forgive me!"

And so *I* ended up comforting *him*. But I didn't mind – I was just grateful to hear his apologies and promises it wouldn't happen again.

It did calm down after that one occasion. But it was a new dynamic now; one in which the rules had changed. Now I knew that it could happen again, if he was provoked again. Now I had to be wary, and careful.

So I kept my eyes down when we were out together, never letting my gaze rest on any other man no matter how briefly or inadvertently. I tried to avoid going to the toilet, and if I needed to go I would pray there was no queue to delay me.

I'm not proud of this, but sometimes I lied to skip the queue. "I'm pregnant," I might tell the other women, "do you mind . . .?" Or, "I'm so sorry, but I have to use the toilet right now. I've got a dodgy tummy, and if I don't go now . . ." I'd leave it to their imaginations what might happen, and it always worked.

Looking back it's hard to believe I lived like that, in fear and terror. But it happens so gradually that you slide into it. It helps, of course, if you have little self-esteem to begin with, which I did, and which – I'm now convinced – he knew immediately. That was the source of my attraction for him.

Then I got pregnant.

I stared horrified at the blue line, that bleak evening in early January. We had always been so careful – Mark was adamant he didn't want babies at all. Something about his own dreadful childhood and how he was inflicting that on nobody. And to be honest, I didn't want a baby either. I was too young, too dependent on Mark, too messed up myself. An abortion was the obvious solution. It really was the sensible decision – absolutely everything pointed to it.

But yet, I couldn't. This baby existed now, and something primeval in me stirred. I swore to protect it no matter what. It would be safe within me until it was time to be born.

But I had yet to tell Mark. My stomach churned and my palms were slick and foetid as I approached him.

But he surprised me. Not that he was thrilled, I can't say that. But he accepted it philosophically enough. "What's done is done," he said. "We'll make the best of it."

So that was grand. At least, it was grand until later that evening. He opened a bottle of wine with his dinner as usual, and as he drank it I noted that he was becoming quieter and quieter. Then he had two very generous whiskeys.

There was a palpable tension in the air. I busied myself with clearing up the meal, and tried to ignore the leaden atmosphere, but my heart was beating too quickly and I was aware of the acid taste of apprehension in my gut.

"Tell me . . ." he said at last, conversationally.

"Yes?" I asked, my voice squeaking a little. I had learned to distrust that pseudo-chatty tone.

"Who exactly is the father of that baby you're carrying?"

Dear God! I gasped with the shock of the question.

"The father?" I repeated stupidly. "You are, of course!"

He was shaking his head.

"No. I've been thinking about it. We have always been so careful. There's no way you could have conceived with me. You must have been screwing around on me, got pregnant and are now trying to palm the bastard off on me."

"No!" I tried to make my voice firm, and I looked him straight in the eye, *willing* him to believe me. "That is absolutely *not* what has happened. I know we were always careful, and I don't know how it happened either, but I have been with nobody but you, and you *are* the father, Mark."

"Lying bitch," he said calmly. He took another swig of his whiskey. I stared at him, transfixed with fear and uncertainty. I didn't want to do the wrong thing and by so doing provoke him to anger. But any action could be the wrong thing, and so I did nothing.

Then he erupted anyway. From being outwardly calm he transformed into this hatred-spewing, spittle-flying, obscenity-yelling monster. He stood up abruptly, knocking over his glass and not noticing, and came for me.

He called me names I can't repeat, I can't bear to think of them. He grabbed my shoulders and shook me violently as he accused me of sins of which infidelity was the slightest. All his anger and hatred at his own mother, his own father, his other girlfriends, at everybody and everything, up to and including Life itself — came rushing out onto my bowed and shaking head.

"You'll have an abortion," he told me. "You surely will. I'm raising no man's bastard."

"Okay, okay, I will," I promised him through my tears. Anything, anything, once he stopped this assault.

But that didn't appease him. Perhaps I had given in too quickly, before he had the satisfaction of spewing his anger.

"We won't even wait for an abortion. I'll knock that bastard out of you now!" he roared at me. "I'm not having my woman carrying another man's child in my house!"

He lifted his fist and aimed for my stomach.

"*Nooooo!*" I yelled, and I curled myself over my stomach, determined to protect my baby. It was probably too early for any blows to damage the baby (no matter the damage they would have done to me), but neither he nor I was thinking of that.

I slipped under his blow and turned away, and fled towards the door to the hall. He reached for me, but slipped on his spilled whiskey. There was a poetic justice to that, although I didn't have the leisure to appreciate it then. But it meant I could reach the door.

"*Come back, you bitch!*" he was yelling as I reached the hallway, grabbed my bag from its place on the banister newel-post, opened the front door and fled the house, slamming the door behind me.

Where to? If I ran out onto the street he'd surely be able to catch me. I ran to the gate and pulled it open, but instead of leaving the garden I darted back to the side of the house and began to crawl into the hedge, ignoring the scratches from its thorns.

I was only half-hidden when the front door opened, spilling its light carelessly onto the front garden, and he ran through the open gate and out onto the street, cursing me as he did so.

I pushed further into the hedge until I was satisfied I was hidden. My heart was banging hard against the inside of my ribcage like a bird trapped behind a window.

I heard his footsteps on the road slow and then stop, and then start again, slowly this time, unsure. He was clearly wondering which way I had gone. He walked a little bit one way, then the other, clearly unsure as to what to do next.

I stayed where I was, hunkered uncomfortably, bitterly cold in the January night with no coat to warm me. I clamped my jaws fiercely together, to prevent my teeth from chattering. They say there are no atheists in foxholes – well, there are none in suburban hedges either, when a violent man is hunting, and you're his quarry. I fervently prayed that it wouldn't occur to him that I was hiding.

It worked. Cursing mightily he came back into the driveway, passing within a foot of me, and back into the house. I waited, unsure whether it was a trick or not, and after some time, when I judged it to be safe, I carefully unfolded myself and extricated myself from the hedge.

Cold, cut, bruised, shaking, I walked as briskly as I could down the road, taking random turns to shake off the pursuit which I knew rationally wasn't there at all. Eventually I arrived at a pub and went in, grateful for its warmth. I ignored the stares I got and made my way to the toilets. Once there I took out my mobile phone and dialled it.

After a few rings I heard a voice I hadn't heard for over a year.

"Mum?" I said. "Mum, it's me! Can you come and get me?"

I burst into tears and I couldn't talk, couldn't answer her frantic, "Of course I will – where are you?"

★ ★ ★

I didn't see Mark again for five long years. My father and brother went to collect my belongings and I never asked what transpired between them and him. I allowed my family to nurture me and love me and heal me, and in time I gave birth to Ella who is the light of my life. I try not to read too much into it when she loses her temper.

And yesterday in Grafton Street. I hid in the doorway of the shop and watched Mark with this other woman. I saw her ingratiating smile targeted towards him, and his possessive hand on the back of her neck. I noted his grim expression as he surveyed the other men on the street, and the way his grip tightened at her neck. I realised that he hadn't changed, that he's still crazy, even after all these years.

Ella said, puzzled, "What are you looking at, Mummy?"

"Nothing, darling," I told her, "nothing at all."

I smiled down at her and, taking her hand, left the doorway, and walked in the opposite direction.

Also by Tracy Culleton, published by Poolbeg

More Than Friends, Loving Lucy,
Looking Good

5

Unfinished Business
CATHERINE DALY

The accident that was to change everything happened at half past three on a Friday afternoon in August. Most people were winding down at the end of their week, preparing for the weekend, but all Rosemary could think of, was that she needed to be home by half past five in case Edward thought of something else he needed for his important weekend conference. Rosemary was fairly confident she'd packed everything he could possibly need to impress his colleagues and competitors at the event, but it would be just like Edward to think of something at the last minute and then sniff and tut, in that distracted way of his, implying it was her fault for not preparing for every eventuality.

She sat on the kerb, behind the now parked car, trying not to cry and reassuring concerned onlookers that she was all right. Which wasn't true. She felt like she had done twelve rounds with Mike Tyson. Her ribs hurt so much that she winced with each breath, her head pounded, especially if she moved it, and she had to keep wiping blood from her eye with a soggy tissue, blood that was running down from a cut on her forehead. But worse, far worse than any physical injury was the sickening realisation that now Edward would realise where she had been all afternoon. When the young policeman asked Rosemary if he could follow her to the hospital, to take a statement about the accident, she could only nod weakly. She was at least grateful that he wouldn't upset her husband by turning up at home in a squad car, causing the neighbours' curtains to twitch.

Casualty was quiet and she was seen quickly. She reassured the doctor that she had not been knocked out, and he examined the cut on her head.

"Two stitches will sort that out for you, Mrs Regan. It looks a lot worse than it is. There are a lot of blood vessels under the scalp, and they bleed like fury if you cut them at all. The only scar, and I promise it will be a tiny one, will be under your hairline – your face is just grazed."

Rosemary thanked him.

"Right, so, I'll just get Staff Nurse O'Reilly to clean you up, and then I'll come back to put in the stitches. Your ribs aren't broken, you'll be glad to hear, just badly bruised. Have the painkillers helped?"

She nodded, but the doctor didn't seem convinced, mistaking the worried look on her face for distress.

"Are you sure? I can prescribe something stronger." She tried to smile, but only managed to pull off a grimace.

"I'm fine, honestly," she said. "Just ... look, I'm fine, really."

"If you're sure . . ." The doctor seemed to hesitate at the curtain screening off the cubicle, but then the lure of a far-too-rare coffee break decided him and he pulled back the curtain to leave. "I'll see you later, so. Don't forget; if you begin to feel the slightest bit sick, or groggy, push the call button at once.'

"Of course. But I didn't really hit my head, just scratched it on the car as I fell."

The doctor didn't answer, just made his escape at the same moment as a severe-looking receptionist pushed her head between the curtains.

"Mrs Regan, we haven't been able to contact your husband at the number you gave us. Apparently he always takes Friday afternoons off?" The woman's severe expression hardened, as if she was implying that Rosemary was wasting valuable health-service resources by giving the receptionist misleading information.

Rosemary tried to look as if she'd merely forgotten about Edward's early finish on a Friday, but it was news to her. In fact she had always believed Friday afternoon to be set aside for the partners' meetings. And Edward, more often than not, returned home late after them.

"Sorry to have wasted your time," she apologised. "But it's not necessary to contact Edward, is it? The doctor seems happy enough with me. I'll call a taxi and make my own way home." She felt a faint glimmer of hope.

"I don't think that would be wise." The receptionist shook her head, her vast medical knowledge lending weight to her assertion. "Not wise at all. You never know with head injuries. It's best if I keep trying to reach your husband. Does he have a mobile number I could try?" She bustled off with the information Rosemary reluctantly supplied – a woman with a mission, ready to track Mr Regan to the ends of the earth.

"Now, Mrs Regan, let's get that wound cleaned up so that Doctor ... Good God, Rosie! What are you doing here?" The male nurse stopped in his tracks, and a huge grin spread across his face. His warm brown eyes danced with delight at seeing her.

"I'd have thought that was obvious. I've been throwing myself under cars in every city in the country in an attempt to find you." She felt strangely upset that she hadn't known he had moved back home. "Staff Nurse O'Reilly, I presume? Welcome back, Mark."

"My God, Rosie, I haven't seen you since . . ."

He rushed forward and looked as if he was going to hug her. She flinched automatically. He stopped, and a professional expression replaced the split second of hurt she saw on his face.

"Sorry, Mark. It's my ribs. They hurt like hell." She tried to grin. "You can owe me that hug."

"You've certainly changed, Rosie," Mark said, smiling again.

Changed for good or for bad, she wondered, but didn't ask. Why should she care what an ex-boyfriend thought? She was a married woman now.

"You look so elegant, so stylish, so – grown up!"

Bad then, she decided.

"And you still look so . . ." A distant, wistful look came over his face.

Maybe not so bad. She knew he was remembering the long-forgotten Rosie, in jeans and T-shirts, with wild, untamed long auburn hair. The Rosie with her heart on her sleeve and her foot in her mouth. So sure of what she wanted from life. A long way from Rosemary, in a Jaeger knitted suit, a bloodstained white blouse and pearls. A woman who rarely voiced her opinion without checking first with Edward what her opinion should be.

"Mrs Regan." He rolled the name over in his mouth, tasting it. "You got married then."

"Yes, Edward's his name, an accountant. He has his own firm. Set up on his own seven years ago, just a year after we got married. He's doing well. There's three partners now . . ." Stop it, she thought, you'll be giving out his school grades next.

"Still married?" Mark asked. The question took her by surprise and her shocked expression made him laugh.

"Sorry, I'm afraid I'm just an old cynic. Fifty per cent of all marriages – blah, blah, blah. This might sting." He applied some moistened gauze to her temple.

The young policeman came in at that point, and asked her a few more questions about the accident.

"It was my own fault. I was in a hurry. I needed to catch that bus, get home before . . . I crossed without looking," she babbled.

"Another witness suggested the driver wasn't looking where he was going. If you want to take it further . . ."

"No! Absolutely not!" she cried. "I mean, no real harm done, best to forget about it." She lowered her voice. "My husband doesn't need to know *where* the accident took place, does he?"

The policeman went pink and snapped his notebook shut. "As the incident is closed, it's up to you what you tell him, madam." He scuttled out.

Mark was cleaning grit out of the grazes on her hands now.

"It's not what you think," she said, not sure why she felt she had to explain herself to him.

"I don't think anything." But as he looked up at her, she could see he was dying for an explanation.

"I was at work. Edward doesn't know yet that I have a job. I will tell him, of course. There just hasn't been a right time." She hadn't found a right time in the six weeks since starting her part-time job. "He can't understand why I would want to work – it's not exactly as if we need the money."

"Has our super-efficient Julie managed to reach him yet?" Mark changed the subject. "If you have no lift home, I'm finishing up soon." He glanced at the address on her chart. "I live out your way – I can take you home, make sure you're all right until . . ." He looked into her eyes. "I'd like to . . . I mean . . . we could have a drink maybe, catch up on old times . . ."

"It was a long time ago, Mark."

He had broken her heart when he left to study nursing. She couldn't understand why he turned down an offer closer to home, and he was angry that she insisted on staying at home, in the town they had both sworn to escape from, the first chance they got. Stubbornly, she broke it off with him, and then was devastated when he didn't come begging for the forgiveness she longed to give him. She married Edward less than a year later. On the rebound, but she had married him. And that still meant something, didn't it?

"Any kids?" Mark tried to lighten the mood.

"No, we're . . . well . . ." She longed for children, but how could she explain that after seven years of refusing to discuss it, Edward had recently announced that he was too old, at forty-four, to start a family?

"Oh well, plenty of time. You're only thirty." Mark looked sad for a moment. "It was kids that tore apart my one lasting relationship while I was away. I wanted them; she didn't. Amy's a doctor. She said she'd never make consultant if she had children."

"Do you miss her?" She was glad to take the spotlight off herself.

"At first. But it was never going to work . . . we met too soon after . . ." He couldn't meet her eyes. "It was a mistake, that's all."

Rosie's hand was now cleaner than when she stepped out of the shower, but Mark kept stroking it with the damp cotton wool. Even through the thin layer of latex of his surgical gloves her fingers recognised his touch. She hoped he couldn't feel her pulse racing. Maybe she was suffering from concussion after all.

"Rosemary! My dear! What happened to you?" Edward went pale as he pulled back the curtain. She closed her jacket to hide her bloodstained blouse; he was very squeamish.

"Don't worry. It's not nearly as bad as it looks, Mr Regan." Mark stood up to leave. "I'm just finished here. Dr White will put in those stitches and then you can go." He was gone before she could even thank him, let alone say all the things she wanted to say, but were probably best left unsaid.

Edward leaned over and kissed Rosemary on the cheek. She smelled alcohol and garlic. Not unpleasant odours. White wine, fresh garlic, as if he'd just stood up from the table.

"I was meeting a client all afternoon with Jeanine, the new trainee," he explained without meeting her eyes. "I only just heard what happened. As we're going to be out of here soon, I'll ask her to wait and give us a lift home."

"You didn't drive to the restaurant yourself?"

"Eh . . . no. My car's still at the office. Back in a minute." He was gone.

Suddenly Rosie needed to go to the bathroom. She poked her head between the curtains. From the corner of her eye she spotted Edward beetling towards the waiting area. A young woman, who seemed to be in her early twenties, with long blonde hair and wearing navy trousers and a white T-shirt, stood up. She looked angry. He said something to make her smile, and then brushed a strand of hair out of her face. A gesture Rosie recognised. Edward used to brush her hair back like that, before he persuaded her that she would look much better with short hair. The woman laughed at something he said, and sat down again.

Edward returned to Rosemary as the doctor cut the thread on the last stitch, then signed her chart with a flourish.

"That's it. You're free to go now. You can come back in ten days or so to get those stitches removed, or go to your own doctor. This is a prescription for a course of antibiotics and some painkillers. Those ribs are going to get sore." He scribbled a few lines onto a sheet of paper and thrust it at Rosemary before leaving.

"Rosemary . . ." Edward hesitated, hopping from foot to foot. It was a habit of his that annoyed his wife. It was as though he was trying to look vulnerable, or indecisive, which he never was. "As you're going to be fine, would you mind awfully if Jeanine and I went back to the office for a couple of hours? It's just that . . ."

"That's all right, I understand." She smiled a smile that didn't get past her lips. "Unfinished business. You go on out to her. I want to leave a thank-you note for the nurse." She ignored his look of impatient irritation and went to the desk.

Rosemary wrote down her name and phone number

on a page ripped out of her diary, and asked at reception if there was any way of leaving a message for a member of staff. She named him.

"Mark?" the receptionist said. "He should be out in a moment and you can give it to him yourself. He's just getting changed."

Rosie remembered how he had offered her a lift home and the opportunity to 'catch up on old times'. She crumpled up the note she had been writing, shoving it back into her pocket.

"Good, I'll wait for him. Mark and I are old friends." Her smile spread beyond her lips, lighting up her eyes for the first time in far too long. "He offered me a lift home actually, and I think I should take him up on it. My husband has some unfinished business to attend to."

She turned as a door beside her opened and Mark emerged.

"That lift home . . ." she said as their eyes met. "Is your offer still open?"

He grinned, and to Rosemary's surprise, she blushed and her stomach flipped.

I think I have some unfinished business myself, she thought as he looped his arm through hers and led her to the staff carpark.

ALSO BY CATHERINE DALY, PUBLISHED BY POOLBEG

A French Affair, Charlotte's Way,
All Shook Up

6

Tiaras At Teatime

MARTINA DEVLIN

"I'm Bella, I'm four and I have a vulva."

Deirdre's gaze, fixed expectantly ahead after ringing the doorbell, travels downwards a couple of feet until it lands on a figure all of 39 inches high, wearing a diamante-studded pink cape. "You have a Volvo? That's lovely."

"No, a vulva. It's what girls have instead of a penis. I expect you have one too. My mum does."

"Does she?"

"Yes, but not my daddy because only girls are allowed to have them. It means we can't wee standing up like boys."

Deirdre wonders how this minuscule human being – one with such an anatomically correct vocabulary – was able to reach the lock to open the front door.

Almost as though she can read her mind, the little girl volunteers, "I've had the door open a crack, waiting for you."

"You knew I was coming?"

"Of course – my mum told me. She's taking forever to get ready, my mum. She changed her clothes three times and dropped her lipstick on the carpet. It's all covered in fluff."

An emotion that might have been sympathy, under different circumstances, catches Deirdre by surprise as she steps into the porch. It's crowded with Wellingtons, umbrellas and coats. Family debris, she notes with a pang.

Bella pivots on tiptoe, sending her cape swirling around her in a glittering spiral.

"I'm a princess."

"Where's your tiara? All princesses have a tiara."

"What's a tirara?" The rotation stops abruptly and a pair of grey-green eyes latch onto Deirdre's.

"It's sparkly and sits on top of your head like a hairband."

Bella's pupils dilate with gratifying awe. "Would I look pretty in it?"

"Drop-dead gorgeous." Deirdre bends to secure the bow on the cape, which is slipping off Bella's shoulders.

"I want a tirara! Can you get me one?"

"I hope you're playing nicely, Bella." A woman's voice floats down from the half-landing on the stairs.

Deirdre watches her as she descends and comes to a halt behind her daughter. "Hello, Deirdre."

Deirdre sees a woman in her early forties with chestnut hair the same shade as her own, cut sleek to the base of her neck and tucked behind her ears; the toasted complexion of someone who has lived for years in a hot climate; sherry-gold eyes that are watchful; crescent lines either side of a mouth that isn't smiling but gives the impression of being willing to, with any encouragement.

Deirdre isn't ready to provide assistance in that department.

"Come inside, you're welcome to our home." Karen steps backwards, pulling her daughter with her to make space.

"We have pink and yellow cake for tea," confides Bella. Her accent is as English as if she had grown up in Newmarket instead of Nairobi. "I picked it. It's my next favourite after octopus cake, but Mum says we can't buy birthday cake unless it's somebody's birthday. It's not yours, is it?"

"No, my birthday's on the —"

"Fifth of December," Karen finishes her sentence for her.

Deirdre compresses her lips. Clever of her to remember; even smarter if she'd bothered to spend more than the first three birthdays with her.

"It was snowing when I went into labour with you," continues Karen, leading her towards the living room. "I remember thinking we could build a snowman in the front garden to show the new baby."

"I've never seen a real snowman, only ones in books." Bella careers around, whinnying and tossing her hair. "That's because we used to live in our real house in Africa where it doesn't snow, but now we live in our new house in Ireland in a country called Dublin."

"Back to front, dumpling," Karen corrects her. "But this is your real house now. Won't you take a seat, Deirdre? Bella, stop snuffling. We won't feed you sugar lumps even if you are a pony. You know I've explained sugar will hurt your teeth and make them squeak."

Bella perches on the arm of Deirdre's chair, staring intently as though auditing the contents of her nostrils. "I'm watching you," she announces.

"Leave Deirdre in peace."

"She's not bothering me, honestly."

Bella leans closer to Deirdre. "We have blue water in our toilet. In Africa the water was white when you flushed. Well, sometimes it was brownish white. But here it turns blue. Would you like to see?"

"She's fascinated by the coloured water in the loo," Karen explains. "She wants to flush it a hundred times a day. She thinks it's the most exciting thing about Ireland."

Deirdre and Karen sit opposite one another, each woman's gaze making a foray across the room and sliding off the other's face. Deirdre's attention is caught by a pair of bronze figures to the left of the French windows: attenuated stick insects but for their protruding stomachs. One is of a woman with a water jug on her head, the other a man with a drum resting on his hip. They must have come from Africa with the Fairfaxes. Philip Fairfax, Karen Fairfax, Isabella Fairfax. Her almost family. Deirdre looks for further signposts to their lives there, on another continent, and spies an ebony woodcarving on the mantelpiece, a purgatorial tangle of faces and limbs.

"Some tea? Or perhaps you'd care for coffee? We also have herbal tea if you prefer. All tastes catered for." Karen's teeth appear, and disappear just as abruptly.

"Bella, why don't you show Deirdre how beautifully you can write your name while I put the kettle on?"

There's something about her clipped 'some tea' which tells of that stretch of years among expatriates. Deirdre realises her mother has spent longer outside Ireland than living in the country – Kenya probably seems more like home than anywhere else.

"Can you write your name? That's very clever – show me."

"I'd like it better if you drew me a picture of a princess wearing a tirara. And will you make it really sparkly?"

"I could try. I'm not very good at drawing."

"You can use my gel pens. They'll help." Bella smiles reassurance at Deirdre, who finds herself reaching out to touch a dimpled cheek.

"If you like, I'll bring you a tiara the next time I come to see you."

Without warning, Bella slides off the arm of the chair and flings herself on Deirdre. "Thank you! You won't forget?"

Nonplussed, Deirdre looks down at the caramel head with a snatch of pink scalp showing through at the crown. "I won't forget."

Bella twists away as abruptly as she hugged Deirdre. "Mum, did you bring the pink and yellow cake?"

"I certainly did," Karen replies, above the clatter of a laden trolley. Her hand trembles as she pours and liquid slops over onto the saucer. "I'll take that one," she says swiftly. "I don't know what's wrong with me today."

Bella crumbles Battenburg cake on Deirdre's cream linen trousers while the tea ritual is observed. Then she wanders off to her room to play with her Barbie dolls, leaving the others alone.

"It feels odd to have a sister twenty years younger than me — it feels odd to have a sister at all."

"Your eyes are the same shade of grey-green," remarks Karen. "Jasper, a jeweller once called it."

"Is she your only child? Apart from ..." Deirdre stumbles, unable to finish.

The older woman shrugs helplessly. "I was eighteeen when you were born, a girl in many ways."

"But a mother, all the same." Deirdre is inflexible.

Karen stands and starts stacking the tray to avoid responding.

"Why did you leave me anyway?"

There, it's suspended between them. The question that haunted her childhood is out in the open.

"Mothers tend not to leave their children behind, even when they walk away from a marriage." Deirdre twists the knife.

Karen's eyes scamper around the room, searching it for an answer. The folds of the curtains, the flock of the carpet, the hands of a cloisonné clock on the mantelpiece are all scrutinised as though they could field a credible explanation on her behalf.

Then an expression of resignation settles on her features, she replaces the tray on the coffee table and sits back in her armchair.

"I didn't love your father when I agreed to be his wife. I thought perhaps the love would follow, once we settled into marriage, but it didn't. When I discovered I was pregnant I was all at sea. I didn't know what to do for the best, so I was grateful when he took control and said we should marry. Jim seemed strong and dependable and I clung to that. He offered me a way out of the trap I felt I'd stumbled into – but gratitude never developed into love. And I discovered that traps come in different shapes and sizes, and who knows but that your escape hatch will turn into your prison?" The palms of her hands are moist and she rubs them on her sweater. "I don't know how mature teenagers are nowadays, they're probably intimidatingly capable, but I was far from that. I was at my wits' end, to tell you the truth, and marriage seemed my only option. Either that or . . . abortion. I suppose there was adoption too but, well, then everyone would have known I was pregnant and unmarried, wouldn't they? I didn't even consider turning to my family. All my father and brothers thought of was the farm. I didn't have the words to tell them how I'd insisted on coming to Dublin to work and landed myself in the oldest trouble known to woman. I was the serpent in my own Garden of Eden." Her front teeth catch her lower lip and dig in viciously.

Deirdre senses her mother is scarcely conscious of her presence.

"Mine isn't an original story; I suppose few people's are. I discovered I was pregnant and thought marriage was the solution. It never occurred to me that I could have a baby and raise it on my own." Karen twists a pearl ring on her finger, first clockwise, then anti-clockwise.

"How did you meet?" Deirdre knows so little about their life together. Her father would occasionally let slip a tantalising ribbon of information but generally he was uncommunicative on the subject of his wife.

"I grew up on a farm in County Wexford, near Enniscorthy. When I was seventeen my mother died and I didn't want to take her place in the household so I asked my father if I could leave school and find a job. He agreed, although I think he was surprised by how quickly I was offered a post. A teacher helped. I loved books and she had a cousin with a bookshop in Dublin, so they agreed between them that I should work there. I rented a bedsit in a house in Rathmines and your father had a small flat on the floor below me. We introduced ourselves in the hallway collecting our post one morning. He was a lot older than me, twenty-two years my senior, and in some ways I was in awe of him. But he loved reading, the same as I did − it was an instant connection between us. That and loneliness, I suppose. I remember long conversations about books. He'd recommend novels I should read, and he used to bring me to see plays and lend me the book afterwards." She smiles, the darkness in her eyes ebbing. "I saw *Juno and the Paycock* with Jim – he was a great admirer of Sean O'Casey's – although I preferred the production of *Waiting For Godot* we managed to buy tickets for just before curtain-up. Your father wasn't keen on Beckett – he found him godless." A trapped nerve ticks in her cheek. "Sometimes we'd go for meals – not often because money was scarce. I earned next to nothing in the bookshop; a church mouse would have been richer than me. Jim was doing well at the bank, mind you, but he had to send money home to his mother. I had the impression there were debts in the family but I never asked and it seemed to tail off after we were married, apart from the odd sum. She didn't make old bones, his mother, so perhaps the debts died with her. To be honest we were at our happiest when the money was tightest, Deirdre. You might find that out for yourself one day."

Deirdre thinks of the windfall brought by her father's death and winces. "How did you come to get pregnant?"

"The usual way." Karen's mouth crooks in a parody of humour. "A combination of drink, affection and opportunity. It was my eighteenth birthday and Jim knocked on my door with a bottle of champagne. I'd never tasted it before, it tickled my throat on the way down and I thought it was heavenly. We sat on my bed – there was nowhere else to sit, the room was that small – and drank it out of teacups. We were only together that one time. I never even undressed. Sure I was as green as grass." Frowning, Karen pulls her hair forward to mask her face. "I decided to end it with your father after that slip –"

Her hand flies to cover her mouth. How will Deirdre react to her conception being described as a slip? Deirdre hasn't noticed, however, grappling with the realisation that her father's halo has been tarnished. A forty-year-old man, a teenager and a bottle of champagne in her bedroom . . . Deirdre's frown is a match for her mother's.

Karen continues. "I knew he was in love with me and while I admired Jim and was fond of him, I couldn't love him back. It just wasn't in me. I thought I'd try my luck with one of the big bookshops in London. I had a few pounds saved up to tide me over and I handed in my notice. Jim asked would I reconsider if he were to marry me, and when I shook my head he said he wouldn't stand in my way. I was young, he said, I shouldn't have my youth stolen. But it was already too late. A few days before I was due to leave I discovered I was pregnant and your father stepped in. I was thankful, believe me, but not, I subsequently discovered, thankful enough to spend my life with him."

Deirdre feels obliged to intervene. "My father was a fine man."

"He was, but he wasn't the man for me. We made each other miserable for almost four years, with me feeling imprisoned and him feeling like the jailer jangling the keys. There was you, of course. We both loved you." Her face, which has become self-intent, clears. "But you weren't enough, my dear. Babies never hold marriages together. They only postpone the collapse."

Deirdre decides she's heard enough for one day. She'd wanted the story, but she hadn't counted on the complexity of emotion it would stir up. "So you ran away to England, found a job and intended to send for me. But my father put up a fight, you subsided without much opposition and later you moved to Nairobi with the man of your dreams." She's reciting a lesson drilled into her. "And although you initiated divorce proceedings a few years ago, my father beat you to it by dying. Game, set and match to Jim Scully, a decent man who did nothing worse than get a girl pregnant and try to do right by her." Her voice would have corroded metal. "Meanwhile, you replaced husband and daughter, didn't you, Mother?"

She calls her 'Mother' deliberately, for the first time. Baiting her.

"Bella," says Karen, "why have you cut off Highland Barbie's hair? And where did you find the scissors to do it? You know they're too dangerous to play with."

"I used my play scissors for cutting paper. I wanted her to have the same hairstyle as Deirdre. Don't you think she looks just like you?" Bella holds the savagely shorn doll towards Deirdre for inspection.

Deirdre decides to be flattered that her sister imagines a doll, whose vital statistics would measure 42-18-32 if she were life-sized, resembles her. "We could be twins. Do you have any other Barbies?"

"Millions. That's a lot, you know. Would you like to play with them?"

"I'd love to, but I have to go now, Bella. I – I'm tired."

"But it's nowhere near bedtime. It's not even dark outside."

Karen gathers Bella into her arms, almost like body armour. "Your big sister can see your Barbies next time. There will be a next time, Deirdre?"

The air grows dense between them and Deirdre fumbles for an answer. "I'm not sure. You've hurt me once already – what's to stop you doing it again?'

"Nothing. You could hurt me too, though. Or you could hurt Bella. That's a chance I'm willing to take."

The child glances from her sister to her mother, sensing the tension. "What about my tirara? You promised you'd bring me one next time."

Deirdre turns away, unable to meet her gaze.

"Mum?" Tears well in the little girl's eyes.

Karen drops a kiss on the crown of her head, soothing her. "Your father taught me one lesson I carried through life, Deirdre."

"What was that?"

"You have to learn to love like you've never been hurt. There's no other way to do it."

"I don't know if I can manage that."

"None of us do, that's the catch, none of us do."

ALSO BY MARTINA DEVLIN, PUBLISHED BY POOLBEG

Temptation, Venus Reborn

7

The Hitch-hiker
ANNA DILLON

Climbing back into the car, Teri Wilde shoved the summons into the door pocket, snapped on her seat belt, then smiled at the blank-faced Garda Sergeant and gently eased the BMW away from the kerb. It took an enormous effort of will not to floor the accelerator and shower the bored-looking officer with gravel. She was in enough trouble already. This was the third time this month she had been stopped for speeding. And the second time by this particular sergeant.

"Are you aware that you were doing one hundred and thirty kilometres in a one-hundred-and-twenty-kilometre an-hour zone?" he asked patronisingly, leaning into the car, filling it with the odour of damp sweating waterproof clothes and musky aftershave.

She blinked quickly, eyes watering, her contact lenses misting.

How were you supposed to answer that? What were

you supposed to say? "Yes, I knew. That's why I was doing it," or "No, I didn't know. Why do you think I was doing it?"

Neither answer would be acceptable, she guessed, so she just shook her head and shrugged. She didn't even bother trying to come up with an excuse; she reckoned he'd heard them all. She watched as he pulled out his book: how many points had she on her licence now?

She reckoned the police officer was jealous. He sat there behind his little radar gun and he saw this fire-engine-red BMW 7 Series speeding toward him with a pretty young woman behind the wheel, and even if she wasn't speeding, he was going to stop her, just for a look-see. And one-thirty wasn't that fast; the limit on this part of the motorway was one-twenty; ten kilometres over the limit was nothing, barely even noticeable. The car would go a lot faster. She knew: she'd pushed it to up to a hundred and sixty kilometres on the Athlone bypass.

It was also so unfair. While she'd been speaking to the Garda, dozens of cars had sped past, brake-lights blazing as they suddenly realised there was a police car lurking, partially concealed by the red BMW. Why hadn't *they* been stopped?

Teri glanced in her rear-view mirror. She could still see the cop standing on the road, watching her; she thought he might have been grinning. The young woman scowled. She reckoned she'd accumulated enough points now to lose her licence, though maybe Brian would know someone.

Brian *always* knew someone.

So: was she going to tell her husband? She hadn't told him about the two previous tickets. But there was a lot she didn't tell him nowadays.

Teri rounded the curve and, once out of sight of the police, changed gears and shoved the accelerator to the floor. The heavy car surged forward. The needle moved smoothly up to one hundred, one-ten, one-twenty, one-twenty-five kilometres an hour. Now that she knew where the speed trap was, she knew this next section of the road was clear. Holding the car at a steady one-twenty-five, Teri cruised down the dual carriageway. She didn't think she was driving that fast: cars still passed her – either cap-wearing boy racers in their souped-up toys or balding executives in their company cars. It was obviously some sort of affront to their pride to have a woman ahead of them.

If there was a possibility that she was going to lose her licence, she was going to have to tell her husband . . . and Brian was not going to be pleased. He'd make that disappointed face, shake his head and tut-tut – all of which just infuriated her. There were times when he seemed to forget that he was her husband, and not her father.

Brian Wilde was nearly twenty-five years her senior, and indulged her outrageously, buying her everything she wanted – and lots of things she didn't. This car was a sixth wedding-anniversary gift; it hadn't made any difference that she neither needed nor wanted a new car. "The moment I saw it, I just knew I had to get it for you," was all he'd said when she protested at the extravagance of the gift. "It makes me happy to make you happy."

And there really was no response to that.

Six years married: seven in three months' time. A lot of people had predicted that it wouldn't last more than a year. These were the same people who thought – no, who *knew* – that Teri had married Brian for his money. They found it impossible to accept the fact that she genuinely loved him. Teri's lips twisted in a sudden grim smile. She *had* genuinely loved him. Past tense. But now?

Things change.

People change.

They had been deeply in love when they married, but over the last couple of years the differences – in background, education, tastes, age – which had once drawn them together, had become points of friction between them. Everything he said or did got on her nerves. She'd also begun to notice that Brian was increasingly irritated by the same habits in her that he'd once found charming.

As the carriageway ended and the road narrowed, Teri slowed the car minimally. The petrol light began flashing on the dashboard and she suddenly realised that the needle was hovering close to zero. She swore softly; she had meant to fill up the tank at the last petrol station but her encounter with the Garda had driven the thought from her mind. She wondered how many miles were left in the reserve tank.

A road sign flickered by: Balbriggan – Drogheda – Dundalk – Belfast. Brian was due to fly into Belfast airport from London that morning for a meeting with the managers of the hotel group he owned. He wanted to drive down to Dublin afterward himself, but she had insisted on going north to collect him. Belfast was less than two hours from the capital in her BMW, and she thought the long drive would do her good . . . and give them a couple of hours alone together so they could talk. They rarely seemed able to find the time to chat together any more. When they first started seeing one another eight years ago, they'd done nothing but talk. God, the things they'd talked about – everything, *anything*! She'd been fascinated by his wealth of knowledge, his wide range of experience, the stories of his travels. Brian in turn had been entranced by her vivacity, her enthusiasm for living, her eagerness to learn about fine wines and good food and the theatre, all the things he knew about which she had only dreamed of until then. The twenty-five years between them was almost an added bonus: they could each bring something special to the other.

Brian and Teri had been exact opposites; that's where the attraction lay. The attraction quickly turned to affection and then drifted into love, and then there came a point when they spoke of marriage as inevitable.

Teri frowned. Lately, she found herself wondering if they had ever really been in love. Had she still been in love with Brian when she'd had her first affair three years ago, and another less than a year ago? Both were brief impassioned events which had left her elated and disgusted in equal measure. Didn't the fact that she'd needed the affairs tell her something was very wrong with the relationship? She should have got out then: it would have been easier, certainly the more honest thing to do. She remained in the marriage because she was genuinely fond of Brian. Her lips twisted in a bitter smile as she added the second part to the sentence: and because she'd become used to the good life. So, what did that make her?

She wanted to tell him. Needed to talk to him – not to hurt him, never that – but simply to explain how events had spiralled out of control.

The bright red, orange and yellow lights of a petrol station loomed on her left. She indicated and slowed, cutting across the road and pulling into the station with a squeal of tyres, ignoring the blare of horns behind her from the cars she'd cut off.

The young male attendant had eyes only for the car, even as she climbed out with her skirt hitched up, showing a length of tanned thigh. "Fill it, please," she snapped at him. She glanced at her tiny diamond-encrusted Dior watch: Brian's plane was due to land in an hour and a half, and she really wanted to be there in time. He hated to be kept waiting.

Teri was pulling out of the station when she noticed the hitch-hiker.

He was sitting on an army rucksack by the side of the road, and from his weary expression and the despondent slump of his shoulders she guessed he'd been sitting there a long time. He was young – early or mid-twenties – and handsome, his long blond hair pulled back off his face into a tight ponytail. His face was oval, with pale blue eyes over full lips and a pronounced jaw, and his faded T-shirt was stretched across a muscular torso. He reminded her of someone, but she couldn't think who, maybe some movie star or singer. She glanced in the rear-view mirror: the young man had glanced at the car, then obviously dismissed her, knowing his chances of getting a lift from a single woman in a car were practically nil. Teri never picked up hitch-hikers . . .

Tapping the horn, she indicated and pulled in to the side of the road.

She watched him in the mirror, reading his expressions as they washed across his face: the quick flare of hope, then indecision, and finally relief. He gathered up his rucksack and ran easily down the road towards her. Teri lowered the electric window on the passenger side. Crouching beside the door, he peered in, and she was once again struck by the remarkable familiarity of him.

Maybe she'd met him somewhere . . . at an event . . . a charity gig?

"Thanks for stopping," he said. "I'm looking for a lift north." He had the faintest trace of some accent she couldn't identify.

"I'm heading to Belfast," she said. "Dump your bag in the boot." She pulled the lever that popped the boot-lid open and watched as he heaved the bag inside, then brushed the dust off his clothes. "You look like you've been waiting a long time," she said as he climbed into the car. He exuded an earthy scent; musk and sweat, she decided. Very male.

"I really appreciate this. Not many lifts today," he replied non-committally.

"Have you come far?"

"A long way," he told her. "When I left school I decided to take a year off and hitch my way around the world. I'm on the home stretch now – heading back."

Teri was impressed; she remembered Brian telling her that he had done the same. "Why?" she wondered, asking him the same question she had asked her husband.

He shrugged and grinned. Glancing at him, she decided he was even younger than she'd thought. And very attractive. "Why not?" he said, giving her the same answer Brian had. He swivelled toward her. "I'm Mark," he volunteered.

"Teri." She changed gear. "Hitching around the world – it sounds so crazy."

"Didn't you ever want to just do something crazy, Teri?"

"All the time," she told him. Then she realised with surprise how bitter she sounded.

"Why didn't you?" he asked, settling back into the

leather seat.

She threw back her head and laughed. "Oh, Mark, I wish it were that simple."

"It is, really. If you want to do something – then do it. Be true to yourself."

"It's really not that simple," she insisted. "I'm married. I have a husband, responsibilities . . ."

"Oh."

She was conscious that he had glanced pointedly at her hand.

"I didn't see a ring."

"I don't like wearing jewellery," she defensively. To an extent that was true. If she wore a lot of jewellery people were more convinced than ever that she'd married Brian for his money. But the wedding band had first come off at the time of her first affair, three years ago. Now she habitually took it off when she was not with Brian – and on occasion when she was. She didn't think Brian ever noticed; he was too preoccupied with his business to notice. At any rate, he'd never said anything. "I'm driving to Belfast now to pick up my husband," she went on hurriedly.

"He's a lucky man."

Teri glanced at him sharply, unsure if he was being sarcastic or not. "Why do you say that?"

"Not many wives would drive from Dublin to Belfast to collect their husbands. You must love him at lot."

The quick answer – the stock answer – would have been, "Yes, I do," but somehow the truth came more easily. "I'm not sure how I feel about him any more."

Mark shot her a quick look, then turned to stare through the passenger window. Glancing sidelong at him, Teri caught his reflection in the glass and once again was struck by his familiarity. Where had she seen him?

"Why are you going to pick him up then?" he wondered.

"I want to talk to him. I need to talk to him. I need to tell him how I feel . . . how I have been feeling over the past couple of years. I want to see if we can . . ." she paused, then said, "sort things out."

"Sounds to me like you still love him," Mark said shortly.

Teri opened her mouth to reply, then shut it again, not sure how to respond. She eased her foot off the accelerator, and kept the needle hovering around one hundred and twenty kilometres an hour. "Will you continue your education, once your year of travel is over?" she enquired politely, wanting to take the conversation away from herself.

"Absolutely. I want to do so many things – there are a lot more courses I want to take." He added with a laugh, "I might be a student until I'm forty!"

"That's nice," Teri said absently. "I was never really interested in school. Sitting in a classroom hour after hour listening to teachers droning on just bored me to tears. It was only when Brian – that's my husband – began teaching me things that I got interested in learning. He teased me because I was always asking so many questions." She took a deep breath. "He doesn't bother teaching me any more."

"Do you bother asking him those questions?"

Teri shook her head. She'd stopped asking him questions about three years ago.

"Maybe you should take some time off," Mark said quietly. "Go on a trip. Make some time for yourself."

"Alone?" she asked, surprised. "I'm not sure Brian would like me going off on my own."

"Did you ever ask him?"

"No, I guess I didn't."

"Maybe you should."

"Maybe I will."

"I'll bet he says go. If he loves you, he will."

Teri nodded. Maybe Brian would. Although, instead of going alone, maybe they should have a holiday together. A quiet holiday, away from phones and faxes, internet and email. Just the two of them, rediscovering that initial attraction.

"What do you do for fun?" Mark asked, swivelling in the seat again to look at her.

"Fun?" She hadn't thought much about 'fun' in a long time. It seemed such a childish idea. "I go shopping," she told the hitch-hiker.

"But what do you and your husband do together?"

"Nothing" was the answer, but she didn't verbalise it.

They drove on in silence for a while. She could feel his unspoken criticism. Was her life so obvious? Flash car, expensive clothes, businessman husband who travelled and left a dissatisfied wife at home?

"You don't understand how it is, Mark. Life is never the way it looks from the outside."

"You seem to be doing all right."

"I'm not talking about material things. I'm talking about time! When I was your age – and that's not so long ago – I used to think I had all the time in the world. When I got married, though – and even before I got married – there were always demands on my time. Now I don't seem to have a moment to myself."

"Even when your husband's away?"

"Especially when he's away. There's the house to run, and social engagements, and the charities I volunteer time to, and once you get on the merry-go-round you never get off," she finished lamely.

It was the merry-go-round that had led to her first affair. With Brian away, she'd given herself over to the social whirl, filled the empty hours with trivia and a handsome stockbroker with a blonde wife and three blonde children at home.

"Sure you can. Just step off."

"You're only a kid!" she flared. "You don't know what you're talking about – you simply don't understand!"

"Maybe I understand more than you think," he said softly. "What I think I'm hearing is guilt."

"Guilt! What are you talking about?"

"You." Mark smiled. "You don't need to be Sherlock Holmes to work it out. You've told me you're driving north to collect your husband so you can grab a couple of hours to have a chat together. To sort things out, you said. Must be an important chat."

Teri glanced at him again. He really was good-looking. That unlined skin, those white even teeth. Teri felt the old restlessness stirring in her. I wish I was his age, she thought, and had just met him, and both of us as free as the wind. At that moment he turned and looked at her, his eyes locking with hers, and she had the profound conviction he knew exactly what she was thinking.

"I'm hearing guilt," Mark smiled. "You've done something. You're torn between admitting it to your husband and keeping quiet."

Teri squeezed her lips together and said nothing.

That was her dilemma. Should she tell Brian about the affairs, admit everything and allow events to unfold, or should she simply say nothing and attempt to rebuild her marriage?

"Maybe he knows," Mark said quietly, not looking at her.

"What do you mean by that?" she demanded.

"You admitted he's clever and successful. Maybe he knows and all he's waiting for is for you to admit it."

"You're studying psychology – right?" she snapped.

"No, business studies," he said.

"Brian did business studies," she said. "I had an affair – two affairs," she went on quietly, shocking herself with the admission to this perfect stranger. "Do you think Brian could forgive that?"

"Does he love you?" Mark asked, very softly.

"Yes," Teri admitted.

"If you were honest with him, then yes, I think he would forgive you. People in love can forgive just about anything."

Teri drove in silence for several miles, then she nodded. "You're right. I'll tell him. I was afraid to tell him before this. I didn't want to hurt him."

"If he already knows, then by not telling him you're hurting him all the more."

"Very deep for a business student."

"Business is life," he muttered. "Understand one and you understand the other."

"Brian says exactly the same thing," she said.

★　★　★

They drove across the non-existent border in silence. Teri thought the young hitch-hiker was dozing. She was glad she'd picked him up and he was right, of course: she needed to be honest with Brian. She'd tell him. And if they split up, then she'd do as Mark suggested: step off the merry-go-round and take some time for herself.

"Where do you want me to let you off?" she asked, when she felt him stirring.

"You're going to the airport? That'll do me, I suppose."

She laughed. "You can't hitch a ride on an airplane."

"No." He continued to gaze out the window. His silence was beginning to make her uncomfortable.

She wheeled the BMW into the short-term parking lot and glanced at her watch. Brian's plane would already be down; she'd have to hurry. Impatiently, she popped the lid of the boot as she hauled up the handbrake.

"Grab your bag," she told her passenger as she climbed out of the car, expecting him to get out on his side.

But when she walked around the car he wasn't there.

Nor was he still sitting in the passenger seat. Standing behind the car, she looked around, completely confused now. "Mark . . . Mark?"

Teri glanced into the boot. There was no sign of his bag. She walked around the car, head swivelling left and right. Where had he gone? She didn't think he'd just grab his rucksack and disappear without saying a word.

Teri slammed the boot shut and walked towards the terminal building. Had she imagined the entire encounter, dreamed it? But he had been so real. She'd smelled his heat, the earthy odour of him, heard his wheezing laugh. He had been so familiar, the line of his jaw, the tilt of his shoulders.

He had looked so much like Brian.

Suddenly, icily chilled, she realised just how much. And Brian's middle name was Mark.

★　★　★

The professionally sympathetic airline official sat beside her and held her hands.

"We tried to get in touch with you, Mrs Wilde, but your mobile was off. Your husband took ill on the flight and the plane turned back. There was a nurse on board and she did what she could to make him comfortable. I'm afraid he passed away before the flight landed."

Her lips were so dry, it took an effort to part them. "When was this?" she managed to whisper, feeling the world start to spin around her.

"About ninety minutes ago."

Ninety minutes ago she was picking up the hitch-hiker from the side of the road.

"Did he say anything?"

"The nurse said he kept repeating your name . . . and that of a young man."

"Mark."

ALSO BY ANNA DILLON, PUBLISHED BY POOLBEG

Consequences, The Affair,
Seasons, Another Season, Season's End

8

Pigs Might Fly
ANNE DUNLOP

Lucy Streaghorn lived at the end of a long wet lane in a small cold farmhouse with harsh overhead lights and lino on the bathroom floor. The farmhouse faced a yard of piggeries and her six brothers carried the Pig Smell into the kitchen on their boiler suits and Wellington boots and woolly hats. They spoke with their mouths full when they ate Pig for dinner, they belched and farted Pig afterwards and they didn't excuse themselves.

The Pig Smell lingered, baked into the bread, washed into the dishes, ironed into the laundry from the downwind clothes-line. It followed Lucy down the long, wet lane to work in the morning. Like a faithful friend it was waiting for her when she got off the Magherafelt-Bellaghy bus in the evening.

"You're imagining things," said Lucy's mother, who'd stopped smelling Pig years before.

"I'm not imagining things," said Lucy. "People laugh at

me in Magherafelt – nudge nudge, sniff sniff – when they see me coming."

"Townie people have delusions of grandeur," said Mrs Streaghorn comfortably. "Where there's muck there's money, Lucy love, and don't you forget it."

There must, Lucy thought, be a more fragrant way to make a fortune.

★ ★ ★

Lucy Streaghorn worked in a Hairdressing Salon and Beauty Parlour called Curl Up And Dye. The salon was owned by Aunt Ruth, a dirty, overweight lump of lumber who lived in a tarted-up council house in Magherafelt. Few people believed on first acquaintance that the brassy Ruth with her scuffed black stilettos, plunging necklines and Jingle Bell earrings was in fact an inspired businesswoman who, in addition to the salon owned a fleet of superior chip vans. The Chip Smell lingered, dyed into her 'big' hair, painted into her cigarette-stained fingernails, etched into her wrinkles.

"What smell?" said Aunt Ruth who had stopped smelling Chip years before.

"Aunt Ruth," said Lucy desperately, "I think you and my mother have something broken in your noses. Some inherited genetic defect in the olfactory organ."

Aunt Ruth gazed in wonder at her graceful, androgynous niece. She was genuinely bemused by Lucy's aseptic obsession.

"Where did you learn all the big words, Lucy?"

Thanks to Lucy, Curl Up And Dye was a deodorised oasis with fresh flowers in summer and scented candles in winter. Lucy's immaculate white Beauty Parlour overalls were boiled in an on-site washing-machine. She used the luxury shower unit by the Turbo Tanning Beds twice a day. Personal Hygiene Certificates, the Bronze Award, Silver Award and Gold Award, were framed on the Beauty Parlour wall. Lucy could not have been cleaner but just occasionally the Pig Smell would catch her unawares, slipping in through an open window, jumping out from behind a customer, mocking her freaky, squeaky clean efforts.

"Not the smell thing again, Lucy." Ruth worried, when she noticed her niece's sad eyes and dilated nostrils. "It's driving your mother mad."

Lucy Streaghorn was an extremely successful beauty therapist. One may scoff at provincial Northern Irish market towns, Magherafelt is no exception, but Aunt Ruth's salon was booked up weeks in advance. It was an apolitical beauty parlour - Mrs Protestant's money was the same colour as Mrs Catholic's. No birth, death, marriage or First Holy Communion was complete without Lucy's omnipresence.

"You're a clever, clever girl, Lucy," Aunt Ruth praised her. "Just please don't start chasing after me with a Brillo pad and a can of air-freshener."

The day Aunt Ruth won 'Northern Ireland Businesswoman of the Year' her rough-and-ready bravado deserted her and she elbowed her way to the front of the queue in Curl Up And Dye.

"Lucy love," she said, thrusting a photograph of Princess Diana under her niece's nose, "can you make me look like this for the newspaper photographs in Belfast?"

"Aunt Ruth," said Lucy nervously, "I can't perform miracles."

But she did her best.

She scraped Ruth's make-up off with a shovel. She cut off all her burnt orange 'big hair', leaving just the six inches of regrowth. She removed her Jingle Bells earrings and tidied them into a plastic bag.

"Save them for the Christmas Tree, Aunt Ruth," she advised.

Ruth stared at her naked face in the uncompromising Beauty Parlour mirror and was horrified. "Maybe I should wear a paper bag over my head for the photographs!"

But Lucy had only started. Off came the tight black pencil skirt, the laddered black stockings and the scuffed black stilettos. Aunt Ruth was hosed down in the luxury shower unit, boiled up in the sauna, pummelled senseless on the massage table. While she was face-packed, deep-conditioned and body-wrapped, Lucy personally scrubbed at her cigarette-stained fingers with a Brillo pad and bleach.

Aunt Ruth emerged looking like a million dollars.

★ ★ ★

The next six months were the most lucrative of Lucy's career. Aunt Ruth became Curl Up And Dye's 'Over-Forty But Who's Counting?' cover girl. Before and After photographs, published exclusively in *Ulster Tatler* encouraged posh ladies to drive out of Belfast and down the motorway to Magherafelt in swanky white Sports Utility Vehicles for the 'Over-Forty But Who's Counting?' Beauty Mornings.

At first Lucy was over-impressed and slightly intimidated by the scrupulous attention the hypercritical 'Over Forty' clientele paid to every grooming detail at the salon. My goodness, thought the impressionable girl, how important they are! What sort of careers can they have?

Cynical Aunt Ruth soon set Lucy straight. "Bless you, Lucy," she said laughing, "but any one of them could be you or me. The only successful thing most of them ever did was marry a rich man. That fancy Mrs Doctor Dawson that was just in, complaining that the Mini Facelift isn't lifting far enough, I know her from years ago when she was just plain Jane Dawson working in one of my chip vans to finance the good doctor through his finals a fourth time. That's why she calls herself 'Mrs Doctor Dawson'. Just in case anybody forgets that Tony finally managed to pass the exams . . ."

Lucy didn't hear Aunt Ruth's caustic opinion of Mrs Doctor Dawson. She had heard only as far as 'marry a rich man'.

She gazed at her aunt with shining eyes. Aunt Ruth had, unwittingly, unlocked the secret of the universe for Lucy. Of course there was a fragrant way to make a fortune.

All she had to do was marry it.

★   ★   ★

It was at one of Aunt Ruth's 'Over-Forty but Who's Counting' Beauty Mornings that Lucy met Jackie Diamond. By then Lucy had attended to many high-maintenance Over-Forties but it was safe to say that Jackie Diamond, with her fabulous skin, sparkling eyes and designer everything, outshone the lot of them. The rest of the salon clientele backed off and watched respectfully as she removed half a ton of gold from her ears, neck, wrists and fingers and threw it casually into her designer handbag before starting her treatments.

Jackie Diamond told Lucy that she lived on an island in the Arabian Gulf called Bahrain. For thousands of years Bahrain was a desert island. Then oil was discovered and Bahrain quantum-leapt from the Middle Ages into the 21st century. Expatriates flooded in from all over the world to find the footpaths paved with gold and money growing on trees. After a few years digging up the footpaths and harvesting the money-trees the expatriates were ready to return home, their fortunes made, their families showered with the fruits of their labours.

"Well, I never did!" said Lucy as she massaged and plucked and waxed and exfoliated. "I thought the Middle East was just a big sand-hill full of Muslims."

Jackie Diamond was the Cabin Crew Manager of Ex-Pat Air, a small exclusive airline which ferried the gold-plated workforce in and out of Bahrain.

Jackie's job was to recruit sophisticated, poised, glamorous girls and train them as air stewardesses. She taught them how to make small talk with the Ex-Pat passengers; how to shake and stir cocktails; how to play Special Requests on the Grand Piano in the upstairs lounge area of the aircraft; how to graciously receive chocolates and flowers and thank-you letters for services rendered but tactfully rebuff the amorous advances of any Ex-Pat millionaire who fancied his chances with a woman in uniform.

Jackie's air stewardesses lived in luxurious seafront apartments in suburban Bahrain.

Maids cleaned twice a week and there was a swimming pool on the roof and a fully equipped gym in the basement.

They carried credit cards and spare uniforms in their

hand luggage. They slept in Five Star hotels in jet-set cities. They ate Room Service. They shopped internationally. Their luxurious seafront apartments were crammed with World Traveller souvenirs: leather picture-frames from Dhaka, silk cushion covers from Delhi, Christmas decorations from Manila, mosquito nets from Tanzania, mountain bikes from Trivandrum, life-sized wooden giraffes from Nairobi.

They saw the world and got paid for doing it.

"Many of our air stewardesses are from Northern Ireland," said Jackie. She flicked through a glossy magazine and pointed out her advertisement to Lucy. There was a map of the world to show you where Bahrain was, a photograph of Jackie Diamond with her sparkling eyes and big smile and the caption: *'You too can get these wrinkles sunbathing by Five-Star-hotel swimming pools in exotic locations'*.

"I'm interviewing later this week," Jackie announced. "If you're interested, come on Friday afternoon."

"Muslims don't eat Pig, do they?" said Lucy thoughtfully as she was leaving.

The following morning, while Aunt Ruth was drowning a hangover in the flotation tank, Lucy went to the Travel Agent in Magherafelt for a Worldwide Holiday Brochure. In it she read that Bahrain was green and pleasant, the legendary site of The Garden Of Eden. The water was not poisoned, there were no endemic diseases, there were no creepy crawlies. It was hot in summer and occasionally in winter it rained.

Then she went to the library where she read that though Muslim women could not marry non-Muslim men, Muslim men were free to marry Presbyterian girls from Northern Ireland.

She went back to the Travel Agent.

"I'm just curious," she said. "How much does it cost to fly Ex-Pat Air to Bahrain?"

The Travel Agent tapped at her computer keyboard. Her eyebrows shot up at the price of the fare. "Have you just married a millionaire?"

"Not yet," Lucy told her.

★　★　★

Lucy's family were not impressed when she told them about her air stewardess interview.

"There are worse things than the smell of Pigs," said Samuel, her oldest brother, firmly.

Aunt Ruth said, "Why don't I turn the roof space above the salon into a centrally heated studio apartment with subtle lighting and wall-to-wall carpeting for you, Lucy love, and you need never go near the Pigs again?"

"It's not just the Pigs," said Lucy quietly.

The night before her air stewardess interview Lucy had a nightmare. She dreamed there was a bag of gold with her name on it in the Pig Houses. It was winking at her from the far side of the Farrowing Crates. To reach the gold she had to cut the teeth and take the tails off eight litters of baby Pigs.

No suffocating Pig Smell is going to stand between me and my gold, thought Lucy.

She rolled up the sleeves of her immaculate Beauty Parlour overall, pinched a clothes-peg over her nostrils and jammed the first wee pig under her armpit.

"This is for your own good," she told the nervous piglet. "Bored baby pigs have sharp little teeth and they nip, nip, nip at each other's tails."

When the eight litters were finished Lucy took the clothes-peg off her nose and grabbed her gold.

Stop, thought Lucy in the dream, I can't smell anything! No Pig Smell. Sniff sniff at her hands. Sniff Sniff at her hair. No Pig Smell.

Lucy woke up screaming. Pig Smell was bad, but no Pig Smell was worse. If she couldn't smell it, it could be making a fool of her behind her back. She'd not even realise why the townies were still laughing – nudge nudge, sniff sniff – when they saw her coming.

★   ★   ★

Lucy took her seat in the interview waiting room with the flotsam and jetsam of wannabe Ulster air stewardesses.

There were poised girls, sophisticated girls, glamorous girls. There were even beautiful girls.

A lesser girl might have panicked in the face of such competition. But not Lucy. The 'Over-Forty But Who's Counting?' clientele had taught her well. Lucy surveyed the curvaceous, heavily made-up brunettes around her with professional detachment.

Oh dear, she thought, what a lot of moustaches need waxing.

Lucy strode confidently into the interview room, chest out, chin up, tummy in. Jackie Diamond liked what she saw. She did not sneer at Lucy's cheap little suit, her plastic handbag or the simple chignon in her hair. Instead she noticed that Lucy's tights had no ladders and her unpretentious shoes were polished until her pretty pink smile was reflected in them.

Lucy sat when invited but did not cross her legs. She spoke when spoken to and looked Jackie in the eye but didn't eyeball her. She was charming and intelligent and quietly spoken.

"Miss Streaghorn," said Jackie with satisfaction, "I knew it the moment I laid eyes on you. I knew you looked like an air stewardess."

The rest of the interview passed on a hazy, dazzling high. Lucy smiled and nodded and smiled while Jackie confided that she too had left a small town for the bright lights of Bahrain.

"It all seems so long ago now," said Jackie laughing. "It's amazing how quickly the rough edges get smoothed out. Now there isn't an Eligible Arab in the Gulf who isn't proud to have me on his arm. And let me assure you, Lucy, they pay handsomely for the privilege."

A tiny chill pierced through the haze of Lucy's happiness. It was just as Aunt Ruth had remarked – admiringly – when Jackie was at the salon earlier in the week.

"That one knows the price of everything and the value of nothing."

"Any questions, Lucy?"

Lucy shook her head. "No, Jackie."

"Not even a little bit curious about the fabulous wealth of the Eligible Arab oil barons?"

Lucy shook her head again. "No, Jackie."

The interview was over. Jackie shook her hand. "Welcome on board, Lucy."

Lucy stood up to leave.

"It's true, you know," Jackie insisted suddenly, "they *are* so flamboyantly wealthy they can abandon a limousine in the desert when it runs out of petrol . . ."

Lucy calmly gazed into Jackie's sparkling eyes.

There was nothing in Jackie Diamond's eyes except

dollar signs flashing.

★   ★   ★

What a strange, almost surreal bus ride back to Bellaghy!

Lucy's family were grouped around the kitchen table drinking tea when she got home.

"I've got the job," she announced.

Her wonderful news was greeted with silence. Mrs Streaghorn looked close to tears.

"But I've decided not to go."

There was Pig meal in Samuel's nostrils but she kissed him anyway.

"You're right, Samuel," said Lucy. "There are worse things than the smell of Pigs."

The last word went to Samuel. "That perfume you're wearing, Lucy, you've enough on to knock Pigs down!"

ALSO BY ANNE DUNLOP, PUBLISHED BY POOLBEG

Pineapple Tart, Kissing the Frog,
Dolly Holiday, A Soft Touch

9

A Heartbeat

GEMMA ENGLISH

Rachel drove to the lake and sat in her car for a while, waiting for the last of the evening strollers to pass on by. She got out of the car and walked to a bench looking out over the lake. She took a bottle of wine out of her bag and placed it on the bench beside her. Then, taking great care not to break it, she took a glass from the bag. It was a silly-looking glass with a picture of the Arc de Triomphe on it. They'd got it when they were on honeymoon and it was one of Luke's favourites. When they were celebrating he'd drink from it.

And this had been one of his favourite places.

She opened the wine and poured a large glass. She looked back out over the lake and suddenly she was at a loss. What do you do? What do you do when the love of your life walks out one day and never comes back? With no warning, he's just gone. In a heartbeat. What do you do when you realise he'll never come back? Not ever. And how do you cope when life starts to move on? It starts to move and you're not ready for it.

She drew her knees up to her chest, buried her face and sobbed. She cried until her body shuddered and her ribs ached, her head throbbed and her eyes were swollen. When she finally stopped crying there was that horribly familiar feeling. She had begun to refer to it as 'The Nothing'. It was that dreadful moment when you're all cried out and the stress and loss that's been building for the last while is gone, but it's not fixed. Nothing is fixed and it feels as though nothing will ever fix it. Is there any cure for a broken heart? Everyone says time heals a broken heart, but time wouldn't bring Luke back. Time would only make him more distant.

The last eight weeks had been the longest of her life. And yet her memory of them was sketchy. Yes, there were entire days that were so burned on her memory that she could repeat verbatim everything everyone said. Those days were so real to her she could still smell the perfumes and feel the gut-wrenching sickness as people huddled around her and then left her to be alone. And then there were days she couldn't remember: she made dinners, she knew this because she remembered eating them, she did grocery shopping and even closed his bank accounts. But she had no recollection of how she did it or what she said to people as she went about it.

As she sat there memories of those eight weeks flooded in, unwanted and unstoppable. She closed her eyes but that only made them more vivid. They played like a movie in front of her.

★ ★ ★

She'd been sitting at her desk in work when her manager approached her. He called her into his office. As she walked the twenty feet to his office her mind raced. Was she being sacked? What had she done? When she walked in and saw Carol from Personnel sitting there she knew she was being sacked. But why?

"Rachel, we have some dreadful news and I don't know how best to tell you," said her manager.

"Am I being sacked?" She looked from one to the other and saw the look.

That look would haunt her forever.

"I only wish it was that simple, Rachel I truly do."

"Rachel, we were contacted by the Gardai this morning," said Carol. "They wanted to confirm your details before they contacted you. We thought it might be easier coming from us."

"The Gardai? What's happening?"

"There's been a crash, Rachel," said her manager. "It appears Luke's car sideswiped another and then veered into a wall. I'm so dreadfully sorry, Rachel, but Luke didn't survive the impact. He died this morning."

Some time later – she couldn't say how long – her manager handed her a cup of milky tea, then sat down beside her and put a hand on her shoulder. He was clearly out of his depth. His sympathy was palpable but he didn't know what to do with it.

She sat and thought back on the morning she and Luke had shared. There were no tears, no words, she just sat there staring into space. Luke got up at 6.30 as usual and left the house at 7.15.

Had he said, "See you later" or was it, "See you, love"?

She hadn't heard him properly. She had been tuning in to a new station on the radio and the kettle was boiling beside her. Why hadn't she stopped for one minute and looked at him? What was he even wearing? They might ask her what he was wearing and she wouldn't know. She'd have to say she wasn't looking at him, that she pretty much ignored him this morning. He was in the kitchen when she came in; he put down a mug of coffee and went out the door. He shouted a goodbye from the door and she'd muttered some nicety in reply.

And so that was the last time she would hear him speak. How strange! Life really throws you some curveballs sometimes.

Then things began to fall into place for her. They had a case of mistaken identity here. It was someone really like Luke, someone driving a black Avensis, late thirties, perhaps even called Luke Harper. There must be at least ten Luke Harpers living in Dublin. This was someone else's Luke. She was very sorry for their loss but it wasn't her loss. Her Luke was in work in Donnybrook. She'd ring him and there he'd be. She'd hear his familiar voice and he'd laugh and tell her to stop worrying. She'd go right now and ring him.

She stood up.

"Where are you going?" her manager asked. His voice seemed very far away.

"This is all a big mistake," she said. "I'm going to ring Luke. This is all a huge mistake."

"Rachel, I'm sorry. It's no mistake," he said. "They have his driver's licence and a folder with some of your stuff was in the back. It is Luke. He's been taken to St Vincent's Hospital. They need you to go over there and identify him. You shouldn't go alone — is there anyone we can call for you?"

The room fell in on top of her. The walls spun and a

voice from the depths of her soul screamed, bloodcurdling and raw.

"Not my Luke, not mine, not mine!"

★   ★   ★

Her friend Jennifer came into the office and brought her out to the waiting taxi. They travelled in silence holding hands.

She rang her mother and Luke's mother from the taxi. As the taxi pulled up she saw Luke's parents, holding each other for support, and then her own parents pale and old beside them. Because she was Luke's wife and officially his next of kin, she was the one to identify him. They were led into a room and a cover was removed from his face.

It was his lovely face. His cheek was bruised and his eye had swollen up but it was Luke. So pale but still strong-looking. She expected him to open his eyes and smile at her, but he didn't. She stared at his face for as long as she could, committing it to memory: this was what he looked like. This was her husband.

Things were a blank until the funeral. She remembered a stream of white coats. Doctors gave her advice on every topic from counselling to what to eat over the next few days to keep her strength up. Then came the social workers: they sympathised and held her hand. They told her what to expect and confirmed that she was not alone in this; there were families playing out this scene in every hospital in the country, every day. She was not alone. Had she any children? No? It was probably for the best – she was a young woman and with the grace of God she'd go on to remarry and have a family in time.

Then there was the funeral, her mother-in-law at the

top of the church, sobbing uncontrollably. Grown men openly crying as they hugged her and then each other. Her friends looked suddenly very old and very young at the same time. Drawn faces, pale and tear-stained. She noticed everyone's fine lines as they smiled and drew her close to them. Then their hair, so rich and youthful against their pained expressions and the black clothes. It didn't fit. She didn't fit. She was only thirty-four; she'd only been married four years. She wasn't a widow – surely she was too young to be a widow? What was going on here? The church was black. These weren't strangers; they were her friends.

She looked around and saw Richard and Sinéad. They were both crying. Richard was Luke's best friend – they'd all been out together last Saturday night. Jason and Susan came over and hugged her; it was Jason's birthday soon and they were all going out. Well, they should have been.

Rachel sat down as a huge wave of grief came over her. There were so many things they'd planned to do and suddenly all the plans were for nothing. All the working and overtime to pay for the house and the cars and the better life. All for nothing.

After the funeral everyone went back to Rachel's house. They drank and talked quietly about how shocking it was. There was a murmur of voices and the clink of glasses, but no real noise.

No noise except for the sound of Luke's mother sobbing every few minutes. Her words echoed in the house. "My baby boy! My wonderful baby boy! Murderers, rapists, drug-dealers all walking the streets and my child is dead! Why is that? Tell me!"

Luke's brother and sister comforted her. Everyone else tried to ignore her outbursts. People took Rachel out into the kitchen or the garden, asking about the flowers or the wine they were drinking. Anything but acknowledge Mrs Harper's grief. Nobody knew what to do – everyone was out of their depth here.

Then the funeral was over. The week after the funeral was long. People called in to see her. Everyone was still crying and when they left there was an odd silence in the house. Luke was everywhere but nowhere. In every room he'd left his mark. There were photos of him, his DVD collection, his mug in the press and his books on the shelves. The simple everyday things that reinforced the fact that he wasn't coming home.

There was a lot to do, a lot of forms to fill in and documents to sign. Closing accounts and paying for funeral expenses.

And then there was the laundry. She couldn't bring herself to wash his clothes. They smelled of him and if she washed them she'd wash him off them. She did the grocery shopping and only when she was unpacking did she realise she'd bought him some beer and his favourite flavour yogurts. Then there were all the meals she bought, two of everything. It's the small things that were the hardest to take. Taking his jeans in off the line, post addressed to him, looking through a drawer and finding a note in his handwriting. An entire video with nothing but *Match of the Day* taped back to back. She sat for a while fast-forwarding to find a space to tape *Desperate Housewives* before she realised what she was doing. His weekends revolved around *Match of the bloody Day* and now here they all were, taped over and over again and he wasn't here.

In all her 'little chats' with the social workers since Luke died, none of them had mentioned the fact that something like a bank statement through the post or a pair of boxers in the laundry would cut her to the bone as sharply as any eulogy or well-written verse on a Mass card. The little things were the hardest to deal with. And let's face it, life is full of the little things. She'd never expected life in general to hurt her as badly as it did.

Two weeks after the funeral everyone else had gone back to work and the phone didn't ring half as much as it had before. People were leaving her to grieve alone and in some ways she welcomed it. She could lie on the couch all day, crying and staring at photos, banging her fists off the walls and screaming in rage that he was gone and she was still here. She could sink into the bath and talk to him; she'd tell him everything that had happened since he'd gone and how much she missed him. She watched TV until the early hours of the morning and then woke at dawn, her stomach clenching when she realised it was six a.m. and there was nothing to do all day.

She went to his grave every single day, bringing flowers and trinkets. She'd look at the ground and couldn't help but wonder what he was like down there. Was he still the same? One day she had to plunge her hands deep in her pockets to stop herself from digging into the soil to rescue him.

She stopped going to the graveyard after that. She didn't trust herself.

Then it was his 'month's mind' – a Mass attended only by the closest friends. Everyone said the same thing. It seemed no time at all and already a month had passed. A friend's baby had been born and another's parent had passed away since Luke died. A lot can happen in the blink of an eye. People had moved on, the talk was not of Luke but of Lily, the new baby girl, and how much like a tiny doll she looked. Rachel sent a card and a small dress but she didn't visit. They didn't need her crying down on their new baby.

Her mind had been full of babies before Luke died. They had been talking about having a family. They were in no rush when they first married but now they felt the time was right. They were looking forward to the future – two maybe three children. Rachel had been looking up the internet on how best to start the process. Would she take vitamins before they tried or while they were trying?

It was all irrelevant now. The vitamins were worthless if you didn't have a partner to help. She believed she'd never have a baby. By the time she met someone new, became serious about them and decided to have a baby, it would be years.

She blanked that thought. It was defeatist and she could no longer deal with such negative energy. That was what the doctor had told her yesterday when she went to see him about a sick cert. She'd been so down in the dumps, not just about Luke, but about everything. She asked about medication for depression; she needed something to kick-start her back into the world. It had been eight weeks and she was still unable to clear out his wardrobe or wash his laundry. She wanted something to help her over this first hurdle and allow her at least look at the rest of her life, even if she didn't much like the idea of getting out there and living it. She needed help in opening the blinds in the morning – as things stood they were down all the time and even though she knew this was bad she couldn't bring herself to open them. She needed help. Americans took Prozac and were always cracking on about how great it is. She wondered if he'd prescribe her some.

He listened and finally agreed to give her some medication. Only for a month and then she would have to come back and see him. They might need to look into counselling and getting her back to work. He agreed that a month of Prozac might just be the kick-start she needed. He had to ensure she was in good health, all things considered, before he wrote the prescription. Was she taking any other drugs, even over the counter? He was sorry to ask – he looked very grave here – but just to be sure, could she be pregnant?

Rachel began to shake her head, then stopped. It had been eight weeks since Luke died. And a little longer since her last period. It was just stress, of course. She had missed periods at stressful times before . . . less stressful times than this.

She told the doctor so but he insisted they check it out before they went any further.

The doctor pulled out a test from his cabinet, gave her a sample jar and sent her off to provide a sample.

She wasn't even nervous as he dipped the test in the sample. It would be negative.

His face was mixture of delight and sorrow as he told her the news.

She was pregnant. She and Luke were having a baby.

★   ★   ★

And that was how Rachel found herself out by the lake, with a bottle of wine and Luke's favourite glass. Calm now, she looked out over the lake and felt a little glow of happiness begin to push the sorrow away.

A new life, a new heartbeat.

She lifted the glass and drank a toast to Luke. Just a

little sip, of course.

"Congratulations, Luke," she whispered. "You're going to be a daddy."

She raised the glass high and threw the wine in the lake. Then she wrapped the glass back up and went back to the car.

The following morning she opened the blinds and did the laundry.

ALSO BY GEMMA ENGLISH, PUBLISHED BY POOLBEG

Three Wishes, The Trouble with Boys,
Tangled up in You

10

What Do We Want!
ANNE MARIE FORREST

The crowd move as one. I like this. I like being part of this mass, all these people who left their homes this morning to come here to make their voices heard. It's – I don't know – comforting being part of something this big, part of these thousands of people marching along in unison, all drawn together in a common purpose.

I look down at Lizzy and I smile. She looks up at me, and she smiles back. I give her hand a little squeeze. I love the feeling of her tiny little hand in mine.

We march on. One foot in front of the other, all together.

Whatever about me in my anorak and jeans, Lizzy fits right in with our fellow protestors. By the time I saw the 'outfit' she'd put on her this morning, we were running late and anyway I didn't have the heart to make her change, she was so delighted with what she'd picked out. She's wearing a rainbow sweater, a too-small summer dress she unearthed from somewhere, red tights, pink hat, striped scarf and a sheepskin jacket she has 'on a borrow of' from Katie, the seven-year-old who lives downstairs from us. Yeah, she looks a right little hippy chick, a mirror of so many of the adults around us. What is it about protests? Why are hippy-types always drawn to them? Do they care more about things than the rest of us? I don't really know – this is the first time I've ever been on a march.

"Mum!" Lizzy tugs my hand now. "Belinda wants to get a Happy Meal too when we go to McDonald's."

I glance around, worried that anyone might have overheard – talk of McDonald's Happy Meals would not, I think, go down well with some of those around us.

"Well, maybe she can share yours," I say.

"But she wants her *own* Happy Meal!"

You see, even though Lizzy might be dressed for the occasion, her reason for being here is very suspect: because I promised I'd take her to McDonald's later for a treat.

"Hush!" I glance around. "We'll see, okay?"

"Humph! We know what *that* means, don't we, Belinda?"

I'd better explain Belinda – Belinda's not actually real, she's just one of the host of imaginary friends my daughter has. Even now while Lizzy has her right hand in my mine, she's holding out her other, like she's catching Belinda's.

Anyway, where was I? Oh yes, you've probably guessed by now I'm not exactly a sandal-wearing, lentil-eating type, not that I've anything against sandal-wearing or lentil-eating but it's just not me. And I'm not normally a "WHAT DO WE WANT!" placard-carrying type of person either – in fact I feel I'm usually a little too passive, but there comes a time when enough is enough, when something really hits home.

It all started in the playground in front of the house where me and Lizzy live in a rented flat (apartment is too fancy a word for it) on the top floor. The house is an old red-brick one on an old Georgian Square near the city centre. Now, I happen to think we're very lucky to live there but unless you consider lino and chip wallpaper state-of-the-art, then, well, our flat is definitely not state-of-the-art. Neglected, I think would best describe it, but its years of neglect mean that the high ceilings, the old fireplace, the shutters, the coving and the centre rose all remain intact. But neglect has a downside too. It means no central heating, a crack in the window, a constant fight with the damp and I won't even get into the state of the bathroom. But I like it, especially the way the sunlight comes streaming in the big windows in the morning.

And the thing is, it's not going to be our home forever. No, I have plans for Lizzy and me. Although, sometimes, I fear all my plans will come to nothing. Sometimes, I wake in the middle of the night in a panic, thinking I'll *still* be here when my little four-year Lizzy, the light-of-my-life, has long since grown up and flown our little nest. I fear then that, in my lonely state, my only visitor will be our lecherous landlord but, whereas now I view his weekly Saturday-night visits as a necessary evil, maybe, as I grow older and lonelier, I'll start looking forward to them. I've never understood why he doesn't just let his tenants set up a standing order to his bank account (actually I probably do: "Ho-ho! And have the taxman after me!") and I don't really understand why he has to collect the rent on a Saturday night either but, as this little arrangement continues over the years, maybe, in time, we'll become the 'friends' I know he'd like us to be now. Maybe then I'll welcome him in and we'll sit at the table supping tea — I just know he's the supping kind — and eating the Kimberly Mikados I buy each week especially for his visits. And, after he's told me about all his properties and the problems he has with rogue tenants, he'll get up from the little table, squeeze his way between it and the old-fashioned cooker (he buys most of his stuff in those auctions where they sell off the contents of dead people's houses), put his outsized hand on my now outsized bottom, and whisper in my ear, "Will we have a shag?" and then we'll move to the other side of the room and, as I lie under him, under the candlewick bedspread (in my head my duvet has morphed into this pink bedspread), I'll be happy for this bit of human comfort.

But it's only in the middle of the night I contemplate such awful futures. In the daytime, I know it won't be like that because, as I say, I have a plan for Lizzy and me, and my plan is this: to finish college and then move to Galway. Even though I don't have much free time in college — I'm always in a rush to get away to collect Lizzy from her crèche — but, whenever I do have a spare moment, I find myself logging on to Myhome.ie looking at all the houses in the west, houses that are so cheap compared to Dublin. I'm not saying I'll be able to buy one of these but maybe me and Lizzy could rent a little cottage somewhere.

Lizzy may have imaginary friends, but I guess I have imaginary houses and imaginary futures. With sea views, fitted kitchens and ensuite bathrooms.

Usually I have sense enough not to talk to Lizzy about these houses but, the other day, I saw this little house on a cliff, on the internet, and one of the photos showed a girl's pink room with a little window seat overlooking the sea. So, that day, I found myself asking her as we walked home from the crèche, "What if we were to move to another home? What kind of room would you like?" And she looked at me with those beautiful eyes (the same beautiful eyes as her father – that's where all this really started, but he's a whole different story, and, quite frankly, not worth the effort of telling) and said that she didn't want a room of her own, that she'd only like a new home *if* she could go on sleeping in my bed.

See! That's part of the problem. She doesn't know any better.

Anyway, back to why we're on this march. As I was saying, one of the things I do like about where we live is the fact that there's a playground right outside the front door. We just have to walk down a few flights of stairs and cross the busy street and she has an entire playground to play in – but not entirely to herself, of course. Most of the kids and their mums are nice, but there's a few who ruin things for everyone. Anyway, last Friday, I got away from college early and collected Lizzy at three, time enough to go to the playground before it got dark. Now, Lizzy is a bit of a daredevil on the swings and slides *if* there are no other kids around but she's a little shy when there are others but, this day, she was getting on fine. She took her place in the queue for the slide again, and again, and again, so I relaxed on the bench, took out one of my textbooks and decided to make a start on the essay I had to write for the following Friday. Ten minutes later, Lizzie came running over.

"That boy told me to fuck off!"

"Don't talk like that."

"I'm not talking like that – I'm telling you how the boy was talking."

"I don't want you to ever use that word again!"

I shouldn't have snapped at her. I wasn't annoyed with her. I was annoyed that she had to hear words like this. Like, where does a four-year-old boy get these words?

"Just stay away from him then, and go on the swings instead."

So, I went back to my book but, the thing is, she didn't go over to the swings and when I looked up to check on her she was nowhere to be seen.

I panicked. I stood up, looked around the park and, then, when I still couldn't see her, I let my eyes dare travel beyond the park railings. And there she was, in her little pink hat, running across the road with a car bearing down on her at speed. It was like I was looking at it in slow motion. I can still see it all now. Lizzy standing rooted to the spot in the middle of the road. The look of horror on the driver's face. The sound of the skid. It was over in a matter of seconds.

I ran out, picked her up. She was unharmed. But almost immediately I had this man, the driver, shouting at me, "What the hell was she doing running out in front of me like that! Children shouldn't be allowed to be on the road!"

I walked away from him and carried her back into the safety of our own home.

"What were you doing running out on the road? Haven't I told you often enough never ever to do that?"

"But I saw Paddy getting on a bus."

"Okay." I had to think about this. It seemed to me that Paddy always turned up when she was feeling vulnerable. Like at crèche – I know she doesn't like going. Maybe now if I had comforted her, rather than snapped at her, when that boy told her to 'fuck off' then she wouldn't have needed Paddy now. She wouldn't have run across the road. "Okay, if you ever see him again, don't ever run after him, okay?"

Yes, my child definitely has an over-active imagination. Lizzy is rarely Lizzy but more likely to be Beauty, or Snow White, or Princess Fiona, or a poor girl whose wicked stepmother won't give her any food. And I'm rarely Mummy. Sometimes I'm the Beast to her Beauty, the seven dwarfs to her Snow White (all seven of them), the Shrek to her Fiona, and the wicked stepmother to her poor girl.

It's less tiring than you might think. I can go about my everyday business but I just have to 'be' them, and answer her when she uses their names. We do sometimes get funny looks when we're out, and someone overhears her: "Beast, can I get some sweets?" Or "Grumpy, will you give me the money so can I pay the lady?"

Really, for a household of two we're pretty crowded and I haven't even got into the animals. For a couple of weeks she went around with a parrot on her shoulder – which she used to talk to all the time (more strange looks). Then we had a dog that slept on the end of our bed ("Mum! Don't sit there. You'll squash Buster!") and for a while we even had a pony living with us, well, not actually with us in the flat – Lizzy used to tie him up outside on the street. And now we have Belinda – a little Chinese girl who wears a red dress and her hair in pigtails – and Paddy, a leprechaun with a little beard and a soft green jacket.

This leprechaun turns up everywhere.

Anyway, this Paddy was the reason she ran across the road that day, and the fact that she ran across the road was the reason we're now on the march.

I know people always harp back to a time when kids played on the streets. Now, I can't say I remember playing on the road – there wasn't a need, we lived in a nice big house with a big garden, and played there with our friends, or in their own nice big gardens. But still, I don't see why it has to be that cars own the streets. That day when she was nearly knocked down, I was annoyed with her at first, then me, then the driver, and then just cars in general. Where we live, there must be hundreds of kids around but they have to be escorted back and forth to the playground and then corralled in behind fencing, all to protect them from the traffic.

So when I saw the poster on the notice-board in college – RECLAIM THE STREETS MARCH – I decided, why not? It's not that I think after this march we'll suddenly have leafy boulevards, with just the odd car driving slowly by. But I just felt I needed to show that I wasn't happy.

"Mum! Mum! Look, we're going to be on telly! Wave Mummy! Wave Belinda!"

I look to where Lizzy's waving and I see a camera focused on our section of the march. My first instinct is to turn away. It's one thing to be on the march. It's another thing to be seen on the march by everyone, and I guess by 'everyone' I mean my mum. I can see her coming in from that same big garden I was telling you about, switching on the TV to see us on it. I can imagine her saying to herself "What next? First she goes and has a baby all on her own, then she decamps into some inner city slum, and now she's marching on the streets! And what has she got the child dressed in?"

In fairness to my mother, she did offer us a home with her when Lizzy was born and I guess the sensible option would have been to move in. But my mother's personality is as big as her house, and I was afraid of getting swallowed up. And while she's great at doling out advice and giving opinions, she wouldn't be so good on the nappy-changing side of things. No, it's better to be where we are in our little flat, planning our own future.

So I put on my biggest smile and wave to the camera and then, as it pans away from us and on to others, Lizzy shouts out: "Mum! Mum! Look, there's Paddy!"

"Oh yes!" I pretend to see him and wave.

Right then, something happens. Suddenly the crowd starts pushing. No longer are we marching as one. Suddenly this peaceful protest has become anything but and people are pushing and shoving from every direction. Now the crowd begins to surge. It seems like everyone is shouting. I am terrified, and if I am terrified how must Lizzy feel?

"Mum, what's going on? Why are all these people shoving?"

"Don't worry, love. I'm with you. Just hold on to me, everything is okay."

But it's not. It's chaos. I see a Garda on horseback and I see a young skinhead firing a bottle at him.

"Mum! Mum!"

"Hush, pet, hush!" I scan around me, trying to see how I can get out of here but we're hemmed in from every direction. I'm gripping her tightly but I can feel the crowds coming between us. "Hold on, Lizzy! Just hold on!" I feel her little hand being pulled away from mine. *"Lizzy!"* I scream.

I can hear her voice, shrieking, "Mummy, Mummy!"

I can't see her anywhere.

"Lizzy, where are you?" I'm shouting. "Hey! Hey! Let

me through, I'm looking for my little daughter! Please, get out of my way!"

And then, someone, or something hits me on the head.

I'm not out for long, but long enough for two civil defence guys to haul me out the crowd, and long enough for Lizzy to have disappeared without trace. I get up. I plunge back into the crowd searching for her. There are still people shoving and pushing everywhere. I see a window being smashed. How could I have put Lizzy in this situation? But I didn't know it was going to be something like this. I thought we were marching to reclaim the streets, not turn them over to hooligans! There's one of the Garda on horseback high over the crowd. I push my way over to him but he's too busy defending himself, too busy pushing back the crowds to be of use to me and, anyway, I can't reach him, and I have no hope of catching his attention. I push my way out of the crowd again, thinking I might be able to see more from the edge. I see another Garda on horseback and I run over to him.

"Please, you've got to help me!"

"What?" he shouts down at me.

"I've lost my four-year-old daughter!" I shout at him.

He looks around from his high perch, but even I can tell him he's not going to see her from up there. She's lost beneath the underbelly of the crowd. Oh! Sweetest Jesus! I can't bear this! But now he's asking me for her name and a description and then he gets on his radio.

Now I feel my own phone vibrating in my pocket.

"Mum, th —"

"I saw you and Lizzy on the television! How could you be so stupid, Jane! Taking her into something like that!

Get out of there, right now!"

"Mum! Lizzy is missing!"

"Oh my God!"

"I lost my grip of her!"

"Oh no, oh no, oh no! Okay – have you told the Gardaí?"

"Yes!"

"Right, you stay where you are. Keep looking for her and I'll come in immediately."

I do stay where I am. I do keep looking. But, as the streets empty, my heart sinks further and further. There's still no sign of her.

I see my mum rushing over.

"Mum! They haven't found her yet!"

She gives me a quick hug, then goes over to the nearest Garda to explain the situation again to him. Maybe she thinks her word will carry more weight, but he tells her they're doing everything they can.

She comes back.

"Okay, I'm going to stay here in case she turns up but I want you to start walking home."

"She's a four-year-old! She's not going to find her own way home!"

"Just start walking in that direction."

So I do. I retrace our steps. The streets are all littered now with debris. Ever since the moment my little Lizzy was born, I feared that something would happen to her and, as I look around, all I see now are threats; in everyone I see a potential paedophile or child trafficker; down every lane, I see a potential crime scene. When I find I'm nearly as far as home, I press on hurriedly, just in case she did manage to find her way back.

When I turn the corner, I see her, a kaleidoscope of

colour, sitting on the steps leading up to the house where our flat is.

I run to her. I pick her up and squeeze her so tight she begins to protest.

"Mum, you're hurting me!"

"Lizzy, Lizzy, my baby, you're safe!" I shower her sweet soft head with kisses.

"Of course I'm safe, Mum! I'm with Paddy and Belinda."

"How did you get here?"

"Paddy brought me."

It's only now I notice the man – a stranger – still sitting on the steps watching our little reunion. He lifts a Happy Meal box from his lap, puts it on the step, gets up and walks over.

"I found Lizzy wandering in the crowd looking for you. We waited for ages but then I thought the best thing to do was to bring her back here. I thought it was the one place you would definitely turn up."

"Why didn't you just hand her to a Garda?"

"I called into Store Street and told them I had her but I thought she'd be better off with me. At least she knows me. I work at her crèche."

"But I've never seen you!"

"Just in the mornings."

Now I look at him, really look at him. Yes, he's small (ish), and he is wearing a velvet green jacket and he has a beard, but he's no leprechaun!

"Are you really Paddy?"

He nods.

And I find myself laughing. "I thought she'd made you up! I thought you were a leprechaun!"

He's smiling now. "I've been called a lot of things in

my time."

Lizzy is sitting back down on the steps of the house, unperturbed by the events, busy tucking into her own Happy Meal.

Seeing me looking at her, he tells me: "She told me you'd promised her one – I thought it would keep her mind off things."

I nod. "Thanks." Then I remember Mum. "I'd better ring my mum – she's still looking for Lizzy."

I ring, tell Mum we've found Lizzy and she says she'll be right up. Then I go to search for my keys and find I've lost them. We'll have to wait until Mum comes. I go to sit on the steps. Lizzy is still tucking in. She looks up. "Don't sit on Belinda!" she warns.

"Okay." I move over.

Paddy is smiling at us. "I'd better be going."

"No, wait," I say. "Until Mum gets here with the keys. You might as well finish your meal."

He smiles, sits down and picks up his box. Then he looks over at Lizzy.

"Lizzy, I don't think Belinda is eating her Happy Meal," he says, pointing at a spare box. "Do you think she might give it to your mum?"

Lizzy thinks for a moment, then picks up the box and passes it to me. "Okay, but you can't have her free toy – Belinda wants me to keep it for her."

"Okay." I look over at Paddy. "You bought Belinda a Happy Meal?"

He grins. "What can I say? I'm a sucker."

And the three of us sit there, munching away.

Every now and then, I sneak a look over at Paddy. And when he catches me, he smiles. And I smile at him.

"So do you live around here?" I ask between bites.

"Yeah, just around the corner."

And I keep on sneaking glances at him and thinking, if my daughter were to imagine a friend for me, she couldn't imagine anyone nicer. And suddenly I'm not imagining a life for us in a little cottage in Galway. Suddenly right here, right now, is looking pretty good.

ALSO BY ANNE MARIE FORREST, PUBLISHED BY POOLBEG

The Love Detective,
Something Sensational, Dancing Days
Who Will Love Polly Odlum?

11

Secrets & Lines
GER GALLAGHER

I often heard my mother say that you can tell a woman's secrets by looking closely at the lines on her face. If they are etched deep into the forehead then the chances are that she is hiding something deep inside, was what she used to say. Of course *her* face was as smooth as alabaster; she had lived a life of charm and virtue and could hold her unwrinkled brow high with pride. I often wonder what she would say if she could see me now. She would probably step closer and examine the creases that spread across my freckled forehead, especially the one in the middle that runs a little deeper than all the others.

My name is Suzie Jenkins and, until I resigned three years ago, I worked in Farlanes department store in Chicago for seventeen years as a store detective. That's where I met my husband Jimmy. He was the store manager. I was eighteen when I first started working there, and on my twentieth birthday I married Jimmy. We rented an apartment for the first five years and then, when we could afford it, we bought the house out by the lake. Jimmy was good with his hands and he spent hours every evening hammering and drilling until he'd fixed the place up real nice. He built a deck at the side of the house and in the evenings we liked to sit there, drinking beer and listening to the sound of the water as it lapped gently against the boathouse.

I have tried to pin down the exact time it all started, but I don't think there was such a time. It was as if we were infected with the same thoughts and just acted on them instinctively, without any discussion. At first it was pretty harmless, just a piece of merchandise every now and again. A toaster for the kitchen, a rug for the living-room floor, and as always I never said anything. Jimmy said it was a perk that came with the job. Farlanes had a reputation for being stingy employers and it was well known that a lot of the staff used to steal. My job included carrying out random searches on the workers as they left the building every evening but, being the coward that I am, I only ever picked on the ones that would never dream of taking anything they hadn't paid for.

We were happy for a long time, childless, but happy with our own company. We never had a lot of money, and I certainly never needed much. Jimmy was the one who liked to spend. He also liked to gamble. He played poker with the guys from his bowling team every Saturday night, and sometimes he would blow his entire wages in one night. When that happened, he would load up the car with the items he had stolen from the store the previous week and drive out of town to a car-boot sale. That would usually go some way to making up for his losses.

I know I should have confronted him back then but, as

I said before, I am a coward and besides I knew it would have been pointless. Jimmy was the boss and, as he never tired of telling me, he knew best.

Almost six months had gone by before I realised that although Jimmy was stealing less merchandise, he always seemed to have lots of money. We went out to dinner every weekend and always to a swanky restaurant. But the most noticeable change of all was that Jimmy began to look really well. He had his hair cut short which really smartened him up, and he started buying fancy clothes from expensive shops in town. Up until then he had never bothered with his appearance – a pair of old jeans and a Van Halen T-shirt were his usual Saturday-night attire. I wasn't really sure whether I liked his new look – some evenings he took twice as long as I did when we were getting ready to go out. On the night of my thirtieth birthday I was sitting in the kitchen, waiting, while Jimmy fixed his hair in the bathroom. When he came out, he had this big smile on his face and he came over all shy and bashful and pushed a little box into my hand. Inside was the most beautiful diamond ring I had ever seen; it made the one he had given me for our engagement look like something that came free in a cereal box.

"Oh Lord, Jimmy!" I gasped. "Where did you get the money for something like that?"

I knew as soon as the words had left my mouth that I had said the wrong thing. Jimmy's face darkened.

"Sweetheart, don't you like it?" he muttered crossly.

"Of course, I love it! I've never seen such a beautiful ring!"

"Well then, that's all that counts," he said with an unconvincing smile.

I knew right then he was up to something, but being

the way I am, I let it go for a couple of weeks. Besides, it was always better to choose my words carefully whenever I was tackling Jimmy.

One Saturday night I decided to wait up until he came in from his poker game. It was three o'clock in the morning and Jimmy was very drunk. He smiled at me as he staggered across the room and when he emptied his pockets, hundreds of dollars fell out onto the table. I sat up and stared at the notes as they floated downwards.

"You've got to tell me, Jimmy," I whispered.

He looked at me, swaying slightly, and a coy smile played at the corners of his mouth.

"Come on, Jimmy. I'm your wife – you need to tell me where the money is coming from."

He looked about the room as if he was checking to see whether anyone else was there.

Then he nestled down on the couch beside me and took my hand like an excited child.

"You know the Thursday lodgement?" It was the biggest take of the week – Thursday was late-night opening and Jimmy was responsible for lodging the money in the night safe.

"I've taken registers 4 and 5 off the system," he whispered, hardly able to contain his excitement. "No one knows they exist any more and all the proceeds go to yours truly," he said, prodding his thumb into his puffed-out chest.

My jaw nearly hit the coffee table. Those two registers were Farlanes biggest earners; they were in homewares and could take in thousands of dollars a week.

"Christ, Jimmy," I moaned, "if anyone found out, you'd be done for!"

"*I'd* be done for!" he shouted, jerking his head back

and looking at me with one eye closed. "Come on, Suzie, where do you think I've been getting all the extra cash? Do you think I got a big pay rise and forgot to tell you?" He stood up unsteadily and began to walk around the room. "Don't play the innocent with me! You've known from day one that I've been on the take." He wagged his finger at me.

"I know, Jimmy, but don't you think two registers a week is pushing things a bit far?"

He turned on me suddenly, clearly annoyed that I was stating the obvious. "Well, I haven't heard you complaining, Missy. You've been enjoying the spoils just as much as I have."

"Come here," he said, pulling me up from the couch. He took my hand and led me through the kitchen and out onto the back porch. It was a still balmy night and the almost full moon threw a silvery light on the lawn as we picked our way down the path that led to the boathouse. When we got there he fumbled inside the door for a light switch, still keeping a firm grip on my hand. Inside the dimly lit shed he pulled me towards the old rain-barrel. With one arm, he reached down inside and pulled out a dirty old sack. Letting go of me, he turned the sack upside down and tipped the contents on to the floor.

"How much?" I asked flatly, keeping my eyes fixed on the sea of notes at my feet.

"Twenty-two grand," he said proudly. "Another year or two and we can move out west and buy that home in Malibu we always talked about."

"Jimmy," I gasped, "what on earth have you done?"

★ ★ ★

I tried to live as normal a life as I could, but knowing what Jimmy was up to affected my nerves badly. I was paranoid that everyone in Farlanes was looking at us. If Jimmy came home with anything from the store I flew into a spin, but it had no effect on him. Even comments from his poker buddies about us winning the lottery didn't stop him. I purposely stopped spending money in an attempt to compensate for his extravagance, but as I became more frugal his lifestyle became more lavish. It all came to a head the day I came home and found him cutting the lawn on the brand-new John Deere ten-thousand-dollar sit-upon lawnmower. I stepped out of the car and gawped in disbelief as he held up his tin of beer and waved over at me. I waved back, and tried to disguise my panic with a terrified smile. What the hell was he thinking of?

Jimmy began to get careless, and pretty soon after that the fighting started. The management at Farlanes became suspicious, checks were carried out and still Jimmy continued to rob them blind without a care in the world. I could feel that things were moving towards a bad end.

When I confronted him he shrugged me off and called me a nag; when I persisted, he exploded and waved his arms wildly in the air. "Goddammit, woman, don't you know how I hate all these questions!"

One Saturday night I went too far, and he hit me. My eye blew out pretty bad, I wore dark glasses to work and told people I had an eye infection. He never did say sorry. We hardly spoke for a week, then on the weekend he came home with flowers and we made up, but it didn't last long. About two weeks after that he hit me again, only this time it was harder and I had to get stitches at the hospital. After that, things got pretty nasty and I began to get really scared of Jimmy. I wanted to leave but he wouldn't hear of it; he knew that I knew too much. I had put up with a lot from him over the years but he always managed to win me over because he was such a charmer.

But the day I came home and found him in bed with Jean from homewares, even his charm couldn't save him. Jean was the kind of girl that all the guys fancied. Her yellow hair-extensions fell down to her shoulders in soft curls and her lips were always drawn in a Cupid's bow with the reddest of lipstick. Jimmy never liked me wearing make-up, he said it looked cheap, but it sure as hell didn't put him off when it came to that tramp. It was his day off. I had felt sick all morning and decided to clock out at lunch-time and go home. I thought it strange that Jean's car was in our driveway, and even stranger when I saw her dress draped over our kitchen chair. I could hear them in the bedroom, his deep laugh followed by her silly high-pitched giggle. Without a second thought I went over to the cabinet where Jimmy kept his hunting rifle, checked to see that it was loaded and without a moment's hesitation walked into the bedroom and shot them. *Bang! Bang!* One bullet each, it was so easy.

Getting rid of them was the difficult part. It took me the best part of three hours to pull their bodies down to the boathouse. That was almost four years ago, and I am still attending a chiropractor every month for the injuries I sustained.

I put them into the old rowing-boat that had been lying there forever – neither of us liked the water and it had lain there rotting for years. As I pushed it off from the jetty I noticed that the water bubbled up through the holes that were dotted along its sides. Like a magical illusion, it seemed to sit just on top of the water as it drifted out into the yellow dappled sunbeams that danced on the surface of the lake. I didn't hang around to see it go down, but I know it sank very quickly. By the time I got back to the kitchen and prepared to clean the place, there was no sign of anything out there.

I stayed on at Farlanes for another few months. Apparently even the dogs on the street knew that Jimmy and Jean had been carrying on behind my back for years. The management came to the conclusion that the two of them had carried out an elaborate plan to rob the place and then split with the money. I, on the other hand, got all the sympathy. Staff lowered their voices and smiled sweetly whenever I passed by. People called by the house with home-made muffins and pot roasts every evening until I thought I would scream. Don't get me wrong. It's not like I didn't appreciate their generosity, it's just that it made me feel so guilty, especially when Jean's mother called and suggested that we start going to church together.

I eventually resigned, telling people that I wanted to start a new life. Which was true. It was kind of creepy living out by the lake knowing the Jimmy and Jean were somewhere at the bottom of it. I got myself a passport and took all the money from the rain-barrel and moved to Ireland. It seemed as good a place as any to lie low for a while. I rented an apartment in Ballsbridge and, after I settled in, I applied for a job in security at a fashionable department store. I was offered a position, but when the time came to start I found that I couldn't go back to doing the same thing again. I guess my heart just wasn't in it. When I turned down the job, they very kindly suggested that I apply for the vacancy in the Cosmetics Hall. At first

I wasn't sure, but I decided to take my chances, and within two weeks of filling out an application I was offered a job working for a company that makes a very exclusive anti-ageing cream.

I love my work. All the girls in cosmetics are so friendly and made me feel so welcome when I first started. We go out together for lunch most days and we laugh and gossip about the staff in other departments over our cappuccinos. I like having girlfriends. I don't know why but I never had any before, I guess it was probably because Jimmy didn't like me spending time with anyone else but him.

I have also made good friends with a lot of my regular customers, and their skin consultations have become more like therapy. The deeper the lines, the more they like to talk. The confessions rarely surprise me. Most of the time I can guess their story before they even open their mouths, and I can't help thinking of what my mother used to say because now I know it's true. The lines on the face betray the secrets that lie beneath. Like all those women, I have tried to erase the past with the ultimate age-defying anti-wrinkle lotions. But like all those women, I know that there is only so much a face cream can do and our lines will always run as deep as our secrets.

ALSO BY GER GALLAGHER, PUBLISHED BY POOLBEG

Broken Passions, A Life Left Untold

12

The Suntan Man

Suzanne Higgins

The rain was really spectacular. With her two daughters safely deposited at the school door, Rebecca decided to wait a few moments just to let the worst of the weather pass before driving home. She glanced at her watch. She still had an hour before the dishwasher man was due.

For three long weeks she had been waiting for that bloody guy. When the dishwasher began to make odd noises, she ignored them.

"Big mistake," the repairman had said when he first visited almost a month ago. If she had paid heed to that rattling sound she could have saved the vertical loop flushing-plug. Of course, back then she had no idea how important flushing-plugs were and they were very hard to come by for old machines – particularly the vertical loop variety. He would have to send off for it and even then there was no guarantee. Rebecca begged him but he still couldn't say with any certainty. Then she pulled out the big guns. The kettle was put on and the fresh scones were presented. (She had long since given up bribing repairmen with biscuits – they were so past that.) After an hour of sitting, listening to his complaints about the dreadful plumbing of his new townhouse in Turkey, he finally agreed to 'do his best'. If there was a vertical loop flushing-plug available in Europe, he would find it for Rebecca.

Still no sign of the rain easing off, she noted now as she glanced at her watch again but God forbid she wasn't there to greet him. She had to pick up the fresh scones on the way home too. There was nothing for it – time to go, she decided as she hurriedly put the car into reverse. The next thing she felt was the dull thud of two cars colliding. Pulling forward again, she re-parked before getting out to assess the damage. The school gardener, who she had bumped into, was very nasty about the whole thing and started to rub his neck ostentatiously.

Five minutes later, they had swapped insurance details and Rebecca had admitted liability – anything to get out of the rain. Caroline Kennedy, one of the elder lemons in the school had seen the entire episode and she waded in to help Rebecca. She had put five daughters through the school and now it was only her youngest who remained under the care of The Sisters of Perpetual Faith and Sufferance. She wasn't easily inhibited.

"Rebecca, are you all right? Are you hurt?" She gave the gardener a withering look as she guided the younger mum away from the accident.

Caroline had a huge sunshine-yellow umbrella and she pulled Rebecca underneath it.

"Oh, Caroline, I'm such an idiot! I was rushing to get out of the car park and now I've done Godknowshowmuchdamage!

That's another few thousand euro down the drain."

"Don't worry about that. What about you?" Caroline asked with genuine concern.

Rebecca, usually an upbeat person, was finding that recently life was really getting her down. On hearing Caroline's kind words, it was a little like a floodgate opening. She burst out crying.

"I'm sorry. This isn't like me, you know," she sobbed.

"Come on." Caroline turned Rebecca around and guided her towards her own car.

"What? Where? I have to go home. The repairman is coming at ten."

"You'll be home by then if you must – but first of all I'm buying you a huge sticky bun and a freshly brewed cup of coffee. You need it, girl!" She and Rebecca got into Caroline's large Mercedes Benz. "I'm taking you up to The Royal. You can let off all the steam you want and when you're feeling better, I'll take you back to your car. Now tell me – can you feel that car seat warming up yet?"

Rebecca hadn't been to The Royal since its major refurbishment, and rumour had it that it was seven-star luxury. She had been dying to try it out. It felt good to be minded and so she let her body relax into the comfort of the heated car seat.

The hotel was everything she had expected and more.

"God, I love what they've done with this place," she enthused, momentarily forgetting about all her problems.

"Isn't it perfect?" Caroline agreed, catching the eye of one of the staff. They took the Queen Anne chairs next to the fire and within minutes they were digging into hot scones served with cream and jam.

"None of your low-fat spreads here, thank you very much," Caroline grinned. "Life is simply too short not to enjoy the very best at every available minute."

She glanced at Rebecca. "Don't you agree?"

The younger woman nodded without conviction. Caroline could see Rebecca was troubled. "You can tell me," she encouraged the younger woman. "God knows I have a few years on you. There's nothing you can say that would shock." And so Rebecca did just that. She talked to Caroline about her daughter Ruth's terrible mood swings. She told Caroline about her godforsaken dishwasher and its friggin' vertical loops. Then there was the leaking roof which had only been fixed last year, combined with the crash and the fact that she thought she would never see the sun again.

Caroline nodded empathetically. "Look, maybe you didn't do too much damage to the other car this morning," she suggested. "And regarding your daughter's mood swings – keep reminding yourself that it's just a phase. Believe me I've had four girls go through puberty and it's like living with multiple personalities. It's a heck of a rollercoaster. Only one more to go and then I'm finished," she chuckled.

This made Rebecca laugh. "I guess I only have two daughters. It should be easier," she agreed.

"It is wretched not to get away to the sun, though," Caroline continued, pouring them each a second coffee from the large silver pot. "The Irish weather can be very depressing," she sighed and raised the fine bone-china coffee cup to her lips.

Rebecca shrugged. "Well, I guess I'll just have to grin and bear it. I don't have much choice, do I?"

Caroline glanced around the empty tea room. "Perhaps there is something you can do to cheer yourself up a bit."

"What?"

"There is a man – I'm not sure if you've heard of him. He's called the Suntan Man. Ring any bells?"

Rebecca looked blankly at her coffee companion and then shook her head. This wasn't a solution. The last thing she needed was a suntan. Knowing her luck she'd get burnt! And anyway, she was permanently wrapped up thanks to the Arctic Irish conditions.

"Trust me, Rebecca. It's what you need. Basically he gives you a massage but he rubs in suntan oils – not your ordinary lavender type of oils. The long and the short of it is that you'll feel wonderfully refreshed and relaxed afterwards and the bonus is the next morning when you wake up you'll be brown as a berry too." She smiled encouragingly at Rebecca but the younger woman was not convinced.

"Look, as it is, your dishwasher is getting more attention than you are! You said you ignored it at first when it started to make the warning noises. Don't make the same mistake with yourself. You need a little maintenance too, girl. Have you considered the state of *your* vertical loop flushing-plugs?" Rebecca laughed again. "I'd say they're a mess."

"The Suntan Man," Caroline repeated as she handed Rebecca his phone number. "You won't find him in the Yellow Pages so don't lose that number. He only comes by recommendation so tell him you got his name from me." Then she dropped her voice to a whisper. "Trust me, he's tanned up and rubbed down most of the mums in the school. How else do you think they stay looking so good right through our long dark winters?"

Caroline sat back and tapped the side of her nose as if to say, 'mum's the word'. Then she moved the conversation on to more mundane territory. Just as they were preparing to leave, the text came through.

"Well, that's just typical," Rebecca groaned. "He's cried off again!"

"Who has?"

"My dishwasher guy. This is the third time he's cancelled. It's driving me nuts!"

Caroline shook her head sympathetically. "Rebecca, for a house to run smoothly, the mother must be happy and contented. If she's in good form, the family will function well. If she's not, the whole house of cards comes tumbling down." Caroline studied the younger mum. "You are not happy. Until you sort yourself out you cannot hope to have your family content." They got up to leave.

"Call the Suntan Man!" Caroline ordered as they headed out.

★　★　★

It had been good to let off a little steam but by that evening, Rebecca was back into her rut of school lunches and chasing the girls up to do their homework. And it was still a battle to get them to bed by ten o'clock. By the time Johnny got home she was fit to be tied.

Rebecca had started having a glass or two of wine every evening just 'to take the edge off the day' as she put it. Sadly, however, taking the edge off the day was adding the edges to her and in all the wrong places. The final straw was when Johnny tried to get romantic with her later that night.

"It's a bloody Monday," she argued.

"So what?" he laughed incredulously. "What law says we can't have sex on a Monday?"

"Johnny, I'm exhausted."

"You're always exhausted," he grumbled as he turned his back to her and drifted off to sleep.

Rebecca lay awake and studied the blackness of the ceiling. She could hear the drip-drip of the leaking roof in the hall outside her bedroom door. How could he possibly expect to have sex with that annoyance in the background? Rebecca thought about her smashed-up car, her smashed-up house and her utterly knackered dishwasher. She fretted over her expanding backside and the only thing that was growing faster – her overdraft. Added to all of this was her strained relationship with her daughter and husband. Could life get any worse, she wondered miserably as her eyes glassed up for the second time that day.

And then she thought of Caroline's advice.

★　★　★

She made the call the very next morning as soon as the girls were in school and Johnny had gone to work.

It was only half an hour before his arrival when Rebecca began to panic. She had to shower and exfoliate before this guy saw her body.

Then, having shed a full layer of skin and washed her hair just for good measure, Rebecca opened the door to the Suntan Man. To her enormous surprise and delight she was greeted by a tall good-looking young guy. He had to be over six foot three with sandy blond hair and cheerful blue eyes. Physically he looked extremely fit and more like a ski instructor than a masseur.

"Mrs Mullen?" he enquired with a slightly shy grin.

Rebecca was hooked in an instant. "Please call me Becca," she said, and smiled like a schoolgirl.

"Hi, Becca, I'm Chris – the Suntan Man."

"Welcome!"

Chris had come prepared; he had a huge medical-looking bag full of creams and exfoliants. He could shimmy and buff or wax and polish her to within an inch of her life.

"Me or my car?" she laughed nervously but he was able to put her at ease.

He offered a selection of services from Brazilians to tangas. (At first she thought he was offering to dance with her!) He'd even brought his own masseur table, which he quickly assembled in her drawing room.

"Okay!" He clapped his hands together and began to rub them vigorously. "I need to warm these up so I don't freeze you," he laughed. "Now, Mrs Mullen, eh Becca, if you can just remove your dressing-gown and lie down, we can get started.

Uncertain of home-massage etiquette, Rebecca had come up with the brainwave of wearing a bikini under her dressing-gown. She took her dressing-gown off and quickly hopped up onto the massage table, lying face down.

Whether he thought her bikini idea smart or stupid, he didn't pass any comment. He concentrated instead on making a thorough skin assessment. His attention to detail was spectacular as he studied every square inch of her shoulders, her back, her thighs, calves and even her feet. It was all thoroughly professional and as such she didn't feel threatened or scared.

Then Chris began his magic. Starting on her back, he kneaded her flesh and rubbed her muscles. He never hurt her but rather urged her skin back into life. Unaware that she had just had a full exfoliation (mainly because she didn't tell him), Chris gave her the full treatment. She didn't feel him undo her bikini top but, by the time she realised it, the woman was beyond caring, such was her state of ecstasy. He buffed then polished her and finally he began to blend in the exquisite-smelling suntan potion.

Chris explained that he personally mixed the oils as he started his 'tapping treatment' on her pulse points. She listened idly as he tapped her in places where she had never been tapped before. It was a secret combination of tanning agents, antioxidants and ylang-ylang and there were a few other ingredients mixed in which he couldn't tell her about.

"Because then you'd know too much," he whispered into her ear as his hands pushed down along her back and right under her bikini bottoms!

When he had finished, she was in a state of utter bliss. "Those pulse points," she mumbled as if she were drunk, "you really got 'em good." She wanted to nod off but Chris interrupted her daydreams.

"You're going to have to sit up while I do your front," he explained. "If you lie down, your back will get smudged."

Rebecca did as she was told and that's how she ended up sitting in her drawing room practically naked, getting covered from head to toe in some secret feel-good cocktail.

By the time he had finished, Rebecca was in a happier place than she had been for many months.

"God, Chris, you really have a gift," she enthused as she shoved the fifty-euro fee into his hand and a further five euro for good measure.

He smiled winningly at her. "Yeah, I enjoy my work. You have terrific skin by the way but I'm worried about the tension in your shoulders and the skin on your lower back. It's very dry. I really think you need a course of treatments to get back into good condition."

"Really?" she asked, feigning more concern than she actually felt for the state of her lower back.

"You don't want to have dry skin with Christmas just around the corner."

"Christmas? God, we haven't even had Hallowe'en yet!"

"It's only ten weeks away. You'd need to be working on the condition of your skin now to have it in good nick for the Christmas party season. I'm sure you'll be wearing a few backless numbers over the holiday season," he smiled mischievously at her, "and it would be good to get rid of the tension in your shoulders too." Then his tone turned slightly serious. "To be honest, I would recommend a twice-weekly intensive massage and moisturising course for the next two months."

Rebecca didn't even need to think about it. After all, your health came first and this was practically a medical emergency. "'K," she agreed like a five-year-old.

★ ★ ★

It was some weeks later when an incredibly radiant and gloriously tanned Rebecca Mullen met Caroline Madden in the school carpark.

Caroline winked at the other woman and tapped the side of her nose.

"Thank you so much for giving me his number, Caroline. The Suntan Man has put the pep back in my step."

"And your car?"

"Oh, it wasn't so bad. Nor was the gardener's. Even the ruddy dishwasher got fixed last week. Don't get me wrong – Chris hasn't solved all my problems. It just seems easier to cope with the trouble and strife of life – even Ruth!" Rebecca smiled.

"No less than the dishwasher, you just needed a little attention," Caroline whispered.

"Even Johnny and I are getting on much better. He loves my new tan!

"I bet he does!"

"Yes, he reckons that the Suntan Man is the secret to my staying sane and he wants me to keep up with at least a treatment a week in the New Year."

"Has he met Chris yet?"

"Oh yes – Johnny thinks he's gay. Can you believe such nonsense?"

"Never!" Caroline pretended to look shocked and remembered the day she discovered her masseur was, in fact, gay. In all the time he had been tanning her up, she really believed that they were on the verge of a rampant affair. In reality the only thing that was rampant was her imagination.

Judging by the twinkle in Rebecca's eye, she was in the very same place right now.

"Anyway, Johnny and I are having a wonderful time at the moment. When you feel so good in your skin, it really has a positive effect on your – well, your romantic life, doesn't it?"

"Definitely," Caroline agreed. Things were working out perfectly, she realised with some personal satisfaction.

But they were interrupted by the sound of metal crunching in the school carpark.

A young mum who Rebecca vaguely recognised got out of her car and began to cry as she saw the damage she had done to the school bus she had just reversed into. Caroline smiled at Rebecca. "Will you tell her or will I?"

Also by Suzanne Higgins, published by Poolbeg

The Will To Win, The Woman He Loves, The Power of a Woman

13

Female Intuition
MELISSA HILL

There was no doubt whatsoever in Shauna's mind that Des was seeing someone behind her back. All the signs were there. The whispered phone calls and secretive texts, the sudden interest in his appearance, the extra nights 'working late'.

"I think he's seeing some woman from work," she confessed to her friend Martha the day after Des had yet again arrived home late without a proper explanation.

He'd barely said a word over the dinner Shauna had painstakingly prepared for them, and not long afterwards had blithely informed her he was tired and heading for bed.

In all the years they'd lived together, Shauna could never remember him going to bed before she did – or indeed showering beforehand. It was a classic sign, wasn't it?

"What on earth makes you think that?" Martha said,

apparently as shocked by the notion as Shauna was.

Typical, Shauna thought sourly. Everyone thought the sun shone out of Des Morrissey's ass — handsome Des with his startling blue eyes and honest, friendly smile. The man could charm anyone, from stuffy clients at the bank to the old biddy neighbours on their street, who — to Shauna's great amusement — were forever asking him to do little jobs around the house for them.

"I just know," she replied petulantly, rather stung that Martha wasn't taking her concerns seriously. "All the signs are there."

"You don't know anything for certain," her friend insisted, throwing an eye towards her toddler son, Ray, who was playing on the kitchen floor beneath their feet. "The late nights don't necessarily mean an iota. Remember, he's a busy man with an important job."

Obviously much more important than she was, anyway, Shauna thought resentfully. Des worked as a financial advisor for one of the biggest banks in the country, and while his well-paid job ensured they could afford their lovely house, a top-end BMW and two foreign holidays a year, it also meant that he spent much more time at the office than he did with Shauna. But this was different. She just knew it.

"Call it female intuition — whatever you want," she insisted. "I just *know* that something is going on. And," she added, taking a deep breath, "I think I know who it is — who *she* is too."

Martha's eyes widened. "What?"

Shauna nodded tearfully. "She phoned the house the other day, and I recognised her voice."

"Whose voice?"

"That bitch of a secretary of his — Jodi."

Martha laughed. "His secretary? But that is such a cliché! Sorry," she added quickly, when Shauna flashed her a look.

"She's very pretty – all glossy hair, high cheekbones, and long legs. And I know for a *fact* that she fancies him."

The last time Shauna had popped in to see Des at the office, Jodi had gone out of her way to interrupt their time together, and had used every opportunity to flirt with Des right in front of Shauna's nose. And she didn't like the way the other girl was over-friendly with her either, addressing her by her first name when she barely even knew her!

Then late one evening last week, Jodi had, brazenly, phoned Des and Shauna's home number. And as soon as she heard Shauna answer, the other girl had gasped theatrically and tried to pretend she'd phoned the wrong number – knowing full well that Shauna would recognise her voice. This, along with his weird, secretive behaviour, had really sent Shauna's suspicions into overdrive, and convinced her that he and Jodi were seeing one another behind her back.

"What am I going to do?" she asked Martha then. "How do I stop this?"

"Shauna – I doubt very much that . . . oh, darling I told you not to do that!" Martha broke off as her son clattered headfirst to the ground, his piercing cries putting a swift end to their chat.

As she headed for home, Shauna felt somewhat heartened by Martha's assurances, but they still didn't make her feel any different. There was definitely something going on – she knew just it. Her female intuition was screaming at her.

As she approached the house, she spotted his BMW in

the driveway. So, he was home early today – for a change.

"Hi, darling!" he called out as she went inside. "Where have you been?"

"Just over at Martha's," she replied, joining him in the kitchen and doing a double-take when she realised he was preparing dinner.

Weird, Shauna decided, worrying even more. When was the last time he'd made her a cup of coffee, let alone dinner? "You're making dinner?"

"Don't sound so surprised!" Grinning, he continued chopping vegetables. "I thought it might make a nice change," he added, before turning to face her. "Look, love, I know I've been a bit preoccupied with work lately, and we haven't had the chance to spend much time together." Then, drying his hands on a towel, he opened a cupboard nearby and to Shauna's utter amazement, produced a huge bouquet of sunflowers.

Shauna was lost for words and all of a sudden, a lump came to her throat. That was it – the final piece of proof she needed. Now she knew for certain that he was up to something behind her back. Why else the dinner and the flowers? Weren't they both classic signs?

"I hope you like them," he said, when at first she didn't react. "Sunflowers are still your favourite, aren't they? It's hard to keep up with you sometimes." He reached forward and kissed her tenderly on the forehead, Shauna still unable to speak.

Just then, the telephone rang, startling her out of her reverie.

"I'll get it – you've got your hands full there," he said, before practically sprinting down the hallway – evidently all too eager to get to the phone before she did, she thought derisively.

"It's for you," he said, handing her the cordless phone, his face impassive. "Your mother."

"Hi, Mum," Shauna tried to keep her voice light. "How are you?"

"Grand, love – I just thought I'd call and see how you were. I haven't heard from you in a while."

At the sound of her mother's warm and friendly voice, Shauna almost burst out crying. With all that was happening – especially today, she wanted more than anything to confess her suspicions to her, but she couldn't do it.

Besides, her mum – like Martha – just wouldn't believe it. Quiet, reserved Des, seeing some woman behind Shauna's back? The very idea would seem ludicrous. And of course, it went without saying that Cathy would go ballistic should Des do anything to upset her precious daughter. No, there was no point in saying anything at this stage, at least not until she knew for certain – and *especially* not to her mother.

"I'm great," she lied, trying to keep the tears at bay. "Sorry I haven't been in touch – things have been busy."

"How's Des?" Cathy asked, and for a second Shauna wondered if she could read her mind. "He sounded a little bit preoccupied when he answered the phone."

"Oh, he was just in the middle of making dinner when you called so – "

"Des – making dinner?" Cathy laughed, evidently highly amused by the notion. "Well, I never!"

Shauna and her mum chatted on for a few minutes, until Shauna eventually found trying to sound carefree and light-hearted too much of a strain. "I'd better let you go," she said. "Dinner's nearly ready."

"OK, love – we'll talk again soon. Keep in touch."

"I will and say hi to Da – "

"He's here beside me – he says hello, too. Come and see us soon, won't you, pet? It's been a while, and we miss you."

"I will, Mum – bye." Shauna hung up, suspecting that her mother might be seeing a hell of a lot more of her from now on, should her suspicions about Des prove correct.

Nevertheless, Cathy's timely phone call had given her an idea.

"I thought I might go to Galway next weekend," she mentioned casually the following morning over breakfast.

Des looked away from the paper he was reading. "On your own?"

"Why not? I know you're too busy at the moment to come with me."

"Well, that's true … but how will you get there?"

Although Shauna could drive, there was no question of him letting her take the car. For one thing he needed it for work, and for another, she knew he didn't trust her behind the wheel of his precious Beemer.

She shrugged. "I could just take the train there and back. It's only for a few days."

"Are you sure?"

She couldn't be certain, but Shauna thought he sounded relieved and more than a little pleased. Well, he would, wouldn't he? With her out of the way for a few days he could get up to anything he liked. He could stay over at *her* place or even . . . no, he wouldn't dream of bringing the little bitch here to their house, would he?

Shauna didn't think so, but she couldn't be sure. She wasn't sure of anything where he was concerned these days. Which is why she had to find out once and for all if he was up to something.

So, on Friday lunchtime, when he dropped her off at Heuston train station, Shauna kissed him goodbye, and behaved as if there was nothing out of the ordinary.

"See you on Sunday night," she said, heading straight for the ticket office.

But instead of buying a ticket for the Galway train, Shauna waited until the Beemer had safely driven away before heading directly for the Luas stop and taking the next tram into town.

Little did he know she'd no intention of visiting her mother – instead she was going to find out once and for all what was going on with him and Jodi. Enough was enough. She wasn't going to be lied to any longer.

Having spent an hour or so wandering around the shops, Shauna decided it was time for action. Taking out her mobile phone (having first made sure that her number was concealed) she dialled the bank's main reception.

"Des Morrissey, please," she said crisply, when the call was answered.

"May I ask who's calling?"

"Shauna Morrissey," said Shauna, assuming her haughtiest tone.

"Hold one moment – I'll just put you through." If the receptionist was surprised she didn't try his direct line instead of going through the switch, she certainly didn't show it.

Shauna waited for what she suspected would be the inevitable reply.

"I'm sorry, Mrs Morrissey, but your husband seems to have already left for the evening."

Shauna smiled. This was too easy. "Could I speak to Jodi then? His secretary?"

"Hold on."

Again Shauna anticipated the receptionist's eventual reply.

"I'm very sorry but I'm afraid Ms Moore has also left early this afternoon."

"That's fine," Shauna replied pleasantly. "Thank you for your help."

"No problem, Mrs Morrissey. Have a good afternoon."

Shauna's heart raced in her chest. She'd been right! The two of them had evidently jumped at the chance to sneak some quality time together while she wasn't around. How dumb did they think she was? And how dumb was *he* to think he could get away with it?

Shauna marched resolutely towards the nearest taxi rank.

So, she'd ascertained that he and Jodi really *were* together – now all she had to do was catch them in the act. Rattling off the woman's address to the taxi-driver (which she'd checked out before her supposed trip to Galway), she sat back in her seat and contemplated what to do next. If, as she anticipated, his car was parked outside the other woman's apartment, and they were inside together, what should she do? She couldn't just arrive unannounced at the door, couldn't she?

But as it turned out, when they reached the address, there was no sign of Des's car. Which meant only one thing . . .

As the taxi-driver eventually reached Shauna's own house, Beemer sitting in the driveway, she spotted the closed upstairs curtains, and realised that what she'd suspected for the last few weeks, what she'd been dreading the most was really happening. No prizes for guessing what was going on in the bedroom – or who with.

How could he *do* this to her? How?

Even though she'd suspected it – had facilitated it today to a certain extent – she still couldn't help but be outraged. She'd hoped that her suspicions were unfounded, that they were – as Martha suggested – simply the result of paranoia on her part. But there was no denying it now. He'd lied, deceived, and as far as she was concerned had broken every ounce of trust they'd ever had between them.

Incensed, Shauna paid the driver and got out of the taxi, before not-too-quietly driving her key into the front door. Stepping into the silent hallway, she slammed the door behind her, leaving the happy couple in no doubt that they were no longer alone.

Within seconds, she heard the bedroom door open and Des appeared on the landing.

"Shauna!" he exclaimed, his shirt half-opened, and his trousers undone. "What are you doing here?"

"What am I doing here? I live here!" she cried from the bottom of the stairs. "Or have you forgotten that already?"

"Of course not. But look, darling . . ." White-faced and with eyes filled with guilt, he glanced surreptitiously towards the bedroom door. "Look, let's go downstairs and talk about this, okay?"

"Well, aren't you going to introduce me?" she continued, her voice dripping with scorn.

"Shauna –"

"I can't believe you would do this to me!" she yelled, as he ran downstairs. "I can't believe that you would go behind my back like this!"

"Shauna, love – I was going to tell you –"

"You were going to tell me what – that you and the

silly cow are *in love*, is that it?"

"Now hold it right, there, madam." Suddenly, his tone changed. "You don't know what the hell you're talking about."

"Don't I? Don't I?" Shauna was screaming now, her face puce with anger. "I know *exactly* what you're up to! This little fling been going on for a while, hasn't it? Who knows, maybe it was going on when Mum was still around!"

"How *dare* you say something like that to me!" he shot back. "I was faithful to your mother since the day I first laid eyes on her! She was one who walked out on *me*, remember?"

With that, he marched resolutely into the kitchen, leaving Shauna standing alone in the hallway.

Immediately she felt guilty. She should never have said that. Who knew better than she did how much Des had suffered when he discovered her mother had been having an affair? And who knew better than she how hard it was for him to come to terms with the fact that Cathy – his wife of thirteen years – was leaving him to set up home with someone else?

When she and Des had split almost three years before, Cathy and her new man Danny had wanted Shauna to come and live with them in Galway, but she had wholeheartedly refused. She loved it here in Dublin, loved her home, her friends, her new school . . . but most of all, she loved her dad.

"I'm sorry," she sniffed, going after Des. "I didn't mean that. But you were sneaking around behind my back –"

"Honey, I didn't think I had a choice," he said, his tone softening. "Obviously I knew something like this would affect you – after all, you've been the only woman in my life for the last few years. I was just waiting for the right time to tell you. The last thing I wanted was for you to find out like this."

Shauna sniffed. "Is it *her*?" she said, unable to hide her disapproval that the horrible Jodi was seeing her father. "Is it Jodi?"

For a brief second, Des didn't seem to realise who she was talking about. Then his eyes widened. "Jodi? Jodi from work?"

She nodded.

"Shauna – Jodi is happily married with a young child," he told her, smiling. "There was never any *question* – "

"Then who . . .?" She looked at him, puzzled

"I know you'll find this hard to believe, which is why we didn't want to tell you until the time was right but – "

"Hi, Shauna."

Stunned at the voice – one she knew well – Shauna turned to face the woman who had quietly entered the kitchen.

Martha looked shamefaced. "I tried to convince him to tell you sooner – especially when you said you had your suspicions." Her gaze locked onto Des's. "Still, as you can imagine, we weren't sure how to break it to you . . ."

Shauna couldn't believe it. Martha and her father – together!

Martha, the lovely single mother for whom Shauna often baby-sat, and her single, separated father . . . well, this was . . . this was cool! Okay, so she'd always dreaded sharing Des with another woman, but Martha . . . well, Martha was her friend so it wouldn't be half as bad!

But how silly must she have sounded telling Martha that she thought her dad was seeing Jodi. And how awful must poor Martha have felt, unable to tell her the truth until Des agreed to it. Her cheeks went pink as she recalled the horrible accusations she'd flung at her father earlier.

Des looked affectionately at Martha. "We got to know one another properly a while back when she asked me to cut down some trees in her back garden."

Shauna remembered teasing Martha about being as bad as the other biddies on the road, getting her dad to help with bits and pieces round the house. Little did she know that it was to be the start of a romance – a secretive, clandestine romance that had sent Shauna's imagination into overdrive! But yet, when she thought about it now, weren't they just *perfect* for each other?

"I can't believe you kept this from me," she said, shaking her head in bewilderment, although inwardly she felt relieved.

"So what do you think?" her father asked, as he and his 'other woman' regarded her warily. "Do you mind?"

Shauna made a face. "Duh! I don't mind at all," she replied, smiling at the two of them, and congratulating her female intuition for being – once again – spot on.

ALSO BY MELISSA HILL, PUBLISHED BY POOLBEG

All Because of You, Wishful Thinking,
Never Say Never, Not What You Think,
Something You Should Know

14

Get Lost
MARY HOSTY

I'm finding it easier than I thought. In fact I never imagined it could be so easy. Today, for instance, I slipped past him on the main street and he didn't even notice me. He's only programmed to spot beautiful women, you see. Actually it's comical to watch. A beautiful woman appears on the horizon and he starts to do that peculiar strutting thing with his fat veiny legs that I've seen stallions doing in the field at the end of the village. Only they do it much more gracefully. His chest plumps out and his chin seems to take on a life of its own as it spears the air with his version of youthful arrogance and his *'Hey, look at me – am I not the hottest oldest, fattest and baldest man in town – if not in the whole world!'* attitude.

I'm beginning to think that surrendering beauty is a very small price to pay for peace of mind. My fabulously glamorous, immaculately-turned-out sister is worried that I'm losing my mind. Each morning it takes her sixty-five minutes exactly to shower, groom and apply her magnificent mask for the world. She always looks stunning with smooth porcelain skin and a dark halo of glistening wavy hair framing her violet eyes. I can achieve that stunning look too but these days I'm quite enjoying being invisible.

Getting lost – I call it!

And it's so gloriously simple and easy!

In the past few months, I have sometimes found myself wondering why I was ever so flashily, fluorescently visible in the past – more like a brash cockatoo than a swan. Looking back, it seems that if I was not in a state of in-your-face, height-of-fashion, just-stepped-out-in-this-week's-newest-fabbest-outfit, I wasn't fully existing somehow. That was how I'd met Elgin in the first place. He was setting up in business and he wanted a trophy wife alongside him. I ticked all the boxes apparently. (I'll digress briefly to tell you that his mother had a thing about marble, hence the name Elgin, and her daughter was called Carrara. Perhaps if she'd had a third – it might have been named Connemara). I was working as a model when we met and I expect that he didn't really see beyond my long wavy mane of strawberry-blonde hair, my carefully practised catwalk strut and dazzling sky-blue eyes. Though I would never have considered myself beautiful, I had turned myself into the sort of girl who men stopped and stared at. It was quite nice to be admired. I would be lying if I said otherwise. Being beautiful is no burden to a woman – or at least I used to think that was so. These days I'm not so sure.

But there is scarcely a shred of that tall curvaceous blonde left. These days I wear flat shoes. My hair is light brown and pulled back in an unruly ponytail. My eyes without the expensive cobalt-blue contact lens, my eyes are actually a washed-charcoal colour and without elaborate layers of make-up and expensive clothes, I am quite nondescript to look at. And now that I'm in the background more, I've begun to notice a lot of interesting stuff about people. Probably I'm a better judge of character. After all, it was a monumental case of bad judgement that first led me into the arms of Elgin Flavin, part-time solicitor and trophy hunter and full-time gobshite.

My mother – a history teacher – told me the other day, when I broached the subject, that there is a long and illustrious history of women making themselves unseen. She told me over coffee in that nice little New-York-style deli in the village, that if you trawl back through history women of all ages have thought nothing of making themselves invisible to the outside world.

"Oh, come on, Mam – that's all a bit Lady of Shalott, isn't it?"

"What, dear? Is that some sort of *Desperate Housewife* thing? I do find it hard to keep track these days."

I grinned patiently at her. Age has begun to tangle up her memory and though she hides it, I can see that it frustrates her.

"It's an old poem by Tennyson – you remember:
"Or when the moon was overhead,
Came two young lovers lately wed;
'I am half sick of shadows,' said
The Lady of Shalott."

I finished off with a little flourish of my spoon and a brave smile.

Then it was her turn to smile patiently at me. "Very pretty, darling – but all that Camelot stuff – not real history. I'm talking about real women clad in those lovely medieval hoods that hung in elegant folds and hid their faces from unwanted attention, women who stayed behind the scenes and yet wielded great power. Oh dear – once a history teacher – I should know better than to lecture you. But what I really wanted to tell you was that your Great-Aunt Bridget carried out an astonishing feat of invisibility a little over fifty years ago."

"What?" I was in a desperate rush. A man was coming to view my house. The estate agent said the man was very keen to buy. I couldn't afford to keep him waiting. But I also wanted to hear about Great-Aunt Bridget. Mam very rarely yielded up family gossip.

She leaned forward and took a deep breath. "Your great-aunt . . ."

"I'm sorry, Mam – but I really have to go . . ."

I could see the disappointment in her eyes. We always meet up twice a week – but still I knew she was lonely and it made me feel horribly guilty any time I rushed away from her.

"I'll see you on Thursday for dinner – I promise," I said, pulling on an old grey coat and a thick black scarf that hid the bottom half of my face. "Then you can tell me the story over a nice bottle of wine."

I hugged her and left.

Back at the house, I waited for the man to arrive and reflected on what it would feel like to sell my home – the place where all my dreams had stirred, where the happy-ever-after life I'd always wanted had been planned and brought to the brink of fulfilment. The house where love had died. I wondered if a prospective buyer might sense it – the dark cloying stagnancy of a failed marriage.

The man arrived punctually and looked over the house

with the estate agent. He asked a few basic questions about structural repairs and fixtures and fittings. I offered freshly brewed coffee. I thought the smell of it might entice him to buy. It's a pretty little place. I have done quite a bit of restoration work on it and the walled courtyard garden at the back is probably the prettiest on the street.

The estate agent had gone outside to take a call on his phone.

"Why are you selling?" the buyer asked. His name was Thady. He was an engineer with one of the big construction companies in the city, looking for a small house in a quiet village – somewhere to chill out at the weekends. He sipped at his coffee and spoke with little inflection in his voice. He seemed to have that knack of dealing politely with people without ever really engaging in any actual communication. It suited me fine.

I explained that I was moving to be closer to my new job. Which wasn't entirely a lie. And anyway why burden him with my dead marriage, knowledge that might put him off buying the house. Besides I do have a new job, but it's very far removed from my previous career as a catwalk model.

That was almost a week ago and I have heard nothing back from the estate agent. I need to sell the house quickly. I'm paying rent on a new apartment nearby and divorce is an expensive business. The house was in my name and though Elgin did make a half-hearted effort to lay claim to half the proceeds of the sale, in the end he gave up as it would have meant declaring his gambling debts – and that would be the end of his last few straggling clients.

I started my new job on Monday.

"You can't be serious," Jane said when she heard I was going to work in a library. "Libraries are ghastly places – full of used and smelly books that have been manhandled by God knows who. You'll never meet anyone remotely interesting or successful in a library. Libraries are for losers." Jane has an arsenal of such maxims. She's a hedge fund manager with one of the big commercial banks in the city centre. She drives a top-of-the-range Mercedes and owns a penthouse overlooking the bay. She lives on carrot juice and Botox. She takes muscular young lovers and smothers them in sex, attention and presents – until she tires of them. I love her dearly – for her fierce arrogant honesty most of all. But she lives in a world far removed from the lives of many people – most of all mine.

My first day in the library was nerve-racking. I kept putting the books in the wrong place and talking too loudly. The boss is a woman about my own age with a permanent fish-eyed glassy smile. I ought to describe her more kindly and perhaps her permaglaze-smile hides a broken heart or shattered childhood. But she hasn't gone out of her way to make me feel welcome. Quite the reverse! She ignored me completely on the morning I arrived and then, in the first afternoon, she drew me into the office and introduced herself as Mrs Davis. I shook her limp dry hand and thanked her for taking me on. "Yes, well, it's hard to get library staff," she said, by way of an encouraging reply and then hissed at me that autobiography and biography were not the same things and that children were not allowed to use the Internet. She warned me that there was a small nest (her word) of university students ensconced in the reference room and that I was to watch them carefully to prevent stealing books and kissing and touching.

That was the extent of my induction programme and I spent the rest of the day being shown the ropes by Lucy, who looks about ten years younger than me – probably late twenties. She's very sweet and by the end of the day I was finding my way round the system. In spite of the fish-eyed boss, I'm beginning to feel quite comfortable here, mainly because there's no chance of Elgin coming in. He's not a library person. I won't make the obvious joke about books and bookies.

I saw him when I was on my way home, sitting in his favourite spot – the bar next to the bookie's. I stood at the window for quite some time, observing him through the semi-frosted glass. He had been studying the form and his swollen fingers held the biro like a large and languid spider fastening onto a long stick insect. I could tell by the expression of pure smuggery and delight on his bloated face that someone has given him the tip of a lifetime – a sure-fire winner, a dead cert. He carefully measured his attention between pint, racing page and the large plasma-screen telly on the wall. The racecourse was clearly visible on the screen. In a matter of moments the race would start and my ex-beloved would begin his orgasmic tirade at the telly – starting with low moans of encouragement and building to a crescendo of abandoned whoops of elation or bellows of despair.

I didn't linger. I find the sight of him painful. Every place I go in the village reminds me of him, of our life together, our marriage and the vile dead thing it became. Even though he doesn't see me, he is all too visible to me. Some days I feel horribly exposed, like the whole place knows the creaking and rattling of my broken heart. It's like walking round with a great big open wound that everyone can see. Jane says I should leave altogether, move away and start again. She says that's what loads of people do in my situation. She tells me I'll go mad from it all.

Maybe she's right.

But it would seem like running away. And besides, I can't leave Mam.

Back in my little apartment, I curled up beneath the bedclothes and wept for the time I had lost and the love I had misspent. I stayed like that for a long time. But despair is really quite boring. It saps all your energy and about the only good thing that can be said for despair is that it can help you to lose weight. I hauled myself out of bed, showered and threw on a pair of jeans, white T-shirt and a toffee-coloured linen jacket. Apart from the shapeless black suit that I wear to work, it's the smartest outfit I have these days.

I was meeting my mother for dinner. Over the years we have fallen into the routine – a three-course meal and a bottle of wine, then a stroll home to her house at the end of the village. I still enjoyed the dinner. Mam is great fun and easy to please. She loves her nights out and has an endless supply of light-hearted conversation. But lately I had begun to dread the stroll through the village. Even though he'd scarcely notice me in my present guise, the possibility of bumping into Elgin on the street, the awkwardness, his jovial bluster and fake bonhomie, as if he hadn't entirely wrecked my life – is always with me. I wondered if I could persuade Mam to get in a takeaway instead. Not likely.

"I wanted to tell you about Great-Aunt Bridget," she said, once we were seated and had ordered our food. "This is a big family secret – and I don't intend telling anyone else – not even Jane – so don't you go telling her."

"I won't," I said, biting into a glistening plump green olive.

"She fell in love," my mother said like it was a trip to town or a stroll in the park. "With a rather nasty man as it happened."

"Anyone I'd know?"

She shook her head. "He owned a lot of property in the town. He had a few shops. He was married and, though she never encouraged him, he used to pursue her all the same. One day he'd tell her he loved her and was going to leave his wife and the next day he'd accuse her of leading him on and trying to destroy his life. Aunt Bridget was no fool but his behaviour confused and intrigued her. Then sometimes he would turn up with expensive gifts. He kept it up for a long time and in the end she fell for him. Peavoy – that was his name. The family has died out now."

I shook my head in sympathy with my aunt. The food had arrived and Mam was tucking in hungrily to her Sicilian chicken breast. I poked wearily at some pasta with funghi.

"His wife was a nice woman and Aunt Bridget felt awful about her position. Every week she tried to end her relationship with Peavoy and every week he'd bully, blackmail or bribe her to remain as his mistress. Once he bought her a beautiful horse. Bridget loved horses and it was the sort of present he knew would tie her to him more forcefully. She was only twenty-one – scarcely more than a girl. What chance did she have? One evening he beat her."

I speared a slice of mushroom with my fork. "Why?"

Mam bit her lip and looked across at me. "Why does any man beat a woman?"

I said nothing.

"Why did your husband beat you?" she said quietly.

I'm not sure if she was really expecting an answer – and I don't think I could have come up with an answer anyway – since I don't know. Elgin never ever actually sat me down and explained his reasons to me. He did not sweep me into town, to dinner at the best restaurant, or lean across the table and stare into my eyes and say *"My darling Ruth – the reason I beat you to a pulp all those times is because . . ."*

We sat in silence for a few moments and then Mam continued with her story. "When Peavoy continued to beat Aunt Bridget, she realised she would have to escape somehow. She thought of running away to the city – but like you she was a home bird. She loved her parents and she loved her brother. In the end she became invisible."

I gave a small mocking laugh, which my mother ignored.

"She began by visiting his wife and confessing everything."

"Brave," I said.

"The wife was very influential and in spite of the circumstances took a great fondness for Bridget. She got your great-aunt a job at the stables of a big horse-trainer out the road. Aunt cropped her hair, dressed up as a boy, changed her name to Bill and lived out the rest of her days running the horse-trainer's stables – one of the happiest women or lads in the district."

"This Peavoy – he must have found out!" I said, throwing cold water on her cute little story.

She shook her head vehemently. "It was the best kept secret in town. Only Peavoy's wife, the trainer, Bridget and her parents and brother (my father) knew. Whenever he or anyone in the village asked where she'd gone, they were told she'd moved to London to look after an elderly aunt. Peavoy stomped round for a year like an angry bear trying to trace her, but in the end he gave up and started tormenting some other young girl. They say that when the trainer's wife died, Aunt Bridget and he became lovers in secret – but I never found out if that was true or not. You see – she found a way of becoming invisible from Peavoy without leaving her family."

I felt angry suddenly at my mother's cosy little happy-ever-after tale. I felt angry with my aunt for running away and hiding, at her family for condoning her actions. I felt angry with myself for wanting to do the same. I wanted to run up the street to that bar beside the bookie's and grab my ex-husband by the thick hairy folds of his neck and tell him how he and all bullies like him wrecked the lives of so many people. But I didn't.

"What a story!" I exclaimed brightly. "What an amazing story!"

"And now it's our secret," my mother beamed, "and who knows what might come out of it."

I didn't linger to ask her what she meant by that. But I suspect she was suggesting I might take a leaf out of Aunt Bridget's book and disguise myself as a boy to hide away from Elgin. Mostly I think she was worried I might leave her and this was her subtle way of conveying that anxiety.

Work yesterday was a little better and apart from the fish-eyed boss, my colleagues are a pleasant bunch, especially Lucy who has sort of adopted me. I couldn't get Aunt Bridget out of my mind though. I'd initially scorned her disappearing act but now I began to think of the calmness and strength of mind she must have possessed to live such an extraordinary life in such an ordinary place. Every single day of the life she chose to live must have presented a challenge of some sort. She was brave, I decided, and with a sense of the humour and absurdity of life.

But thinking about her life made me feel more torn than ever – on the one hand wanting to run away and put all the past behind me, and on the other determined that I should stay and live my life on my own terms without feeling intimidated by anyone. If I ever married, I thought, here is where I would like to rear my children. If I have children – with the one ovary he didn't punch into a septic useless pulp.

Jane has bought me an iPod and after work yesterday evening I took a brisk walk down along the riverbank. I listened to some old Willy Nelson songs. Not fashionable, I know – but who else sings of human regrets like him? I sat on a bench and watched the water rippling by. A teenage boy came and sat beside me. He was listening to his iPod too, though I doubt it was Willy Nelson. I don't think he even noticed me. Occasionally, he threw a stick for his dog but mostly he just stared at the water and listened to his music. There we were – the two of us on a bench, doing virtually the same thing and never engaging with each other at all.

We were living in parallel universes. Side by side – but never connecting! The phrase lingered in my head and I mulled over it for a long time before I fell asleep last night.

This morning when I woke I felt as though a leaden shroud was slowly lifting from my shoulders. I phoned Jane.

"I'm staying put," I said. "Damned if Elgin Flavin is going to bully me out of the village that I love. If he can go on living here – then so can I. After all, I was here first!"

"Are you sure?" said Jane. She was on her way to the airport – Buenos Aires, I think.

"Yes. I've just realised. I simply have to imagine myself in a parallel universe . . ."

"What?"

"I sat beside this boy on a bench yesterday evening and . . ."

"You're breaking up. Can't hear you. Got to go. Love you!"

I will tell my mam this evening.

This afternoon the estate agent called. Thady the engineer wants to view my house again. He's almost certain to buy. I felt unaccountably pleased. I remembered that he was pleasant and tactful in his manner, that he was careful in his dealings with both the estate agent and me. Such a man would bring good people to the house, maybe at some point, even me.

I've just caught sight of myself in the mirror and I don't think this invisible thing is going to work. I've grown tired of the mousy shapeless hair, the dark tracksuits and neglected complexion. "'*I am half sick of shadows,' said the Lady of Shalott.*"

It's time to become visible again.

Nothing flashy, mind! Just a new style and a few highlights! Oh and I've seen the most amazing pair of 3-inch heels!

ALSO BY MARY HOSTY, PUBLISHED BY POOLBEG

A Perfect Moment, Learning To Fly,
The Men in her Life

15

A Visit To Uncle Arthur

LINDA KAVANAGH

Evie put on her hat and took a last look around the bedroom. Yes, she'd packed everything she needed. Before she picked up her suitcase, she took a last glance at herself in the mirror. She saw a plump middle-aged woman whose coat had seen better days, and whose hat was practical rather than fashionable. The short brown hair was sprinkled with grey, and her jaw-line was already showing the first signs of sagging.

But while her conscious mind took in all of this, another part of her brain saw only the woman that *he* would see: the woman who would excite and delight him, who would sparkle and titillate him with her wit and coquetry. She gave a sexy pout in the mirror and, pleased with the result, picked up her suitcase and headed downstairs.

From the dining room, she could hear Joe snoring. Peeping in the door, she surveyed him as he slept, the newspaper fallen from his lap onto the floor, his mouth wide open, the few remaining hairs on his head awry. She sighed. He'd been handsome once, but that was a long time ago. At one stage – it was hard to imagine it now – all the women at the factory where they'd both worked had set their caps at him. But he'd chosen her, and now they'd been married for – could it really be almost forty years?

Back then, they'd been fresh, young, excited by life and each other. But the years had taken their toll – maybe they did in every marriage – and now their days were mediated by long-established rituals and habits. They rarely actually spoke to each other any more, probably because there was little they needed to say to each other.

"Joe – I'm off."

"W-what?" Joe surfaced from his netherworld of dreams, immediately picking up the newspaper and his glasses from the floor.

"I'm off to catch the train."

"All right, love."

Joe yawned and closed his eyes again, and Evie knew that already he'd drifted off to sleep again.

Then just as she was about to close the door, she heard him say: "Don't forget to give my regards to Uncle Arthur."

Although her husband couldn't see her face, Evie blushed. Uncle Arthur had been her own invention – a great-uncle on her mother's side who didn't actually exist. And every year, Evie went to visit this mythical relation. It was her own special time, when she broke away from traditions and conventions, becoming a totally different woman.

"Yes – of course I will."

Evie sighed as she closed the living-room door. Their

daily lives were so humdrum and boring that she needed to break out. She needed the excitement of the unusual, and now she was off to find it. Suitcase in hand, she stepped out the front door and closed it firmly.

At the train station, Evie bought several magazines to read on the journey. It was all part of the ritual, part of the sheer luxury of treating oneself, while the glossy pages had an almost illicit feel to them as well. She gazed out of the window and thought with excitement of the wonderful weekend that lay ahead. Her eyes darted to her suitcase, wherein lay some scanty items of clothing that would certainly have surprised the other occupants of the carriage!

Her eyes sparkled with anticipation, and she had to make a conscious effort to compose her expression into one more suited to a middle-aged woman on an errand of mercy to an elderly uncle.

The rural scenic beauty was a spur to her excitement. She ticked off the landmarks as the train rumbled along. Yes, there was the old mill, which meant that she'd come halfway, and further along the waterfall, where swans were gathered with their clutch of patchy brown cygnets. How fortunate that we are not all judged on our appearance, she mused, watching the adult swans fussing over their dull offspring. If people were judging me right now, they would never guess that I, too, will soon be transformed.

As the familiar landmarks flew by, Evie found that she didn't want the journey to end yet, for it was part of the exciting build-up to her special weekend. She looked around the carriage at the other middle-aged occupants, and wondered what they would think if they knew where she was going, and what she was about to do. And she hugged her secret to herself with relish. It was a wonderful secret – one that made it possible to cope with all the other boring days of the year.

In a sense, the weekend had a far greater lifespan than merely two days. There were the weeks of anticipation, as she looked forward to, and prepared for, the big event – she had to shop for new clothes and make-up, and hide them away so that there was no chance of Joe finding them. And she had to carry on her normal daily life, even as the joy of anticipation was bubbling up inside her.

Then afterwards, there were the days of sated delight, and the unfamiliar soreness of frenzied sexual activity. And, of course, the spring in her step that made other men look curiously at this once-again frumpish woman, who seemed to be harbouring a special secret of her own.

At last, the train pulled into the station and Evie, complete with precious suitcase, alighted and made her way to the nearest hairdressing salon.

"Mrs O'Brien? Oh, yes – you've an appointment with Nigel. He'll be with you in a moment."

Contented, Evie took her seat in front of the mirror. And she watched as Nigel, in the role of sorcerer, performed his wizardry on her dull, tired locks, transforming them into a wreath of auburn curls that made her plump, plain face come alive and almost look pretty.

"Really, my dear, you should have your hair styled more often," Nigel intoned. "Once a year is hardly enough, and you do have such lovely hair."

Evie thanked him, tipped him well, and left. Then she headed for the beauty salon across the road, where she had a manicure. Afterwards, she hailed a taxi, which took her across town to one of the most stylish hotels in the vicinity. Having checked into her room, she showered (taking care to use the protective plastic cap supplied by the hotel) and luxuriated in the comfort of the big guest towelling dressing-gown that had been hanging on the bathroom door.

She checked her watch. In just two hours, she would be meeting him. By longstanding arrangement, he, too, would have checked into the hotel under an assumed name, and later she would meet him downstairs in the piano bar, where he would immediately buy her a Martini. Then they would talk tentatively and shyly about the events in their lives since their last meeting a year ago. Then there would follow another Martini, then another, and he would tell her how beautiful she looked, and admire whatever new outfit she was wearing. And she would blush like a young girl, thank him shyly and return the compliment.

Having applied her make-up carefully – it took time, since it was not something she did regularly – Evie slipped into her new red satin dress. It had a plunging neckline, which showed off her ample breasts, and clung to her body like a caressing hand. She surveyed herself critically in the mirror, but could find no fault with her appearance. He would love the dress, she knew. And he would compliment her, unlike the sleepy, unobservant spouse she had left behind.

She clipped on her new matching red earrings and stared at her reflection defiantly.

She felt no guilt at being fully appreciated as a woman. She felt entitled to shake off the shackles of suburban mediocrity once a year and to be, if only for a short time, a real *femme fatale*.

When she entered the bar, her heart skipped a beat. He was there already. For a moment, before he caught her eye, she studied him, and her heart was filled with an overwhelming tenderness. For years, they'd been meeting like this, each of them slipping away from the humdrum life they each led at home, and spending a brief and magical weekend together.

Every year, it was exactly the same, but no less exciting for all that. They had initially thought of registering for a double room as Mr and Mrs Smith, but Evie herself had demurred, wishing to keep the mystery and excitement alive between them. She knew from everyday experience that sharing the same living quarters destroyed all the mystery. So she preferred to return alone to her own room in the early hours of the morning, after a night of passionate lovemaking, hugging her secret joy to herself as she took a long luxurious bath before going to sleep. Too much intimacy was a killer of passion, she knew, thinking of dear old Joe who never seemed to notice whether she was wearing face-cream and curlers or not.

"Darling!"

The word, when he spoke it, was the most beautiful word in the entire English vocabulary. It sent a frisson of delight up her spine as she slid her beautifully manicured hand into his. Tenderly he took it, studying it as though it was a thing of incredible beauty, and kissing each red nail in turn. She could never imagine Joe doing anything so romantic.

"Same as usual?"

She nodded, and the barman brought her a Martini on the rocks. She toyed with it before drinking it, watching the glistening cubes of ice swirling around in the glass. She was determined to soak up the pleasure of every moment of this special weekend. Then slowly she sipped it, savouring the taste and gazing rapturously into the eyes of the man before her.

"Did you have any difficulty getting here?"

"No," she said, smiling, "did you?"

He shook his head, all the time gazing at her, as though he couldn't tear his eyes away, even for a second. "You look wonderful," he said softly. "Your hair is the colour of autumn leaves, and that dress . . ." He held her away from him as he surveyed the overall effect, then clasped her to him tightly.

As he kissed her hair, Evie could feel the heat of his lips through her scalp. She could hardly speak for the lump in her throat. She was so happy that she wouldn't have cared if she'd died at that precise moment. She was with the most exciting man in the whole world, and she would tell him so as soon as the lump in her throat dissolved.

Instead, she buried her face in his collar and breathed in the aroma of his aftershave.

She loved its tangy bitterness, and the smell of it would stay with her for the rest of the year. "I love you," she whispered, uttering the sacred words that she never said to poor old Joe.

After the third Martini, he took her hand and led her out onto the small dance floor, holding her close as the group of resident musicians played a medley of old romantic favourites. At first, they were alone on the floor and, dreading to be the centre of attention, Evie fought a moment of panic and shyness before giving way to the magic of the moment. In a way, being out there on their own made her feel as though they were the only two people in the universe.

She gave a small involuntary chuckle, and he smiled down at her quizzically. "I was just thinking," she said, "of what the neighbours would say if they could see me now!"

"They'd see a beautiful woman, in the company of a man who adores her." Tenderly, he kissed her hair. "God, I want so much to make love to you!"

"Not yet," she told him gently. "The night is still young. Let's make the most of it."

So they drank more Martinis, and did both the tango and the rumba when the musicians played a selection of well-known South American numbers. In fact, their ability on the dance floor and their pleasure in each other was so obvious that the other revellers in the bar stood back and watched them with delight, applauding them loudly when each dance ended. Evie was surprised at the applause; she had been lost in the joy of their ritual mating dance, and blushed when she realised that others might have seen through its purpose.

Later, they dined in the hotel's beautiful restaurant, then arm in arm took the lift to his room. Once in the door, there was no further politeness or pretence. They tore off each other's clothes with the frenzy of two people who could wait no longer for release.

Then they were touching and caressing each other, lost in their own special world where no one else existed.

Afterwards, they lay sated, comfortable in the silence that enveloped them. Then they made love again, this time more slowly, savouring each other's bodies, and filled with the wonderment that people of their age could behave like rampant teenagers.

As the first light of dawn became visible through the curtains, and the first strains of early morning birdsong could be heard, Evie crept from his bed and slipped back to her own room. In her mirror, she surveyed the ravages of the night's activities. Her mascara and eyeshadow were smeared, her hair all awry. But she knew that she exuded that indefinable glow that this special weekend always produced. And with joy in her heart, she cleaned her face, took a shower, slipped into bed and slept like a newborn babe. Later in the day, they would have lunch together, then perhaps take an afternoon sightseeing trip, followed by a final night of lovemaking before going their separate ways once again.

All too soon, the weekend was over. And on the morning of departure, they stood together on the small balcony outside his room, gazing out across the grounds to the horizon, where already the sun was beginning to rise. Soon, they would have to pack their cases and begin their separate journeys home.

"Same time next year, love?"

Evie nodded, hardly trusting herself to speak. This had been the most wonderful weekend ever. "I wish it could be more often," she blurted out, then wished she hadn't said it, knowing it would only hurt him.

He looked at her sadly. "But then it wouldn't have the special magic that it has now, my darling. If we could do this every day of the week, it wouldn't be special any more." Then he laughed as he hugged her. "Besides – I wouldn't have the energy! I'm not getting any younger, you know."

"You'll always be young to me," Evie told him tenderly.

★　★　★

The house was quiet as Evie let herself in. In the living room, Joe lay sprawled across the couch, asleep as usual. He was snoring, his mouth wide open, his jaw sagging. Her eyes swept over his body, taking in the big paunch, the almost bald head with just a few wisps of hair carefully swept across it. And suddenly, she was overwhelmed by a tumult of affection for him which this simple gesture of vanity produced in her. Even at his age, she thought, he can feel insecure.

As though sensing her presence, he opened his eyes, yawned and sat up. "Had a good weekend, pet?" he asked. "How was Uncle Arthur?"

Evie smiled at him. "He was fine. In fact, I've never known him to be so lively."

Joe's eyes twinkled. "So you think there's life in the old chap yet?"

"I'm certain of it," said Evie. "How was your weekend?"

Joe grinned. "I'd say it was about as exciting as yours."

Evie blushed, and suddenly Joe was on his feet, catching her around the waist and kissing her. As he did so, she caught a whiff of his tangy aftershave, and was transported back to their passion of the previous two nights.

"As I was driving home, I thought about what you said," Joe said, looking shyly into his wife's eyes, "and I think you were right. Just because we've been together for almost forty years, it shouldn't mean that romance is limited to one weekend a year . . ."

He held her at arms' length as he had done in the hotel bar, and looked earnestly into her eyes. "Evie, my darling, I really do want to make love to you right now." Evie was speechless, but happily so, as her husband carried her upstairs. He hadn't done anything so romantic in their home since he'd carried her over the threshold nearly forty years before!

"Does this mean I won't be visiting Uncle Arthur any

more?" Evie asked him, as they reached the top of the stairs.

Smiling, Joe shook his head. "No, of course not, my love – I wouldn't miss our special weekend for anything." Then he gave an impish grin. "But maybe Uncle Arthur ought to visit here as well!"

In the bedroom, they began to undress each other, and Evie wondered what on earth the neighbours would think, if they knew . . .

ALSO BY LINDA KAVANAGH, PUBLISHED BY POOLBEG

Love Child, Love Hurts

16

Old Flame
ERIN KAYE

For the first time, since the heady days of their courtship nearly twelve years ago, Alison West was nervous about meeting her banker husband, Neil.

She was waiting for him in the Costa coffee lounge in the Arrivals Hall at Edinburgh Airport. She glanced at the monitor suspended from the ceiling and the word '*landed*' appeared alongside Neil's flight number. Her heartbeat quickened and she felt suddenly faint. How would he respond to what she had to say to him? Would it come as a surprise? Would he be distraught? Or would he be expecting it?

She stood up on unsteady legs, took off her cashmere-blend jacket and folded it across her knee. Then she sat down again, twisted her hands fretfully in her lap and stared at the frosted automatic doors through which Neil was shortly due to discharge.

She pictured his travel-tousled fair hair, his unbuttoned

collar and his silk tie all askew. She imagined how he'd pick her out from the crowd with his quick green eyes, his tired face pinched by anxiety and his left shoulder weighed down by an overnight bag. She pictured the lopsided work-worn smile with which he'd greet her when he spotted her in the crowd and her stomach churned.

The opaque doors slid open for the umpteenth time and Alison's heart filled with dread. A pilot and two air hostesses came out pulling small, wheeled suitcases behind them, the women's high heels clip-clopping on the hard flooring. They walked briskly, chatting to each other, and completely ignored the small crowd assembled to meet friends and family.

Alison let out a sigh and stared at the oversized and overpriced chocolate-chip cookie in front of her and regretted buying it. What was she thinking of? She'd reached the age where any transgression from a healthy, wholesome diet was reflected in the relentless thickening of her waistline. She touched her slightly protruding stomach and then sat up straight in her chair. The improvement in posture brought immediate results – the little pot belly disappeared.

Still, she reminded herself, she wasn't in bad shape for a thirty-nine-year-old mother of two. She might be a little bit overweight but she wasn't too wrinkly (yet) and she had a pretty, dimpled smile – not, she reflected, that she did a lot of smiling these days.

Her rich auburn hair may have dulled in recent years but she hadn't yet had to resort to dyeing it. And her mother, Susan, was always remarking on her good legs and good teeth – she meant well but she made her daughter sound like a mare. Alison thought that if that was the best her mother could come up with, she'd rather she didn't bother.

Normally she wouldn't be here to collect Neil from the airport. Generally, he took his car as their busy schedules were just too jam-packed for romantic drop-offs and pick-ups at the airport. She had a busy job as an English teacher in George Herriot's, one of Edinburgh's most prestigious private schools, as well as the children to look after – eight-year-old Kirsten and six-year-old Callum.

But today Neil's car was in the garage for repairs, the children were at their Granny West's and here she was, childfree for a few precious moments, with time to think.

Her life, it seemed, was rushing past her like a video on fast-forward. When she took the time to really look at her children they astounded her by how fast they'd grown. Kirsten was so independent all of a sudden and when had Callum turned from a Mummy's boy into a child too big to be seen kissing her at the school gate?

Alison sighed and pressed the space between her eyebrows with her index finger. She was tired. Tired of putting a meal on the table every night, weary of making packed lunches and supervising homework and emptying the dishwasher at eleven o'clock at night. Fed up striving so hard and conscientiously at work without the recognition she felt she deserved. And she was tired, most of all, of being alone. She felt like a single mother a lot of the time, so frequent had Neil's business trips away from home become.

He said that he was working on some big corporate deal and she believed him. Maybe she was wrong, but he didn't strike her as the type to have an affair. Not with a woman anyway. If Neil was having an affair, it was with his work. But he was, Alison believed, tiring of her, just as she was tiring of him.

Their marriage had become stale, their sex-life non-existent. Maybe they'd taken on too much buying the four-bedroomed house in the Grange, one of Edinburgh's most sought after and expensive residential areas. Neil was working longer and longer hours, leaving her to keep the home fires burning as well as juggling a full-time job.

It was the tedium of her daily existence, she concluded, that had finally led her to seek out some excitement in her life. Something, anything, to brighten her day and distract her from the daily grind.

It all started innocently enough nearly three months ago when, late one evening just before bed, she'd logged onto her computer and found a message waiting for her via the Friends Reunited website. When she saw the name Seamus Teague her heartbeat quickened. She glanced quickly over her shoulder, but of course there was no one there. The kids were in bed, Neil was away on business and she was all alone on the third-floor galleried landing that served as a study.

A flood of memories came crashing in on her like a tidal wave. Nearly twenty years had passed since she'd last seen or heard from Seamus. She'd met the handsome Irishman at Leeds University and, just turned seventeen and fresh out of a Catholic girls' school, she'd immediately fallen in love.

He was olive-skinned with shoulder-length dark curly hair and brown eyes and he was a whole two years and eleven months older than she. Alison was enchanted by his disdain for authority and his irreverence for almost everything polite society held dear. Looking back his humour had been a bit cruel, but harmless, and you couldn't help but laugh at his wicked jokes. Alison smiled, remembering.

Seamus had returned her affections for a while – long enough to bed her – and then his interest waned. She had not minded then – it was enough to be loved and to learn how to love physically. It had been, and still was, the greatest adventure of her life. Her first love.

But what on earth could he want from her now after all these years? She clicked on the short message and read it. He was married with two kids, he said, and he worked as a software engineer with IBM. He lived in Harrogate. His life sounded, well, surprisingly conventional.

"I think of you often, Ali. How has your life turned out?"

Alison hit the reply button and her fingers hovered over the keyboard. She knew what she *should* do. She should send back a short, polite message saying that she was very happily married, thank you, and discourage any further correspondence.

But she did not.

"Seamus," she wrote, **"how lovely to hear from you after all these years. I often wondered what became of you. I have wonderful memories of our time together at uni. It was good, wasn't it? You ask about my life. Well, it's a long story . . ."**

Before she knew it she'd written a full page about herself – her children, her job, Neil, the death of her father last year whom Seamus had once met. She even hinted at her unhappiness within her marriage. She hesitated for only a moment before hitting the reply button and the message was sent.

"What's eating you?" said her friend and colleague, Shona, who was an art teacher, the next day at work.

"Oh, nothing," said Alison, wondering if she had been a little indiscreet in her email. Sharing things with Seamus that she shouldn't have been sharing with anyone except Neil, such as the unsatisfactory state of their marriage.

There was a silence during which Shona raised her carefully pencilled eyebrows and waited.

"Oh, it's just that I'm fed up with Neil being away all the time." Somehow it was easier to put it all in writing than broach the subject with Neil. An email felt anonymous in a way, impersonal, as though she was telling the computer and not a person.

"I thought you said that it was temporary," said Shona. "That he was working on some big deal."

"He is but it just seems to be dragging on forever. And I'm a bit fed up here too."

"With Herriott's?" said Shona, sounding surprised.

"Not with Herriott's itself. With my job. I love the kids but I think I'm ready for a new challenge – but I don't want to leave here. I don't know what to do."

"Alistair will be retiring soon," said Shona, referring to the deputy head.

"Don't be daft. I wouldn't stand a chance of getting his job."

She couldn't wait to get the kids in bed that night to read Seamus's reply.

"I know exactly what you mean about marriage being hard work. My life hasn't turned out exactly the way I'd imagined either. You know, I think letting you go was possibly the biggest mistake of my life . . ."

When Neil came home two days later she omitted to tell him about the emails. Had he been there that first night, maybe she would have. They had never kept secrets from each other, not once in all their married life. But these emails were private correspondence, Alison told herself, between friends. Nothing more. All they were doing, after all, was emailing each other. That wasn't a crime, was it? So she suppressed the guilty feelings that told her otherwise and kept her lips sealed.

The next few weeks turned into months and life carried on as before – Neil working unsocial hours and travelling a lot and Alison's late-night sessions at the computer keyboard. Seamus made her laugh with anecdotes about his workmates, his boss and his attempts at learning to ski. He never once mentioned his wife or children.

"You shouldn't feel bad about what's happened between you and Neil," he wrote to her one day. **"People change, they grow apart. It happens every day."**

He understood her perfectly. And if she was going through some sort of mid-life crisis, then so was he. She took solace from the fact that she was not alone.

And then one day she logged on to post what had become a daily epistle to Seamus. And there it was – a succinct two-word message from him that conveyed more than a hundred carefully penned words could have done.

"Let's meet," it said simply.

Alison blinked and swallowed. Up until now she had not acknowledged to herself that she was having a relationship with Seamus. He was only a pen-friend, wasn't he? But she knew this to be much less than the truth. He was a former lover. She knew what he looked like, sounded like, even smelt like.

And she knew what a reunion would mean. The very act of meeting, without either spouse's knowledge, would be tacit agreement that she was ready to embark on an affair. Was that what she wanted? And yet what was the alternative? To sit here night after night, alone and unloved?

That night Alison sat for a very long time with the knuckles of her right hand wedged in her mouth, thinking.

The opaque doors into the Arrivals Hall slid open once more and Alison stood up. She saw Neil as soon as he walked through them, scanning the crowd. His face lit up with a smile when he saw her and Alison's pulse began to race.

He walked over and threw his arms around her. Alison squirmed uncomfortably in his heavy embrace, wondering what had brought this on – Neil wasn't big on hugging and kissing in front of strangers.

"It's been a hell of a week," he said into her hair and sighed heavily. "It's been a hell of a ride. But we did it, Alison. We pulled it off. They signed the deal."

"That's great, Neil," said Alison flatly.

He pulled away, held her at arms' length and looked into her eyes. She blinked and looked away.

"We need to talk," she said.

"Yes, I know we do," he said eagerly. "Let's sit down here. Can I get you a coffee? Tea?" he said, looking into her empty cup.

She sat down and said, "Nothing, thanks. Listen, Neil, I –"

"I've something to tell you, Alison," he said, stealing the very words she had been about to use and pulling up a chair.

She stopped speaking and stared at him, waiting. She noticed that his eyes were red-rimmed from lack of sleep and guilt crept over her. She suddenly realised how miserable the past few months must have been for Neil too.

"I want you to know that everything I do, I do for you and the kids," he said. "And nothing means anything to me without you. I love you all."

Alison blushed and glanced at the table. She had doubted his love but had she been wrong?

"I didn't want to tell you all this before," he said, his eyes alive with excitement, "but I'm going to get a big bonus in the next couple of months because of this deal. A very big bonus."

"Good for you," said Alison dully.

"That's why I've been working all these crazy hours," he went on, as though she hadn't spoken. "I didn't know if we could pull it off. We very nearly didn't. But we won through in the end."

"That's great, Neil but I –"

"Just a minute," he said, raising his hand ever so slightly to silence her. "I know that the past few months haven't been easy on you, Alison. I know that you've been doing everything at home and I've hardly been around. But it's been worth it."

"Has it?"

"Yes, because what we choose to do with this money can change our lives."

"What do you mean?" she said warily.

"If we use it to pay off part of our mortgage, you can give up work, Alison. If you want to. I know you're worn out trying to work full-time, run the house and look after the kids."

Alison didn't want to give up her job but it was so sweet and loving of Neil to make the gesture. "But that's hardly fair, Neil," she protested. "That I should get to choose whether I work or not and you don't."

"I want what you want," he said and he grasped her hands and held them between his own. "All I really want in life is to make you happy, Alison."

Alison felt hot tears streaking down her cheeks. Neil brushed her cheek tenderly with the back of his hand and she was consumed with shame. For the past few months she'd done nothing but moan while Neil had been working himself into the ground for her. She thought of Seamus and cringed with embarrassment. How could she have been so silly?

"I – I don't deserve you, Neil," she said.

"I know," he said with a big grin. "Now what was it you wanted to tell me?"

The phone in Alison's handbag rang.

"Oh, it wasn't anything important," she said. "I'd better get that in case something's wrong with one of the kids."

She pulled the slim silver phone out of her bag and peered at the number on the small screen.

"It's work," she said, puzzled, and glanced at her watch. "It's nearly six. What would anyone be calling me for at this time?"

"You'd better answer it."

Alison pressed the green handset button and put the phone to her ear.

"Alison," said the voice of the Herriott's headmaster, Derek McKinley, "I've just come out of a board meeting and I wanted to catch you tonight. Is this a good time?"

"Well . . ." said Alison and she glanced at Neil.

"It'll only take a minute," persisted Derek.

"Okay."

"Look, I'll get straight to the point. The board want you to take over from Alistair when he retires."

"They do?"

"Yes, they've agreed to appoint you deputy head on the back of my strong recommendation."

She was stunned and just managed to mumble, "Thank you, Derek."

He paused and said, "Assuming you want it of course, Alison."

"I – I'd –" she stumbled, as her eyes filled with tears and her throat constricted. She didn't deserve Neil and this good fortune.

Neil stepped forward and touched her lightly on the arm, his features creased with concern. "What is it? Is everything okay?"

"Yes," she said and nodded at him. Then she cleared her throat and said into the phone, "Derek, I think I do want it. But can I let you know for sure tomorrow?" She finished the call and said, "You're never going to believe it, Neil. Derek has just offered me the deputy head's job!"

"Oh, Alison! That's wonderful news! But are you sure it's what you want? You don't have to work if you don't want to."

Alison thought hard for a few moments. This was the opportunity of a lifetime. It was perfect. And what would she do at home all day while the kids were at school?

"Yes," she said at last, "I do want it. But I don't want to carry on living the way we have been. Let's pay off part of the mortgage like you suggested and free up some monthly income. We'll use that to pay for help around the house. And you and I can start living a little. When did we last have a weekend away? Just the two of us?"

"Oh, Alison, let's do it!"

"What about Paris?"

"Or Salzberg?"

"New York?"

"Oh, darling, I'll take you anywhere you want to go. I love you so."

"And I love you," said Alison and meant it with all her heart.

That night just before bedtime, she slipped up to the third-floor landing where she carefully composed a short, deliberately cool email to Seamus.

"No," she wrote, **"let's not meet. It would only spoil the memories. I'm very happily married, Seamus, and I wish you and your family all the best for the future. On reflection, I think it's probably best if we don't communicate with each other any more."**

"Are you going to be long?" called Neil from downstairs.

"Nearly done," said Alison as she pressed the send button.

"Come on. It's late."

"Just coming," she said as she deleted Seamus' contact details from her address book on the computer.

Then she switched it off and went downstairs where Neil was waiting for her.

ALSO BY ERIN KAYE, PUBLISHED BY POOLBEG

Closer to Home, Second Chances,
Choices, Mothers & Daughters

17

Rachel's Holiday (Chapter One)
MARIAN KEYES

They said I was a drug addict. I found that hard to come to terms with – I was a middle-class, convent-educated girl whose drug use was strictly recreational. And surely drugs addicts were thinner? It was true that I *took* drugs, but what no one seemed to understand was that my drug use wasn't different from their having a drink or two on a Friday night after work. They might have a few vodkas and tonic and let off a bit of steam. I had a couple of lines of cocaine and did likewise. As I said to my father and my sister and my sister's husband and eventually the therapists of the Cloisters, "If cocaine was sold in liquid form, in a bottle, would you complain about me taking it? Well, would you? No, I bet you wouldn't!"

I was offended by the drug-addict allegation, because I was nothing like one. Apart from track marks on their arms, they had dirty hair, constantly seemed cold, did a lot of shoulder-hunching, wore plastic trainers, hung around blocks of flats and were, as I've already mentioned, *thin*.

I wasn't thin.

Although it wasn't for the want of trying. I spent plenty of time on the Stairmaster at the gym. But no matter how much I Stairmastered, genetics had the final say. If my father had married a dainty little woman, I might have had a very different life. Very different thighs, certainly.

Instead, I was doomed for people always to describe me by saying, "She's a big girl." Then they always added really quickly, "Now, I'm not saying she's *fat*."

The implication being that if I was fat, I could at least do something about it.

"No," they would continue, "she's a fine, big, tall girl. You know, *strong*."

I was often described as strong.

It really pissed me off.

My boyfriend, Luke, sometimes described me as magnificent. (When the light was behind me and he'd had several pints.) At least that was what he said to *me*. Then he probably went back to his friends and said, "Now, I'm not saying she's *fat* . . ."

The whole drug-addiction allegation came about one February morning when I was living in New York.

It wasn't the first time I felt as if I was on Cosmic *Candid Camera*. My life was prone to veering out of control and I had stopped believing that the god who had been assigned to me was a benign old lad with long hair and a beard. He was more like a celestial Jeremy Beadle, and my life was the showcase he used to amuse other gods.

"Wa-atch," he laughingly invites, "as Rachel thinks she's got a new job and that it's safe to hand in her notice on the old. Little does she know that her new firm is just about to go bankrupt!"

Roars of laughter from all the other gods.

"Now, watch," he chuckles, "as Rachel hurries to meet her new boyfriend. See how she catches the heel of her new shoe in a grating? See how it comes clean off? Little did Rachel know that we had tampered with it. See how she limps the rest of the way?"

More sniggers from the assembled gods.

"But the best bit of all," laughs Jeremy, "is that the man she was meeting never turns up! He only asked her out for a bet. Watch as Rachel squirms with embarrassment in the stylish bar. See the looks of pity the other women give her? See how the waiter gives her the extortionate bill for a glass of wine, and best of all, see how Rachel discovers she's *left her purse at home?*"

Uncontrollable guffaws.

The events that led to me being called a drug addict had the same element of celestial farce that the rest of my life had. What happened was, one night I'd sort of overdone it on the enlivening drugs and I couldn't get to sleep. (I hadn't meant to overdo it, I had simply underestimated the quality of the cocaine that I had taken.) I knew I had to get up for work the following morning, so I took a couple of sleeping tablets. After about ten minutes, they hadn't worked, so I took a couple more. And still my head was buzzing, so in desperation, thinking of how badly I needed my sleep, thinking of how alert I had to be at work, I took a few more.

I eventually got to sleep. A lovely deep sleep. So lovely and deep that when the morning came, and my alarm clock went off, I neglected to wake up.

Brigit, my flatmate, knocked on my door, then came into my room and shouted at me, then shook me, then at her wit's end, slapped me. (I didn't really buy the wit's end bit. She must have known that slapping wouldn't wake me, but no one is in good form on a Monday morning.)

But then Brigit stumbled across a piece of paper that I'd been attempting to write on just before I fell asleep. It was just the usual maudlin, mawkish, self-indulgent poetry-type rubbish I often wrote when I was under the influence. Stuff that seemed really profound at the time, where I thought I'd discovered the secret of the universe, but that caused me to blush with shame when I read it in the cold light of day, the bits that I *could* read, that is.

The poem went something like, "Mumble, mumble, life . . ." something indecipherable, "bowl of cherries, mumble, all I get is the pits . . ." Then – and I vaguely remembered writing this bit – I thought of a really good title for a poem about a shoplifter who had suddenly discovered her conscience. It was called *I can't take any more.*

But Brigit, who'd recently gone all weird and uptight, didn't treat it as the load of cringe-making rubbish it so clearly was. Instead, when she saw the empty jar of sleeping tablets rolling around on my pillow, she decided it was a suicide note. And before I knew it, and it really *was* before I knew it because I was still asleep – well, asleep or unconscious, depending on whose version of the story you believe – she had rung for an ambulance and I was in Mount Solomon having my stomach pumped.

That was unpleasant enough, but there was worse to come. Brigit had obviously turned into one of those New York abstention fascists, the kind who if you wash your hair with Linco beer shampoo more than twice a week, say that you're an alcoholic and that you should be on a twelve-step programme. So she rang my parents in Dublin and told them that I had a serious drug problem and that I'd tried to kill myself. And before I could intervene and explain that it had all been an embarrassing misunderstanding, my parents had rung my painfully well-behaved older sister, Margaret. Who arrived on the first available flight from Chicago with her equally painful husband, Paul.

Margaret was only a year older than me but it felt more like forty. She was intent on ferrying me to Ireland to the bosom of my family. Where I would stay briefly before being admitted to some Betty-Ford-type place to sort me out 'for good and for all', as my father said when he rang me.

Of course, I had no intention of going anywhere but by then I was really frightened. And not just by the talk of going home to Ireland and into a clinic, but because my father had *rung me. He* had rung *me*. That had never happened in the whole of my twenty-seven years. It was hard enough to get him to say hello whenever I rang home and it was one of the rare occasions when he answered the phone. The most he ever managed was "Which one of you is that? Oh, Rachel? Hold on till I get your mother." Then there was nothing except banging and bashing as he dropped the phone and ran to get Mum.

And if Mum wasn't there he was terrified. "Your mother's not here," he always said, his voice high with alarm. The subtext being, "Please, *please* don't let me have to talk to you."

Not because he didn't like me or was a cold unapproachable father or anything like that.

He was a lovely man.

That I could grudgingly admit by the time I was twenty-seven and had lived away from home for eight years. That he wasn't the Great Withholder of Money For New Jeans that my sisters and I loved to hate during our teenage years. But despite Dad's lovely manness he wasn't big on conversation. Not unless I wanted to talk about golf. So the fact that he had rung me must have meant that I'd really messed up this time.

Fearfully, I tried to set things right.

"There's nothing wrong with me," I told Dad. "It's all been a mistake and I'm fine."

But he was having none of it. "You're to come home," he ordered.

I was having none of it either. "Dad, behave yourself. Be . . . be . . . *realistic* here, I can't just walk out on my life."

"What can't you walk out on?" he asked.

"My job, for example," I said. "I can't just abandon my job."

"I've already spoken to them at your work and they agree with me that you should come home," he said.

Suddenly, I found myself staring into the abyss.

"You did WHAT?" I could hardly speak I was so afraid. What had they told Dad about me?

"I spoke to them at your work," repeated Dad in the same level tone of voice.

"You big stupid eejit." I swallowed. "To who?"

"A chap called Eric," said Dad. "He said he was your boss."

"Oh, God," I said.

OK, so I was a 27-year-old woman and it shouldn't matter if my father knew I was sometimes late for work. But it *did* matter. I felt the way I had twenty years earlier when he and Mum were called up to the school to account for my on-going dearth of completed homework.

"This is awful," I said to Dad. "What did you have to go ringing work for? I'm so embarrassed! What'll they think? They'll sack me for this, you know."

"Rachel, from what I can gather I think they were just

about to anyway," said Dad's voice from across the Atlantic.

Oh no, the game was up. Dad knew! Eric must have really gone to town on my shortcomings.

"I don't believe you," I protested. "You're only saying that to make me come home."

"I'm not," said Dad. "Let me tell you what this Eric said . . ."

No chance! I could hardly bear to think about what Eric said, never mind *hear* it.

"Everything was fine at work until you rang them," I lied frantically. "You've caused nothing but trouble. I'm going to ring Eric and tell him you're a lunatic, that you escaped from a bin and not to believe a word you said."

"Rachel," Dad sighed heavily, "I barely said a thing to this Eric chap. He did all the talking and he seemed delighted to let go of you."

"Let me go?" I said faintly. "As in, fire me? You mean I've got no job?"

"That's right." Dad sounded very matter-of-fact.

"Well, great," I said tearfully. "Thanks for ruining my life."

There was a silence while I tried to absorb the fact that I was once more without a job. Was God Beadle rerunning old tapes up there?

"OK, what about my flat?" I challenged. "Seeing as you're so good at messing things up for me?"

"Margaret will sort that out with Brigit," said Dad.

"Sort out?" I had expected the question of my flat would totally stump Dad. I was shocked that he'd already addressed the matter. They were acting as if something really was wrong with me.

"She'll pay a couple of months' rent to Brigit so that Brigit has breathing space to find someone new."

"Someone new?" I shrieked. "But this is my home."

"From what I gather yourself and Brigit haven't been getting on too well," Dad said awkwardly.

He was right. And we'd been getting along a whole lot worse since she'd made that phone call and brought the interference of my family tumbling down on top of me. I was furious with her and for some reason she seemed to be furious with me too. But Brigit was my best friend and we'd always shared a flat. It was out of the question for someone else to move in with her.

"You've gathered a lot," I said drily.

He said nothing.

"An awful bloody lot," I said, much more wetly.

I wasn't defending myself as well as I normally would have. But, to tell the truth, my trip to the hospital had taken more out of me than just the contents of my stomach. I felt shaky and not inclined to fight with Dad, which wasn't like me at all. Disagreeing with my father was something I did as instinctively as refusing to sleep with moustachioed men.

"So there's nothing to stop you coming home and getting sorted out,"said Dad.

"But I have a cat," I lied.

"You can get another one," he said.

"But I have a boyfriend," I protested.

"You can get another one of those too," said Dad.

Easy for him to say.

"Put me back on to Margaret and I'll see you tomorrow," said Dad.

"You will in your arse," I muttered.

And that seemed to be that.

Luckily I had taken a couple of Valium. Otherwise I might have been very upset *indeed*.

Margaret was sitting beside me. In fact, she seemed to be constantly by my side, once I thought about it.

After she finished talking to Dad, I decided to put a stop to all the nonsense. It was time for me to grab back control of the reins of my life. Because this wasn't funny. It wasn't entertaining. It wasn't diverting. It was unpleasant, and above all it was unnecessary.

"Margaret," I said briskly, "there's nothing wrong with me. I'm sorry you've had a wasted journey, but please go away and take your husband with you. This is all a big, huge, terrible mistake."

"I don't think it is," she said. "Brigit says . . ."

"Never mind what Brigit says," I interupted. "I'm actually worried about Brigit because she's gone too weird. She used to be fun once."

Margaret looked doubtful, then she said, "But you do seem to take an awful lot of drugs."

"It might seem an awful lot to you," I explained gently. "But you're a lickarse, so any amount would seem like lots."

It was true Margaret was a lickarse. I had four sisters, two older and two younger and Margaret was the only well-behaved one of the lot. My mother just used to run her eye along us all and sadly say, "Well, one out of five ain't bad."

"I'm not a lickarse," she complained. "I'm just ordinary."

"Yes, Rachel." Paul had stepped forward to defend Margaret. "She's not a lickarse. Just because she's not a, a . . . junkie who can't get a job and whose husband leaves her . . . Unlike some," he finished darkly.

I spotted the flaw in his argument.

"My husband hasn't left me," I protested in my defence.

"That's because you haven't got one," said Paul.

Paul was obviously referring to my eldest sister, Claire,

who managed to get ditched by her husband on the same day that she gave birth to their first child.

"And I have a job," I reminded him.

"Not any more, you don't," he smirked.

I hated him.

And he hated me. I didn't take it personally. He hated my entire family. He had a hard job deciding which one of Margaret's sisters he hated the most. And well he might, there was stiff competition among us for the position of black sheep. There was Claire, thirty-one, the deserted wife. Me, twenty-seven, allegedly a junkie. Anna, twenty-four, who'd never had a proper job, and who sometimes sold hash to make ends meet. And there was Helen, twenty, and frankly, I wouldn't know where to begin.

We all hated Paul as much as he hated us.

Even Mum, although she wouldn't admit to it. She liked to pretend that she liked everyone, in the hope that it might help her jump the queue into Heaven.

Paul was such a pompous know-all. He wore the same kind of jumpers as Dad did and bought his first house when he was thirteen or some ridiculous age by saving up his First Communion money.

"You'd better get back on the phone to Dad," I told Margaret. "Because I'm going nowhere."

"How right you are," agreed Paul nastily.

ALSO BY MARIAN KEYES, PUBLISHED BY POOLBEG

Anybody Out There?, The Other Side of the Story, Angels, Sushi for Beginners, Watermelon, Lucy Sullivan is Getting Married, Rachel's Holiday, Last Chance Saloon

18

The Dinner Party

Nicola Lindsay

I knew I shouldn't have come! One look from that
Suzanne one sitting opposite me with her fair, frizzy
curls and scarlet lips, is enough to curdle the crème fraîche
in the carrot and coriander soup. James warned me about
her. What was it he said? "The trouble with Suzy is, she's
never content. Always on the lookout for more and
better." He didn't admit it but I think they may have slept
together in the not-too-distant past. The way she keeps
giving him that knowing little smile – as though he and
she share a thrilling secret that no one else knows about –
it's a dead give-away. I wonder in what way he didn't
come up to scratch? Or was it *he* who dropped her? Now
I've met her for the first time, I can't help being surprised
that he ever went out with her in the first place. I can't
imagine her ever being tender towards a man – towards
anyone. There's a dangerous, spiky quality about her that
makes me feel uncomfortable.

That's the trouble when you're my age and have been safely married for twenty years – and then, suddenly, you're not. Your self-confidence takes a nosedive. During those twenty years, I never looked at another man. Well, I *looked* but I never let on I was looking; never made eye contact or gave so much as a flicker of an 'I'm interested' glance at anyone. So, when I find myself invited to a dinner party by a gorgeous-looking man who's ten years younger than me and apparently interested and I'm sitting at a table with six strangers – well, it's all a bit nerve-wracking, really. You see, I've forgotten the rules; forgotten how people play silly games. I'd also forgotten how important it is in a situation like this to be able to gracefully fill any gaps in the conversation with some interesting or informed remark. Right now, I couldn't tell you my own phone number, let alone come out with anything the slightest bit witty or entertaining. I think the part of my brain that's responsible for wit has quite possibly atrophied from lack of use. I mean, you don't have to be terribly bright when, most of the time, you're on your own or mumbling inanities to a couple of daft dogs, do you?

You can't help wondering about all these individuals' past history. How did they meet James? When did they meet him? How well do they know him? Biblically or otherwise. The candlelight makes eyes glow and gently shadows cheekbones, making everyone look slightly mysterious. Its trembling golden light gives me the feeling that I'm suddenly a lot more attractive too. There is a large, ornate silver bowl, filled with roses in the middle of a very beautiful tablecloth that looks as though it might have been hand-embroidered with delicate white flowers on white.

I'm just thinking how perfect it all is when a voice says, "How lovely the table looks, James. You *are* clever."

"Thank you, Pamela."

James smiles at her. She's a lot older than the rest of the women at the table – early sixties probably. Terribly elegant with her grey hair swept up into a flattering topknot. She's dressed in dark green brocade and is wearing several very beautiful rings and gorgeous earrings that look as though they cost the earth. Her husband's Italian. Roberto Something-or-other. My mind always goes blank when I'm being introduced to new people. She doesn't pay him much attention, even though he seems rather nice – although he's an awful flirt – and vain. Checked himself in every available mirror when we moved from the drawing room to the dining room. His wife certainly doesn't like me. She's managed to keep an animated conversation going on without once catching my eye or even glancing in my direction. It takes years of practice to be quite so devastatingly exclusive.

Now she looks at James and murmurs, "I always remember how marvellously welcoming your mother made anywhere the two of you lived. You must have inherited her divine good taste."

"Yes, Mother was always a splendid hostess. Even after father died, she took great care not to let standards drop. It was a gift she had."

I catch a fleeting expression of sadness on James' face. I'm sure he told me his mother died over five years ago. He's talked a lot about her in the few weeks we've been seeing each other. So many things seem to spark off memories of her. They must have been very close. I hadn't realised that he'd lived with her until her death though.

Green-eyed Suzanne leans towards him. There's a slightly malicious edge to her voice. "She was too good at everything, Jamie. She spoilt you for anyone else. No one else could possibly aspire to her high standards."

Bill, Suzanne's partner of the moment, notices the flash of anger in James' face.

"Do you remember those camping holidays with her down at Brittas when we were at school, James? They were tremendous fun, weren't they?" he says, quickly.

I can feel some of the tension leave James' hand, resting on the table to the right of my plate. He nods at Bill and then turns to me.

"Bill and I were at the same school. Our parents were great friends and after Dad died we spent a lot of the school holidays together."

Suzanne interrupts, sounding irritated. "The trouble is though, some people never grow up. Bill would still drag me off to a camping site if I let him. Can you imagine me in a tent? I mean, I ask you?"

"Might do you good, Suzy. You've grown soft and lazy in your old age."

Séan sounds amused. It seems he has known her since they shared digs together in their student days when he was studying architecture and she Drama.

"Oh, shut up, Séan! You're every bit as bad as they are." Suzanne turns to Séan's wife, Jenny. "What do you think, Jenny? Aren't all men just little boys at heart?"

Jenny is dark-haired, about my age, with an intelligent, lively face. She looks fondly at her husband and smiles slightly. "Oh, I don't know. I've always thought men were rather like dogs: noisy and in your face but you knew what they wanted from life. We women on the other hand remind me of cats. Much more manipulative and deceitful. I think men are rather nice, on the whole."

Suzanne, however, doesn't respond to this amicable observation on the difference between the sexes. Looking sour, she takes another mouthful of soup.

Bill looks as though he's about to say something to her and then changes his mind. Instead, he asks Jenny how her children are.

Roberto offers me some bread, which I decline. He looks at me with his dark eyes and says, "I hope you're not slimming, Hilary. Beautiful women must always have plenty of curves." He waves his hands around in an exaggerated figure of eight.

His accent is delightful, as are his handsome brown eyes. I can't help noticing that his wife is pencil-thin. He must have to be careful not to cut himself on the corners when they're in bed together.

I smile at him. "Oh, no! I'm not thinking of my weight. I just want to leave room for the *coq au vin* and the pud."

Pamela, without taking her eyes off her plate, says in low voice, "*Pud!* I didn't think anyone used *that* term any more for dessert."

Feeling like a gauche teenager, I feel myself colour slightly. Jenny, sitting diagonally across the table from me, catches my eye, raises her eyebrows slightly and makes a little 'oops!' shape with her lips. I've decided that I definitely like her!

First course disposed of and the *coq au vin* is brought in by James. When Jenny and I offered to help carry in the dishes from the kitchen, Suzanne informed us crisply that *she* would help James and that too many cooks in the kitchen would be a bad idea. I wasn't offering to cook anything for God's sake – just carry some plates.

Pamela is telling everyone at the table about the marvellous holiday she and Roberto have just spent in Italy, staying in a little place they own in Santa Margherita on the Ligurian coast. Suddenly, she leans across Séan and eyeballs me for the first time this evening.

"And where did *you* go for your holiday this year, Hilary?"

Should I tell a lie? I'm tempted to say I spent weeks of passionate lovemaking on an exotic Caribbean island with the Depps but she'd be sure to find out that wasn't true. Anyway, James knows that I didn't.

"I stayed with friends in the West of Ireland early on in the year," I admit, lamely.

"Really? How nice."

Those three words speak volumes: lack of interest, confirmation of the sort of boring person she thinks I am and above all, totally dismissive. She turns and smiles at Séan. "I hear that you and Jenny spent a glorious three weeks in the South of France. No wonder you're both looking so relaxed and bronzed." Pamela then turns her attention to James. "James, dear. What did you get up to all through August? We got back at the end of July and you seem to have disappeared. I rang – several times."

Am I wrong or does she sound just the slightest bit put-out?

James is suddenly looking uncomfortable. The reason he wasn't around was that he and I spent most of any spare time we had getting to know one another. It involved a lot of sitting up until the small hours, talking: about books, films, travel, our likes and dislikes. We had so much to learn about each other. James is the first man I've met who seemed interested in finding out about me without trying to do it in bed. Although, I have to admit,

I'd love to move on to that stage before too long. I'd rather like to reassure myself that all my bits are in good working order after such a long period of self-imposed celibacy.

He smiles at Pamela. "Oh, you know! Pressure of work with everyone away enjoying themselves. Someone had to stay behind and keep the show on the road."

I feel a sudden stab of disappointment. Why didn't he just say that he and I were doing a lot together and that there hadn't been any time to go visiting Pamela and Roberto? I get the feeling that, if anything, she's even more jealous of my new relationship with James than the green-eyed Suzanne.

I make an enormous effort to look lively and involved in the conversation. Giving Pamela a dazzling smile, I remark, "We managed to pack in quite a few visits to the theatre this summer, didn't we, James?"

"Yes." He gives a minimal and rather absent-minded nod.

He's staring vacantly down at his plate, blond hair falling over one devastatingly blue eye. But I want more than just 'yes'. I want him to at least sound enthusiastic about our evening sorties together. What's wrong with him?

Pamela and Suzanne are both looking unbearably smug. I open my mouth to speak, to distract them from James' apparent lack of enthusiasm and to keep a flow of conversation going but my mind has gone completely blank. I can't think of a thing to say. They all look at me, waiting, jaws suddenly immobile, knives and forks poised over their plates. As I sit here, leaning forward slightly with parted lips, there is absolute silence for at least ten seconds, although it seems more like half an hour. I get a strong urge to laugh but instead, I lunge for my glass and take a large gulp of wine. James, looking rather frozen-faced, gets up to refill people's drinks. I wouldn't mind a little encouraging smile at this point but he's steadfastly refusing to look at me. I obviously don't know him as well as I thought I did. I knew he was shy, sometimes rather inarticulate – but he's never before shown signs of being a prig.

We've now moved on to the crème brûlée and it is delicious. However, I'm having trouble enjoying it. I keep thinking that I'd much rather be back in my own house, dressed in a track suit, cuddled up with the dogs in front of a crackling fire, watching some good telly with a large gin and tonic for company. James seems to have joined the Pamela-Suzanne camp. He's only spoken to me a couple of times in the last twenty minutes. When he did, his eyes rested on my face only very briefly. Now he's holding a conversation with Suzanne and Roberto about sailing. He knows I hate boats. I thought he did too. One by one, the others join in. It seems that everyone at the table is deeply into sailing. Everyone that is, except me. I stolidly spoon my way through my pud . . . sorry . . . dessert.

I think my face must be registering the fact that I'm not having a great time. Then, gentle Bill, down at the far end of the table comes to my rescue.

"What sport do you enjoy, Hilary?"

I'm not into sport at all but I'm grateful for any friendly attention. I reply with the first activity that floats into my head.

"Swimming," I blurt out. "I like swimming."

What was it they said about my swimming when I was at school? Something along the lines of, 'Hilary has no stamina but has style'. Translated, I suppose that means: 'If up against it, Hilary will drown gracefully'.

"You must come and swim with us at the sports club. We play quite a lot of water polo. It's great fun. Very competitive!"

Oh, God! I'm really sunk now.

Then the coffee arrives on the scene. Thinking that perhaps it would be a good idea to stay sober – especially as I'm driving, I turn down offers of cognac and Grand Marnier and take a surreptitious look at my watch. If I can just manage to sit it out for another twenty minutes, then I'll plead an early start in the morning and leave. They've moved on from water polo to ice hockey and abseiling. I'm definitely out of my league here. I had no idea James had such athletic friends. He must have been pretending when he told me that he had no time for sport of any kind. I sit quietly, sipping at the excellent coffee and wishing I could vanish into thin air. I'm sure they'd never even notice I was gone.

I'm suddenly aware that total silence has filled the room. *Everyone* is looking in my direction, waiting to hear my answer to a question that I wasn't aware of being asked.

"Sorry?" I say, apologetically.

Suzanne stares coldly in my direction. "We were wondering if you'd seen the latest Arnelli film." I hear the distinct sound of ice cubes tinkling in her voice.

I frantically search my mind for a shred of information on recently released films. I know I read something in a magazine in the dentist's about a film that was making people talk. Then it comes to me.

"Oh, you mean that awful film about the creep who sleeps with his mother? No, it's not the sort of thing I'd enjoy. In fact, I think the whole Oedipus thing is pretty unpleasant, really. What sane man ever wanted to go to bed with his mother?"

I suddenly have the feeling that time has stopped. I look from one frozen face to another. They all seem to be doing their best *not* to look at James. He is very white – and very still.

"Don't mind her, darling. We all know she didn't mean to upset you." Suzanne's voice is silky with compassion.

It hits me like a thunderbolt. How could I have been so slow and stupid? All those references James constantly made about his mother, his ambivalence about sex. Panic-stricken, I get to my feet, aware that a cold sweat has broken out on my forehead.

"It's getting late and I have to go. I'm sorry." I somehow manage to give them a collective smile although I know it probably looks more like an alarming goblin-like grimace.

James, face like a marble statue, is looking straight ahead and doesn't move. No one speaks as I noisily push back my chair and stumble to the door, clutching my bag. I'm feeling dizzy. I wrench at the handle – which then comes off in my hand. This is becoming like a nightmare. No, it *is* a nightmare. The kindly Séan materialises beside me and gently takes the handle from my shaking hand. After some patient poking and fiddling, he manages to get the door open. He looks as though he wants to say something but I brush past him with a muttered, "Thanks."

As I flee out of the house and past the window, I see that Pamela and Suzanne have moved over to where James is sitting. It looks like oil painting or a tableau from a wax-works. All the figures seem strangely frozen in a haze of candlelight. The older of the two women is holding James' head against her breast and is stroking his silky hair with her long, slim fingers.

ALSO BY NICOLA LINDSAY, PUBLISHED BY POOLBEG

Butterfly, Tumbling Jude,
Eden Fading, A Place for Unicorns,
Diving Through Clouds

19

Thursday Nights
KATE McCABE

Carmel hated Thursday nights. It wasn't so bad in the summer when the weather was warm and there were loads of people around and nobody paid her much attention. But in the winter, it could be brutal. There were nights when the wind would sting your skin till it felt raw. If it rained, there was nowhere to take cover since the council had demolished the band shelter because the young ones were using it for drinking parties. And the looks she got from some of the men who passed by, as she waited patiently beside the bushes, made Carmel's cheeks sting worse than the wind ever did. As if she was on the game or something!

Yet she couldn't stop herself looking forward. Every Monday, she would be counting the days till Thursday came around and she saw Barry again. And he always came. He might be a little bit late sometimes depending on if the traffic was bad. There had even been a few occasions when he was early and he was waiting for her at the harbour wall opposite the coffee shop before she got there. But he always came. That was one thing could be said in Barry's favour. He always turned up.

It was her mother who had commented on it first. Her father never had much time for Barry. He used to say if it was raining soup Barry would be out with a fork. Her father believed men should have regular jobs if they were going to provide for their wives and children. So he didn't think much of Barry's ambition to become a big rock star. He used to say he was whistling in the wind. And he didn't hide his belief that Carmel was wasting her time with him and would be better off with some fella who had a trade or profession and decent financial prospects.

But her mother disagreed and said Mr Roche was old-fashioned and wasn't living in the real world. Things had moved on since he was a young man. Kids now had much more confidence than they did in the old days. They had more ambition and more imagination. That's why we had produced people like Bono and Bob Geldof who could go anywhere in the world and talk to presidents and popes as if they were bosom pals.

Her mother had a soft spot for Barry. She always had a nice cup of tea and some apple tart for him whenever he called. The pair of them got on like a house on fire. Barry used to run her down to Raheny in his car every Sunday afternoon to visit her sister. And afterwards, he picked her up again and brought her home. He did it every Sunday without fail unless he had some gig planned. That's why Mrs Roche always had a good word for Barry. Even when Mr Roche said he was a waster and would go to the dogs and take Carmel with him.

But back then, her parents' views didn't matter much

to Carmel. She was madly in love with Barry. She had been in love with him since the night she first met him in the Baggot Inn after a gig by his band, The Perfectionists. The moment she clapped eyes on him, she knew she was smitten. He had been dressed in black from head to toe. He wore black trousers and a black shirt and black boots and black shades. He had designer stubble on his chin and a cigarette hanging from the side of his mouth and he drank bottles of Bulmers cider by the neck. And when he smiled his blue eyes twinkled like stardust. Carmel thought he was the epitome of cool.

They got chatting and he offered her a lift home. He was living in Portmarnock then and she was living with her parents in Baldoyle. Carmel was thrilled to sit beside him in the passenger seat of his silver Audi as they went shooting along past the Bull Wall with the windows down and the breeze blowing her hair all over her face. And later when he took her in his arms and his warm lips encircled hers, Carmel felt sure her heart was going to melt.

They began to go steady. Barry was twenty-eight and had his own pad. He spent his days hanging around the flat practising guitar chords and listening to CDs and learning new material. At weekends, the band held rehearsals in the garage of the drummer's house and most nights they played sessions in pubs around the town. Carmel thought it was all madly exciting. She was nineteen and worked as a sales assistant in Brady's chemist shop. He was her first real boyfriend. She loved being with him. It made her feel so alive. She loved the lifestyle and the parties afterwards. She loved listening to him sing and the way he gazed straight into her eyes as she sat at a table beside the stage with the groupies and the hangers-on. She loved the envious looks she got from the other girls.

Barry was always talking about the future. He had big plans. When they were alone together, he would tell her he didn't intend to spend his entire career playing in pubs. He was going to get an agent for the band and secure a record deal. Then they'd be on their way. All they needed was a lucky break. He had no doubt that they were going to make it big. You just had to look at the reaction they got at their gigs.

Carmel believed him when he talked about the grand house he was going to build up on Howth Head where they could look out over Dublin Bay and the cars he would buy and the boat that he would keep in the marina. Of course, he would be away from home quite often because they would have to do a lot of touring at the beginning to consolidate their fan base. Barry had already picked up the marketing jargon. But once they were established, they'd be able to cut back and maybe only tour every couple of years. But he would always do a concert every Christmas at the Point Theatre, probably for some charity. It would be his way of repaying his loyal Dublin fans.

Mr Roche scoffed at Barry's plans. He said it was all pie in the sky. He said it would suit him better if he took his head out of the clouds and settled down to a regular nine-to-five job. Mrs Roche defended Barry and said her husband had no creative spirit and Mr Roche laughed and asked how many hungry mouths that would feed.

In the end, all the arguments about Barry began to get on Carmel's nerves so she moved out of her parents' house and went to live with him in a new flat in Clontarf. He had been encouraging her for months. He kept saying they would save money since two could live as cheaply as one.

By now, he was very excited. He had managed to get hold of an agent who drew up a career plan and promised to launch The Perfectionists with a recording contract within three months. He also guaranteed to get them concert engagements as support to some big bands. Barry was over the moon. He went out and bought a whole new wardrobe of clothes and put down a deposit on a new Fender Jazz guitar which cost over €1000.

Carmel was excited too. She desperately wanted Barry to succeed. He was working so hard on his musical career that he deserved a big break. And she wanted to silence those critics, including her father, who kept saying that the venture wouldn't work. But the record contract never materialised and the one support date the agent secured for them disappeared when the concert was cancelled at the last minute because one of the musicians was admitted to hospital suffering from a drugs overdose.

Barry was devastated. Some of the older musicians told him he shouldn't get too downhearted. The industry was full of sharks. People promised you the sun, moon and stars and disappeared when the going got rough. It was a cruel business. It had even happened to the Beatles when they were starting off.

Carmel just cradled his head in her hands and stared into those bright blue eyes.

"Don't give up," she whispered. "I believe in you. You're going to make it."

By now, she was six months pregnant. Barry said he was delighted but she knew he was only pretending. He didn't really want the responsibility of a child, at least not yet. He wanted to wait till his career was on a more solid basis. It looked like her father's prediction was coming true. But Carmel didn't care. She loved Barry. And now they were going to have a baby together. Surely it would only be a matter of time before Barry's luck changed and his career took off.

The baby was a little boy and Barry wanted to call him Antoine which was the real name of his hero, Fats Domino. But Carmel said they should call him James after her father. She wanted to keep her father sweet. She was beginning to think she might need him.

With the arrival of little James, things began to change. She had to give up her job to look after him so now they were relying entirely on the money that Barry could earn from playing gigs in the pubs. It was never enough. It seemed that they were always short of something. It was a struggle every week to pay the rent, not to mention food and baby clothes and all the other necessities.

And Barry began to get grumpy and bad-tempered. He resented the time and attention Carmel was paying to the baby. And he complained that James woke him up in the morning when he should have been getting his rest after playing and partying till three or four a.m.

They started to have arguments, something that hadn't happened before. Barry said he couldn't think straight with a baby always screaming for attention. Carmel said maybe he should take her father's advice and get a steady job. He could still play music in the evenings. But Barry was outraged at the suggestion. He said music *was* his job. He was a professional musician. How was he supposed to make his big breakthrough unless he gave it all his energy?

In the end, Carmel decided she couldn't take any more. All the fights and arguments were bad for the baby. And they were getting her down and making her depressed. Barry said maybe a short separation might be a good idea. It would give them time and space to sort themselves out. So she packed her stuff and all the baby things and took a taxi back to her parents' house.

Her father received her with a grim face. He said this was exactly what he had predicted. He said he hoped she had learned her lesson and got a bit of sense. And he didn't want to see that waster near the house again. If he ever turned up, Mr Roche said he wouldn't be responsible for his actions. Mrs Roche was sad that things had turned out like this but she was glad to have Carmel and little James back home again.

Now that she was living with her parents, Carmel began to get her life back together. Her mother offered to mind the baby so that she could return to work. She went to see Mr Brady at the chemist shop and he gave her the old job back. Barry said he would pay her maintenance for little James; he was his child and he insisted on looking after him. Carmel said he couldn't come to the house because her father could get violent so they agreed to meet at the harbour wall in Howth on Thursday nights at seven o'clock so that Barry could hand over the money. Sometimes, they would go to the coffee shop and have a chat and Barry would update her on all the news.

Carmel convinced herself that the separation was only temporary and they would get together again when Barry's career took off. He was still optimistic. He was still talking of making the big breakthrough. There were plans for a series of concerts. There was even talk of The Perfectionists going to London to relaunch their career. Barry said Dublin was too small. There were more opportunities in London. A friend he knew had offered to put them in touch with an agent over there who would get them gigs and engagements. London was where it was all happening.

Carmel wanted to believe him. She still loved Barry. She wanted the three of them to be together again. But the months went by and nothing happened. Barry always had some excuse. Somebody had let them down or some piece of bad luck had occurred that messed up their plans. The winter passed into the summer and back into the winter again and every Thursday night, regardless of the weather, Carmel went out to Howth to meet Barry.

Sometimes she brought little James with her so that he could see his father. Barry bought him small toys and presents but Carmel could see that he wasn't really interested in the boy. The talk was all about himself and the band and the big breakthrough he was hoping for. He didn't even ask her about herself and how she was getting on at the chemist's shop.

And things were happening there. A new pharmacist had come to work with Mr Brady. His name was Gavin Dunne and he was from Wexford. He was twenty-nine and tall and had a mop of curly fair hair. One evening he asked Carmel if she would like to come out with him for a meal and she agreed. After that, the relationship developed. Gavin was great company. He was always in good humour and he lifted her out of herself. Eventually she told him about Barry and little James. Gavin said it didn't matter. Everybody had things in their past. He told her he loved her. She brought him home to meet her parents and they both took to him at once.

And then, just a few weeks ago he asked her to marry him.

Carmel mulled over the proposal. She was twenty-four. A life with Gavin would mean a new start. She would have security and James would have a father. Mr Roche said she'd be crazy to turn him down. Here was a man with a good job, a decent man who would look after her and her little boy unlike that waster she had got caught up with. She should jump at the chance. It might never come again.

Carmel decided to accept Gavin's offer. He was overjoyed. They set the wedding date for Easter. The hard bit was going to be telling Barry. She decided to get it over as soon as possible, at their next meeting on Thursday. She was dreading the encounter. When the day arrived, she hurried home from work and put on a pale pink sweater and calf-length brown skirt, with her new knee-high leather boots. She brushed her hair vigorously and carefully applied her make-up, right down to eyeliner, shadow and mascara. Then she put on her new winter jacket with the fleece-lined hood, grabbed her bag and caught the 31 Bus for Howth.

She was praying that he wouldn't be late. She hated that lonely promenade by the harbour wall with the wind blowing in from the sea and those dirty-minded men giving her strange looks.

But he was on time. Carmel had barely stepped off the bus when she saw his car turn into the carpark. Next minute he was strolling confidently towards her, his long legs encased in black jeans and his black leather jacket pulled tight across his chest.

"Howya?" he enquired, giving her a quick peck on the cheek. He reached into his pocket and took out the envelope. "Here's your money," he said.

Carmel took it and put it away in her bag.

"Have you got time for a cup of coffee?" she asked, pointing to the misted windows of the café across the road. It would be better to break the bad news to him while he was sitting down.

"Yeah. In fact, I've got something interesting to tell you."

He pushed the door open for her and held out a chair while she settled herself.

"You're looking good," he said, smiling into her face with those big blue eyes.

"Thank you."

"Would you like a piece of carrot cake?"

"Sure," Carmel said.

He went to the counter and ordered, then came back and sat down opposite her. Leaning forward, he said smilingly, "We're getting a new drummer for the band."

"Oh! What's happening to Lefty?"

"He's had enough. He's packing it in." Barry was grinning. "This new guy's shit hot. It's what we really need. I've always thought the drums were our weak spot. Now we'll really take the town by storm!"

He was hugely excited. She could see it in his face. She felt excited herself.

"That's brilliant news," she said.

"Yes," Barry said, squeezing her hand. "This could be it, Carmel. This could be the breakthrough we've been waiting for."

She thought about the news she had to tell him about marrying Gavin. Would it be fair to break it to him now, when he was so happy? No, she decided. It wouldn't be right. The news could wait for one more week. She'd tell him for definite next Thursday night.

"Tell me more," she said, leaning forward and stirring sugar into the coffee that the waitress had just set down.

ALSO BY KATE MCCABE, PUBLISHED BY POOLBEG

The Beach Bar, Hotel Las Flores

20

Skin Deep

Jacinta McDevitt

So I keep thinking. Thinking that maybe if it hadn't been in the fool's month. And on the last day. It was like a last chance to catch me out. One more day and I might have been nobody's fool. So I keep thinking. Thinking that maybe if I'd found it some other time. Or, better still, not at all.

But I did find it. I found it by accident. Lurking. Hiding. On the back of my knee. The right knee. Either knee would have been the wrong one. So it makes no difference which knee. But I keep thinking that it does. That maybe if it had been some other person's knee. But it wasn't. It was very definitely my knee and the right one. And there it was. Just waiting for me to find it. So I did a twirl. And found it.

My husband kissed it when I showed it to him. Kissed the little pin-top imposter. Said he loved it. Said he loved me. My friends said it was so cute, they wished they had a beauty spot. Just like my one. They could have mine. I didn't want it. From the moment I saw it I didn't trust it.

"We'll have to remove it," the specialist said, barely lifting her dark, tightly permed head. "We'll have it off in no time," she said, licking her lips.

And she was true to her word. It took no time at all to remove it and it was fine. No pain. No pain is fine with me. Only three stitches.

"We'll have to wait ten days for the results but it looks fine to me," she said as she patted me better. So we were all fine. And that was that. It was fine she'd said and she was the expert. She knew what she was talking about. She knew her moles. Knew how to excavate. Could wax poetic on all manner of burrowing things. Especially mine. She'd be in touch in ten days to confirm just how right she was and how fine I was.

I nearly missed her telephone call. I answered it just before I went out. I was all set for a bit of retail therapy. I'd seen a dress. Very expensive. An-arm-and-a-leg job. Glamorous. Lush. Black velvet. To my knees. I was going to treat myself. I deserved a little treat after all I'd been through. But just before getting my treat I made the silly mistake of answering the phone when it rang. Big mistake. So silly of me.

I recognised her voice immediately. Soft, businesslike. I should have recognised the doom and gloom in it. But in those days I didn't know doom or gloom. I had never met them before.

"Is it about the results?" I asked stupidly. Well, she wasn't ringing me for the good of her health, was she? Of course, it was all for the good of mine. The fine results. I should have known by her tone of voice that fine wouldn't come into it. "*Don't you dare use that tone with me!"* I should have shouted at her but instead I just listened.

"I'm afraid the result of the test is A typical."

Well, well, what about that, I thought. It sounded good to me. An A. My first. I'd always wanted an A in English or History. Now I had an A in moles. An A is always good, isn't it? Well, no! On the subject of moles an A is a very bad grade. In fact, it's a fail. And what do you get for a fail in moles? Cancer, that's what you get. But I knew I couldn't have cancer because that's what other people get. But not me.

So now she wanted to see me. Well, I wanted to see her too. I could explain her mistake to her. Face to face. Tell her how wrong she was. Then we could chat about something else. The weather. The price of a pound of mince. All she wanted to chat about was how terrific she was at chopping up cancer. But I had places to go, dresses to see. Why didn't I just tell her I was busy? Too busy.

"Very busy at the moment. Very, very busy. Fully booked up for chats."

I should have said: *"In fact, I can't see anyone for a cancer chat for at least twenty years. Yes. I'm sure I could fit you in then. I'll pencil you in for 2.30 p.m. twenty years from today and you can chat about my tiny little mole then. Of course, if I have a cancellation before that I'll give you a ring. But don't hold your breath. The chances of that happening are about as remote as a young healthy mother getting skin cancer. Ha. Ha."*

"I'm so awfully, awfully sorry," I should have said to her. *"But you'll just have to go peddling your long, sad face and smart blue suit and matching eyes to some other poor sucker. Have a little chat with them. Pick on an older sucker. This sucker is not available. Do you hear me? Not available for you or any little bit of cancer gossip you might like to share."*

But instead I just whimpered and listened. I even agreed to see her that very day for more of a cancer chat.

I rang my husband first. He was out to lunch. Couldn't be found. Stuffing his face with some tender, juicy, cancer-free flesh. With onions and all the trimmings. I rang my sister next. A sucker who's always available for chat.

"Hi!" I whispered. "I'm all alone and I have cancer."

She was calm. Said she'd be right over. Then she told me that she loved me. Twice. I held on to the phone. Kept the connection until she arrived. Her eyes were bloodshot. Make-up streaked on her face. Black lines ran from her eyes. Like a sad clown. What had happened to her? Who had upset her? She squeezed me. Told me everything would be all right. I believed her.

In the doctor's surgery she sat beside me. Close. We closed ranks. The doctor, as promised, chatted on and on and on about moles. My big sister took tear-stained notes and prayed on a string of tear-drop pearls that hung around her neck. She wrote down the three types of skin cancer. Jotted down that I had the worst type. I wondered was the worst type very bad or just bad. I soon found out. The worst is very, very bad. Another fail. Only eighty per cent survival rate.

"And what about the other twenty per cent?" I heard my sister ask.

Yes, what about the poor unfortunate twenty per cent?

"They don't survive." The mole doctor looked sad.

"Do they die?" I asked.

Now she looked very sad. She nodded her head up and down and up and down. Like a bloody ornament in the back window of a car but sadder. So I decided to keep quiet. Not to make her any sadder. This was too much for her. I kept quiet. Ask no questions, be told no lies. Sit. Listen. Let my sister ask all the questions. She's always been nosey.

The sun edged its way in the roof light of the doctor's rooms. Listening. Waiting to hear the damage it had done. Beaming.

And I wished the wracking noise would stop. Someone's heart was being broken in this room. I could hear it. I never knew that a heart could be broken. So I was thinking, what's love got to do with it? Just words. Of songs. Figures of speech. Until now. And the sobbing. The sobbing was going through my brain. It was so very, very close. My sister was crying too. Not taking notes now. Holding me and I'm sobbing. Listening. Paying attention in case of another test at the end of it all. We couldn't afford to fail another test.

We learned all manner of science and fiction. There was a satellite cell in my leg, near the original wound, that had to be removed. That was all right then. Remove the satellite. They'd sent a man to the moon in one of those. He came back fine.

And where are all these tears coming from? Who knew I had so many? I wish they'd stop. They can't be coming from me. I feel nothing. Gone way beyond feeling. Orbiting the room now. Ground control to mole.

The doctor was dying to cut into me again. Cut in about a centimetre. Avoid the tendons. Then maybe do a skin graft. She was getting very enthusiastic. But what did I care? If it would cure me she could cut the whole leg off. I don't need it any more. It's probably worn out. Past its best-before date. I've been using it now for the past thirty-six years. Only thirty-six . . .

I didn't believe her when she told me the skin would

grow again. Pull the other leg, I nearly said but just giggled instead. I wondered what else would grow. More moles. A crop of them. Crop, flock, gaggle, herd, army. Please don't tell me any more, I nearly shouted in a whisper. Just do what you have to. Put me asleep. Wake me up. Better. Fixed. A cancer-free zone. Please. Please.

So another something new I learned was that cancer is a frequent flyer. It travels. Goes all over the place to all sorts of exotic destinations. Kidneys, lungs, anywhere. It's not selective. It hops and hides. Has an open-ended pass. Final destination, most desired address: the bloodstream.

Some cancers are home birds. They never travel. But mine, of course mine is a traveller. I have made travelling easy. There are no borders in my body. Freedom of speech and freedom of passage are my beliefs. I will die for my beliefs. I nearly laughed but thought it would be rude so I cried some more instead.

"Melanoma . . . melanoma." The doctor keeps saying it. Over and over she says it. It sounds so nice. Not like the killer it is. Cancer sounds like a killer. Shut up, Cancer! Let Melanoma speak. Melanoma. Soft and kind. Like semolina. Semolina, melanoma. Melanoma for the adult; semolina for the child.

And what about my child? She hasn't even had a birthday. "Hey, you, God! Do you hear me? Up there in your ivory tower with the pearly gates. Where are you in my hour of need? I flocked with all the others to Mass every Sunday and high day and holiday. Novenas, rosaries, Stations of the Cross. It's payback time. I don't want this cross, God. Are you listening? Listen."

Oh, God, what about my little baby? My little girl? Don't take me away from her. Not yet. No one loves her like I do. Loves the bones of her. Kick her, I limp. I am limping now, God. All the time. Is that not enough of a cross for me? Well, come on then, God. Give me pain, lots of pain. I can take it.

The sobbing sound is getting worse. I can't bear it. I can't hear myself talking to God for all the sobbing I'm doing. And I can hear a pigeon too. On the roof light. It's making that noise. You know the sound. I can hear it in between the sobbing. And the doctor talking. Pontificating and cooing. Vying to be heard. If my cancer made a noise we could find it. Speak up, Cancer. Tell them where you are. Then it's open season on cancer cells. We'll bag the lot. But it's mute. Like me. Shh! Keep quiet! I might be dreaming.

"There'll be a wound," the doctor said. A big, kick-ass wound. She told me we'd have to mind the poor wound. Look after the poor wound. The wound had to be given a chance to heal. Well, fuck the wound, I say. What about me? Heal me. *Me.* "And there's a free theatre tomorrow," she said. All delighted and excited, she said she could start cutting into me tomorrow in the free theatre. Roll up, roll up, no tickets needed, standing room only. But I know I won't be in any humour to be entertained tomorrow. If there is a tomorrow.

At last my husband is here. Holding me. Didn't he get the short straw all the same? My life partner. Life. Not a chance. I can feel his guilt. He loved it. Kissed it. Befriended it. Now he's crying Judas tears. He's never cried any sort of tears before. This cancer thing is really taking control.

We've had a charmed life, him and me. No need for tears. Until now. He's all bent. Twisted. Out of shape. And for a moment, just the briefest of moments, I get a glimpse of what he will be like when he is old. I want to hold him. But I will never grow old. Old like them, my mother, father.

"If only," they say. "If only," they keep saying.

So I think of pots and pans and tinkers. While they talk of Padre Pio and St Jude and maybe a little holiday. Maybe Lourdes. They calmly play let's pretend and jolly hockey-sticks. And there, there, everything will be all right. I wish they'd stop. But it's how they cope. I don't want them to cope.

"*Look at me!*" I want to shout. "*Show me how you really feel. Let me feel it. Scream for me. Scream! I can't. If I do I'll know it's real.*"

Another cry. My baby. Smiling up at me. She is the same to me. Always. Loves me for me. Warts and all. Now moles. She doesn't know what is growing in me. She has no fear. It's all in the here and now for her. And that's all I have. She puts her arms up to me. Chuckles. Wants to be held. Tight. I cling on.

Everyone is with me but I will be alone. Except for the cancer. That will be with me. Growing. Lurking. And I keep thinking that it will be loyal. It will befriend me and stay until the end. And is this the end? If it is, it is a very strange ending. Not at all how I had imagined it would be. So I keep thinking about that. You know, the end.

ALSO BY JACINTA MCDEVITT, PUBLISHED BY POOLBEG

Handle with Care, Sign's On

21

This Place
ANNA McPARTLIN

Darcy woke. Instantly she knew it had been a long sleep. She could hear her own heartbeat and listened to its rhythm drum-drumming like the boy in the school band who led the march on cold days in March or tick-tocking like her grandfather's grandfather clock which dominated his tiny home in a rural area lost to progress many, many years ago while she was still a child. She examined her own hand – small, shrivelled and interestingly almost wand-like – then again maybe the clouds before her ancient eyes just made it seem that way. This place was warm and although small she had room enough. She didn't want for anything. The last time she was truly awake she had ached but sleep had cured her of that. This place would be a new start for an old soul. Her journey had been long and painful but now in the stillness she felt a certain excitement without really having a clue why.

* * *

Michael woke. He was groggy and sore from the journey and yet content to have finally arrived. In the stillness he too could hear the beating of his own heart and the echo that was hers. There were no windows and he couldn't see a door. The place was small and not difficult to explore. He listened for signs of life outside the four walls. Faint sounds floated around him, confirming that there was a world outside and he wasn't dreaming. Back to back as they were, he knew she wasn't aware of him and he could sense that she was happy in isolation. He stretched and waited for her recognition. She rested beside him while he lay awake, alert but patient. This place would be a new start for him too and he wasn't desperate to leave. Now that they had found one another again, he was determined things would be different.

* * *

He couldn't recall the first time that they had met. They had been the offspring of neighbours and were born only two weeks apart. He was the older of the two. She had been one of seven but he was an only child and described as a miracle. His mother had lost nine others and had nearly lost him twice. She had spent the entire pregnancy in bed and Darcy's mother had told him that once he was born she had to be taught how to walk again. He had wondered at the time, then a mere child, how in nine months his mother could have forgotten but Darcy's mother had threatened to give him a clip around the ear and warned him to be good to his mother who had suffered Hell's brimstone to bring him into the world. Of course, with the moniker of 'miracle' came spoils and as the only son of a well-to-do farmer he was spoiled. Darcy's father, while blessed with a large family, was not as fortunate as his neighbour when it came to economy. His farm was smaller by five fields and eighteen cows and although he had more chickens he had not one horse and he had nine mouths to feed including his own. Darcy's father would sometimes admit to a certain jealousy of his neighbour but this would only come after beer and, although drunk, he would realise the insensitivity of such a statement so the comment would come in the form of a whisper. Darcy's dad wasn't a nasty man, he was just a tired one. He viewed the leisurely life that came with his neighbour's being a father of one and, although in his heart of hearts he wouldn't give up one of his children, he sometimes wished for the peace that came with an empty house.

Sitting on her tired dad's knee, his second-youngest girl pitied him because she too saw the life that her best friend had and envied him – but then what did Darcy know?

★   ★   ★

It wasn't all plain sailing for the young Michael. His father, although well heeled and a cheery addition to any party, wasn't as happy as his neighbour would have guessed. He wasn't content with one child and a wife that was not able to provide him with the family he believed he was entitled to. With each miscarriage came fresh misery and his wife's delicate mind would fracture a little more but he wouldn't give up. Contraception was illegal and he wasn't going to be emasculated by any woman, not even one he once loved, and so the cycle continued and each loss became another brick in the wall that separated them. He then lost himself in his farm and she in her only son.

As the child grew older a new problem emerged. Michael had turned into what his angry father described as 'a mammy's boy'. He didn't play hurling or football with the other boys, instead preferring to play-act with a girl from the farm next door. He didn't like work either. He was physically sick the one time he was asked to help calving and his weak arms couldn't hold a woman's purse not to mind carry a pail of milk. He was bullied in school by boys who saw in him all the weaknesses his own father had seen and come to loathe. The boy was as weak and disappointing as his mother had been. He could have done something to protect his child but in those days a good beating was considered character-building.

★ ★ ★

Darcy was the tough one. She had to be tough to be even noticed in a household made up of three boys and four girls. She shared a bed with two of her sisters and had arm muscles from spending nights tugging the blanket. She was happy though and unknown to herself she was the light in Michael's otherwise dull world. To the outsider she had nothing and he had it all. Walking together hand in hand they stood out, she dressed in her sister's hand-me-downs and with an effortlessly dirty face, just a scrap of a thing and always ready for battle, and he in the finest clothes and sparkling clean, tall and lean and with a pretty girl's face.

Once and while still very young she had admitted to her best friend that she was a little envious of his finery. He was thoughtful and wanted to share with her his experience, hoping that while wearing his clothes his friend would see the world did not instantly become a better place. She was concerned by the possibility of his nakedness and so they agreed to swap clothes. He stood in his father's barn in her bit of a dress and she in his velvet pants suit. She marched and saluted and laughed out loud when he danced a jig, his legs wild and her frayed frills flopping. They didn't see his father enter and his father didn't seem to care that the little girl from next door witnessed her friend's savage beating. She ran home to her own father's arms dressed in little boy's clothes and sobbing. Her dad wrapped her up and told her to keep away from the poor child. That evening Darcy's father went to his neighbour's home to return the boy's clothes. The doctor was leaving and Michael's mother was a ghostly shade of pale. Her husband was nowhere in sight. She offered to pay for the dress which had been stained in her son's blood but he refused and left her be.

In the middle of the night Darcy woke and, despite her father's warning, concern led her out of her house and through the fields to her friend. In the days when houses weren't locked she slipped inside her neighbour's back door and, with heart in mouth and the memory of his beating fresh, she crept up the stairs and into his bedroom. He was lying awake, his body bruised and painful. She slipped into his bed and he laid his head on her chest. She told him that everything would be okay and that she would take care of him and sometime after dawn they promised one another they would be together forever.

★   ★   ★

At seventeen Michael had escaped the farm and his father's control. A year before he had finished school, his father succumbed to a stroke which left him partially paralysed and dependent on the care of those who had been such a disappointment to him. Luckily for the man, his wife and son were better souls then he and they took care of him in a kinder way than Darcy thought he deserved — but then his kindness was one of things that she loved in her friend.

Despite his religion Michael was accepted into Trinity. Although a disappointment on the field, he was a smart boy who excelled in the classroom. He studied engineering and, with a nice allowance now controlled by his mother, he lived in what some would describe as luxury. Certainly that is how his best friend Darcy described it. She was not college material and, even if she was, the money for such things simply wasn't in the pot. Instead she followed her friend to Dublin a year into his course. She worked serving breakfasts and lunches in Bewleys on Grafton Street and most days he visited with her. She would take her break and they would sit together smoking and drinking coffee. She'd tell him about a man who had queued for ten minutes, not for eggs but instead to ask her out, and he'd laugh when she described how awful he looked as a reason for her saying no. She'd tell him the business of all who worked with her and he'd laugh at her mock shock at their antics and little jokes about the ones she didn't like. He didn't ever talk about girls and, although it was unspoken, each of them had an inkling as to why. Darcy would never question her friend about anything that made him wrinkle his forehead. She loved him too much for that. He would tell her stories about the boys and girls in his class and about the work he was doing and what he dreamed of accomplishing once his course was completed. She was always welcome in his lodgings too. Her own were a lot bleaker and she shared a room with two other girls – at least this time she did have her own single bed. She would often be waiting for him when he'd finished a late class. She'd feed him with a new recipe the cook in Bewleys had taught her. She had talent – the old woman had told her so and her best friend didn't disagree.

★ ★ ★

Darcy was working late one evening when Michael came in. He was upset, so upset that she feigned illness so as to be let off her shift three hours early, forgoing the badly needed pay. Hand-in-hand, with Michael on the verge of tears, they went back to his apartment. He sat head in hands while she lit two cigarettes, handing him one before making tea. He took a long drag and blew the smoke into the room so that it mingled with hers. She put the teapot between them and waited for him to speak.

The pot of tea was gone and they were both on their sixth cigarette by the time he did so but Darcy had always been patient. He told her that he loved her and that she was his best friend. She told him that she felt the same way. He said that he wanted to make love to her.

It was a shock that she wasn't prepared for. She had never seen him as a sexual object and believed he had never seen her in that way either. She wondered why and he cried. He begged her to consider him and she worried that his proposal was indecent but he seemed so desperate and she did love him. He asked her to trust him but of course she did. He begged her to help him and although she didn't understand she agreed, so desperate was she to take away his pain.

He pulled his chair toward hers so that they were sitting opposite one another. Then he leaned in for a kiss and his lips felt numb against hers. He pulled away with fear in his eyes. She didn't know what to do for him so she kissed him again. He got up soon after and asked her if she wanted a drink. He took out a bottle of whiskey and despite not liking even its smell she agreed. They sat at the table drinking glass after glass and smoking cigarette after cigarette and at some point in the evening, when they were both drunk enough, hand in hand they went into Michael's bedroom. He stripped himself and she did likewise. They slipped under the covers and lay still for a moment and then suddenly he was on her and kissing her hard on her mouth as though she was an enemy he was trying to hurt. She battled against him and their strengths were evenly matched. They trashed around until suddenly he was inside her. She watched the surprise which was written on his face as they both moved rhythmically. He watched as a sharp pain registered on hers and he wanted to cry. She was leaking and he was not sure whether or not she was uncomfortable. He didn't kiss her again and she didn't want to be kissed. Afterwards he flopped down on top of her and cried in her arms. She held him and put her hand through his hair, much as his mother had done when he was a boy. She told him that everything would be okay and they pledged to be together forever. At the time they believed it but, of course, it was untrue. They had made such a huge mistake. But that was all a long time ago.

* * *

Darcy smiled. It had been days since she'd registered her old friend's presence but in this place time meant nothing. She, like he, had been busy remembering the past. She had just recalled a game they used to play as children, one in which he would hide and she would follow the clues that he left her to find him. And then he would find her. It would take him most of the night before coming up with appropriate clues for the game but he loved it, and seeing the joy in her face when they found each other was enough to ensure he put much time and effort into it.

And now, as though he had just found her, she opened her eyes and he was facing her. He was looking at her, hopeful and silently begging her forgiveness.

"It's been a long time," she said.

He smiled with tears in his eyes and, nodding, he agreed that it had been. "I was always with you," he replied.

"It didn't seem like it," she answered honestly and without any bitterness.

"You know I loved you," he said.

"As much as you could," she replied.

"I want to make it better," he whispered.

"You can't," she replied kindly, suggesting it to be a matter of fact as opposed to an attempt to hurt him.

"Then allow me to make up for it," he begged.

"Okay," she nodded and his face flushed. "Explain it to me."

His joy faded.

"Please," she said and he nodded.

"Where do I start?" he asked.

"That day," she said. "That day you begged me to make love," she reminded him.

As though he needed reminding. After all, that was the day it had all gone so wrong.

"I was scared," he said.

"Scared of what?"

"I was scared because I had kissed a man," he said.

"And you liked it," she said.

He nodded.

"So why me?"

"I didn't want to like it," he admitted sadly. "I wanted to like it with you."

"But you couldn't."

"No," he said, shaking his head from side to side. "I didn't. Inside you I knew that I wanted him," he admitted, heartsick.

"But it was too late."

"The baby," he agreed. "Yes, but not just that you were pregnant – it was more than that. How could I have come out as a gay man back then?"

"Impossible," she agreed. "But I knew."

"I know. I know, and that's why I loved you."

She wiped away a tear. "We could have worked it out."

"A gay man and a single mother?" he asked, almost laughing at the lunacy of such a suggestion.

"We could have moved away."

"And do what?" he asked.

"We could have pretended like we did when we were kids," she said, her eyes suddenly filling up. "It wouldn't have been the fairytale but it could have been okay."

"I couldn't see a way out, Darcy."

"But you did. You left me alone!" she cried. "How could you leave me alone?"

"Madness," he admitted. "If I had my time over again," he mumbled.

"After you left I got sick and I lost the baby," she said quietly. "Did you know that?"

"Yes," he nodded. "I told you I was always with you."

"I never did have children after that," she said. "Some sort of infection," she remembered.

"I know your world seemed empty. You never got over what I had done. You blamed yourself."

"You're right," she said. "You see, I knew what you were and I let you talk me into that bed and if I hadn't maybe you wouldn't have −"

He shushed her. "No," he comforted. "It was you who kept me going as long as I did." He smiled. "Without you I would have jumped many years before."

"You took part of me with you!" she cried.

"I didn't mean to."

"All I ever wanted was to care for you."

"And I you," he said. "But I couldn't back then − I was too weak."

"And now?"

"And now we've got a second chance," he smiled. "We can go through the world watching out for one another just like we said we would."

"I would like that," she smiled. "It was so lonely without you."

"No more," he grinned.

The walls seemed to be closing in on them now. Darcy was disappearing to somewhere unseen.

"It's okay," he said. "It's time to go."

"You'll be right behind me?" she asked.

"You know I will."

"Michael," she said.

"Yeah?" he smiled.

"Did you notice anything about yourself?"

"What?" he asked, a little alarmed.

"You're a girl!" she laughed.

He looked down. "Wow! I suppose I asked for that!" he said smiling, getting ready to follow.

★ ★ ★

In the hospital a new mother rested with her twin baby girls in her arms. Looking down upon them, she promised her girls the world and they in turn sucked their fingers and gazed happily into her face.

The past would now be forgotten and left behind in that place. The slate was once again wiped clean.

"Together forever," they had once pledged and they hadn't lied.

ALSO BY ANNA McPARTLIN, PUBLISHED BY POOLBEG

Apart From The Crowd, Pack Up the Moon

22

The Mermaid

SHARON MULROONEY

The golden chain lay curled around itself on the dusty bedside table. She lay in her own place, on the crumpled pillow. She stared at the delicate filigree of the heart-shaped locket, wondering if the etchings were anything more than the whim of the engraver on a particular day. Did he think of that heart living on, long after his own had stopped? Did he imagine it being passed down through generations, or worn by only one person, and buried with them? It would lie under the ground, never diminishing, while the bones and flesh of the wearer faded into the soil. Or melt in the searing heat of a crematorium fire, chemically bonded with the person's ashes forever.

She blinked away the images, feeling the sleepy stirring beside her. David would be fully awake soon, sliding his hand across her flat stomach, finding her secret places, taking and giving pleasure. She glanced at the window.

Daylight had crept into the sky in her tiny moment of distraction. The certitude of the birds singing in complete darkness had lifted her spirits. She had lain there for an hour, full of expectation of the dawn. But she had missed the moment. Now the greyish yellow light was slowly unveiling the anonymous shapes of the night, revealing mundane reality. The leaning gatepost that David had promised to fix when she had come to him with a splinter. Dark red blood had welled suddenly on the tip of her pale finger, pierced by the tiny sliver of wood. She had held it up like a child, and he had taken her hand and deliberately licked away the blood, never taking his blue eyes from hers.

"I'll make it better," he had murmured and she had believed him.

The twisted branches of the cherry tree were no longer sinister, but tipped with tight pink buds of blossom. The cat slunk back from its night-time foray, to the comfort of the stove and a dish of food. David's hand traced its morning journey, and she turned towards him, clinging to him as she often did in a way that made him thrust deeper inside her, to claim her as she seemed to be claiming him.

★ ★ ★

The well trodden path from the bus stop was fringed with long dewy grass that brushed against her jeans, damply marking her strides. Someone slouched ahead of her, rucksack dangling from one shoulder, his body language declaring a complete lack of interest in the nine o'clock lecture. She held back, slowing her natural pace to match his, not frustrated enough to overtake him. He might speak to her. Better to walk at a snail's pace and arrive at the west door of the Arts Faculty building at least a minute behind. She hated small talk. It seemed so pointless. She didn't need to make any friends. David was enough.

She touched the golden locket, smooth and warmed now by her skin. She traced the filigreed twists with the tip of her finger, wondering what her father was doing now. The chain had been a gift when she left home to go to college. Tears had streamed down his face as he stood waving her off on the bus. She had waved back, embarrassed by him. He had never given her presents as a child, and she had opened the black velvet box on her breakfast plate with more curiosity than expectation.

"It's to remind you of home."

His brimming eyes had betrayed him then too, and she had looked away to give him time to collect himself before saying thank you and kissing his cheek. Right now he would probably still be sitting at the breakfast table. He had no reason to hurry. He had been made redundant from the bank when they closed the branch in Roscrea. Too young to stop working, too old to get another job. He couldn't face a move at his age, he said. He would keep the house nice for her to come back to at the weekends. He would do some gardening, maybe take up a new hobby to pass the time. The days would seem long, without her daily return from school. She had nodded, pretending empathy.

She checked her watch. There was time for a quick coffee before her tutorial. The refectory was humming. No one spoke to her, and she avoided making any eye contact. She had nothing in common with her fellow students. To them, reading lists were a foreign land. Essays were written at midnight with a bottle of beer perched on the table for company. Mornings were a blur. Evenings were for going to the student union bar or sitting on each other's beds, talking endlessly. She wondered what they talked about. At the end of every day she returned to the quiet haven of David's house in Greystones. After they had dinner together, she would work at his big scratched mahogany desk. Occasionally she would glance across to where he sat in the yellow glow of the standard lamp, reading student papers, or dozing with a newspaper. She could see his pink scalp through the wisps of his soft sandy-coloured hair. He would sense her gaze, and look up. There was warmth and love in his smile and his indigo eyes. Now that the weather was improving, they sometimes took a stroll in the mellow evening light, and she would inhale the damp air, full of spring promise. Yesterday she had seen among the dead leaves and loamy earth the delicate bell of a single white snowdrop. The tiny green shoot had pushed its way up out of the long darkness and now it was standing, mutely declaring the end of winter.

The noisy morning passed. Students stridently argued in the tutorial, then clattered down flights of stairs, joking, laughing about their exploits of the night before. They ignored her. She was different, and felt like she always had been. She spent a few hours after lunch in the library, relishing the peace. The most ebullient student wouldn't dare to cross the librarian, a stern man in his fifties who patrolled the silence with protuberant eyes. She scribbled untidy notes, the ideas for her essay flowing effortlessly. She felt an excitement she had never experienced before. She had merely served her sentence at school – putting in only the time and effort that it took to earn her passage to UCD. Now she was discovering a world of literature, the richness of which she had never dreamt. Every book she opened was a joy, and she could almost feel a physical expansion of her mind. David said she was one of the brightest students he had ever taught. She had waited behind to ask him a question after one of his early lectures, still not confident enough to speak in front of an auditorium full of her peers. He had considered her question and given her an explanation, looking into her eyes as he spoke. In his eyes she had found an echo of something familiar amidst the strangeness of her new life. He had asked her out for a drink. As they talked, sitting in a pub away up in the Dublin Mountains, far from the madding crowd, she had found an easy familiarity with him.

★   ★   ★

Tonight it had been her turn to cook. It was nice to alternate, after eight years of cooking every evening. Her father had never learned, even after her mother died. He would expect her phone call this evening. It was Wednesday. The middle of the week. On Friday he would meet her off the bus, kiss her and buy fish and chips on the way home, as a treat.

She and David were sitting at the table, plates with leftovers pushed to one side.

"Going to ring your dad?" David asked, lighting up a cigarette, the only one he allowed himself each day. He thought of himself as a man of great self-discipline. Order prevailed in every aspect of his life – his bookshelves, his CD's, his student files labelled and alphabetically organised.

He was never seen in her company on the campus. He had asked her not to talk about them to anyone else.

"It's no one else's business but ours, is it, darling?" he had said, after the first time they were together. He had stroked her hair and she had understood, just as she had when her father first came to visit her room at night.

She wondered what would happen if she didn't ring her father this evening. Would the strident ring of the old-fashioned telephone in the hall shatter the companionable silence? Would she answer, to hear him asking if his little princess was all right, in the soothing voice that calmed her after childhood nightmares?

"Maybe later," she murmured, and stood up to clear the table. David stubbed out the cigarette, holding and savouring the final inhalation. He nodded and moved across to the wing-backed chair beside the fire. Later he made love to her and then he turned away and slept while she lay staring at the sliver of moonlight on the ceiling. Was her father asleep too, snoring gently, or was he lying awake, fretfully wondering why she hadn't phoned? She felt oddly calm. Her dreams were haunted by the mermaids and sirens of her essay on female mythology. She had read about a mermaid stranded on the beach after losing her magic comb. The mermaid couldn't return to her ocean home without it. The comb had been hidden by a lonely little girl called Freya who wanted to keep the mermaid as her friend. The sea had roared and storms had lashed the shore, while the mermaid paced, in human form, searching for the comb that would release her to the waves. Finally, Freya had returned the precious talisman. The mermaid swam away, never to be seen again.

She shot awake, gasping for breath outside her drowning dream. The telephone was ringing. She stumbled downstairs, her pale body luminous in the moonlight, and sat on the stairs while a stranger told her that her father was dead.

★   ★   ★

The snowdrops were fading here, under the darkness of yew. Crocuses lay like strewn confetti on the fine green turf. The sandy gravel path did not crunch as she walked towards the dark, heavy door. She had asked David not to come. She wanted to say goodbye alone. Three or four other mourners were gathered outside. They nodded to her, customers of the bank driven by protocol rather than any particular empathy. She and her father had kept themselves to themselves. She passed through the door, her lips set in a straight line, and sat in the front pew. The service was short. She had given the priest no words for the eulogy. The pallbearers were provided by the funeral home. She followed the coffin, her hands clasped tightly. The locket lay glowing against the fabric of her new black dress.

At the graveside, the priest said words that seemed familiar although she didn't remember her mother's funeral. She was only nine. She had cried a lot. Now the priest was signalling the moment when she should throw a handful of soil onto the coffin. She reached up and lifted her hair from the nape of her neck, then unclasped the locket. It felt heavy in her hand as she paused for a moment. The chain curled warmly in her palm. A dull tinkle as it fell on the wood. An indrawn breath as a neighbour looked at her husband, eyebrow raised.

She turned away.

"Ella!"

The shout echoed in the silent moment that followed. She lifted her eyes. David was striding along the yellowish sandy path, waving something. She had forgotten to hide the letter. A postage stamp with a rampant red dragon on the creamy envelope. Her offer of a place at the University of Cardiff.

She was free.

ALSO BY SHARON MULROONEY, PUBLISHED BY POOLBEG

More To Life,
Matthew, Meet Matthew
Daddy's Girl

23

Costa Del Solo

ALISON NORRINGTON

My boyfriend, Toby, is having an affair with my best friend, Fiona.

They think I don't know, but I do.

They think I haven't noticed the way they try to keep a polite distance from each other whenever we're all out together.

But they'll realise that I know soon. Give it a day or two and they'll miss me.

Everybody will.

★   ★   ★

'*Sun, Sea and Sangria!*' it screamed, in curly swirly text. Aoife fiddled with her elastic-band ball, whilst gazing out of the office window.

Dublin was raining.

Again.

Blinking away more tears, she stared at the happy faces

on a holiday ad in the travel agent's window. Lobster-red people, photographed clustered on golden beaches. Aoife wondered whether they'd left behind a replacement temp at their offices in Cork, a relief postman covering their round in Leixlip, or a woman in Drumcondra with no idea her builder had taken his two weeks' holidays and would soon be appearing on travel posters all over Ireland.

"Aoife!" Ms Gregson, her boss, called from her office.

Her door was closed, which meant she was having another sneaky cigarette. She always called Aoife to check whether 'management' were on the prowl.

Aoife looked up, ignoring the mountain of paper littering her desk.

"Forget the sun and sea – pass me the sangria," she muttered, "Valium, sleeping pills – anything to numb this pain."

The betrayal stung and she couldn't think straight. Only a couple of hours ago Toby had slipped up, confirming the suspicions she'd tried to ignore and now she was either staring vacantly at nothing, or rushing into the toilets and blowing her brains into tissue paper as she sobbed uncontrollably, unsure who she hated more – Toby for being tempted by Fiona, or Fiona herself.

"I wouldn't mind," she told her elastic-band ball, "she's not even *that* attractive. Nice legs, and I'd never normally mention it, but vague halitosis on occasions."

"*Aoife*! In my office, now!"

Gregson's voice was like rusty nails in the bottom of a metal bucket and Aoife would have leapt out of her chair. But now, heavy and weighed down with disappointment and humiliation, her stomach churned at the memory of all those evenings spent with Fiona. She'd confided how Toby liked her to rub her bare feet up his trouser legs whenever they were out for a meal. Aoife imagined them laughing at her as she'd even gone on to explain how her corn plaster had once peeled off and stuck to the hairs on his leg. Fiona knew *everything*.

"And I was cocky as anything about it all," she sniffed at the scantily clad holidaymakers on the poster. "Fiona knows about the too-tight condom that rolled up and pinged off at high-speed, landing on the hotel-room lampshade. She knows about Toby's liking for baby oil and how he'd always wanted me to cover the mattress with cling film and for us both to roll around on the slippery oiled surface in the nod! I was simply feeding her material to seduce him! And she *knows* how badly I take rejection, how I *always* have to be the dumper and *never* the one-to-be-dumped."

She could no longer hear Gregson's yelling voice or the hopping telephones. She was strangely drawn to the 'Sun, Sea, Sangria' advert, but tried to dismiss it. It was a ludicrous idea.

"Aoife Kelly," Gregson hissed through the small crack in her door, "get your butt in here! *Now!*"

Aoife knew the routine. Gregson was afraid to emerge and let the cigarette smoke out, so Aoife had to go to her. As she rose from her chair, her phone rang and, irrationally, she turned to answer it, immediately regretting it.

It was her mother.

"Oh Aoife, *dear*. Any more news? Have you spoken to that pig, Toby?"

"He's not a pig, Mum," she whispered. She knew she was defending him. It was the teenager in her.

"He *is* a pig. So what are you going to do? And what about Fiona? It's surely a mistake. She's such a nice girl."

"Nice girl! Nice girl!" Her voice was getting louder, but she couldn't control it. "I'll give you nice girl! Did I ever tell you how she takes photos of her boobs on her mobile and Bluetooths them from her phone when we're out? Or how she's always said I should take off my Nanny McPhee shoes and jump straight into bed with Toby's gorgeous brother? Have I? Have I?"

"Aoife! Please!" her mother chided. "Anyone could be listening!"

And then it came out. The ad called her and before she knew it she was saying, "I just want to get away from them, Mum! I need to get away from here, from the humiliation. I'm – I'm – I'm going to Spain!"

"Aoife Kelly!" her mother barked. "Spain? Who with?"

She shrugged, still fourteen despite her thirty-four years. All she needed was badly applied black eyeliner and a few spots. She pouted. "I'll go alone if I have to."

To which her mother shrieked so loudly it caused Aoife to draw the handset away from the side of her head.

"You? Alone? You've never done *anything* alone! You can't even *eat* without company? You were a *teenager* before you'd go to the loo without me or your father coming up the stairs with you! You *always* make someone else go to the bar. You can't buy a pair of *knickers* without a full committee meeting! Aoife Kelly, I'm surprised you can even manage to *have sex* without a friend there beside you telling you you're doing the right thing! *Please!*"

And it was true.

It was then she realised, in a zoom-the-camera-in-close shot of clarity, that she had *never* been truly alone. She'd drifted from school boyfriend to new-office boyfriend in a virtually seamless string. With every job move or promotion, Aoife had traded in her current guy for a new one – always The Dumper.

Leaving her mum squawking into the phone, she turned and strode right into Gregson's office, blurting it out in another moment of madness, "Ms Gregson, I need to take three months off work. My boyfriend is shagging my best friend and I need to get away. Is there any chance you could keep my position open for me?"

Gregson looked as if she wanted to laugh, but managed to twist her lips into a thin straight line. "Three months? On what grounds, Aoife?"

"On health grounds," she plucked from deep within her too-many-hours-watching-*Oprah* archives. "Based on the fact that I need to find myself."

"Jesus, Aoife!" Gregson crowed, illegally sucking the last out of her cigarette and throwing the butt out of the open window. "You think any of us *know* who we are? No chance!"

Feeling the blood coursing through her head, the rushing in her ears as she heard her mother's wicked-witch-of-the-west cackle, impulse reigned as she blurted out:

"OK then. I quit."

★ ★ ★

The Costa del Sol. The home of sherry, flamenco and numerous clichés about Spain. Crammed with tourists in the summer and home to the idle rich with a huge ex-pat community. I look down at my legs and realise for the first time that they're nearly as white as the glaring Lego-brick houses with small black windows and nutmeg roofs that surround me. It had been a typically Irish summer and my ivory legs are proof of that. Sitting on the harbour wall, looking out at the luxury yachts bobbing happily in the marina, I'm a little light-headed. It's either the intense heat or hunger. It's all happened so quickly and I haven't eaten since the in-flight excuse-for-a-meal. I enjoyed my walk into the Old Town of Marbella – up Calle Huerta Chica and into Plaza de los Naranjos, and I'd sat outside a café, in the shade of the glossy orange trees.

The prospect of travelling alone was terrifying and I know, if I hadn't acted completely on impulse and booked the flight and apartment as pure knee-jerk reaction to Mum's comments, I'd still be bored at my desk at Cunning Stunts Modelling & Casting Agency in rainy Dublin. It's hard to believe that I'm really here, in the warm bath of mid-September sunshine.

Alone.

I've *never* been completely alone and I'm trying to be brave enough to insist that I've done the right thing. But Mum is right. I've never done anything without a general consensus.

By early afternoon I've made my way to the rich, sunlit streets of Puerto Banús. It's strange, walking alone, hundreds of miles away from Dublin and yet, a four-hour flight and my old life seems weeks away. I push my hands into the pockets of my six-summers-old shorts, the heat causing ripples before my eyes as the dire state of my 'holiday' wardrobe begins to dawn. I haven't been 'away' in five years. I've already had to discard my white shorts as they wouldn't go up past my knees and I nearly strained a ligament trying to pull them on. And my arms! My semolina skin is almost baulking with disgust at the relentless glare of sunshine. It's only a matter of time before I'll be harpooned. Jesus, I hadn't realised I'd put so much weight on! I look down at myself. My clothes look cheap. Back in Dublin I'd always manage an appreciative wink or a look or even a chat-up line here or there, but now, only a few hours away from home, I look ridiculous. Only a few weeks ago I'd delighted in telling Toby how the guy from Accounts had smarmed me with a 'I've lost my phone number, Aoife – can I borrow yours?'. Toby had laughed. It had annoyed me that he was never jealous. Now I know why. He's been with Fiona the whole time. I hate him. But I don't want to.

"He's like a bloody jackdaw," I inform my fingers as they fidget, yearning for the familiarity of a few elastic bands to shape and snap into a ball, "attracted to anything shiny. Like Fiona's tawdry shiny eyeshadow that highlights her crêpey lids."

A cockney voice makes me jump as I feel the heat of breath in my ear,

"First sign of madness, you know? Talking to your hands?"

I look up and, blinded by the dazzling sun, it looks like Peggy Mitchell standing before me, her hair a candyfloss blonde halo. I blink a few times and move my head so that the sun is behind her. It's either Peggy Mitchell from *EastEnders* or the old lady from *The Titanic* film, overly made-up. She's smiling at me, her pink lipstick smeared across her bleached teeth.

"You just got here?"

"Yeah," I smile, "how did you know?"

"How did I know?" she laughed. "Just look at your arms, white as a bloody polar bear you are. Irish?"

I nod.

"Mmm." She rubs her wrinkled hand – a huge brown raisin with long, pink fingernails jutting awkwardly –

267

along my white rectangle of shin. "You need high factor lotion for that lily-white skin. You'll burn before the day's out."

As she speaks I realise for the first time that I haven't given any thought to sun protection. I'd literally left work and headed straight for home where it had only taken me half an hour on the internet to find a cheap flight to Malaga and a decent apartment that was empty from September for three months. I'd cleared my bank account, leaving just enough to cover my half of the rent until Christmas, had scrawled a quick note to Jemma my flatmate and had quickly rung my parents, lingering in the moment that I told Mum I was going away for a while. *Alone.* I'm sure she thinks I've cracked.

Daydreaming, I realise that 'Peggy' is still rambling on about tourists glowing in the dark due to sunburn.

"C'mon," she says, clucking and fidgeting, "come on over to my bar. You could do with some company and it'll do you good to get out of this midday sun."

So I follow, the blonde leading the blonde, as we make our way across to a small wine bar. Its entrance is typically 'roses-around-the-door' – only they're bougainvilleas. It takes a few seconds for my eyes to adjust to the cool darkness of the bar after the bright, hot day but once they do I'm pleasantly surprised – air con, cool leather and dark wood.

"So? What's your poison?" she grins, turning and holding a tumbler up to the optics. I shake my head. "Just water, please."

As she slides in a Neil Sedaka CD for atmosphere, I notice the sign behind the bar:

'DRINK TRIPLE, SEE DOUBLE, ACT SINGLE'

– and it makes me smile as I realise that I've spent so many years relationship-hopping I've never really had the chance to act single. Before I realise it she's back, holding her glass aloft as she passes mine across.

"My name's Trudy. Cheers! And you are?"

"Aoife," I smile at her, "my name's Aoife. Cheers!"

Sipping at my water I watch as she sinks the entire glassful. I'm dying to ask her why she raised 'PhilunGrant' to be such a couple of thick-necked book-ends, or why they always call themselves 'the Michews', but before I can get my words out she's smacking her lips, and making an '*ahhh*' sound. She leans in on the bar and comes close.

"So, what's happened then, darlin'? How come you're on your own?"

Without warning, I burst into tears.

★ ★ ★

It feels better knowing that I've poured it all out. I've never understood why it's so much easier telling a complete stranger though.

I'm still blubbing a little when I say, "I had no idea he wasn't happy. I only just bought him sat-nav for his car." I begin to wail a little. "I wish it was only programmed for the North Pole! It's *never* been just *me*!"

She frowns, straining to make sense of my blurted, choked gabble.

"On the DART every morning . . . meet friends . . . travel together. It's a habit . . . terrified about being alone."

"Okay, love," Trudy pulls up a bar stool and sits behind her bar, opposite me, "let me tell you all about being alone. I moved here thirty years ago. Bet you can't even remember thirty years ago, can you?"

I shrug. "I was four."

"Thought as much. Thirty years ago life was different. Thirty years ago was the hottest summer for two hundred years. Concorde began taking passengers from London to Paris and Pan's People were flicking their legs about on *Top of the Pops*. Men wore tight pants, had long hair, big collars and women loved it. Thirty years ago I was about your age and I was married. Unhappily married."

I was rooted to the spot. This kind stranger was about to tell me her life story and I wanted to know it all.

"My husband was horrible to me. He fancied himself as a John Travolta type and was playing about all over London in his white suit. I stayed at home and pressed his big-collared shirts and polished his shoes, only for him to dress up and go missing again for the night. I was a wreck. He made me feel ugly and fat and unlovable. I was on those appetite depressants for months!"

"They're called appetite *suppressants*," I offer.

"Yeah," she smiles warmly, "whatever. And then one Christmas I'd just had enough. We were at a works 'do' and some slimy fella came over and asked me for a kiss under the mistletoe. Well, I laughed it off. I had to. I knew that George would have gone bananas. 'Kiss him under the mistletoe?' I'd said to George after, 'I wouldn't kiss him under anaesthetic!' But George didn't believe me. Beat me into next week, he did. I was used to it and spent years blaming myself for making him lose his temper. It was always *my* fault. If only I hadn't made fun of his cousin, or if only I'd been more understanding when he talked about his hard day, or his difficult childhood, or whatever the hell was bugging him at the time. It took me a long time to pluck up the courage, but eventually I realised. I had to leave him. Terrified of being on my own I was, but what was the option? Stick with him and spend the rest of my life hiding my bruises? No way. But it was hard. Very, very hard."

"So what did you do?"

"I was lucky, darlin'. We had money. There's thousands of women who can't get out of it that easily. I took his money and I moved out here and bought this little bar."

"So you've been here for thirty years?"

"Yep. Thirty years this Christmas."

"So what happened then?" I feel like a child at story-time in the library. Here I was, feeling sorry for myself and Trudy was putting my life into perspective.

"Nothing really. Nothing and everything! I changed my life."

"Weren't you afraid of being alone?"

"'Course I was, darling! I was at first, but you soon get used to it. And Christmas took on a whole new meaning. Christmas shopping? Let's be honest! I'd rather be buying presents for myself! And George? Well, we're all older – I know the sun has damaged *my* skin. But I don't buy in to that anti-wrinkle-cream crap. When they start trying that stuff out on testicles I'll start to take notice. If they can get the wrinkles out of *them* then I'll buy it! But you should see George now. Sixty-odd with a comb-over hairdo like a pedal-bin lid! God moves in mysterious ways eh?"

★ ★ ★

I lie in a cool bath back in my apartment. Trudy insisted that I share a bottle of wine with her and so we'd sat and talked about being alone, over a couple of bottles of Pinot Grigio and a bowl of olives. Trudy reckons that wine is adult fruit juice, meant to be shared, and I love her relaxed and wizened look on life. In anger, humiliation and desperation I booked this solo trip to the Costa del Sol. I was dreading feeling like the sore thumb, sticking out from the Noah's Ark of couples, doing it 'two-by-two', but after talking to Trudy I feel free. The cool water laps around my parched and clammy skin as I rest my head back in this strange bathtub, as I watch a huge mosquito walk across the wooden loft hatch-door. I wonder at what the next few weeks will hold? No doubt I'll have moments where I'm swamped with the couples that surround me. Of course it'll feel odd going into a restaurant and asking for a table for *one*. But I'm sure I'll get used to it. Trudy says her son, Aaron, owns two of the large yachts in the marina, but she says not to get too caught up in the grandeur of it all. Once you scratch the surface "It's more Albert Square than Times Square," she says – ironically, considering she looks so like Peggy. She's already suggesting that I make friends with Aaron. But I'm not sure. Perhaps it's better if I keep a slight distance for now. Maybe I will check out his boat, but I want to make the best of this Costa del Solo. I need to get to know Aoife Kelly again.

And there'll always be plenty more fish in the sea . . .

ALSO BY ALISON NORRINGTON, PUBLISHED BY POOLBEG

Three of a Kind, Class Act
Look Before You Leap

24

The Spa
ANNA O'MALLEY

"You should go."

Maddie Callaghan gave a derisive snort, then chucked the invitation on the kitchen counter. "I don't think so."

Simon wasn't to be put off. "Why not? You might even enjoy it."

"*Enjoy*? A class reunion? A room full of high achievers still sneering after fifteen years? I don't think so," she repeated as she savagely smeared peanut butter on a slice of bread.

"Go on. It'll be a blast," her husband persisted. "I had a ball at mine as I remember it."

"As *I* remember it, you crawled home at four in the morning, one eyebrow shaved off, had a hangover for Ireland, and whinged that you were getting a brain tumour for a good three days after the event!" She waved the peanut-butter-encrusted knife at him. "Do you want an orange or an apple, Milo? Katy, eat up your Coco Pops, or you'll be late for school."

Milo, who was playing with his Game Boy, either didn't hear her, or chose not to answer. He was going through a feigning-deafness phase which was driving Maddie crazy.

"Orange or apple, Milo?" she repeated ten decibels up the scale, then when she still got no reaction, reached over and swiped the Game Boy out of the seven-year-old's hands and switched it off. "No Game Boys at the table. Orange or apple?"

"Ah Mu-uum! I just got to Level Five!"

Simon ruffled his second son's hair. "*Five*? Good on you, son!" Then he looked up at Maddie. "Exactly my point. I had great *craic*, and so will you."

Giving up on Milo, Maddie tossed an orange into his lunch box along with the peanut-butter sandwich and a carton of liquid tooth-rot. "No, I won't, because I'm not going."

A rapid thump, thump thumping down the stairs followed by an eerie silence put an end to the discussion as Maddie and Simon, closely followed by Milo, rushed out to the hall to find Jesse sitting in a banana box up against the side of the hallstand. He appeared to be unscathed.

"Did you just come down the stairs in that box?" Simon asked, disbelief tingeing the statement.

Jesse nodded, not sure if he was in trouble.

Maddie and Simon exchanged bemused glances, then Simon said, "Show me."

Jesse, eight and a half and a serious but thoroughly good-natured child, obliged, dragging the banana box up to the top of the stairs, sitting in it and pushing himself off. He clattered down the stairs once more, this time deftly steering past the hallstand and ending up on the doormat.

"Cool!" Milo gasped, seriously impressed.

"You're not to do that again, Jesse," Simon said, attempting a different kind of serious. "You could hurt yourself."

Jesse looked crestfallen. "Aaah ..."

Fighting the urge to laugh, Maddie backed him up. "Your dad's right, Jess. It's too dangerous."

Katy was still playing with her Coco Pops when they all returned to the kitchen. She was a picky eater, her daily intake of food consisting of half a dozen Coco Pops, a slice of toast, a Cheese String and a couple of olives, if they were lucky. Thankfully she still insisted on taking a bottle of milk to bed with her, which Maddie didn't discourage as at least it was some form of nourishment.

"So will you go?" Simon asked again, as he was leaving for work.

"Oh, let me see," Maddie replied, then after a theatrical pause, continued, "Oh drat! I just remembered I have to push hot needles into my eyeballs that weekend."

Simon was dropping the kids off at school as he didn't have an early meeting, so after they all left, Maddie made a fresh pot of tea. The invitation was still sitting on the counter, the corner smudged with a dollop of peanut butter.

Unlike Simon's do the previous year, a hastily thrown-together haphazard event, the invite to the Sancta Maria College Reunion looked very classy. Cream deckle-edged card with a small printed RSVP slip.

You are invited to the Heather Springs Spa for a reunion of the class of '89.

There was a very formal covering letter which stated

that the reunion was to take place over a weekend. Friday night to Sunday. A welcome buffet and drinks on the Friday night followed by a day at the spa. Tickets cost €350 which covered the two nights' accommodation with breakfasts, a light lunch and dinner on the Saturday, and one spa treatment.

How very appropriate, she thought.

The letter was signed: *Davina Hughes-Livingstone, Past Pupil's Committee Chairperson.*

Reaching for the phone, Maddie dialled and when she heard the familiar voice at the other end of the line said, without preamble, "Davina Hughes got herself a hyphen."

"No better woman," Phoebe said. "You got one too then. Are you going?"

"Hot needles."

"Oh, I don't know. A spa weekend? I quite fancy it myself."

"Three hundred and fifty euro I haven't got for the dubious pleasure of spending time with a bunch of people who made my life a fecking misery?"

"Oh, come on!" Phoebe said, sounding a touch miffed. "Hardly a misery. We had fun, didn't we?"

"Well, *we* did," Maddie back-pedalled. "But being a social pariah has left me psychologically scarred."

Phoebe laughed. "Feck off! What happened to 'Dyslexic Goths Rule KO'?"

"I'm just not sure I could face it. They're all so fecking competitive. Anyway, we could get together any time."

"But we don't." Phoebe said. "This is a perfect opportunity to get some chill-out time together. No kids. No husbands, and anyway, I dare say the other crowd won't even remember us. We can ignore them, enjoy the food and the treatments and chill for a couple of days.

What's wrong with that?"

Maddie paused for a moment, caught on the hop. She'd never expected that Phoebe would actually be up for the Weekend from Hell, but she did have a point.

"But I've nothing to wear," she bleated, looking down at her rounded stomach. "And I'm fat!"

"You're not fat. You're five months pregnant," Phoebe reminded her. "What did Simon say?"

"He's all for me going. The man's a sadist."

"There you are then. Promise me you'll come, otherwise I might have to share with Davina the Dreadful."

After she had hung up the phone with a vague promise that she'd think about it, Maddie poured herself a cup of tea then rummaged in the drawer for the Rennies. It was the heartburn that had finally made her give in and go out to buy the pregnancy-test kit. She'd been in serious denial despite the two missed periods; the prospect of another baby, just when she'd thought she was home free with Katy starting school, had left her depressed. It wasn't so much the baby as the pregnancy. She hated being pregnant, hated what it did to her body. She felt fat and unattractive and right up to the birth of all three of her children had felt as if she'd been taken over by some alien being, suffering recurring nightmares involving Sigourney Weaver. Katy's pregnancy had been particularly horrendous with terminal heartburn and projectile puking 24/7. Then there were the swollen ankles. Although by no stretch of the imagination could Maddie be considered vain, she was extremely proud of her good legs, inherited from her mother's side of the family, and was horrified when pregnancy caused them to melt downwards, settling in a puffy mass around her ankles.

Stretching out her legs she examined her feet. Ankles

only slightly puffy as yet, but it was early days. I bet Davina bloody Hughes-Livingstone doesn't get swollen ankles, she thought. Or Lorraine Hennessey.

Lorraine Hennessy. Prefect, Head Girl. Captain of the basketball team, now a TV journalist anchoring the *Nine O'Clock News*, totally professional, not a hair out of place. Lorraine had always been extremely bossy and had a scathing turn of phrase, her ire usually directed at Maddie and Phoebe or anybody else not in the golden circle. *VIP* magazine had done a spread showing her *'lovely Sandymount home'* with a smiling Lorraine sitting in her 'landscaped garden' in jeans and pristine white T-shirt, looking *fabulous, dahling*. Maddie was wearing jeans and white T-shirt too, but there wasn't a non-bio detergent made that could take the blue sticky-sweet stains out. God, she thought, I'd even fail the sodding *Daz Doorstep Challenge*! How sad it that?

Maddie and Phoebe had both fancied themselves as rebels at school, but their rebellion was pretty tame. Teenage angst, a lot of sighing and, when the rest of their classmates were going to discos in girly gear, they opted for the Goth look and high-top Docs. It was a great disappointment to her when her mother admired the inky-black dye-job on her hair, complimented her on her Goth make-up, and hadn't even objected when she'd briefly attempted smoking, but then her mother had been a child of the sixties, had flirted with hippydom and rather liked the black clobber and stylised make-up. Also, having been something of a rebel in the small rural community in which she had grown up, she empathised with her daughter and was quietly pleased that she refused to conform.

Maddie had met Simon at work. She was a junior art director at a small advertising agency, Trollop & Co, and he was an account executive. They'd hit it off straight away, sharing the same sense of humour. A further plus, and probably the clincher, was the fact that they both liked Billy Bragg, had all his CD's, and their first date had been a Billy Bragg gig at the Stadium. Simon was her first serious relationship and she his, and almost from the start Maddie couldn't imagine spending her life with anyone but him, which surprised her as she'd never in her wildest dreams imagined she'd meet a man she'd want to spend ten days with, let alone a lifetime. She'd fallen pregnant with Jesse and they got married. Not because there was any pressure from the families, but because they wanted to. Milo was born a year and a half after Jesse, and Katy followed just as Milo started playschool. Apart from the gruelling pregnancy, Katy had been a cranky baby with colic, dairy intolerance and an aversion to sleep. With the two boys to care for and Simon working long hours, it was an arduous three years, then suddenly everything seemed to clear up at once. During the preceding dark sleepless nights though, while she'd paced the floor with Katy wailing inconsolably, she had fantasised about a life after babies.

Her career in advertising had been cut short, and she realised that it would be virtually impossible to pick up where she had left off, but nonetheless she was determined to do something. The question was, what? Simon was supportive but of little help, unable to come up with any suggestions. Phoebe, on the other hand, who also had three children very close in age to Maddie's, could understand exactly where she was coming from. Phoebe had always been in a better position, having trained as a primary school teacher, so childbearing and childcare had caused the minimum disruption to her career – to her life in general. It was she who suggested the Fine Art course. It appealed to Maddie because, apart from her obvious interest in all things artistic, she had gone the graphics route and, although she painted when she had the time, the energy and the inclination, the prospect of studying techniques and art history was very appealing. Truth be told, she wanted a project. Something to get her teeth into and most of all she wanted to prove to herself that she could do it. Jokingly Simon called her a 'housewife savante' and, although she had laughed, she felt it was an apt description. Outside of changing nappies, wiping snotty noses, making peanut-butter sandwiches and ferrying her three offspring to their various after-school activities, she had little time for much else in her life. Scary too to realise that she knew all the words of the Bob the Builder song and could name all the Teletubbies.

The downturn in the economy meant that Simon was working horrendous hours, fighting to keep the agency afloat, so they rarely got out together. Ironic that with sex so thin on the ground, the one time they had managed to get it together in three months she'd got up the duff so to speak.

But now with the prospect of at least another four years before she had the time for herself, her Fine Art course was out of the question.

"Not necessarily," Phoebe said. "So you can't do it this year, but next year you could — at a push."

"It's too hard," Maddie protested. "How could I manage it with a toddler? I'm stuffed."

"Oh, don't be such a drama queen!" Phoebe had chided. "It's only two days a week. Where there's a will —"

"There's a relative," Maddie cut in and that was the end of that conversation.

Despite her best efforts to avoid it, she was no match for Phoebe and Simon when in conspiracy mode, and she found herself *en route* for Heather Springs Spa with Phoebe on the last Friday in September. Milo had just got over the chickenpox a touch too quickly for her purposes, and Jesse and Katy were showing not a sign of a spot so there was no excuse. Milo's illness however had banjaxed any chance of a haircut or leg-wax and she'd had to make do with a home hair colour and stealthy use of Simon's razor. Phoebe had come up trumps though, having purloined a gorgeous Lainie Keogh number for her to wear from her sister who was a size sixteen. She'd been dubious at first when she'd seen the shapeless-looking knitted garment until she'd slipped it over her head. Despite her reservations, the cut was perfect, the effect stunning and it complemented her neat basketball bump. Also, because it was long, it hid her rapidly disappearing ankles.

"There, you see," Phoebe said with the smugness of the righteous.

To which Maddie muttered ungraciously, "One Lainie Keogh doth not a weekend make."

Heather Springs Spa was a large Georgian pile set in parkland. Phoebe remembered it in a previous incarnation as a hotel, having attended a wedding there some ten years previously. There was no one about when they walked into Reception.

"Wow! They've spruced this place up," she commented. "Pity though. I kind of liked the faded elegance look."

"That's me. Faded elegance," Maddie muttered, catching sight of herself in a long gilded mirror. He face was flushed and shiny and her hair flat to her head.

The receptionist checked them in, giving them their room key, and directed the porter to show them to the room. He picked up their bags and they followed him up the magnificent staircase. The rooms had no numbers, just names such as Beech, Oak and Maple which was a tad confusing for Maddie who had no sense of direction. The porter told them something of the history of the house as he led them by a circuitous route to their allocated room. Apparently the house had been owned by the first Lord Somebody-or-Other who lost it in a poker game in the mid-1800's to Lord Somebody-or-Other-Else, and Daniel O'Connell had slept there once. Phoebe misheard and muttered a sarcastic "Hurrah!", assuming he meant Daniel O'Donnell. The room, Willow, was pretty if a touch Laura Ashley. Two wide single beds, a moderate bathroom, TV etc.

Maddie threw herself on the bed. "Oh the luxury of sleeping alone for a change!"

Phoebe picked up the welcome pack and flicked through it. "There, you see, I told you you'd be glad you came."

Maddie got off the bed and wandered over to the window. Their room was at the front of the building two floors up. A red Audi TT had just drawn up and, as she watched, Lorraine Hennessy got out, went round to the boot and took out a Louis Vuitton suitcase. She was wearing jeans and a fitted white shirt, with a camel sweater tied loosely around her shoulders. It was a look Maddie could never manage to carry off. It was the same with scarves and shawls. When she attempted to do anything with a shawl, scarf or sweater the result was always more Armenian refugee than Victoria Beckham.

"It says here they do those seaweed wraps," Phoebe

said. "I've always fancied one of those. It's supposed to get rid of all the toxins."

"Speaking of toxins, Lorraine Hennessy's here," Maddie said.

Phoebe hurried to join her at the window and, as they watched, a round woman dressed entirely in deep purple descended the steps to meet Lorraine. There was a perfunctory hug and they both headed up the steps and out of sight.

"I wonder who that was?" Phoebe said.

"Tinky Winky," Maddie said, feeling instantly thinner.

They both enjoyed a swim in the pool, a spell in the Jacuzzi and a leisurely shower afterwards, so the Welcome buffet was well under way by the time they ventured back downstairs to the small drawing room. It was an impressive oak-panelled room. High ceilings and a stunning marble fireplace which was big enough to roast an ox in. Maddie couldn't see Lorraine Hennessy but there were a number of familiar faces amongst the crowd of around thirty – Marian Dwyer, Molly McEvoy, Sandra O'Rourke to name but three. They were standing in a group at the buffet table talking and surveying the food. Marian too was pregnant, almost ready to pop by the look of her, which was a comfort, and compared to Tinky Winky, who was shovelling food onto a plate at the other end of the table they both looked positively sylph-like.

"It's Davina," Phoebe hissed.

"What?"

"Tinky Winky," Phoebe said.

"You're kidding." Although Davina had always been what Maddie's mother termed hefty, she had ballooned out in the intervening years and her hair was painfully thin, styled in a sort of long comb-over.

"Hi."

They both looked round. Marian Dwyer was standing close by now, and noticing that their gaze was firmly on Davina whispered, "Poor Davina. Steroids, you know. Brain tumour, benign but inoperable, so she's been on medication and radiation."

Major guilt trip. Maddie glanced at Phoebe who looked fairly humbled too.

"That's awful!" Maddie said. "Is she going to be okay?"

Marian shrugged. "Hopefully. I know she was always on the big side but the rotten steroids have blown her up like a balloon. And her hair. Did you notice her hair? It's falling out in lumps." She glanced down at Maddie's bump. "When are you due?"

Glad of the change of subject, Maddie said, "Oh, the twenty-fourth of December, can you believe? Hospital food at Christmas."

"More like induced the day before Christmas Eve," Marian said. "I'm down for an elective section in three weeks. It's not that I'm too posh to push, but my kids are apt to have enormous heads."

"Oh. How many have you?" Maddie asked, interested. Marian had never struck her as the maternal type. Far too ambitious. Got Law at Trinity and was determined to become a barrister.

"Six, and this one," she said pointing at her sizeable abdomen. "Two sets of twins already. How about yourselves?"

"Oh, Maddie's only on number four," Phoebe said. "And I've got a measly three."

"My God!" Marian said. "I'd never have had you two down as Earth Mothers. I mean you were both so Bohemian."

Maddie laughed. "Bohemian?"

"Well, yes. I had you down for artists, or perhaps political activist urban guerrilla types. I never thought you'd settle down."

Maddie was tickled to death. *Urban guerrillas?* And odds on she was serious. The Marian Dwyer she had known and scorned was well known for her irony bypass. "Funny you should say that. I thought you'd be a judge by now or at least a Senior Council."

"Well, actually, I'll be taking Silk next year," Marian said. "And what are you up to yourself these days? Didn't you work at something arty?"

"Advertising," Maddie said.

"Oh, yes. Still at it?"

"Well, actually no. I'm a housewife savante now."

Marian looked flummoxed. "A what?"

"Housewife savante," Maddie repeated. "Oh . . . must have a word with somebody over there!" Grabbing Phoebe's arm, she dragged her away, then when they were out of Marian's earshot, muttered, "How do other women do it? She's got almost seven kids, for feck sake, and she's heading to be a sodding Senior Council!"

"And probably has a full-time live-in nanny and never sees her kids or her old man," Phoebe said.

"Well, judging by the state of her they meet up occasionally. My God!" she uttered with feeling, closing her eyes. "How I'd love a full-time nanny!"

"No, you wouldn't."

"OK, so I wouldn't like a full-time nanny, but I wish ... well, I just wish I could say I'd achieved something."

"But you have," Phoebe said. "You've three and a half gorgeous happy kids."

Maddie glared at her. Abruptly livid, she felt the rush

of a hormonal blub coming on. "Have you any idea how patronising that sounds," she said, tears spilling down her cheeks, then turned and strode purposefully towards the door.

Phoebe hurried after her. "I didn't mean it like that …don't be so bloody precious! Where are you going?

Maddie kept walking. "I have to pee."

After she had run her wrists under the cold tap and splashed her face with cold water she felt better, and the need to cry for no good reason subsided. What was left of her make-up however had disappeared down the plughole and her face was red and shiny again, with black smudges where her mascara had run. She felt bad about biting Phoebe's head off, but she knew that her friend was well used to her heightened sensitivity during pregnancy, so wouldn't take it to heart. There was nothing for it but to go back to the room to repair the damage. Whatever about being *just* a housewife, she had no intention of letting Marian or any of the other members of the super-achievers clique see her looking blotchy to boot.

She was fine nipping up the grand staircase, but after a couple of left and right turns she found herself hopelessly lost and rued the fact that she hadn't had the foresight to leave a trail of crumbs, and that the poncey hotel couldn't use room numbers like everyone else. After passing Maple for the second time she turned a corner and bumped straight into Lorraine Hennessy, who was standing in the middle of the corridor fumbling with her bag.

There was a mutual *oops* and *sorry*, but then Lorraine, noticing her red sooty eyes and blotchy complexion frowned and said, "Are you okay?" She sounded genuinely concerned. "Good grief! Maddie, isn't it? Maddie Egan."

Maddie nodded. "Yes. How are you, Lorraine?"

"More to the point, how are you?"

Maddie self-consciously rubbed at the smudged mascara. "Oh just a touch of hormones. Cry at the drop of a hat these days."

Lorraine rummaged in her bag, a scrumptious soft olive-green suede satchel, and produced a make-up wipe and a small compact mirror. "Here. Try this."

Maddie took the proffered wipe and sat down on the bottom step of a short flight of stairs.

Lorraine watched her as she fixed the damage. "You look great, by the way," she said. "Despite the panda eyes."

Maddie stopped what she was doing and snapped, "Okay, so the real Lorraine Hennessy's been abducted by aliens, right?" She was in no mood to be patronised yet again.

Lorraine visibly winced, then sat down on the stair next to her. "I was a bit of a cow, wasn't I?"

Expecting her to revert to her normal scathing self, this wasn't the reply Maddie had expected. "Um, well … yes, I suppose you were," she said lamely. "You and the rest of the alpha crowd."

Lorraine threw back her head and laughed. "Alpha crowd?"

Maddie snorted. "Like you don't know. You and the rest of the super-achievers. You were horrid to us nobodies."

Lorraine just nodded in agreement, which was a trifle unsettling. Between bitter memories and Marian bloody Dwyer looking down her nose, Maddie was up for a fight, and Lorraine wasn't cooperating.

"You made our lives a misery at every opportunity."

"Only because I was jealous," Lorraine muttered. "I wanted to be like you."

"Oh, piss off!"

"No, really. I was so jealous of you and Phoebe. You were so out there, so 'I don't give a toss!'."

"So what stopped you joining our gang of freaks?" Maddie snarled, well into her stride. "I believe that was the tag you stuck us with. *Freaks?*"

Lorraine winced again. "Ouch!"

Maddie stood up. "And just in case you were wondering. No, I don't have a high-powered job, I don't work outside the home, I have three kids to look after, and this one on the way. And yes, I'd like to have done something with my life. I'd love to have some fuck-off career and do the cover of *VI-sodding-P*, but it didn't pan out. Okay? Happy?"

Lorraine looked up at her and suddenly her face crumpled and she burst into tears. Maddie was appalled. Appalled and embarrassed, and worst of all she had no idea what to do. Lorraine was sobbing now inconsolably, her shoulders shaking, all tears and snot, the whole big banana. Maddie stood by impotently for a few moments more, then sat down beside her again and put a tentative arm around her shoulder.

"Shit! I'm sorry, Lorraine. That was really mean. It was all ages ago. We were kids. I'd no right to be so fecking childish. I'm sorry."

But that just set Lorraine off again on great shuddering throaty sobs. Maddie opened her bag and pulled out a six-foot length of loo tissue she'd torn off the roll and handed it to her. "Here."

Lorraine took it without looking at her, wiped her eyes then blew her nose. "I'm sorry," she snuffled. "I've had a pig of a day."

That made Maddie feel even worse. "No, *I'm* sorry," she repeated. "Please don't cry. I've never made anyone cry in my life."

"Unlike me," Lorraine said before giving her nose another hearty honk.

"Look, that was ages ago. Done with," Maddie said, mortally embarrassed and hoping no one would stumble upon them. "Forget it."

Lorraine gave her a feeble smile. Panda eyes were obviously catching. Maddie used her crumpled make-up wipe to rub away Lorraine's mascara.

"There. That's better."

"Thanks." Lorraine sniffed and after a pause said, "You know, I meant it when I said I wanted to be like you and Phoebe."

Maddie still didn't believe her but had no intention of saying so for fear of another crying jag.

Lorraine looked at her. "Really. I'd have loved to rebel, but my parents had such high expectations, and to be honest I didn't have the guts." She paused again, then looked down at the carpet. "At least not in the way you did." She gave a bitter laugh. "You know what my shrink says?"

"You have a shrink?"

Lorraine nodded. "Oh yes. He reckons I was a bully at school because I felt so powerless at home, but then I'd so bloody much to live up to. My three elder brothers did medicine, you know. Patrick was a Consultant Orthopod by the time he was thirty. My dad was determined I'd follow in his footsteps and do medicine too, but I'd no interest. I always wanted to be a journalist."

"Well, you did that," Maddie said. "You rebelled in

your own way."

Lorraine nodded. "Be careful what you wish for."

"But you like your job. You're really successful," Maddie said.

"You see, that's the problem. I had to be the best, and it still wasn't good enough for them. My shrink says that's why I'm so driven."

"But you got what you wanted in the end," Maddie reminded her. "I'd give my right arm to have achieved as much as you."

"And I'd give my right arm and both my legs to have a gang of kids and a family who don't think I'm an embarrassment."

"So what's stopping you?"

Lorraine gave a bitter chortle. "Surprise, surprise, I'm not good at relationships, so other than a sperm donor, my options are very limited. My shrink says I'm … how was it he put it? Sublimating."

"Sorry?"

"I think he means I'm angry with my father and I'm taking it out on any man who comes into my life. Not much chance of me hooking a husband and having a clutch of sprogs then, is there, if they're all fecking scared of me?" She stood up and ran her fingers through her hair. "Seems to me you've got it all sewn up. You've always had the knack of achieving anything you set your mind to."

They went downstairs together after Lorraine had repaired her make-up. Maddie didn't bother. Suddenly she was feeling better about herself. Grateful for her parents, for Simon, for the kids, for her unremarkable but fulfilled life. And at least she'd never needed a shrink. It just goes to show, she thought.

Phoebe's face was a picture when she spotted the two of them walking in, linking arms. Joanne Porter came over to talk to Lorraine, so Maddie left them to it and wandered back to join Phoebe.

"What was that about?" Phoebe asked, still gobsmacked. "You and Lorraine the Evil One?"

"Oh, she's not so bad," Maddie said. "Listen, I was thinking, about that Fine Art course . . ."

ALSO BY ANNA O'MALLEY, PUBLISHED BY POOLBEG

Redeeming Hope, I'm Sorry

25

Hunky-Dory
GERALDINE O'NEILL

The last track on the UB40 album halted, highlighting the squeaks from the Sky Glider machine and the panting and groaning from the two women. They continued to exercise for a few more moments then came to a halt, breathless and laughing as they looked across Kate's sitting room at each other.

"What are we like?" Kate giggled. "*Desperate Housewives* or what?"

"God, I'm nearly killed!" Paula said, extricating herself from the 'Ab-Strengthener'. "I won't be able to move in the morning."

Kate started bending each leg up towards her chest, in a vague cooling-down ritual. "You should fit into that interview suit easily now, no problem." She gave a few deep breaths. "Has Frank noticed any difference yet?"

"You must be joking," Paula said, rolling her eyes. "He wouldn't notice if I walked up the main street naked with a flower up my nose or anywhere else." She fleetingly thought of copying Kate's cooling-down movements, but moved across the room and flopped into an armchair instead.

Kate was twisting sideways now. "He *must* have noticed. You've lost nearly a stone. Surely he must feel the difference when you're in bed?"

"He doesn't take the time to notice anything about me when he's in the mood," Paula commented wryly, "which is rarely these days. It's as quick as he can get it over and done with."

Kate lifted her training mat from the floor and rolled it up. "Joe was like that before he left, then suddenly it stopped altogether. I knew there was something going on then. I knew he must be getting it somewhere else."

"Do you miss him?" Paula asked.

"Not a bit," Kate replied airily. "Good riddance to bad rubbish! I wish he'd gone long ago. I can do what I like without having him criticising me, and I don't have him mucking up the place any more." She waved her hand around the tidy room. "He had it like a kip with his CDs and books all over the place. Everything is more organised with him gone." She smiled now. "I've more important things on my mind than missing Joe. If I could just pass my driving test, everything would be hunky-dory."

"And if I could get this new job," Paula said, "everything in *my* life would be hunky-dory too. And if things work out with you childminding Ella, we'd *both* be hunky-dory." She checked her watch now. "Jesus, I'd better run or I'll be late for picking her up."

"Don't forget about your hair," Kate reminded her as she went flying towards the door. "You need to do something with it for the interview." She loosened her own long blonde hair out of her ponytail now.

"Cut and coloured?" Paula said, pausing on the doorstep.

"A shorter cut will make you look more professional."

Paula rolled her eyes. "The last time I had it cut Frank said it made me look like a fella."

"Never mind Frank," Kate laughed. "It's the job you're after, not his approval. It'll soon grow back."

★   ★   ★

Kate made a cup of coffee, came back into the sitting room and put on a CD of classical music. Then she picked up her notebook.

She drew two columns on her page. One for pluses and one for minuses. The first plus was the hundred euros a week, cash in hand, that Paula would pay her having Ella for breakfast and then taking her to school and collecting her, then looking after her until Paula finished work. Mind you, she would certainly earn it looking after that spoiled young brat. But a few days of a new, firmer regime would soon put manners on her.

Kate bit her lip. Did she really want the disruption to her nice daily routine? Did she need the money enough? A picture of the new car she wanted flashed into her mind – in a bright yellow or red that would catch Joe's eye when she glided past him in town. An excited tingle ran through her. She just couldn't wait to see his face. Paula's money would pay for the car and membership to a gym – definitely a huge plus.

Another negative was that she would have to be up and out earlier. But, she reminded herself, she would have the mile walk to school and back which would keep her fit and speed up the weight loss.

She smiled. Paula wouldn't have time for walking and exercising if she was sitting in an office all day. All the sitting around would probably make her backside even bigger. It was amazing that however much weight Paula lost, she never seemed to lose it from there. Kate had read articles about weight lodging in particular areas – usually hips and bum – and how you should target them with specific exercises. But there was no point in telling Paula about them. She always knew better. And if she did take the advice on board and slimmed down her bum, she would probably be insufferable.

Paula was okay as far as friends went, but she could be a pain in the arse with her one-upmanship.

Kate could use her new routine to get a few steps ahead herself. With a trimmer figure from the school walk and a spanking new car, there would be no holding her.

★   ★   ★

Paula scrutinised herself in the wardrobe mirror. The suit fitted great and her hair looked tidier – although shorter than she liked.

The hairdresser had put a brown base colour then added a few coppery lowlights. He blew it dry then fluffed out all the feathery strands around her face and neck. When Paula looked in the mirror she felt that a poor-man's version of Sharon Osborne (before the facelift and the new bob) was staring back at her. But – it was worth it if she got the job.

She came downstairs and headed for the desk drawer that contained a packet of cigarettes. "No!" she said aloud to herself. "I'm not starting back again … I can't afford it."

She walked over to the window and stood, arms folded, looking out. What if she didn't get the job? All that money wasted and nothing to show for it.

Frank will go mad, she thought. *Let him!* a little voice replied. *He goes mad about everything anyway. It was my money. I worked hard for it, so he can just bugger off.*

The thing was, she didn't even want to go back to work.

She was quite happy being at home until she discovered how desperate their finances were. Until Frank showed her the bank statement and then the credit card statement. The next morning she booked her computer course. It was lucky she hadn't touched her Children's Allowance or she wouldn't have been able to pay for the course.

Last night she'd tried to cheer Frank up. "If I get the job," she'd explained, "a few weeks' wages will cover the computer course."

All he could say was, "Don't kid yourself, Paula. Nobody wants to employ a thirty-odd-year-old woman who hasn't worked for a few years. They'll be looking for somebody nearer twenty who's fresh out of college. That's what I'd look for if I was looking for a secretary."

Paula hadn't trusted herself to speak.

Then for a finish he had said: "What about Ella? Who's going to look after her, while you're swanning off to work? What about the summer holidays? I won't allow her to become one of those latch-key kids that get up to all sorts of nonsense."

Paula put her head in her hands now, thinking about the £3,000 credit card bill and the sky-high overdraft. *I have to get this job or we're sunk,* she thought. *And Ella will be fine with Kate.*

Thank God for Kate — she's the best friend anyone could have.

★ ★ ★

Kate put the patchwork quilt she was sewing on the sofa and rushed to answer the door.

"I got it! I actually got the job!" Paula whooped, brandishing a Marks & Spencer's carrier bag. "And to hell with the calories! We're celebrating with Cava and carrot cake and handmade chocolates."

A short while later they were sitting opposite each other clinking glasses and working out time schedules for the next few weeks.

"What did Frank say?" Kate asked. "Was he delighted for you?"

Paula topped up their glasses. "I'd never do anything if I waited on Frank to be delighted."

Kate held up her glass. "The best of luck with the new job."

"If you weren't looking after Ella, I wouldn't be doing this."

Kate picked another chocolate. "You know, there are people who live like this all the time — drinking champagne and eating chocolates."

"You mean fat, greedy women?" Paula giggled, the sparkling wine having gone to her head a bit.

"No," Kate laughed, "I mean *wealthy* women. Women who are waited on hand and foot. Women who have fancy houses and cars and expensive clothes and perfume. That kind of thing."

"You mean women who do their food shopping in Marks & Spencers *all* the time?"

Kate shrugged. "Marks & Sparks at the very least — probably Harrod's Food Hall or having everything delivered from an up-market deli store."

Paula took a big slug of the Cava. "I'd love to be like that … If I was twenty again, I'd marry a man who could give me all those things. I wouldn't care what he looked like, as long as he had money."

"What if he was awful looking and really boring?" Kate said, giggling.

"A lot of wealthy men are ugly," Paula pointed out. "Look at that old Onassis fella — you don't think that Jackie Kennedy married him for his good looks, do you?"

★   ★   ★

Kate glanced up from her knitting, checking that Ella was busy at her homework. It was great that she could still do things she enjoyed like the knitting and reading, and mind Ella at the same time.

It was great how things had worked out over all.

In the last few weeks, Kate had passed her driving test and bought her new yellow Ka. And, she had become fond of Ella. They chatted on the walks to and from school and Ella now came running out from school each day, eager to tell Kate all her news.

Although she had the car, they still walked to help get down that last bit to her goal weight.

It was after seven o'clock when Paula came rushing through the door. "The computers went down for two hours and I had a big order that had to be processed for tomorrow morning."

"You can relax," Kate told her. "Frank picked Ella up this evening. He was here at six o'clock."

"Well, that does make a change …"

"You look as though you could do with a cup of coffee. Have you had a hard day?"

Paula sank into an armchair. "Hectic. Thank God tomorrow's Friday. Was Frank annoyed that I was late?"

Kate shrugged. "He didn't seem to be – he was in good form this evening. He had a doughnut and coffee while Ella was watching a programme." She lifted up a small blue square of knitting on two needles. "What do you think of Ella's handiwork?"

"Did she do all that herself?" Paula asked, surprised.

"We've been working on it all week. They're doing a crafts exhibition in school next Wednesday and she wants to take it in." Kate smiled. "It'll actually be a scarf when it's finished."

"Oh, Kate …" Paula suddenly remembered. "Ella has a party at Lisa's tomorrow at six o'clock. Could you drop her off?"

"No problem. Will you leave the party clothes and the present off in the morning?"

Paula rolled her eyes. "I've only just thought of it. It'll have to be money in a card."

"I'm going into town tomorrow," Kate told her, "so I'll pick up a little present then."

"Are you sure? It's putting more things on your plate."

"I'm going to the leisure centre anyway – did I tell you I'd joined?"

"The one in the new hotel?" Paula asked in a high, surprised voice.

"Yes."

"Isn't it very expensive?"

"They do special off-peak rates. I go after I've dropped Ella off in the mornings. You should join, too."

"I wish I could," Paula sighed. "I'm always rushing around and Frank's no help. He still expects me to cook and do everything around the house. He wouldn't think to make me a cup of tea if he gets in before me. If you weren't giving Ella her dinner in the evenings, I'm sure she would starve if it was left up to him."

"Maybe you're being a bit hard on him," Kate said quietly. "He adores Ella. The evenings he calls here, he checks her homework and her reading, and watches her knitting."

"He could show some interest in *me!*"

"Maybe he thinks that you have no time for him ..."

"Well, I've actually got very little feeling for him at the moment."

"Maybe you should think of giving up work for a while."

"You must be joking," Paula said. "At least I get a 'thanks' for the work I do in the office, and I get paid."

"Money isn't everything," Kate said quietly.

Paula checked her watch. "I want to get home and spend an hour with Ella before bedtime." She stood up. "I'll settle up with you tomorrow for the birthday present. She reached and squeezed her friend's hand. "I don't know what I'd do without you."

Later, as she was tidying around, Kate picked up Ella's little scarf and held it to her cheek.

It was amazing how relaxed she'd become with Frank recently. He'd complimented her on how well she looked, and when she'd mentioned having her long blonde hair cut, he said how lovely and feminine it looked and advised her to keep it exactly as it was. Kate ran her fingers through her hair, thinking that she might just have a bare inch off it and maybe a few highlights to brighten it up.

As she washed up, she mused over how things had turned around for her friend recently. Having a job didn't seem to have made things better. Paula had never been properly organised when she was at home, and now she seemed to be using the job as an excuse for doing even less.

★ ★ ★

Paula sat back in her office chair, thinking that going back to work was the same as when she gave up smoking. It made no obvious difference to their finances although she knew their debt was gradually decreasing. Personally, she felt hardly a penny the better off for all her hard work. The overdraft was swallowing up her wages every month and what was left went on paying Kate and her fares and her lunches.

The only positive thing was that Frank's mood had improved and he wasn't so critical. Maybe he was relieved about their money situation improving

He wasn't the type to say it. Paula gave a little sigh. How on earth had they ever got together in the first place? She supposed it had all been physical attraction. Before they had time to get to know each other properly, she was expecting Ella.

But surely there had been more to them that that?

Maybe when the debt was all paid off they might take a holiday. Time on their own. Maybe things would get back to being hunky-dory between them again.

★ ★ ★

Kate did sit-ups in time to her Madonna CD. She was delighted with her trendy new hairstyle and when Frank saw it, he said that from the back she looked like a teenager.

"Young, fit and slim," he'd said. "Your Joe must have been mad going off."

Then, when she was out with the girls at the weekend, she'd run into her ex-husband and his girlfriend, Sarah, in the local hotel. Kate was wearing a short skirt with long suede boots and fishnet tights. Joe's face was a picture. And better still, his girlfriend who was five months pregnant looked pale and dumpy and miserable. God knows what she would look like full-term!

Joe had been waiting when she came out of the ladies'. "What's all this?" he'd said, gesturing towards her outfit. "I never knew you had legs when we were married – you always wore trousers."

She had arched her eyebrows. "Well, now you know what you missed."

Kate took the lasagne out of the oven. She'd made enough for Frank if he came early to join her and Ella again tonight. He was always grateful and he'd even brought her a beautiful hand-tied bouquet of flowers, to say thanks for all the lovely meals she'd cooked when Paula was on a staff-training course.

Joe had *never* bought her flowers.

Not even when she'd lost the twins a few years ago and the other little baby the following year. She'd never got as much as a daisy from him, and hardly a mention of the babies when she'd come home from hospital. Was it any wonder she hadn't wanted to sleep with him since? She often wondered if things would have been different had the babies lived.

Kate grabbed her coat and headed out the door to pick Ella up. She called in at a sports shop on the way to school and bought a new, slightly daring swimsuit.

Paula was going away for the weekend with work and she'd promised Ella that she'd bring her swimming on Saturday, and Frank said he would love to join them too.

They were getting to be quite a little family, she thought to herself. And she didn't feel a bit guilty. All was fair in love and war.

And in the long run, things would work out hunky-dory for Paula too.

ALSO BY GERALDINE O'NEILL, PUBLISHED BY POOLBEG

The Flowers of Ballygrace,
The Grace Girls, Tara's Fortune,
Aisling Gayle, Tara Flynn

26

Stronger Than Before
MARY O'SULLIVAN

A spot of solder, a tweak of the pliers and her work for the day was finished. Somehow, without Jenna noticing, morning had drifted into evening. She switched off the lights in her studio and allowed her eyes to adjust to the dimness. Walking over to the window, she looked across the yard to her home. It was dark and empty. She turned her face towards the west. The last rays of sun were piercing the approaching darkness, tingeing the lake with ripples of orange and fiery red. She watched as sun and water created a work far more beautiful than she could ever hope to achieve.

Turning back to her workbench, she picked up the neck chain she had just been working on and held it up. Amethysts refracted rays of sunset and spilled them around the now almost dark room. Carefully she placed it in one of her trademark purple velvet presentation boxes. Another Jenna Grant piece of designer jewellery was ready for the market.

A corner of the studio suddenly came alive with yelps followed by the scratchy sounds of claws skittering over the timber floor. Jenna stood still and waited as the sounds approached. When she felt the warm fur against her legs she stooped and stroked the thick, rough coat.

"You're right, Baxter. It's walk time," she told the tubby little dog at her feet. He began to yap excitedly as Jenna got his lead and clipped it onto his collar. She locked up her studio and together she and Baxter headed towards the lake.

★　★　★

Dinner finished, Jenna picked up her book and took it into the living room. Baxter trotted after her and curled up at her feet when she settled on the couch. Removing her bookmark, she picked up where she had left off reading last night. The words blurred into each other. Too tired to read, she got up and switched on the television. Flicking through the channels, she rejected one programme after another. Nothing caught her attention. Nothing warmed the coldness inside her. Sensing that his mistress was sinking into one of her lonely moods, Baxter crept close to her and began to lick her hands. She smiled and fondled his ears. "Just you and me now, boy," she said. He wagged his tail and looked up at her with the trust and understanding that was the essence of Baxter. Jenna's eyes were drawn to the photographs dotted around the room. Her past in silver frames, happy moments frozen in time, two-dimensional slivers of lives that been so cruelly shattered and broken.

★ ★ ★

An insistent knock at the door disturbed their peace. Jenna sighed and Baxter retired to his basket. That would be Tessie. Switching off the television, Jenna went to the door to let in her oldest friend.

"God, it's cold out! Why didn't you ring me today? Have you finished your range for Saturday's show?"

Jenna didn't answer as she led the way into the kitchen. There was no need. Tessie usually answered her own questions. She was, as always, wearing clay-spattered jeans and as always she looked spectacular. Tessie, tall and slim with a mane of dark curly hair, could have been a model. Jenna smiled as she put on the kettle for coffee and listened to her friend prattle on. The world of fashion could never have contained Tessie's energy.

"I was brilliant today, even if I say so myself. I threw a batch of pots and had them out of the kiln before lunch. I've just finished painting them now. Shane has a whole range of woodcarvings ready to go too. Were you talking to him today?"

"No," Jenna answered quickly, needing to stop Tessie on this particular line of questioning. Ever since Shane Finchley had joined their crafts co-op, Tessie had decided that he was the ideal match for the pathetic widow she saw Jenna to be. As if anybody, even a gifted craftsman like Shane, could ever replace Paul.

"You should give Shane a chance you know, Jen. He's gorgeous. And kind and funny too. You know he fancies you. You can't stay on your own for ever."

"I have Baxter. He's all I need," Jenna answered as she put two mugs of coffee on the table.

Leaning across the table, Tessie caught Jenna's hand and spoke quickly, as if trying to get everything out before Jenna stopped her.

"It's not right, Jenna. I know you had a terrible break. It was awful but you must face the fact that Paul is no longer here. It's been two years since …"

"Since my husband died."

"Yes. And all you've had for company in that time is a dog for God's sake! Baxter is a lovely little mutt but really, Jenna, you must start to live again."

Jenna withdrew her hand and for once Tessie was quiet. A lump stuck in Jenna's throat, as hard and hot and full of pain as the day Paul had died. That horrific day when his heart, which had seemed so strong, so full of life, had suddenly gone into spasm and stopped beating. And she had not been with him. Nobody had. Except Baxter. She closed her eyes now and allowed the nightmare scene to replay again. Jenna in her studio, crafting her jewellery, Paul calling that he would take Baxter for a walk. Baxter coming back alone, whining, leading Jenna to the lakeside path where Paul had collapsed. And died. No goodbye, no chance to thank him for all the love and tenderness, all the magic his loving had brought into her life.

Opening her eyes, she smiled at Tessie. Her friend meant well.

"I'm all right, Tess. Work keeps me busy. Anyway, if you think Shane is so gorgeous, why don't you go out with him yourself?"

Tessie flicked back her hair and put her chin in the air. "I might. You'll be sorry then. You'll have to fight me for him. Anyway, about the show on Saturday – are you bringing your new amethyst range?"

An hour slipped by as they made arrangements for bringing their work to the Spring Craft Fair in the city. This particular show was one of the most lucrative for the co-op. The money they made usually tided them over between commissions and other fairs. As individual artists, they were each steadily gaining in reputation. There would come a time when they would disband and go their separate ways. But not yet.

"That's settled then," Tessie said as she stood at the door. "You and I will travel in your Jeep and Shane can drive himself. I have accommodation arranged too."

Jenna kissed her friend on the cheek. Tessie was scatty and annoying at times but what would she do without this whirlwind of energy?

★   ★   ★

When Jenna went back into the living room Baxter was still curled up in his basket. That was odd. He always hid when Tessie was around but jumped up the minute she was gone. Walking over to the basket, Jenna stooped down and rubbed the dog's head. There was no excited yap, no leap up. Shaking now, she slid her hand over his ribcage and felt for the deep steady breathing that would tell her everything was all right and that she was stupid to be panicking. His breathing was shallow and very fast. A scream sounded in Jenna's head. Piercing and sharp it whistled around her brain, not letting her think, not allowing her to help Baxter. He was dying. She knew it. She knew death and could feel its coldness in the tiny furry body in the basket. Not Baxter too. She couldn't let it happen.

In her rush to the phone, Jenna tripped over the rug

and almost fell. Grabbing her phone book, she riffled through the pages until she found the number for the veterinary clinic. She dialled the number and cursed as she listened to it ring and ring. Damn! It was supposed to be a twenty-four hour service. Why weren't they answering? When someone eventually picked up the phone, Jenna was on the verge of hysteria.

"I need a vet immediately. My dog is dying. You must send someone out straight away!"

"Your name and address, please," a calm voice asked.

"When will you be here? It's very urgent."

"Just tell me where to come to and I'll be with you soon."

As she waited for the vet with the calm voice to arrive, Jenna cradled Baxter in her arms. His eyes were closed. She longed for him to open them, to see once more the devotion and understanding reflected there. A shiver ran through Baxter's body and Jenna cried, believing that he had taken his last breath. Terrified, she placed her hand on his chest and felt the rapid rise and fall as the dog gasped for air. Had it been like this for Paul? Had he fought against the dying, struggled to hold onto life? Of course, he had. They had plans, she and Paul. They had it all mapped out, the years ahead full of loving and children and laughter. He would have fought for that. For her.

★　★　★

She saw the lights of the approaching car even before it turned into her driveway. Running to the door, she held it open for the vet. The man who got out of the car was tall and dark-haired. Not someone Jenna had seen on her visits to the clinic.

"Don Cleary," he said but he was not looking at her. His attention was on Baxter.

Jenna led him into the living room, keeping a tight hold on Baxter, not wanting this stranger to confirm her worst fears.

"Put him on the couch," he said. "I can examine him better there. How long has he been like this?"

"Not long. Maybe an hour or two. He had his usual walk this evening and he was fine."

"How old is he?"

Jenna stared speechlessly at the vet. How old was Baxter? Ageless. He had been a fully grown dog when Paul had brought him home, sneaking him in for fear Jenna would object to having a stray with mucky little paws around the house. That was six years ago, that day when Paul and Jenna and Baxter formed the little group they believed to be invincible. Immortal. Now this dark-haired stranger was lifting Baxter's jowls, examining his teeth.

"He's quite an old dog," Don announced. "He could be twelve."

"So what's wrong with him?" Jenna asked and then turned her back, not wanting the answer, not wanting to see Baxter's little body struggle for breath. The calm, steady voice reached through her pain. Words, meaningless sounds, washed over her. She didn't need to hear them. She understood. Slowly she turned to face the tall man.

"He's not suffering," he said. "It won't be long now."

Jenna walked over to the couch and sat beside Baxter. She picked him up and held his warm little body close to hers. The breaths were even shallower now. She stroked his ears, incongruously silky with his rough coat. Every touch, each shuddering breath he took brought memories of shared times, of Paul and Jenna and Baxter days, of picnics and hill treks, of happiness and fun. Of hope. Then Baxter was still. The invincible trio of Jenna, Paul and Baxter was finally destroyed.

Don Cleary stooped down and gently removed Baxter's body from Jenna's arms. The cold empty feeling in her arms spread inside, into her heart, into her very soul. That pain, that horrible sharp, heavy weight of loss was pressing on her chest, moving up her throat, spilling over in gushing tears.

"Is there anybody I could call for you?" the vet asked.

Jenna shook her head. She did not want anybody. Not Tessie, not her mother or sisters. They would not understand. To them, Baxter was just a fat, spoiled little mutt. She did not want to hear their well-meaning but unwelcome pep talks. Their 'get over it and get on with your life' speeches. Their 'he was only a dog' exclamations.

"I'll look after Baxter for you if you would prefer."

A sob almost choked Jenna. The implications struck her with a force that was tangible. Baxter must be buried, disposed of, got rid of.

"The garden," she sobbed.

Don Cleary nodded. "Tools? A shovel?"

"The shed."

He walked out then, Baxter in his arms. Jenna threw herself down on the couch and cried. There was no comfort or relief in the tears. The rhythmic sound of shovel hitting earth impinged on her consciousness. She noticed Baxter's empty basket, the furry blanket still holding the imprint of his body. He loved that blanket, always spending time teasing it into shape before finally snuggling into it. She grabbed it and ran into the garden.

"He'll need his blanket!" she said.

Don Cleary, sleeves rolled up, sweat on his forehead, was standing beside the hole he had just finished digging. Baxter lay on the ground beside him, still and silvered in the moonlight. The vet stooped, picked up the dog and held him out to Jenna. She wrapped Baxter up cosily in his furry blanket and taking the bundle in her arms, gave him one last, one final, one never again to be repeated hug.

Then it was over. The dark-haired vet gave the fresh earth on Baxter's grave a final tap with the shovel. Jenna was struck by the incongruity of sharing this intimate and very personal moment with a complete stranger. A kind and understanding stranger.

"Tea? Coffee?" she asked.

"Coffee would be lovely, please," he answered. "I'll just tidy up here. I'll be in then."

Jenna left him to put away the shovel and pick and, going into the kitchen, put on the kettle and got out two mugs. There was solace in carrying out the mundane tasks and comfort in the kindness of the stranger. She had coffee ready when he came into the kitchen. He took his bleeper out of his pocket and put it on the table.

"I'm on call," he explained. "Lambing season. It's bound to beep soon."

"I haven't seen you before. Are you new at the practice?"

"I'm here just two months now. I must say, I like this area. A good mix of town and country."

Jenna looked at him and for the first time noticed his deep blue eyes and dark lashes. Kind, sympathetic eyes.

"Thank you so much for helping me with . . . for burying Baxter. It was very good of you and I appreciate your kindness."

"You're welcome. No problem."

He smiled. Jenna felt the warmth and sincerity of his smile. She knew he understood the depth, the awful pain of her loss.

"Baxter was my husband's dog," she said.

Don nodded and occasionally smiled or muttered a word as Jenna poured out her story to him. The sorry history of Jenna and Paul and Baxter. They talked for an hour. Until his bleeper sounded. He stood and shrugged on his coat.

"An awkward lambing," he said. "I've got to go."

Jenna walked to the door with him. "Thank you so much, Don," she said. "For all your help."

He stood for a moment looking down at her. Then he smiled his warm smile and quickly turned and left. When Jenna went back into the house, the emptiness of it, the loneliness for her husband and for the little creature that had been her comfort totally oppressed her. She cried herself to sleep.

★ ★ ★

The Spring Fair had been a huge commercial success. Jenna had sold her entire new range and won a lot of orders. Tessie had been commissioned to cast a set of crockery for an upmarket hotel chain and Shane Finchley had done well too.

Jenna had been accompanied the whole weekend by the emptiness inside her. It had been so difficult to smile at clients and to listen to Tessie prattle on. On the road home now, she dreaded going back to her empty house.

"You're even quieter than usual," Tessie accused.

"I can't get a word in edgeways with you. Do you realise you haven't stopped talking about Shane Finchley for the last sixty miles?"

"Do you mind?" Tessie asked anxiously. "I did warn you."

Jenna looked across at her friend and laughed. "I'm pleased for both of you," she said sincerely. "I noticed all the longing looks and sighs. I thought you two would never get it together."

"Well, we have now. What's wrong with you then, if it's not jealousy about Shane and me?"

On the outskirts of the town now, they were almost at Tessie's cottage. A good time to tell her about Baxter. The pull-yourself-together lecture would be shortlived.

"Baxter died. Old age."

Jenna had been so wrong about Tessie's reaction. Tears welled in her friend's eyes and she reached across and tightly held Jenna's hand.

"I'm so sorry," she said. "I know what Baxter meant to you."

When Jenna stopped her Jeep outside the cottage, Tessie offered to accompany her home.

"No, thank you, Tess. I'll have to get used to going home to an empty house. May as well start now."

Tessie hugged her and waved as she drove off.

★　★　★

When she went in home Jenna turned on all the lights and switched on the heating. In the stillness, she imagined she could hear the scamper of little paws across the floor. She walked out to the garden and went to the dark scar of earth with the bunch of flowers on top. "Sleep well, Baxter," she whispered to the crusted earth and withering flowers. The silence drove her back inside to the even more silent house.

By the time she had drunk her coffee, it was dark. The lonely night ahead cast a long shadow. Work was the only answer to the emptiness. Jenna crossed the yard to her studio and, taking out her sketchpad, began to work on a new design. Head bowed, fingers busy, she worked steadily for an hour before realising she had forgotten to turn on the studio heater. Stiff and cold, she stood and stretched.

Lights pierced the darkness around the house. A car came up the driveway. She stood still, terrified. Who could be calling at this time of night? Flicking off the studio light, she stood just inside the window and watched as the car parked outside her front door. A tall man got out. Jenna sighed with relief. It was the vet. Don Cleary. The man with the warm smile and kind eyes.

She got to the front door just as he was about to ring. She opened it wide. Her smile of welcome froze on her face. She was stunned by the solemnity of the moment, overcome with the knowledge that she would always remember this very instant.

"She needs a home," Don said, offering the fluffy bundle in his arms to her.

Jenna reached out and took the pup from Don. It was a cross between a Labrador and a collie. Soft and warm with deep brown eyes and a wet shiny nose. The pup snuggled into Jenna and licked the back of her hand.

"Has she found a home?" Don asked.

Jenna put the pup down and watched as she scampered along the hall and made a beeline for the living room. She smiled at Don.

"She certainly thinks so. And so do I. Amy is here to stay."

"Amy?"

"Short for amethyst. Come in and I'll explain."

★   ★   ★

Amy had chewed the leg of a chair and deposited three little puddles on the floor before she settled down for the night in Baxter's basket. Don and Jenna sat together and watched her sleep as they talked. Night gave way to dawn and still they talked. She learned of the long-term relationship Don had left behind when he moved to this area; she told him more about Paul and the tragedy of his passing.

"I don't know how I can ever thank you for your kindness," Jenna said as the first rays of sun shone through the curtains.

"I can think of lots of ways," Don said as he reached up his hand and touched her cheek. His lips gently touched hers and Jenna said her final goodbye to Paul and Baxter. Their memory would always live on in her heart but they would no longer haunt her. They would be warm loving memories now. Her arms slipped around Don's neck as he pulled her closer to his lean, strong body. Amy stirred in her basket and then jumped up on the couch, licking both their faces. At first they laughed in amusement at the playful pup. Then they laughed with the sheer joy of finding each other.

Jenna, Don and Amy, an invincible trio. But this time Jenna knew they were not immortal.

ALSO BY MARY O'SULLIVAN, PUBLISHED BY POOLBEG

Parting Company

27

Sophie Barker's Wedding Diary
SHARON OWENS

"Hello! Oh my God!"

I knew it, as soon as I took the call, that this particular bride was going to be difficult. I made a face at Julie. The kind of weary, dazed expression we pull when we get a giddy one on the line.

"Hello. Maggie speaking. How can I help you?"

"Is that Dream Weddings? Yes? Well, my name is Sophie Barker and I'm about to become one of your biggest clients. He's popped the question at last. Hip-hip hooray! I'm getting married. Oh my God!"

"Congratulations, Sophie," I said, sounding really chirpy and upbeat.

Well, you have to muster up some enthusiasm, don't you? Even though we hear this kind of tearful warble every day of the week.

"How wonderful! You must be over the moon," I added.

The poor woman sounded so excited, I imagined her boyfriend was still down on one knee beside her. She must have had our number programmed into the phone already.

"I have so many ideas, I don't know where to begin," she trilled.

"Well, that's where we come in," I assured her.

Some brides want to live out every romantic daydream and extravagant fantasy they've ever had, on their big day. There's no harm in that, of course. It's only natural. But I find that it's wiser to stay within or at least close to the boundaries of normality. There's less scope for things to go belly-up if you keep the running order fairly standard. We try to steer our clients away from hot air balloons. And the releasing of live doves near overhead power lines. And so on. But it's not always easy. Still, weddings are what I do for a living so I reached for my little gold pencil and began to make notes.

"Chocolate!" Sophie said. "That's the theme I want. Chocolate-coloured silk for the bridesmaids' dresses, chocolate-coloured ribbons draped from the ceiling and chocolate-coloured tablecloths in the marquee."

At no point did she mention the word 'brown'.

An hour later, I had to cover the receiver with my hand so that bride-to-be Sophie Barker wouldn't hear my stomach rumbling. When I'm hungry I make noises like a T-Rex digesting a Woolly Mammoth. Or what I imagine such a thing would have sounded like. Anyway, it's loud.

I pointed at the kettle and raised my eyebrows. It was almost lunch-time.

Julie made two mugs of tea, and opened a carton of chicken and stuffing sandwiches. My favourite kind of filling. She bit into one and closed her eyes with pleasure, just to tease me. Then she pretended to be having an orgasm, holding onto the edge of her desk and shaking backwards and forwards. Julie's the boss so I have to laugh it off when she's being childish.

Having said that, she's the best wedding planner in the business. And she's the absolute Queen of Gossip in this city. Julie knows *everything* about everyone. Two of her best friends own wine-bars and two more are lawyers and the fifth one owns a lingerie boutique. So nothing but *nothing* gets past the coven. As I like to call them. Julie's got a computer for a brain and can cross-reference clients in five seconds flat.

She nearly got married herself once; to a toilet tissue mogul called Bert, but now she's very loved-up with a total Love God (and horse-riding instructor) called Gary.

"So to summarise," I said, trying to wind things up, "that's five heart-shaped tiers, laid directly one on top of the other, without columns?"

"That's right, Maggie," Sophie squeaked with barely repressed ecstasy.

(Maggie, that's my name. I'm Julie's PA.)

"Chocolate sponge, chocolate filling, super-smooth chocolate frosting?"

"That's right. Oh, it's going to be so utterly fabulous!"

"Any decorations in particular?" I finished.

"Oh, yes! Can you please get the baker to cover the entire cake in chocolate hearts? I want the wedding cake to look like, wait for it, *an illustration in a Roald Dahl book.* I want a larger-than-life, simply *scrumptious* fantastical creation. The kind of cake you might dream about if you were a chocoholic who'd been stranded on a desert island for ten years without so much as a solitary sniff of chocolate to ease your suffering."

"I see."

"Does that make sense to you? Lots and lots of *elegantly elongated* chocolate hearts, sticking out in all directions." Sophie almost choked then, having just given so many instructions in the one breath.

"I'm hearing you," I said gently. "What you mean is, too much of a good thing is just not enough, in this case?"

"Yes. That's it. And the cake will go so well with the bridesmaids' dresses." She took another deep breath to continue, but I interrupted her.

"Okay. We'll get some estimates and I'll call you back and we'll arrange an appointment. Cheerio, Sophie."

I hung up and dived on the last sandwich.

"Make sure she pays a hefty deposit before you book anything," Julie said.

Julie always likes to get fees out of the way before we get too involved in any wedding preparations.

"I'm in heaven," I sighed, taking a bite.

"Sophie Barker, now let me put my thinking cap on," Julie said as she passed the tub of butter flapjacks across the desk to me. "Would her intended go by the name of Charles Henderson, by any chance? Does he own a golf-club in North Down?"

"That's the one," I replied. "She did mention that."

I told you Julie was good.

"Oh dear," said Julie. "Charles has a penchant for ladies of the night, so I'm told. Always popping over to London *on business*. Oh well, it's a free country."

"What will we do?" I gasped. "Will we tell her?"

"No way. We'll plan the wedding," Julie said calmly.

"But he's a rat," I protested. "That's disgusting."

"Relax, Mags. She probably knows all about it. He's

minted up to the ears so she's going to turn a blind eye to get her eight-bedroom mansion with an indoor swimming pool and six bathrooms, I'll wager."

"You think?"

"Sure. It's got nothing to do with us. Forget it."

"You're the boss," I said, and I opened a new file.

The following week, however, Sophie came in to the office to meet us. She said she'd had a change of heart.

After an occasionally emotional morning in the office it was agreed that the chocolate fantasy cake was no longer on the wish list. One of Sophie's friends had told her chocolate cakes were too rich on the stomach after a big dinner, and that plain old-fashioned Victoria sponge was the New In-Thing.

So I got my gold pencil out again.

"Now, let's see. You want three heart-shaped tiers of Victoria sponge, with columns this time; duck-egg blue frosting, a kitsch bride and groom on the top, and all the sides to be studded with Love Heart sweets. A post-feminist, ironic, girly, vintage 1950's kind of thing?"

"Got it in one," Sophie sighed, dabbing her eyes with a tissue. "I'm really sorry about this."

"Not to worry," Julie said, making a note to add all Sophie-related phone calls to the bill.

Sophie explained that she was going to wear her hair in an untidy topknot with lots of plastic clips and a yellow plastic flower holding it in place. And the bridesmaids would be wearing shiny pink satin and carrying Frou-Frou dolly-bags.

"Kitsch. I want an explosion of kitsch."

"Okay." I wrote it all down in the order book and crossed out the previous plans.

"I'm very sorry," said Sophie again. "I'm getting a bit

carried away with this wedding, I know I am. But it's going to be the best day of my life."

"We understand," I said. "It's not a problem."

"I promise that's the end of it now, Maggie. There won't be any more changes."

"Righto, Sophie. Leave it with us."

When she'd gone, I looked across the desk at Julie and dared her to say something unkind about Sophie's forty-five-inch waist. Something about Sophie definitely being our biggest client of all time. But she didn't.

"Poor cow's got enough on her plate," was all Julie said as she handed out the sarnies. Salmon and cucumber, this time: not quite as delicious as chicken and stuffing but very nice, all the same. We shared a bag of pretzels, and left salt and crumbs all over the desks.

"I feel bad, taking money off Sophie," I began, as we tidied up after lunch. "Maybe we shouldn't lodge this cheque in case the wedding is called off?"

"Don't get involved, Mags," Julie said. "If that happens, it's not our problem. We'll still have done the work." And that was that.

But the following week, Sophie was back in the office, biting her nails with worry.

"You're not going to believe this," she began. "I don't believe it myself. But my ideas have moved on again."

"Fire away," I said, smiling. I flicked open the book and turned over to a fresh clean page. "We haven't placed any orders yet so we're okay budget-wise."

"Excellent! Well, this time I do want to keep the vintage theme, but I might lose the kitsch elements. Charles has some very wealthy friends, you see, and I'm not being a snob or anything, but they might not get the joke. So I thought we'd just have two heart-shaped tiers of vanilla sponge, jam and cream filling, pale pink frosting, pale pink sugar-paste roses on the top. And could you get them to deliver the cake on a pink glass stand?"

"We'll do our best," I said. "I'll have a look at cake-stands the next time I'm at the suppliers. Okay?"

"Thanks a million," Sophie said quietly. "And we'll go for matt pink silk for the bridesmaids' dresses. I'll fax you their measurements this evening. And we'll have posies of yellow tulips instead of the Frou-Frou dolly-bags."

"And the ceiling-ribbons?"

"I think we should forget about the ceiling-ribbons," said Sophie, in a voice that told us she was terrified of showing Charles up on their wedding day. "It might look like an American prom."

"But that would have been lovely," I said.

"No, the ribbons are history. Sorry. That's definitely the last time I'll be in here to disturb you," she apologised.

"As you wish," I said. I held the heavy door open for Sophie and gave her arm a little squeeze for moral support.

"Bloody hell," said Julie, when Sophie was well out of earshot. The cost of this bash is going down and down. At this rate she'll be handing out biscuits at a bus stop."

"I feel sorry for her," I said.

"He likes them young and foreign," said Julie.

I didn't even ask her how she'd found out that little nugget.

Two weeks later, Sophie sat sobbing on the office sofa.

"I'm in such a state," she wept.

Julie and I exchanged glances. Had she seen incriminating Polaroids in Charles' briefcase?

"Please don't upset yourself," I begged.

Sophie's eyes were puffy with crying. She was dabbing

her damp face with our best tea towel because she'd used up all the tissues.

"I'll be mortified, Maggie, if this wedding isn't perfect. I couldn't bear it if they all laughed at me. I've changed my plans again, I'm afraid."

"Just take your time and we'll take care of it," I patted her hand. "We'll lose some of the deposits but it's your big day and you've got to be happy, haven't you?"

Julie made a pot of tea.

"There's a new fashion now," Sophie wailed. "Just when I had everything settled in my mind, they go and bring out a new fashion. And Charles' friends are very fashion-conscious. I must get this right. So I'm going for all-white wedding. I've lain awake all night thinking about it and I've decided if we keep everything white, then we can't go wrong."

"All-white?" said Julie. "Even the men?"

"No, the men will be asked to wear black-tie. But the ladies will be asked to dress in white, and I'll be in a white sheath-dress and so will the bridesmaids. And we'll have white tulips for the posies."

"Okay," I said. "There go the invitations."

Sophie wept again.

"It's fine," soothed Julie. "We'll order more." I knew by the grimace on her face she was picturing Sophie in a white sheath-dress and the image was not pleasing.

"Make sure the invites are plain white, won't you?" fretted Sophie. "With a fine, silver edge," she added, as her sniffling and sobbing subsided.

"And the wedding cake?" I asked gently.

"Oh, I'm glad you reminded me. I think we ought to go for individual fairy cakes with white icing. Decorated with tiny silver hearts, and presented in silver bun cases.

We can display the fairy cakes on a tiered, transparent glass stand, and there'll be no faffing about with cutting big cakes. And everyone can bring their fairy cake home with them in a dinky little white box with the date of the wedding printed on it."

"Sophie," I said carefully. "Are you sure about this? Because you did seem so sure about the 1950's wedding, didn't you? And I think the frilly pink ball-gown would have suited you so much better than this plain one will."

"Please help me, Maggie? Please, Julie, pretty please?" Sophie sounded slightly deranged. "You said you could do anything. I can't go around organising it. I'm the bride. I'm going on a diet right away, too. I reckon I can lose two stone in three months. And I'm going to get my hair done by a top celebrity hairdresser."

Poor Sophie, I thought. It wasn't as if her husband-to-be was worth all this fuss and preparation.

Julie had been out with her coven the night before. Details had been gleaned.

Charles was rather dull and obsessed with cricket. He had a centre parting. He wore baggy pastel golf-shirts and checked trousers. He smoked cigars and spat on the street.

"I'm worried sick about that woman," I said, almost in tears myself. "What does she see in him?"

"She'll be fine," said Julie. "She's tough as old boots. Mark my words."

And Julie was right, as usual.

The day before the wedding, Charles hit the national headlines in a test case involving a teenage prostitute from Nigeria, her newborn baby and the Child Support Agency. Sophie cornered her beloved in the golf-shop with her father's shotgun and made him eat twenty-seven of the individual white fairy cakes (while James Blunt played on the in-store stereo) before he managed to hit the panic button.

Sophie became a poster girl for humiliated women everywhere, doing the rounds of daytime telly and getting her own column in a gossip magazine.

Mother and baby got a council flat, we got paid six thousand pounds, Sophie got a six-figure advertising deal, and Charles got six months in prison.

Sophie tore the white sheath dress in half, with her bare hands, on her mother's front lawn for the press conference.

Which was all for the best in the end, as she hadn't managed to shift the two stone and would have looked like a cobra swallowing a sheep, in the wedding photographs.

Julie's words, not mine.

ALSO BY SHARON OWENS, PUBLISHED BY POOLBEG

The Tavern on Maple Street,
The Ballroom on Magnolia Street,
The Tea House on Mulberry Street

28

Christmas Tale
MARTINA REILLY

It was first spotted on the 10th of December. The next day, on the other side of the world, it was seen too. At first there was excitement. A new star had been located further out in the universe than ever before. Then the disputes began. Some said that it wasn't a star; its mass and structure and measurements didn't seem 'star-like'. Others said it might be a comet. The prophets of doom said it had to be an asteroid. The astronomers scratched their heads and took more data and ran more tests and tried not to look too alarmed.

★ ★ ★

"Mammy, how does Santa deliver all his presents in one night?"

Abby, up to her armpits in flour, grinned at her oldest child. Joe had just turned nine and was growing ever more sceptical about the Santa Claus tale.

"He sprinkles magic dust and time slows down." Abby cracked an egg and beat it rapidly into the mixture.

"What's the dust made from?" Joe asked.

"How should I know?" Abby shook her head. "I guess it's special magic stuff that you can only get at the North Pole."

Joe smirked. "So, how come no one has ever found it there?"

She was just about to answer him when Clara, her youngest, piped up, "'Cause only Santa knows where it is, silly!" She gave her older brother a punch and added scornfully, "If everyone had it, time would be in a big mess – it mightn't move at all. I'd be four forever and you'd be nine and Daddy would still be here."

Abby jerked at the mention of her husband.

"Daddy's coming back to us," Joe shoved his sister with his elbow. "He's coming back as soon as he can."

"Daddy's coming back?" Clara sounded amazed. "I thought that –"

"Clara, get me the milk, will you?" Abby interrupted her.

"But Joe said that Daddy –"

"The milk?"

As Clara trotted to the fridge, Abby turned to Joe. He had his hands jammed into his jeans and was glaring at her. Abby sighed. For some reason, she'd thought Joe was over all the 'daddy-is-coming-back' stuff. He hadn't mentioned it in ages. "Joe," she began gently. "I don't think it's right to –"

"Daddy's coming back. He told me so."

Abby winced, wondering how it was that Joe could be so sceptical about Santa and yet believe without doubt that his dad was going to arrive in the door any second.

"Joe," she said again, wiping her hands clean on her apron and crossing toward him, "don't you think it's time —"

"He told me he would," Joe interrupted, backing away from her. "He promised."

Clara, sensing something was wrong, abandoned the milk and focused her attention on her mother and brother.

"Dad might have told you he was coming back because you were upset," Abby said softly. "I guess he didn't like to see you unhappy."

"He told me he was coming back because it's true," Joe insisted. His voice rose. "He said when he came that I'd know." He bit his lip. Gulped. "He always told us that we should never break a promise and he promised. He promised me."

"I know but —"

Joe blinked rapidly. He pulled himself up straight. "You *don't* know," he said as he opened the kitchen door. As he slammed it after him, he yelled back, "But you will!"

★　★　★

The light source spotted far out in the universe was not easily identifiable, the astronomers had decided. It was most definitely not a star. It was not a comet or an asteroid. It was simply a dispersal of light. They said 'simply', but it wasn't simple at all. Light did not 'simply' appear without any visible source. Neither did light rotate and re-form into yet brighter light. But this light was doing just that. Something, some energy, was gathering light from different parts of the solar system and coalescing it until a flicker became a beam became a ray.

"A black hole in reverse," one of the most eminent heads had put it. He'd said it with a sort of reverential tone in his voice but those that knew him well knew that he was as baffled as the next man.

And so more tests were carried out. And, as they talked and discussed and threw out vague ideas, the light grew. And then on December 19th, the light began to move.

It wasn't noticeable to the astronomers at first until someone remarked that the telescope needed adjusting. "It's seems to be out a degree," he said. Then, in a sort of shaky voice, he added, "Unless the object is moving."

And that is exactly what the object was doing.

It was moving and growing and the astronomers knew that soon it would be visible in the night skies to everyone in the world.

Something had to be done.

Some story had to be invented to calm the people.

And so the politicians called their spin-doctors and the astronomers worked out just what could be said.

★　★　★

" . . . and now on to the strange light that was spotted in the night sky earlier this week," the reporter on the RTÉ radio show said. "We've got Alan Jones from Astronomy Ireland to tell us exactly what it is. Well, Alan, is it the Star of Bethlehem come to revisit us?"

Alan and the reporter laughed.

Abby turned down the volume on the radio. If she heard any more about this strange light she was going to scream. Everyone was of a different opinion. The people in the know said that it was just dust burning up when it hit the earth's atmosphere or something like that. Abby didn't really care. If they put as much energy into solving the traffic problems in the city as they did to discussing light sources, she'd be a lot happier. She turned her head to see if she could pull into the inside lane and was hit in the eye by a branch from the enormous Christmas tree she'd bought in the market. Really, it was too big, but it had been such a lovely shape that she felt she had to have it. They'd always had a big tree and damned if she was going to let the kids down this year.

★ ★ ★

They all agreed that a probe should be sent up to examine the light. Some sort of probe that wouldn't burn in high temperatures. So, on 20th of December a probe was fired from deep in the deserts of South America. At the speed it was travelling, it would take a day to be in sight of the light.

★ ★ ★

Abby watched Joe and Clara as they decorated the tree, Joe looking serious, with the solemn expression he'd worn ever since his dad had . . . gone. Clara, too young really to appreciate the finality of her dad's going, smiled and joked with her brother oblivious to his silences.

Abby found herself grinning as Joe lifted Clara up to hang a bell on a branch that she particularly wanted. If it hadn't been for her kids she would have curled up and died during those dreadful months earlier in the year. As it was, she was left with an ache inside and an empty space that she couldn't fill, though she'd tried. She'd worked, she'd exercised, she'd baked and throughout it all she knew that it wasn't going to work.

Her husband was gone. He'd died in February. Abby bit her lip to stem the tears she knew were threatening. She'd been dreading Christmas and now –

"Your turn, Mammy," Joe broke into her thoughts. He held out the star to her. "It has to go right at the top. Daddy always put it there."

Abby, glad of the distraction, took it from him and looked up at the tree that, despite having had its top chopped off was still brushing the ceiling. "I think I might need a chair," she muttered. "It's very high."

Joe ran into the kitchen and pulled a chair in for her.

It wasn't going to be enough. Even on her tiptoes, she couldn't reach the topmost branch. Eventually she hung it as high as she could.

"It's not at the top," Joe said sulkily. "It's meant to be at the top."

"Daddy used to do it, honey," she said softly. "He was taller than me."

Joe bit his lip. He stared at the star as it sort of leaned sideways on the branch. "It looks crap," he muttered.

It was old, that was why, Abby thought. Its tinsel points were ragged and bare. The middle part of it was crumpled and torn but somehow they'd never got around to replacing it. She remembered David hanging it up, their very first Christmas together, and how they'd both stood back to admire their handiwork.

"It looks crap," Joe said again.

"Well, it's the best I can do," Abby shrugged. "And I think it looks nice no matter where it is."

"Me too," Clara said staunchly, coming to cuddle her about the legs.

Joe gave them both a disdainful look and stomped out of the room.

★ ★ ★

At fifteen hundred hours on 21st of December the probe arrived at its co-ordinates. At least the scientists were pretty sure it was the co-ordinates. They checked and rechecked and each time it came back positive. The probe was directly across from the moving light source. The only thing was, the on-board cameras were not registering a light source at all.

They reset the probe to move toward the light wondering if it would burn up.

Nothing happened.

They sent the probe in closer again and the on-board camera registered only inky darkness.

The scientists became silent, every man absorbed with the thoughts of his own mortality and 'what-if's'. Every one of them finally admitting that there were simply some things that couldn't be explained.

And every one of them wondering what was going to happen now.

★ ★ ★

Clara was convinced that the light in the sky was Santa. Apparently, someone at school had told her that Santa was travelling so fast, he was making trails of light appear in his wake. She wanted to go to bed at five in case he'd arrive and she'd be up.

"He doesn't come until he knows you're asleep," Abby

explained, enjoying the wonder on her daughter's face. "He's not trying to catch you out, you know."

"And that light up there isn't Santa," Joe said. "He can make time stop so he doesn't have to travel fast."

"Oh, yeah," Clara said, finally convinced. "He can take all the time he wants, can't he?"

Joe nodded. He winked at his mother. He was glad he wasn't a kid any more.

★　★　★

At twenty-two hours, twenty minutes on 24th December, the astronomers studying the light observed something strange. At first the light became brilliantly bright. So bright that some people couldn't look at it. When it reached its zenith, the light began to pulsate and then it stopped. And everything around it stopped. It was as if the planets weren't moving any more. As if the very vacuum of space itself had become completely still.

★　★　★

Abby sat in front of the television, her feet propped on the coffee table, channel-hopping. It was 10.30 and both the kids were in bed. It was nice to get some space to herself. An opened bottle of wine was propped against the sofa.

She'd pulled down the blinds and closed the curtains because the light in the sky was brilliantly bright tonight. It kept throwing shadows onto the television screen so that it was difficult to watch.

She poured herself some more wine and suddenly she had the weirdest sensation. It was as if the very air had become still. As if everything was dulling down. As if the whole world had suddenly come to a complete stop.

A tap on the door made her jump. Wine spilled down the front of her shirt and she cursed slightly. The tapping came again. In horror, she realised that it was someone tapping on the sitting room door and not the front door at all.

"Joe," she called, "is that you?"

The door opened a fraction and a familiar voice, a dearly familiar voice, said, "No, it's me."

Then David, her David, walked into the room.

★ ★ ★

The light in the sky outshone the first beams of a Christmas sun very early next day. It shone on the silent, deserted streets, on the still lazy rivers and seas. It shone on the beaches where the tide was beginning to rise ten hours too late and it shone on the windows of houses where children were beginning to stir.

★ ★ ★

Abby woke up to the sound of feet on the landing. She stretched, wondering how on earth she'd managed to fall asleep on the sofa. Light was peeking in under the curtains. There were two empty bottles of wine at her feet and two glasses. Two glasses?

A picture of David danced across her vision. The last thing she remembered . . .

David!

337

Frantically, she looked around.

There was no sign of him.

Upstairs she heard Clara running into Joe's room and pulling him from the bed.

"David?" she whispered.

The air seemed to be zinging but there was nothing.

Nothing. It had been just the most wonderful dream . . .

Clara and Joe came running into the room and made a beeline for their presents.

Joe stopped suddenly. His voice soft, he whispered, "Daddy?" Then louder, "Daddy!"

Abby started. David was not there.

Joe turned to her with shining eyes. "Daddy was here, Mammy," he said. "Daddy came, just like he said he would. Look!"

Abby turned in the direction he pointed. There, right at the very top of the tree, hung the star they'd bought years ago. Its tinsel points stood proudly to attention.

"He made it shine," Joe whispered. "See, Mammy, how he made it shine."

And it was true.

The tinsel star seemed to be emitting light all on its own.

★　★　★

The light in the sky diminished after Christmas, finally disappearing altogether on 6th of January. Many people offered opinions on what it could have been.

Abby, watching the news on the day the light vanished, laughed quietly to herself at the outlandish explanations. Why couldn't people accept that some things just can't be explained?

"And now," the newsreader turned to camera, "we asked some children from Dublin as the schools would still be shut on 6th January, wouldn't they?"

Joe's face appeared on screen and Abby almost choked on her tea.

"Well, Joe," the interviewer asked, "what do you think it was?"

"Well," he began, "my daddy — he's dead now — he used to say that the Christmas spirit can't be felt, just seen and reflected, so like, I think that's what the light was — it was just the spirit of Christmas."

Abby didn't know if she imagined it, but the star at the top of the tree grew brighter just for that tiny moment.

ALSO BY MARTINA REILLY, PUBLISHED BY POOLBEG

Is This Love?, *The Onion Girl*,
Flipside

29

Happy Ever . . .

ANNE MARIE SCANLON

I'd seen this movie, or variations of it, a million times. Who hasn't? There was one with Nicolas Cage, one with Meg Ryan. Come to think of it, I think that the Meg Ryan one had Nicolas Cage in it as well. When was the last time Nicolas Cage made a decent film? Anyway, Nicolas Cage's poor choices aside, as I said I'd seen it before. I knew how it went. At first I kind of enjoyed it. I knew it was all a dream and was totally intrigued by the details. However, as the week went on I started to get scared.

Let me start at the beginning. On Sunday I schlepped out to the Island to visit Bruce and Fiona. I would have put them off but I'd already done that three times and couldn't get out of it. I hate Long Island except for the beaches and needless to say Bruce and Fi live inland in an area that's all strip malls and yummy mommies in SUVs. Hell, in other words, and that was before the brunch with three couples and their assorted children even got started.

That was hell with a cherry on top.

Bruce and Fi have a slightly different set-up from most of their neighbours and friends. Fi has a kick-ass corporate job (something with computers, I haven't a clue) and earns more money than God. Bruce used to be a graphic designer but gave up his career to mind the kids. Like most men who do this he thinks he deserves a medal, but that's another story. I'd just broken all ad sales records in *Miss Thing* magazine which meant not only was my end-of-year bonus going to be ginormus but, come the following day, I'd be beating off offers from every other glossy in America. Fi made a toast to me during brunch and everyone duly raised their glasses and congratulated me on my great success at work.

When everyone returned to their conversation Bruce turned to me and said in a slightly slurred voice, "Do you know what real success is?" I shook my head – no point in saying 'yes' as he was going to tell me anyway. "All my life I strove for success," he said waving his bottle of beer as he spoke. "I worked hard in school to get the best results. I went after the job I wanted and got it. I got promoted but you know what?" he said leaning in to my face. "It's bullshit, all of it, means nothing. When my kid looks me in the eyes and says, 'I love you, Daddy', that's it, that's success – nothing else matters."

I felt like I'd been slapped. I wasn't married and had no kids, ergo, by Bruce's reckoning my life was nothing but one big fat failure.

Bruce had wrecked my buzz entirely, and during the seemingly endless train ride back to the city I couldn't stop thinking about what he'd said. Maybe he was right. What was it all about if you had no one to share it with? Sure, I'd be earning more money this time next week but what would I do with it – buy more handbags? I couldn't help thinking that I'd blown my one chance at happiness, at real success as Bruce called it, with the only man I'd ever really loved. The man no other man ever compared with. When I was twenty-one, a few months short of my finals at university I'd discovered I was pregnant. Unusually, the father, my fella John, was delighted.

I wasn't so thrilled. John and I had plans. We were going to the States as soon as we graduated. My parents had been good enough to have me before they left Philadelphia so I had an American passport and when John and I got married he'd have one too. It was all planned, all ready to go. John didn't think a baby would interfere with our plans but I knew different. How could you take the world by storm when you had baby puke on your shoulder and had to stop every five minutes to change a nappy? There would be other babies, I told him. We had plenty of time. We had our whole lives in front of us, I said as I got on the ferry. I had to go to England alone – John was 'too upset' to come with me. (He got crap marks in his finals and that was my fault as well.) Anyway, it was never the same after that, and I ended up heading off to New York by myself.

Muffin, my cockapoo (that's a cocker spaniel/poodle crossbreed by the way) was thrilled to see me when I got home. No change there, Muffin was always thrilled to see me. "You love me, don't you?" I said looking into her eyes. She slobbered all over my face so I took that as a yes. I couldn't wait for the day to be over and for it to be tomorrow when I could go back to work and forget all about stupid Bruce and his stupid smug remarks. Poor Muffin got one of the shortest walks of her short life and I hit the sack barely pausing to moisturise my face.

Rarely have I slept as soundly. I even managed to sleep through the alarm the next morning. Or so the man in the bed beside me told me.

"Peg, you'll miss the train!" he said, kicking me. "You'll be in trouble if you don't hurry!"

I hauled myself up in bed. I felt as though I'd been drugged, so much so that I couldn't feel the terror that I knew logically I should feel having a man in my bed, when I knew beyond a reasonable doubt that I'd gone to bed alone the night before. It wasn't as if I had a boyfriend with a key who could have snuck in beside me in the middle of the night. The man beside me turned over, pulling the duvet up around his shoulders and away from me. There was something vaguely familiar about him, which was more than I could say for the duvet which I'd never seen in my life. It was hideous, like something my mother would have bought. Flowery. Very, very flowery.

"Jesus, are you going to move or what?" the man said.

That voice, I knew it. It was John. I smiled a bit in relief. Everything made sense now. I was having a dream. Good, that explained the duvet and, now that I had a bit of a look around, the awful wallpaper. (Who has wallpaper these days?) As I headed towards what I took (rightly) to be the en suite, I noticed a wedding picture on the wall. My wedding picture! I cringed a bit at the dodgy hair but was quite pleased with the dress – not a frill or a flounce in sight.

In the bathroom another shock awaited. I caught sight of myself in the mirror. Holy fuck, my hair, my skin, what the hell had happened? I opened the bathroom cabinet and began frantically searching for my precious tub of Crème de la Mer but couldn't find it. The panic passed when I remembered that this was, after all, only a dream and soon the alarm would go off and the Crème de la Mer would be exactly where I had left it.

"Mom!"

What? Mom? Me?

"Mom, the bus is here. I need money?"

I walked out of the bathroom and collided with a young girl. I got a bit of a land when I got a good look at her. She looked extremely like me when I was younger except with badly applied highlights. She was wearing a belly-top – all the better to show off her pierced navel, low-riding pants and far far too much make-up. I guessed I wasn't sending her to the nuns for the day.

"Mom!" she barked. "Get a clue, would you? Money?"

"In my bag," I said vaguely, stumbling toward the bed. Dream or no, I needed to sit down.

"I looked in your purse," she said, rolling her eyes. "There's nothing in it."

"Jesus Christ, Mel," John said, sitting up in the bed, "keep the fucking noise down, would you? I gave you a tenner yesterday – what did you do with it?"

"Oh, a tenner!" Mel sneered, doing a stage-Oirish accent for effect. "Oh, big deal!"

I heard a beeping noise. Oh good, I thought, there's the alarm. Any second now I'll be awake.

"Christ, he's blasting the horn now. Get down there," John growled. "You've been told before about delaying the driver."

Mel ran from the room calling us both losers and saying she wished she'd never been born. *Ouch!*

Dream? Nightmare, more like. When I headed off to work I discovered two things. One, I apparently worked for PCFT Financial, or so the ID card I found would have me believe. Two, and possibly worse, I was living in Bumlick, Long Island. At the station I bought a copy of

Miss Thing and went straight to the masthead where it said that Lauryn Rosenbaum was the director of Ad Sales. I wondered if Lauryn Rosenbaum was also living in my apartment. I hoped she was taking good care of Muffin. I really missed Muffin.

Work was, well, a nightmare. After a long, overcrowded train journey, I had to squeeze on to a subway where I hoped to Jesus the thing poking me in the lower back was someone's briefcase. And all of this to get to some shite job which was basically doing data inputting. I was bored to bits and in trouble for being late. Every time I heard a telephone ring, or an alarm, a siren, or a loud noise of any kind I thought, at last, here we go, end of dream, awake and back to normal. But no, it didn't happen. I started to think that maybe I was in a coma of some sort and I'd be stuck in this hideous alternative world until I regained consciousness.

When I finally got 'home' after another nightmare subway ride and having to stand most of the way on the train I was exhausted. I just wanted to ring for takeout and flop in front of the telly.

"Where's Roy?" John said as I was halfway through the door.

Roy?

John looked at me closely. "Were you hitting the bottle at lunch-time or something?" he asked.

I had my first good look at him. He'd put on weight and lost some hair but still looked like himself, only now I didn't fancy him. I wondered why I'd ever fancied him.

"Roy?" he said again. "Your son, Roy. Did you forget to pick him up?"

I had a son! I had a son called Roy! Apparently he was also some sort of Immaculate Conception as he was 'my' son and not 'our' son. I had a feeling he was 'my' son whenever he needed to be ferried somewhere but he mutated into being 'our' son when he got good marks in tests or did well at whatever young boys do well at. I found it hard to believe that I'd named a child of mine Roy. What sort of woman calls her son Roy? A quick look at the bookshelves and I realized that it had probably been John's choice. He appeared to have a minor obsession with Roy Keane.

"Oh, for fuck's sake!" John said, storming out. "I'll do it! You can get on with the dinner."

And so it continued. I went to work every day, I collected Roy, came home, I cleaned, I cooked. The cooking was the worst part – I couldn't get over the crap I was feeding my family. Mind you, even if I'd had the time to do more than defrost chicken nuggets and microwave fries, I didn't actually know how to cook anything decent.

John wasn't working; he'd been made redundant from his last job. He couldn't be expected to pick the kids up or do housework or cook as he was far too busy looking for a new job and besides, "I won't be pussy-whipped like that Bruce." Good to know that some things remained unchanged. Apparently part of John's research into getting a new job included watching *Chug-a-lug Girls* and several other porn epics on the Pay-Per-View channel. When I confronted him about this, he shouted at me. It was my fault because I wasn't putting out for him. Even if I'd wanted to, which I didn't, I was too knackered.

I was really pissed off about the Pay-Per-View, not particularly because he was watching porn – rather that than have him pawing at me. No, it was the fact that our cable bill was double what it should have been and we were up to our eyes in debt. Yes, on top of everything else

I got to pay the bills and look after the bank accounts. I pinched myself so often that my arms were covered in bruises. When would it stop, when would I wake up?

John was bad enough – but the kids, they were the biggest nightmare of all. Mel was, to be completely honest, a little bitch. She whined and moaned non-stop. If eye-rolling and saying 'whatever' were Olympic events she'd take the Gold every time. Maybe if I'd held her and fed her and changed her nappies when she was a baby I might have felt something akin to love but I hadn't, so most of the time I just wanted to strangle her. As for Roy, well, he was no trouble whatsoever. No trouble at all, as long as he had his video games. Take away his Game Boy and there'd be a ruck. I tried a couple of times to get him to read a book or even go out and kick a ball around but no, it was the virtual world or nothing. Given our 'reality', I really couldn't blame him.

I was beginning to think that this was reality and the life where I lived alone in an apartment with a doorman, worked at *Miss Thing*, slathered myself in Crème de la Mer, had nice hair and more handbags than Saks Fifth Avenue was something I'd dreamed. As the week went on, all of that seemed to be less and less real. Work wasn't much of an escape. It was easy but boring beyond relief and because I was constantly exhausted I wasn't really all that good at it.

On Friday I was called to a meeting with the boss and someone from HR. They gave me a lecture about the quality of my work, blah, blah, timekeeping, blah blah, too much time off for sick kids. I wondered vaguely why I had to take time off to mind sick kids when I had a husband at home. I was on a warning. If things didn't improve I'd be let go. Back at my desk I had a voicemail from John demanding to know 'where the fuck' I was.

He'd pranged the car (Christ, more money!) and was at the garage and wanted me to leave early to pick him up. Why can't you get a taxi, asshole, I wondered as I ran towards the ladies' room where I locked myself in a cubicle and roared crying. I couldn't remember the last time I'd roared crying – quite possibly it was at a funeral. This never happened to Nicholas Cage, I thought bitterly. No, everything was lovely and fuzzy in his alternative reality – what a sentimental crock!

When I eventually emerged from the stall there was a very glamorous blonde woman in a grey pencil skirt and the most gorgeous shoes standing by the sinks and holding out a hankie for me. I didn't recognise her but then again I didn't recognise most people in this dream/nightmare/reality, so no change there.

"Here you go," she said kindly, handing me the tissue.

"Thanks," I snuffled, dabbing at my eyes.

"So, Peggy what's it to be?" she asked, leaning against the sinks as I tried, without success, to repair my make-up.

"How do you know me?" I asked, risking her looking at me funny and telling me that we'd worked together for the past ten years and had lunch together on the first Tuesday of every month.

"I'm your Guardian Angel," she replied in a matter-of-fact voice.

"You! You don't look much like an angel."

She sighed, a 'not this again' type of sigh, and replied while examining her manicure, "What exactly does an angel look like? No, no hang on, let me guess, big white dress, halo, wings, right?"

I nodded. "All it takes is one drug-addled medieval artist and we're lumbered with that stupid image for eternity," she sighed. "Anyway, enough of that, to business. You may have noticed your life has taken a strange turn of late."

"It's a dream, right?" I said eagerly. "All of this, it's imaginary – you too, you're imaginary."

"No, dear," she replied kindly and produced a lipstick from her Marc Jacobs handbag. "Try this – it's more your colour than that one. No, this is reality. You had doubts, you see. You've let those doubts run your life. Always wondering about what could have been. So we had a kind of cosmic intervention. This," she said, gesturing at the sinks and stalls, "this is what could have been, what was, if you like. This is it."

"It is?" I replied stunned. "Is it?"

"That's up to you, dear," she said. "Now you know. What do you want? Do you want to wake up tomorrow morning in Tivoli Towers alone, or do you want to wake up in Long Island surrounded by a family that loves you."

I opened my mouth to speak but she shushed me.

"However, before you make a decision, remember one thing. Everything changes. Things are bad here at the moment. You're in debt, your husband is suffering from depression and needs to see a doctor and as for your kids . . . well, I don't need to elaborate on them. That said, everything changes. Life isn't static. This life will change and so will the other one. You're three months short of your thirty-seventh birthday. If you don't want this family, you still have time to make another one, or you can try to make this one work. It's up to you. You decide."

You decide. You decide.

I decided.

ALSO BY ANNE MARIE SCANLON, PUBLISHED BY POOLBEG

It's Not Me, It's You! (Non-Fiction)

30

Bumps
SARAH WEBB

Dedicated to Gaye Shortland, who gave me my first break.

Heather was bored to tears. She'd been sitting behind the till for over twenty minutes now, perched on the tall and rather uncomfortable wooden stool, and not one customer had entered the shop. She leaned forward, rested her cheeks on her folded hands, and stared out the spotless plate-glass window at Dun Rowan's main street. After a few minutes spent idly watching pedestrians, her gaze was interrupted by a heavily pregnant woman who stopped and peered in at the shop mannequin, freshly dressed this morning by Heather under the watchful eye of her boss, Hilda.

The woman's forehead was dotted with beads of perspiration, and lank brown hair framed her flushed face. She was the size of a small elephant and Heather doubted that the floaty silk shift dress in coral pink would actually fit her, even though it was supposed to be a maternity outfit.

Bumps prided itself in stocking everything a pregnant woman could possibly need from lacy Elle Macpherson maternity bras, and tights with clever panels which expanded with your growing belly, to exclusive (and very expensive) black tie dresses from top designers, and a range of upmarket creams and potions made from natural products like beeswax and aloe vera.

But in Heather's opinion the owner, Hilda Ramsey, had got it all wrong.

Pregnant women wanted comfortable clothes in cotton that could be bunged straight into the washing machine and didn't need ironing, but that also held their shape and didn't look too hideously tent-like; easy-to-wear pyjamas; slip-on shoes (especially at the later stages when reaching one's feet becomes nigh impossible); and lots and lots of coloured scarves and nice bright jewellery that distracted attention from one's ever-expanding midriff. Plus a kind partner, friend or husband to borrow shirts and jackets from and to paint your toenails. Red toenails, Heather thought, were always a good pick-me-upper.

And Heather should know. She'd had a horrid pregnancy with Alanna, now nearly two, culminating in a thirty-hour labour followed by the terrifying ordeal of an emergency Caesarean after the baby's heartbeat began to get a little erratic. A labour which she'd now managed to almost block from her mind. So understandably, Heather didn't intend to repeat the pregnancy or childbirth experience any time soon, thank you very much, however much her husband Joe encouraged and cajoled her.

Oh, she'd thought about having another baby – she'd thought about it long and hard. Occasionally she woke up at night in a hot sweat, the image of masked surgeon and nurses towering over her. No one had told her what a helpless and terrifying ordeal labour could be. She'd never admitted it to Joe, but at the time she'd thought she was going to die. Of course it was silly, almost no one actually died in labour any more, but towards the end, just before the top-up epidural, she really had thought that her time was up.

The woman waddled away from the window and Heather gave a long-drawn-out sigh. She was completely fed up. If Bumps didn't get more customers and quick, she'd be out of a job. Heather looked at her watch. Ten to eleven. Hilda wouldn't be back until at least three. She had to do something or she'd go crazy. She jumped down off the stool and strolled around the shop, wedge sandals squeaking on the newly laid wooden floor.

"What to do? What to do?" she murmured to herself. She walked towards the right-hand side of the shop and began to tidy the rails of swimsuits once again. She snorted as she straightened the multicoloured bikinis on their hangers. Pregnancy bikinis? Was Hilda completely mad?

"Who wants to show off their stretch-marks on the beach?" she asked the empty shop. She held up a black micro bikini. "How about a thong? Hands up! Anyone – anyone?"

"Talking to yourself again?"

She whipped around. Her husband Joe was standing at the door, grinning from ear to ear. His dark brown hair was freshly shorn and Heather noticed that the barber had missed a spot just above his ear, leaving a slightly longer tuft.

"Thank goodness," she said, putting the bikini back on the rail with a sharp ring of metal against metal. "I thought you were Hilda."

"What were you doing with the bikini?" he asked with interest.

"Just trying to entertain myself. As you can see, the shop is packed as usual. What brings you here?"

Joe walked towards her, a small box cradled in his arms. He'd just started working as the sales rep for Mamma Mia maternity wear after several years managing the Mothercare shop in Blackrock. "Delivering some stock. How's trade?"

Heather wrinkled her nose. "Non-existent. Let's hope it picks up or it's back to commuting for me."

"What about having an event with real pregnant mothers? Local celebrities or something. Isn't Kitty Parker pregnant?"

Kitty was an ex-model and continuity presenter on Irish television and now lived in Dun Rowan with her husband Packie, a wealthy businessman (in the ultra-glamorous waste-disposal and sewage business), in a mock-Georgian mansion, Rowan Manor, on the outskirts of the village. Kitty was a regular on the Irish charity circuit, popping up in all the 'About Town' social diaries and columns, and one of the few women who actually fitted into and bought the clothes in Bumps. In fact, most of their sales to date had been courtesy of Kitty. With her mane of glossy dark-brown hair, wide even-toothed smile, and clear, peachy skin she would certainly be a draw.

"What about a fashion show?" Heather's eyes lit up. "I'm sure Kitty has some other preggy friends. Babies are very in at the moment among the Wicklow chattering classes."

"And long may that last!" Joe grinned. "It's certainly good for business."

Heather smiled back.

It was good to see Heather smiling, Joe thought. She didn't do it enough these days. In fact at the moment, things at home could get a little frosty at times, especially if Alanna was having one of her terrible-two kind of days.

As soon as Joe had left Bumps, Heather picked up a new *Blooming Marvellous* catalogue from beside the till. She winced as she came across a double-page spread of black, orange and rust evening dresses with low-scooped fronts, sequin 'sunburst'' detail on the stomach zone and long, to-the-floor hems. I bet Hilda will buy those for the shop, Heather thought. In rust and orange, not in black of course – far too sensible. Maybe I should rip those particular pages out of the catalogue before she sees them, she mused. Save Hilda from herself.

The dresses and outfits on the following pages were far more sensible and flattering. Layered chiffon trousers in black, dark red, midnight blue and moss green, with matching, cleverly cut tunic tops that could also be worn with jeans for a more casual look.

"I like those," Heather murmured to herself. She looked at the specifications. "Machine washable too. And reasonably priced."

Tucked into the spine on the next page were several order forms. Heather took one out and looked at it. She decided to place a 'fantasy order', trawling through the catalogue and jotting down what she'd order, if she were the buyer. I have nothing else to do, she reasoned, and there are two more order forms for Hilda to use.

Hilda made a brief appearance in Bumps just after four, bustling in, clucking noisily over the lack of sales, as if it was Heather's fault, and bustling out again. She was attending some sort of society ball that evening in aid of what sounded to Heather like 'sick horsemen' and had to dash home to get ready.

Heather closed the shop at five on the dot, pulling down the stainless-steel honeycomb shutter and anchoring it with a heavy clunk. She wondered how long they'd stay open. She had to do something and fast, otherwise it was back to commuting hell. She winced at the mere thought of it. Sweaty armpits, noisy Walkmans, inane mobile-phone conversations about bread and milk and what Daisy said that Clodagh said about Rita. Her energy levels had been much better since she'd started working locally and she was finding Alanna and her demands much easier to deal with. The fashion show could be her last chance saloon.

★ ★ ★

The following morning, Heather lifted Alanna out of her cot and immediately noticed tiny pink spots all over her daughter's face.

"Do you feel okay, pet?" she asked her with concern.

Alanna smiled at her, oblivious. "Okay, Mummy."

"Let's get you ready for Sue's, will we?" Heather began and then checked herself. Alanna couldn't go to her childminder's with that rash. What if it turned out to be chickenpox or something equally contagious? Sue wouldn't thank her for infecting her other wards.

She'd have to take her to the doctor on the way to work. Hopefully they'd get an early appointment.

Unfortunately the doctor wasn't free until ten. Heather rang Hilda who said she'd hold the fort until the doctor had made a diagnosis. "If it's not contagious," Hilda pointed out, "you can bring Alanna straight to her minder's."

Heather wasn't all that keen on leaving Alanna at Sue's when she wasn't well, but didn't have much choice. She'd only been working in Bumps for five weeks now after all, and she wanted to hold on to her job.

So at ten to eleven, reassured by the doctor that the rash was just an allergy, nothing to worry about, having dropped Alanna into her minder's and driven like a maniac, Heather rushed through the door of Bumps and almost collided with Hilda who was practically prostrate, paying homage to Kitty Parker's compact bump.

"Gosh, sorry!" Heather came to a standstill beside the fawning Hilda.

"Poor Heather's little girl is sick," Hilda explained to Kitty. "Some sort of rash," she said, lowering her voice and putting her hand in front of her mouth, completely unnecessarily as they were the only people in the shop. "They were just at the doctor's."

Kitty stiffened and took a small step backwards. Illness of any kind made her a little nervous, especially now that she was pregnant.

"Nothing serious, I'm happy to report." Heather smiled at Kitty and Hilda, eager to set the record straight. "Just an allergy."

"What a relief!" Kitty said. "And how's your daughter feeling – Alanna, isn't it?"

"That's right. The rash doesn't seem to be bothering her at all. And how's baby Parker?"

Kitty put her hand on her stomach and smiled. "Doing well. But I must admit, I'm getting a little bored. Packie isn't keen on me travelling up to Dublin in my condition, there's only so much shopping you can do in Dun Rowan and I've another three months to go! Having so much time on your hands isn't always a good thing."

Heather looked at Kitty. Joe's suggestion popped into her head. "No time like the present."

"Sorry?" said Kitty.

The two women looked at Heather.

"Talking to myself." She smiled at Kitty. "Kitty, would you be available to model some pregnancy clothes, say at a local fashion show? If you were up to it."

"What do you have in mind?" Kitty asked.

"Maybe a Bumps fashion show, if Hilda likes the idea. What do you think, Hilda? And all the proceeds could be donated to a local children's charity." Heather turned towards Hilda. Hilda was staring at her. Heather cringed inwardly; maybe she should have run it by her boss first.

Before Hilda had a chance to say anything, Kitty clapped her hands together. "Oh, please say yes, Hilda! I could ask some of my friends to model – lots of them are pregnant." She paused for a moment before adding cannily, "And it would be great publicity for the shop. Last year's Miss Ireland, Missie Evans, is pregnant. She'd be fantastic."

Hilda was miffed. A fashion show was a superb idea. "I was thinking along the same lines myself," she said, "but Heather beat me to it. Why don't we go out for coffee, Kitty, and discuss it?" Hilda put her hand under Kitty's left elbow.

"What about Heather?" asked Kitty, putting her arms down by her side and taking a tiny step away from Hilda. No one railroaded Kitty Palmer. "It *was* her idea after all."

Heather smiled gratefully at her. Her opinion of Kitty was subtly shifting.

"Someone needs to mind the shop," Hilda pointed out.

"True, so let's have the meeting here," Kitty said, lifting

her chin. As she was already almost six foot, it made her look even taller. She hadn't risen to the top of the Irish television world without learning to a) stand up for herself and b) treat everyone with the respect they deserved, from make-up girls to CEO's. She'd come across lots of women like Hilda in her day – bossy, self-centred women who were quite happy for someone else to do all the work and then to take all the credit.

Kitty won.

★　★　★

Three days later a man with dark blue tattoos on both burly forearms lurched into the shop, his body weighed down by an enormous brown box.

"Where do you want this, love?" he asked Heather. "It's your *Blooming Marvellous* order. There's another one in the van. And I have some clothes on the rail for you."

"Hilda certainly ordered enough stock," Heather murmured.

"Excuse me?"

"Sorry, nothing. You can leave it by the till." Hilda hated boxes being unpacked on the shop floor but the back room was so stuffy in this heat. And today Hilda wasn't in until three, giving Heather plenty of time to price and put out the new stock before her boss arrived. She was glad to have something to do; it was another quiet day in Bumps, surprise, surprise.

When the deliveryman had gone, Heather lifted the transparent layer of floaty plastic off one of the hangers and studied the black dress underneath. Surprisingly it wasn't the impractically beaded low-cut number that Heather had expected to find. She fingered the delicate yet strong material. The dress didn't look like a maternity dress at all – it was carefully draped at the front and had a deliciously light and flirty skirt.

She fetched the spare rail from the goods-in room and hung several different sizes of the dress on it, along with several sizes of cleverly cut moss-green trousers with matching tunic tops. Then she ripped the wide brown tape off the first box with a healthy crack (Heather loved opening boxes and also popping bubble-wrap between her fingers) and began to unpack the contents.

"The wrap-around ballet cardigans," she cooed, lifting one out of its plastic packaging. The brushed cream cotton felt buttery soft in her fingers and she held it up and shook out the folds. "Finally, some clothes that might actually sell."

Just then, Kitty came bouncing into the shop. "Hi, Heather," she said, her perfect white teeth practically glowing against her lightly tanned skin. "What have you got there?"

Heather looked up. "It's some of the new autumn stock."

"Clothes for the fashion show? Can I have a look?"

"Sure." Heather handed Kitty the cardigan. "Feel that."

Kitty ran her fingers over the cotton cardigan, and then held it up to her cheek. "It's so soft. Can I try it on?"

Heather nodded. "Go ahead."

Kitty pulled off her denim jacket, thrust her arms into the cardigan and wrapped it around her body. She stood in front of the mirror. "It's divine. What else is in your Pandora's Box?"

Heather recognised the classical reference and smiled. "Let's have a look. I've only just started unpacking the order."

"Are you sure you don't mind? Maybe you'd be faster on your own?"

"No. Please stay. I'd like the company." Heather realised with a start that she meant it. Apart from the deliveryman, she hadn't talked to a soul all day.

Kitty rewarded her with a huge smile. "Cool!" She pulled out a cream chunky-corduroy skirt and a dark red denim shirt. "Wow! These are amazing. Hilda's getting better." She put her hand over her mouth. "Oops, sorry! No offence intended."

Heather smiled. "You've noticed?"

"Hard not to," Kitty said. "Her taste is a little . . . how can I put this without sounding cruel?"

"You don't have to say anything," Heather reassured her. "I know exactly what you mean. But she's obviously learning. Look at this top." Heather held up a heavy cotton peasant top with a strong red and green William Morris-inspired flowery pattern.

"I'm certainly trying that on. It's fab!" Kitty jumped to her feet, took off the cardigan and pulled the tunic over her head. "I love it!" She moved this way and that, admiring the cut in the mirror. The top nestled under her pert breasts and skirted attractively over her rounded stomach.

Heather found the delivery note in the second box and scanned it carefully. As she read down the list, her heart began to beat a little faster. As she came to the end of the third and last page, the blood drained from her face. There it was in black and white: *Autumn Order c/o Heather Doran.* It wasn't Hilda's order at all. It was *her* order. No wonder it seemed so familiar.

"Heather, are you all right? You look pale."

Heather looked up at Kitty. "I think I've just lost my

job." She gave a groan and collapsed on the sofa. "I'm so stupid." Heather bowed her head and stared at her hands which were resting on her lap, clenched tightly into fists.

"Heather, what's wrong?"

Heather raised her voice. How unprofessional of her, behaving like this in front of a customer.

She gave Kitty a tight smile. "It's fine, really. I'm sorry . . ." She broke off as soon as she saw the sympathetic look on Kitty's face.

"You ordered these clothes, didn't you?" Kitty asked astutely.

"How did you . . .?"

Kitty put her hands up. "Easy, you have good taste. And Hilda doesn't. Simple as that. And I take it that Hilda doesn't exactly know about this order."

"Not exactly," Heather admitted. She explained to Kitty what had happened. "And Hilda's going to kill me. There's thousands of euros worth of clothes here. And I really need this job. I spent the last few years commuting to Dublin and I really don't want to start doing that again, not with Alanna."

"I used to hate the drive up to RTÉ, the traffic was brutal. So I understand, really I do. But surely your husband works?"

Heather raised her eyebrows. "I need to work too or the mortgage doesn't get paid."

Kitty's cheeks coloured a little. "How crass of me! I should have kept my mouth shut."

Heather felt sorry for Kitty. The woman seemed genuinely embarrassed. And it wasn't Kitty's fault that her husband was loaded. "That's okay," she said graciously. "Forget it."

"I've been lucky," Kitty said. "I've never really had to

worry about bills and things. I lived at home until I met Packie, and now he takes care of everything like that."

"Really?" Heather was intrigued. "He deals with all the bills?"

Kitty nodded. "Is that unusual?"

Heather smiled gently. "You could say that." She paused for a second. "What about your mobile-phone bill? Or your credit-card bills? Does he pay those?"

Kitty nodded again. "*All* the bills."

"And shopping?"

"We have a housekeeper. She deals with all that."

Heather's eyes widened. "A housekeeper?"

"Yes." Kitty gave a little laugh. "I know, I'm desperately spoilt. But really, Heather, I'd poison Packie my cooking is so bad. And I haven't a clue how to use the washing machine. I always manage to shrink everything or dye the whole load red or something. Last time I used it I forgot to check the pockets of Packie's black jeans and he'd left a tissue in them. The whole wash was covered in white shards. It was terrible!"

Heather started to laugh. "Kitty, I can't believe you don't even wash your own clothes. *That's* terrible!"

Kitty looked a little sheepish. She shrugged her shoulders. "I know. But Packie says I need to concentrate on other things."

"Like . . ." Heather prompted.

"Well, I was working up until recently. That took up most of my day."

"And now?"

"In the morning I go to the gym. I have Pilates on Mondays and Wednesdays, and on the other days I swim or take a class. And then I buy things for the house."

"What type of things?" Heather was fascinated by

Kitty's admission and wanted to know how the other half lived.

"Curtains – I'm getting new ones made for the bedroom. It's taken me a while to get the fabric just right. Packie wants plain cream, but you wouldn't believe how many different plain cream fabrics there are. I've been into Dublin dozens of times. And I've finally found the perfect fabric in this little place near Temple Bar. It specialises in imported French fabric and it's only beautiful. Velvet with a touch of silk."

Heather found herself thinking about her own bedroom curtains – cotton with a touch of nylon, all the way from China.

Kitty looked Heather straight in the eye. "Frankly," she said, "I'm bored to tears. I'm finding being at home all the time a bit lonely. I'm hoping the baby will keep me busy, but Packie is insisting on a maternity nurse for the first few months and then a full-time nanny."

"A maternity nurse?" Heather asked. "Do they do nights?"

"Yes. Packie says I'll recover from the birth much more quickly if I'm not woken during the night."

Heather whistled. "No kidding. Kitty, take the maternity nurse, I beg you. And if you don't want her, give her to me. Please!"

"But Alanna's not a baby," Kitty said. "Surely she doesn't still wake at night?"

"Hate to break it to you but I haven't had a full night's sleep since she was born."

"Really?"

"Really!"

Kitty smiled at Heather. "We have very different lives, don't we?"

"In some ways. But once your baby arrives, we'll have more in common."

Kitty cupped her hands around her bump protectively. "As long as it holds on this time. We've lost two in the last year, one early on and one at twenty-one weeks. We'll just have to wait and see if it's strong enough this time."

Heather was taken aback. "I'm so sorry. I had no idea."

"That's okay. Packie was devastated – he wants a child so much. When his first wife died he thought he'd never be a dad." She broke off for a moment. "This baby means a lot to him. To both of us."

"Of course."

Kitty looked at Heather and there was sadness in her eyes. Heather suddenly felt sorry for her. So much for her charmed life.

They both said nothing for a moment, slightly awkward after their intimate conversation, then Kitty's eyes rested on the boxes on the floor in front of them.

"So what are you going to do about the order?" she deftly changed the subject. "It was hardly your fault. Surely you can send it all back and explain the mistake."

"I suppose so. But I'll have to tell Hilda what's happened – she'll see the boxes when she comes in later. I'd better ring her."

Kitty said nothing for a moment. "I have an idea. Don't ring her yet, promise?" Kitty clicked open her white leather-covered mobile phone. "Price up the order while I'm gone. I'll be back in half an hour."

"But, I can't . . ." Heather began, but Kitty had already left the shop, leaving the subtle waft of expensive-smelling vanilla scent in her wake. Heather realised that Kitty had left in the tunic top from the rogue order. She put her hands to her eyes and ran her fingers over her eyebrow bones and up towards her temples. "Aagh!" she punched her breath out in a rush. "What is Kitty up to?"

She looked at the unpacked boxes.

"What have I got to lose?" she asked out loud, picking up her pricing gun. "Nothing, except for this crummy job."

★   ★   ★

"I love the new window," Kitty said as she walked back in the door. "It's inspired."

Heather had just finished stacking the ballet cardigans on the round display table at the front of the shop. She'd dressed the window mannequin in a cream skirt with the same peasant top that Kitty had on.

"Thanks."

"And can I buy a few things before the shop gets busy?"

"Busy?" Heather laughed. "Don't hold your breath."

A smile played on Kitty's lips. "And Missie wants to buy some items by mail order. She gave me her credit-card details. Can you post them down to her?"

"No problem."

Kitty beamed. "Excellent. Now I'd better get shopping before . . ."

They both looked over as an unfeasibly tall and slim woman walked in the door. She had the sleek, groomed appearance of a thoroughbred horse, with a mane of dark blonde hair, and a long, equine face. She was dressed in jeans, chunky red surfer flip-flops and a plain white cotton vest, but even in the casual outfit she looked a million dollars.

"Darling!" the woman threw her arms around Kitty

and gave her a smacker of a kiss on either cheek.

"Heather, this is Imelda. We used to model together in Dublin."

"Nice to meet you," Imelda nodded at Heather. She looked around. "Great shop. Kitty was telling me all about it. I'm only five months pregnant . . ."

"Five months!" Heather cried. The girl was as thin as a rake.

"I know, I know," Imelda gave a lop-sided grin. "But I'm almost out of most of my clothes. And Kitty promised me that you'd have jeans that actually fit. I can't stand those ones with the horrible sweaty panel at the front. Hipsters are more my bag."

The door swung open again. "Kitty! Imelda!" A woman with her dark hair pulled back into a messy pony-tail joined the group. Unlike Kitty and Imelda, her belly was huge and her face was pink and flushed. She was wearing a grey tracksuit, silver Birkenstock sandals and carried a candy-striped canvas bag. "How are you both?" she asked in a strong New York accent. "Isn't this place swell?"

"This is my friend, Jen," Kitty told Heather. "She's a fashion photographer."

Within an hour Bumps was thronged with pregnant women of all shapes and sizes, all happily chatting, trying on clothes, and to Heather's delight, spending money.

"Heather?"

Heather handed the large pink Bumps carrier bag to yet another of Kitty's friends and mouthed, "Thanks, enjoy the clothes!" before turning her head towards the voice.

"Sorry for the delay . . ." she began.

Hilda was standing in front of her, over-plucked

eyebrows raised. "Where did all these women come from?"

"Heather!" Kitty shouted over. "You'll have to order more of the ballet cardigans. They're nearly all gone."

"Ballet cardigans?" Hilda murmured. She looked quizzically at Heather.

"I can explain," Heather began but was interrupted by Jen.

"Do you have a Bumps website?" Jen asked.

"It's currently under development," Heather said smoothly.

Hilda stared at her, gob-smacked. She was a complete technophobe and a website had never occurred to her.

"Let me take your details," Heather said, "and your email address. As soon as it's up and running I'll email you."

"Cool."

Heather had another thought. "Hilda, can you man the till for a few minutes? I'm going to ask everyone in the shop for their email addresses. Instant mailing list."

"Sure," Hilda murmured, her nose completely out of joint. "Good idea. I was just thinking that myself."

Two hours later, the shoppers had left and Kitty rested on the sofa as Hilda and Heather cashed up the till.

"So where exactly did all the clothes come from?" Hilda asked as they waited for the end-of-day report from the cash register.

"The wholesaler sent them by mistake," Heather admitted. She explained about her dummy order.

Hilda said nothing. The register pinged to a halt and Hilda ripped the printout off, studied the total and gave a tiny laugh in the back of her throat.

"Heather, look!" she said, pointing at the healthy figure printed in bold.

Heather gave a whoop. "Unbelievable! Our best day yet by a mile thanks to Kitty. Kitty, you're quite a woman!"

Kitty waved her hands in the air. "It was nothing. Besides, it was a good excuse to catch up with some of my friends. And they're all dying to come to the fashion show."

"We should give you a job," Heather said, thinking aloud. She looked at Hilda. "We'll need another person when the internet site takes off."

Hilda frowned. "Ah, yes, I was meaning to ask you about that. Won't it cost a fortune to set up and run?"

"Not at all," Heather said. "I can do it. I took HTML evening classes in Dublin before Alanna was born."

"Would you really be interested in working here, Kitty?" asked Hilda. "After the baby arrives, of course."

"I'll certainly think about it." Kitty looked around. "There's a lot you could do to the place. And I'm always full of ideas." She caught Heather's eye and smiled. "And I might be able to persuade Packie to invest. Hey, we could expand. Go into cool baby equipment and clothes."

Hilda's face fell. She had a feeling things at Bumps were going to change. But if she made money from it, then what the hell? And an investor sounded interesting. Maybe she wouldn't have to work at all.

"Excellent!" Heather enthused. Working at Bumps would be far more fun with Kitty by her side. She had a feeling they were going to make a great team.

★ ★ ★

"You're in good form this evening," Joe commented as he was greeted at the door by a hug and a kiss. "Where's Alanna?"

Heather smiled. "In bed. She fell asleep in the car on the way home and I lifted her out of the car and put her straight to bed. She might wake up later but who cares?"

"In that case," Joe pulled her towards him and held her tight, "why don't we go upstairs and make the most of the evening?"

"Joe!" she said, squirming out of his grip. "What about dinner?"

"I can wait."

"Well, I can't. Maybe later."

"Is that a promise?"

"Get into the kitchen," she commanded. "I even bought your favourite chocolate ice cream."

"I love it when you talk dirty," he joked.

As they chatted amiably over dinner, Heather told Joe about Kitty's friends and about the proposed Bumps website and expansion.

"It's all happening at Bumps," he commented.

"Isn't it great?"

Joe nodded. He hadn't seen Heather this happy since before Alanna was born. He might even broach the subject of a second baby later if he dared.

Funnily enough, Heather was thinking the very same thing.

The End

ALSO BY SARAH WEBB, PUBLISHED BY POOLBEG

Something To Talk About,
Always the Bridesmaid,
Three Times A Lady

WIN A LIBRARY OF
POOLBEG BESTSELLERS!

Be in with a chance of winning 30 Poolbeg titles, one by each of the authors featured in *Thirty & Fabulous!*, worth €300!!

Simply fill in the questionnaire below, return it to Poolbeg by 31st January 2007, and be automatically entered into the draw. The winner will be notified by telephone and email in February 2007.

I am: Male ☐   I am: 18-24 ☐   25-34 ☐   35-44 ☐
Female ☐   45-54 ☐   55-64 ☐   65-74 ☐   74+ ☐

Please rate in order of importance (10 being the most important) what you consider when buying a book:

	0	2	4	6	8	10
Price	☐	☐	☐	☐	☐	☐
Cover design	☐	☐	☐	☐	☐	☐
Blurb (on back cover)	☐	☐	☐	☐	☐	☐
Favourite author	☐	☐	☐	☐	☐	☐
Had heard about the book	☐	☐	☐	☐	☐	☐
Was in a store promotion	☐	☐	☐	☐	☐	☐

(for example 3 for 2 promotion, Book of the Month etc)

My favourite magazines are: _____

My favourite newspapers are: _____

My favourite radio stations are: _____

I buy most of my books at: _____

How did you hear about this book?

Recommended by a friend ☐   Heard/Saw an advertisement ☐   Read a review ☐
Picked it up in the shop ☐   Received as a present ☐   Already a fan ☐
Other _____

Please return to: Poolbeg Questionnaire,
Poolbeg Press, 123 Grange Hill, Baldoyle, Dublin 13

If you do not want to receive our monthly newsletter giving details of forthcoming publications and special offers, please tick here ☐
We will not pass your details on to any third parties

Entrants must be over 18 years of age. Terms and conditions apply. The first entry drawn will be the winner.